RAVE REVIEWS FOR JEMIAH JEFFERSON'S DEBUT NOVEL, *VOICE OF THE BLOOD!*

"Die-hard vampire fans are going to love it."
—*Hellnotes*

"Jemiah Jefferson has proven herself as an author to watch with this novel. If you let *Voice of the Blood* get under your skin, you'll be hooked."
—*Horror World*

"Jemiah Jefferson [is] a welcome voice in character-driven horror fiction."
—Gothic.net

"Jemiah Jefferson draws us into an erotic, violent and tragic world of vampires. . . . *Voice of the Blood* delivers all the bittersweet irony and tragedy requisite of modern Gothic horror."
—*Dark Realms*

DINNER FOR TWO

"Quickly," Daniel whispered from the backseat, his eyes scanning the empty street. The leaves on the trees drooped under the weight of ice. No one, just the freezing mist and the midnight bells lowing from a nearby church.

Ariane rolled up the woman's coat and sweater sleeves, exposing a forearm glossed with an unseasonable tan, waxed smooth and gleaming. Ariane almost winced with hunger looking at it before she lowered her head and took a bite.

And then a deeper one.

The woman's head wobbled. Daniel reached around the seat and worked the plastic latch to lower it back, toward him; her body stretched and relaxed. He wanted to mention the woman's excellent breasts, but it wasn't worth it, watching Ariane suck down blood and knowing that if he didn't hop to it, there'd be nothing left for him.

Ariane lifted her head and gulped the air. "I'm hot," she said in a small voice. Her teeth glistened red between reddened lips.

"She's not dead yet," said Daniel, holding his thumb over the new wound under her chin. "Finish her. Don't waste it."

"No," she whispered. "I'm done. Go for it."

"You're too kind."

There wasn't much left. . . .

OTHER *LEISURE* BOOKS BY JEMIAH JEFFERSON:
VOICE OF THE BLOOD

WOUNDS

JEMIAH JEFFERSON

LEISURE BOOKS NEW YORK CITY

A LEISURE BOOK®

May 2002

Published by

Dorchester Publishing Co., Inc.
276 Fifth Avenue
New York, NY 10001

ISBN 0-8439-4998-8

Printed in the United States of America.

To the Rev. Chris Lotus
and the polar bear twins Ananda and Lilith,
and the people of New York City.

ACKNOWLEDGMENTS

All the thanks in the world are not adequate to show my appreciation for Neil Gordon and his amazing book *Voluptuous Panic: The Erotic Life of Weimar Berlin*, my hero, Elicia Cardenas, Tony Borodovsky, Willow Roberts, Alex Colby and the folks at Nexus Dumbo, "Sweetie" and Joey Arias, Gilad Rosner and the Collective Unconscious, Kevin Sampsell, Lisa Steinman, Alexander Stone, Mykle and Gesina, the fabulous ladies of Crush, Joey Pruett, Don D'Auria and the crew at Leisure, Mehitobel Wilson, Monica O'Rourke, the Horror Writers Association, all the great folks at WHC 2001 who made me feel good, Lawrence Krauser, Colson Whitehead, Celeste Ramsay, and Mom and Dad. If I've forgotten anyone, please give me two hard punches next time you see me.

WOUNDS

". . . They always want to hear *about* . . . and I want to give them the experience itself . . . so they will be terrified, and awaken. . . . They do not realize that *they are dead.*"

—Antonin Artaud

Scene One: "A long time ago in Hollywood . . ."

And why did it, after so many midnights, always come to this?

"Oh my fucking God! Oh my God—I'm puking blood! Oh my—oh my fucking Go-ho-hod!"

Daniel stood across the room, gently scraping flecks of the girl's hardened, dead skin from beneath his fingernails. Already, the formerly florid crimson stain on his shirtfront had darkened to the color of newspaper ink. "Thank you so much for pointing out the obvious," he said to the steamed pane of the window. "I told you it would happen. But did you listen?"

Her litany went on. *"Oh my fucking God! I can't—I Can't breathe . . ."* Her continued wordless screeching belied her for a moment, then the telltale gurgles of true choking started up and the room became blessedly quieter. A long time ago in Hollywood, a beautiful redhead taught him the difference between fake choking and true choking—if it can vocalize, it ain't really choking.

Ariane, the redhead, was still human back then, if he remembered correctly.

Daniel was always misremembering Ariane, thinking that she'd done something miraculous and superhuman, vampiric, when she had not yet been capable of any such thing. He had barely ever known her as a vampire. He definitely wasn't still in love with her, so that couldn't have been the factor that skewed his long-term memory. He hadn't loved Ariane since that night in the airport when they were fleeing for their lives. He hadn't loved anyone since that night. He certainly didn't love the twisting wreck of screeching blasphemy over on the other side of the bed, ruining the pressed linen sheets. Stupid, disbelieving little bitch. She just couldn't take "I'm going to kill you if you don't go away" for an answer.

In the Supernova Gentleman's Club, earlier. "So what happens if you only have a little taste?" The girl's face was moist from the exertion of laughing and drinking and talking. "Like, not even a mouthful?"

Daniel sighed patiently. "It would be like drinking a solution of lye," he explained again. "It would destroy any tissues that it came into contact with, trying to reshape them on a genetic level, or whatever. And even if it didn't destroy those tissues, it would change them into non-human tissue, and then your body would develop a massive infection trying to reject this new flesh that isn't even human. You'd probably die from it. If you were lucky. If you weren't lucky—and I've seen this happen—your mouth would become this glory hole of scar tissue, no teeth, no tongue; just scar. Trust me, you do not want to *have a little taste* of vampire blood."

The girl laughed again, just like the first time he told her, and muffled her mouth in the narrow opening of her cocktail goblet. He had been talking to her for hours, watching her steal cherries from the plastic tub in front of them at the bar, rubbing them against her lips, nipping them away with tiny bites of her small yellow teeth. Maybe she knew he was going to kill her, and the idea excited her. She was on the make, looking for something strange. Daniel was good-looking and bizarre, dressed in a masculine suit but wearing full drama makeup—ruby lipstick, gray-shadowed cheeks, Cleopatra-lined eyes, crunchy blue glitter on his lids. In his hunger, he curled his lip to expose wolf's teeth, and his colorless skin fluoresced creamy lavender, growing paler by the hour. She asked him, flippantly, first if he was a fag, and then if he was a vampire, and he was too bored to lie about either. It was too easy.

"Well, does it hurt?"

"Of course it hurts—look, imagine a mouthful of lye."

"No, when you really . . . I mean really . . . *transform.*"

"Yes," Daniel said, "change always hurts."

She grunted with drunken giggles. "So, Mr. Vampire, what kind of super powers do you have? Can you turn into a bat?"

"No, I can't turn into a bat. That's stupid. And my name's not Mr. Vampire. My name's Thomas."

"I'm Angelika. With a *k.*"

"Yes, you told me."

She shook her head and squinted back toward the empty, tinsel-glittering stage, awaiting the scheduled naked female reinforcements. She didn't work as an exotic dancer but, tolerated by the proprietors, her purpose was to take care of the needs of gentlemen who wanted more than a lap dance, and enough of them did to make it worth her while. Her young face already showed the scoring of professionalism. "So, like I said, we should go on a date."

"I haven't got any cash," said Daniel. "I spent it all, buying you drinks."

Angelika smirked. "That's all you brought?"

"I have to stay for the next set." Daniel yawned. "There's a girl dancing who I really want to see."

"Oh, really? Which one?"

"I don't know her name," Daniel said. "Like you. I don't know *your* name. I know it's not Angelika. Well . . . I could try to guess it. I've got that 'super power.' " He smiled slowly, tingling with anticipation. Parlor tricks, infinitely satisfying; magic; the impossible. He half hoped it would scare her away. Of course, if he really wanted her gone, it would be easy to repel her, but he found himself enjoying her obnoxiousness.

"OK—here goes—if you've really got powers, try to guess my name." She closed her eyes and appeared transfixed in thought, like a game-show contestant struggling with the final quiz question, the one for the new car.

Daniel examined her scrunched-up face. Her fake ID listed her age as twenty-one, the oldest age that might be believable for her; she was closer, he felt, to seventeen or sixteen, a mature sixteen. He reached out and wiped the last daub of lipstick from her bottom lip with his thumb, and rested his palm against her hot drunk-moist cheek. "Allison," he said, calling her awake.

She opened her eyes. "How did you know?" she said.

"You showed me your driver's license about an hour ago. Remember I said I didn't think you were old enough to drink."

"But my fake—I mean my driver's license says Jane." She shook her drooping head. "Jesus Christ, I must be drunk."

Daniel made a small humming laugh and shrugged.

She put her face in her drink again. "So what's the name you think this chick is called?"

"The last time she did her dance, they called her Silver."

"Oh." Angelika sputtered elaborately and rolled her eyes. "*Her?* She's a big buffalo beast. *And* she's psycho. Last time I was in here she tried to start a fight with me for, like, no reason at all."

"I like her dancing." He paused, distracted, also eyeing the empty stage. Angelika put her hand on his thigh, and when that failed to produce a response, threw her arms around him, pushing her spit-glossy lips toward him. He recoiled involuntarily, then covered it by patting her shiny hair. "All right, you beautiful toy, you leave now, and I'll join you at the coffee shop at the corner. Get a coffee and I'll join you. Fifteen minutes." He gently pushed her away, imagining her slipping off the stool and falling onto her ass, a roomful of people looking over.

She smirked again. "Right, OK," she said, sliding bonelessly from her bar stool. "You better be there; I'll be looking for you." Underneath the fur coat, she wore a very tight mustard-yellow velour dress and black herringbone stockings. She looked like she shopped at Hooker Thrift Store. Between her thighs was a bowlegged concavity, her string-bean legs interrupted by giant bony knees like a racehorse. She was cute, in her own disgusting way. Daniel felt a throb of misplaced compassion, and wondered if he should just let this brainless child go on her own way, pick up some other bastard and have *him* rape and kill her. Why should he make the effort to be her special one, the very last trick, the one to remember forever?

But it was too late now. She had had a little taste.

She lay now jerking in a pool of her own fluids, her nervous system jabbering into convulsions as her arteries fed her body the poisoned blood. She would only live a few minutes more; her brain already sent out crazed messages to seizure, and one of them would stop her heart. At least she wasn't squeaking anymore. Daniel used to really enjoy the sound of lungs that begged for air but got only blood; the sound of a fatal throat injury. He heard the sound in countless voices, voiceboxes, inflections, tones, each one unique but universal. But it was a song that he'd heard too many times, and he was sick of it. Now, when it got to the squeak, he got into the habit of just kicking the poor bastard's head in, whoever it was, just to get it over with for them both. He considered it his version of compassion.

That *kick* of her mind into his when he drank deeply from her veins was not its usual mutual ecstasy; she had, at the last minute, been terrified, and the jagged fear in her thoughts blasted him. Yes, the adrenaline was tasty, like fresh cream is tasty—pure nourishment for some part of his vampire body—but such a difference between the adrenaline pumping through the body of a lover and that of a struggling victim. And her mind—a barren wasteland of non-thoughts and non-emotions! She was just a stupid kid from a nasty city, having aborted three babies, veins running slick with liquor and methamphetamine, who had never had any real love or dream or hope about anything. She was too scared even to pray at the last minute. It was a damn shame.

Daniel stood over the biomass in the velour dress and found it silent and still. He had fucked her a little over an hour ago, up against the wall in the room, holding her lank chestnut hair from her forehead as he shoved against her from behind. She had gotten weird about "vampire sex" in the middle of it and started yelling, "Hump me, Dracula!" He lost interest and erection immediately. There were limits to his indulgence. He pushed her against the wall away from him, wiped off, and zipped his pants. Undaunted, she slid down onto her knees on the floor, grunting and touching herself. "Let me drink your vampire blood," she said.

"Don't be stupid."

"Drink my blood, then—or are you full of shit?"

Snarling, he seized her and threw her on the bed. Following her down, he covered her with his body so that she wouldn't struggle, pierced her in the hollow of her collarbone with his fingernail, and put his mouth to the overflowing, crescent-shaped hole. She screamed, of course, as though she hadn't just asked for it. He tried to cover her mouth with his lips, but as she struggled, she bit hard through his bottom lip. She got a big mouthful of Daniel's blood for her trouble. Now she was just a horrid-looking body and this room was on one of trust-fund kid Thomas Arlington's credit cards that still had masses of credit left on it. If only he had just bitten her when she was amused by his caresses . . . ! Stupid!

He rubbed the back of his hand against the fast-healing wounds in his lip and sighed. Nothing to do now but get to work.

He began bundling up her body in the linen bedsheets, cursing how runny she was from both ends, but simultaneously thankful that she was still warm and flexible enough to fold up easily. She was only five feet tall; this would be simple.

In the midst of work, his mind wandered to pleasanter things. The dancer called Silver had danced again that night, but she went this time under the name of Shaneen, coursing and sparking and exploding on stage in ways that made him envious, amused him, disgusted him, filled him with awe. During her first set, he thought to himself that either she couldn't dance or she was a genius. He still hadn't decided during the second but decided that it was immaterial. Underneath red-sequined lingerie (stark as flags against her powdered white skin, shedding spinning particles that softened the spotlights) every inch was smooth; in fact, the only hair visible on her entire body was on top of her head. In the middle of her dance she cast aside her fluffy blond wig like a TV newscaster's scalp. Underneath, short, greasy spikes of dull yellow-silver.

He beckoned her with a twenty-dollar bill and she approached, stopping at the edge of the stage near his bar stool, gyrating her hips slowly, half-tempo against the music, eyeing him emotionlessly. He couldn't smile in the face of such perfect blank neutrality, keeping her near with a succession of twenties. More than anything, he wanted to rub his cheek against her *mons pubis* and catch enough of her skin oil onto his cheek to remember her by scent. He felt that he might have gotten away with it, had he tried it, but there were simply too many different people around, and he just didn't feel that he had the strength to confuse and distract them all.

Instead, he watched the dancer bump and grind, when it would have been just as wonderful to have her standing still. At this distance, it should have been easy to hear what she was thinking; he ought to have had her name and her desires, but she was the only one in the room that he could not read. All he knew was that she did not want him inside her mind. Watching her dance, being in the same room with her with their eyes locked, was like watching television with the sound off. Almost soothing, in a way.

Dead Angelika made a nice small light package, a hobo's bundle that Daniel easily swung over his shoulder. He had changed from the stained cream shirt into the clean blue one, scrubbed his fingertips, rearranged the furniture and rug to hide the stains. Not much could be done about the smell; pity that. If there was one thing he could change about humanity, it would be that they would not void their bowels and lose their bladders at the moment of death. Yes, yes, of course that was impossible. He had shit just the same when it happened to him.

Walking, whistling, through the lobby, he recalled a beautiful monochrome evening in Berlin, in June of 1927. He was walking toward a beer garden where a girl named Mathilde waited for him, and the severe black outlines of the buildings reinforced his resolve. The world flickered cinema-silver. He felt as though, with every step, he was closer to reinventing himself, fostered in the dizzy spirit of that time when Anything Might Happen, and change was a daily shock to everyone. He was twenty-three and an artist, plans rushing through his head to become a new Mephistopheles, a morningstar bringer of chaos, where each thing he did reflected the entropic nature of ideologies, identity, sex, everything. All thoughts flowed into and out of him. That was a significant night, although nothing much had happened with Mathilde; they kissed and drank beer and danced, and then he never saw her again. The last he'd heard, she had gone to the United States to be a movie star. Daniel made a mental note to check the immigration records at Ellis Island to see if she'd ever made it out of Germany.

Angelika's blood, as emotionally unsatisfying as it was, had nonetheless physically reinforced him, and no one asked him any questions as he strode through the hotel with a bundle of bedclothes on his back. He had a great litany that worked magic in these situations: *Hi, I'm your buddy. Don't mind me.* He saw only one person at a time, and each person nodded and never met his eyes. He caught a taxi to Brooklyn Heights. There was plenty of room to hide a body in Brooklyn Heights.

Scene Two: Ricky

Daniel had problems with his personal assistant.

Usually the agency was great about the people they sent into his viper's den; they were all "temps," replaced every three months. Daniel had only killed three of them, which was apparently, to the agency, an acceptable track record. They had to be good-looking, or at least charmingly cute in some way, young, and not too bright. He enjoyed the exposure to whatever insane youth fads were happening at the moment (his permeable mind rapidly picked up on their coarse and gorgeous slang), where the good clubs were, whether or not he would be stared at for wearing leather pants every day, that sort of thing. Thomas Arlington, bless his trust-fund, club-kid, Dalai-Lama-worshipping heart, had been enormously helpful in those situations, and what's more, had already been prone to disappearing for months on end on "spiritual journeys." He had not yet come back from his latest stated destination, Amazonian Brazil, and Daniel could only guess that Thomas's parents would be much happier to imagine their son lying on a bed of peat moss, chowing down on ayahuasca, than to know what actually happened.

Daniel's current assistant, Ricky, was coming to the end of his second consecutive three-month term, and his own arrogance about his place in Daniel's esteem had started to grow out of control. Ricky was very young and wonderful to look at, and once Daniel could comprehend his opaque Scottish accent, hilarious to listen to. Sometimes. And he actually, as an assistant, got things done. Sometimes. Daniel was still in love with Ricky's combination of sex-twink Tinkerbell and football hooligan at the end of the first three months; at the five-month mark, as hazy warm late summer simmered down into a wet and chilly fall, the bloom was off the rose.

Daniel's awakening brain throbbed in tune with frenetic dance music shaking the framed prints on the walls, and Ricky screaming into a wireless phone, dainty in his dainty hands: "No, fuckface, I tell you I want calf on that chair, and you send me suede! Suede is not calf! D'you ken what the difference is there? You know, one's fuzzy and the other one's smooth? Do you get it? Are you completely stupid? Is there any cunt there what knows—right. No, shite-for-brains, I want those delivery cunts out in front of the residence at *precisely* five o'clock. No, pee-em, for fuck's sake. On the dot! One minute earlier and I rip the fuckin' tits off whoever rings the bell. *Be! Fuckin' ! Professional!"* He threw the telephone against the wall, already dented from previous conversations, and relaxed into the orange suede chair with the plastic cover still on it, tossing his cigarette ash onto the floor beside it. "G'morning, sunshine," he called to Daniel, who stood half-dressed in the door to his bedroom. "Yer bookie called. Total washout. And you got this and this in the post, and your old queen of an accountant called. Is it all right if I go early? I have a party to go to. Starts at six. Fuckin' stupid time to start a party if ya ask me."

Daniel sighed and regarded the stacks of bills and catalogues. "Pay these," he said, handing the bills back to Ricky. Ricky got up and turned, head bobbing with the music, to the living room table. "And after you're finished with that, get out. I hate you."

"You what?"

"You foul-mouthed, slobbery, low-bred Glaswegian idiot, I hate your music, I hate your clothes, I even hate the way you smell. Now just write some fucking checks and never ash on my hardwood floors again." Daniel picked up a loose CD case and tossed it with a flick of his fingers at the kid's head.

Without noticing that he had almost been decapitated by a copy of *Spice World,* Ricky blinked innocently. "I can clean that up, Dan," he said.

"Clean it up with your tongue if you would. Actually, what a fine idea." Daniel blinked and smiled at Ricky. "I think you ought to."

Fun with directed thought!

After many years of trying to define this ability, Daniel had decided that it was merely directing a clearly defined intention into someone else's mind; if a consciousness wouldn't do what he suggested, he would just move along onto the physical body and provide it with directions. Eye contact was good—it guaranteed some concentration—but wasn't strictly necessary. Ricky's big eyes, with their deep limpid pupils, provided an easy portal, wide open. Daniel imagined the mind as a house with many, many hallways, all the doors unmarked; but eventually, he always found the right door. It was really easy, once you learned the layout of the place. He pressed against the door—it was heavy; Ricky, frightened, was fighting against him—but Daniel had more power when he was angry. The mental door flew open, and Ricky quivered helplessly.

With great effort, the boy eased onto his hands and knees on the rug, making quiet grunting sounds through his closed lips. Daniel fought down laughter, watching the giant tents of his flared jeans softly collapse onto the floor, great folds of useless denim with nothing to support them except two wee lumps of legs and the heels of monstrously thick-soled shoes poking out of their openings. Stupid kids—if Daniel lived to be five hundred years old, he would never wear giant pants.

Just a stupid kid.

A great spasm of guilt interrupted Daniel; he shuddered, and Ricky sat back down hard. "Forget it," Daniel said huskily, waving his hand. The force of his directed thought had cut off all at once; the shock to them both was profound. "Just go. I'm very unhappy with you."

Ricky got to his feet and collected his music disks, sobbing silently and tearlessly. "What happened?" Ricky mumbled. Daniel opened his mouth to ad-lib an explanation for how Ricky had ended up on the floor, but Ricky continued miserably, "I thought we loved each other."

"You're—" Daniel sat on the couch opposite, watching the patent leather reflect the bright white of his skin in broken tiles of light. "Nothing. I'm sure you do love me. That's why you have to leave."

"You radge cunt," Ricky blurted. He forlornly flipped open the shattered plastic CD case and traced Ginger Spice's generous contours. "Poor Geri; she's all scratched."

"What are you sorry for? You don't even listen to the Spice Girls anymore."

"I do! I just don't when you're about. You're so fucking elitist."

"Then you should be glad to get out of here. Rest assured you won't be replaced, the way you replaced so many other people. Maybe it's time I left New York."

"But how could you? Why would you want to? I have to duck the INS every fucking day I'm here, but it's worth it. It's the greatest city in the world. No other place matters."

"A place can never give you a sense of . . . place," Daniel said. "No sense of home. There is no home for anyone anywhere ever again."

"Listen at you. You're depressed. You need somebody to stay with you. You need *me.*" Ricky sat on the couch next to Daniel, his jacket pockets jagged with CD cases. "You know? I want to be here for you. It's been nice the last couple of months, do you think?"

"Jesus, Richard—*Dick*—you like living in a place with free sex and you've got all the money in the world to play with and a bathroom with gold water taps. You haven't heard a word I've said. I'm not depressed." Daniel stood up again and rubbed the spot on his leg where Ricky's giant jeans had touched him. "I feel like I see things more clearly now. Besides, you don't know, you can never understand what this is like."

Ricky shrugged. "The problem with you is that you're passive-aggressive, like. You let problems build up and never talk them through properly. I know, have a drink. You need a drink."

"You don't know anything. You know I don't drink."

"You drink all the time; I've seen you."

"It doesn't do anything for me," Daniel said through clenched teeth.

"The fuck it doesn't. I'll get it. Scotch?" Ricky was up and moving toward the kitchen, his little raver body lithe and quick. He was so lovely, Ricky, big gold fairy eyes with long fairy eyelashes, a scrub of blond hair, teeth innocent of orthodontics. And Daniel *did* like the way he dressed and the way he smelled. A long time ago in Hollywood, Daniel had known a boy about his age, actually younger by a few years, who every blond boy reminded him of. He mused that, after a hundred years or so, all people he liked or loved conformed to a certain template, an original that touched him deeply, impressed him, and all others after that had been mere imitations. He supposed that this was what people meant when they talked about "running to type"; one of his types was blond teenage runaway boys, even though they unfailingly got him into trouble.

He got up and followed Ricky into the kitchen to find the boy slugging down what appeared to be his second or third shot glass of single-malt whisky. "Brilliant, this," Ricky slurred, pouring another. Daniel approached Ricky from behind and held him in his arms. Ricky giggled sensuously and craned his cheek up to beg for a kiss. Daniel seized Ricky's head and took advantage of the vulnerable throat from the other side.

Thus fortified, Daniel let the limp boy slide from his arms onto the floor, and examined the rest of his mail. It was all bills; he never received correspondence, not even from any of his multitude of lovers who were still alive, in whatever form. He forgot about them for years at a time, then another one who fit a template would come along, and he would obsess on them gently until another walking reminiscence came by to occupy his thoughts. Most of those who had created the templates in the first place were now dead; these simulations were the closest he would ever come to experiencing them again.

Ricky stirred awake on the floor. "Worrappen?" he groaned, touching the sizzlingly tender spot on his neck. There was no blood; Daniel had licked it away.

"You drank too quickly," Daniel said, "passed out."

"That's funny . . ." A small spider hand appeared on the Formica countertop, joined shortly by another, and a scrubby blond forehead. "I never passed out once before I met you . . ."

"I have that effect on people," Daniel said. He felt the alcohol in his blood now, transmitted through Ricky's; a slow drunk drowsiness flowed coolly through his limbs. He helped Ricky to stand.

"So do I get to keep my job?" asked the boy, ever sensible. "If I lose it, I might end up having to go back to Scotland."

"You can stay until the end of your proper term, in two weeks," Daniel assented. "After that . . . it's no longer my problem."

"I thought you'd come round. It's good Scotch, isn't it, though? Only ninety dollars."

"It's excellent," said Daniel. "But there's this little matter of cigarette ashes on the floor."

Scene Three: The click and flash

He waited for her outside the strip bar until her afternoon shift ended.

Out in the street, in milky late daylight, with all the iridescent white makeup washed off, her skin was a sunless translucent pink, eyes like two gunmetal bruises under wet straggles of dishwater hair. She dressed like a bum, and he could smell the unwashed reek on her rain-speckled olive-drab coat. He just stood there lost in the scent for a while, reading through it countless nights of smoking cigarettes, smoking cannabis, drinking liquor, sweating as she walked, sweating as she ran, sweating in her sleep. That coat had come far since its last trip to the laundry, almost all of it on her body; in small rooms full of other people (trains? youth hostels? buses, probably), in rooms full of greasy food, in rooms full of makeup and hairspray and sex. He got so lost in the olfactory history that he almost forgot to follow her.

She took the subway downtown and he went with her, on a different car but the same train. Since he had a car (usually gone all the time with Ricky) or he caught taxis,

Daniel rarely took the subway; the smell, the noise, and the mind-cacophony of everyone else on the train distracted him. He glimpsed the girl hurrying away up the platform and barged after her through a group of disembarking women with shopping bags, spilling their expensive cosmetic contents all over the floor and down the gap. Before they could catch up with him, he had flitted between the tile columns and up the stairs three at a time.

She was tall; she walked with inner-city speed and determination. Daniel wished that he could become invisible, fly, or something. All he could do was dart between street corners, taking a moment to look down the block and note the general position of people and objects and then slip along, winding between people faster than they could see. His fellow pedestrians felt only the brush of chilly leather, hearing a distant rustle and the clapping of soles. Occasionally his predictions of their movements would be inaccurate, and he'd have to flash-dodge or step into the street to avoid collision. He enjoyed himself; this game used his most extraordinary abilities and yet he could not always predict the human chaos of the sidewalks. Tonight was easy—Manhattan, and seven in the evening, threatening rain again. People just wanted to get home.

So did she, he thought as he followed her to a filthy apartment block on the Lower East Side near the Williamsburg Bridge, with a couple of empty storefronts on its ground floor, the windows covered with uneven plywood squares. It was a neighborhood oddly deserted and quiet, as if dreadful things happened so often that the people lay paralyzed in their damp, crumbling homes, instead of daring the street, where broken glass glittered in swept-gem heaps on the corners.

Daniel slipped silently behind her as she dug keys out of her coat, and he began to speak in gentle, even, persuasive tones. "Hi, I know this is terribly unorthodox, but I thought I'd—"

The girl swung around and bashed him in the chest with the blunt plastic cylinder of a heavy flashlight, from which keys crashed and jingled. The plate of bone over his heart, the sternum, the armor that should have protected his insides, buckled like paper. Before he could take a breath she disappeared inside and her footsteps hammered on stairs ascending.

He stood there gasping for several minutes. He had lost the ability to see in color; everything in his line of sight wore a white fuzzy halo of pain, and the buildings looked like construction paper, sloppy rectangles collapsing in on themselves. He rested his hand against the door, bent over, and retched unproductively. A young kid watching the scene from his fire escape laughed and shouted over his shoulder to the apartment behind him in some Slavic language.

"Bitch," Daniel muttered, dripping saliva.

After a few more minutes of limping and cursing through the streets, he hailed a taxi back uptown toward home. Traffic gridlocked at Forty-second Street—trucks and cabs and cars blocked the intersections as if pausing to gawp at the new, vast billboard, featuring two tanned boys with their arms around each other in a clearly sexual and possessive fashion, dressed only in matching underwear. Daniel reached into his coat, withdrew his green cell phone, and called his orange cell phone. Orange was Ricky's favorite color.

Nine rings. "Yeah?"

"Ricky," Daniel said, "why can't you just answer the phone?"

"I was hoping voice mail would pick up."

"It didn't. Are you at home?"

"I'm at a Barn of some kind. There's a brilliant sale on housewares—do you prefer red or yellow drinking glasses?"

"Red. No, wait, no, I don't . . ." He paused for breath as spasms of pain interrupted him. "Listen. Would you please go home and draw me a hot bath? I just got cracked in the chest by a stripper. With a flashlight."

"What? No. Did you clothesline the bitch?"

"Ricky, I have a broken sternum. I really need a hot bath. Please." Daniel glanced at the taxi driver in the rearview mirror; he was a heavyset black man with his hair done in two French braids that spiraled across his skull, terminating in ram's horns resting on tight, greasy naps of hair on the back of his neck. He also had a gun. Daniel decided to let him live. "Do you have any drugs?"

"I have a gram or two of kind buds left from the party."

"Any uh . . . Vicodin or Percodan?" It would help for a little while, anyway.

Ricky shifted to a cocky, knowing tone. "It can be acquired, sir."

"Acquire it and bring it home. . . . I'm in a lot of pain. 'Bye."

Daniel folded the telephone and put it back into his pocket. The pain was always worst as the injuries began to heal; he needed to lie down and let the bones knit themselves properly or he'd have a cavity in his chest for weeks, even months, where the butt of the flashlight had gone in. Bones were tricky things.

"You got a broken sternum?" said the cab driver, sounding concerned.

"Yeah," Daniel said tightly.

"Shouldn't you go to the hospital? That's dangerous. Could stop your heart."

"No, I'll be all right." He felt dizzy. He couldn't stop staring at the black man's cheek, stippled lightly with razor burn spots like Braille. "I just need to get home."

"Traffic is a bitch; I'm sorry."

"I promise I won't die on you, man."

"If you die, you gotta tip me double."

"Funny . . ."

"Healing laughter, I always say."

"Owie laughter," Daniel gasped, sick and dizzy again.

It took another thirty minutes to get up to East Seventy-ninth Street and Daniel's flat. He flung too much cash at the taxi driver and staggered up the pavement to the front door; Ricky opened it with a flourish. "I just finished running the water. And I have twenty vikes."

"Great," said Daniel, "take them."

"What?"

"OK, take four of them. Sit down. Have a drink. Have some of that scotch if there's any left."

Ricky beamed, used to this kind of drug exchange. He bought the drugs for Daniel, then Daniel gave them to him, and then sometimes he passed out. They were very good drugs. "Right."

Ricky helped himself to some clicky ambient music on the stereo as well, and sat down on the new orange calf-leather chair with his overstuffed shopping bags of merchandise. Daniel dragged himself to the bathroom. Underneath his shirt, a hideous bruise spread between his nipples; his heart staggered unevenly.

The hot water took some attention away from the tickly pinprick agony of rebuilding the shattered bone tissue, but not enough, and he lay still and wondered how he might have done things differently. He really hadn't expected her to try to kill him. A punch with that dreadful flashlight would have easily killed an ordinary man, and she'd done it so swiftly and cleanly and simply that he wondered how many other men had fallen to her. She certainly danced with that kind of desperate strength, encapsulating all the force of her body into single gestures, but keeping her center of gravity precise at all times. He had not even seen her expression when she hit him, and the empty space tortured him—a smile, a snarl, or just nothing? Had she had the same blank, serious expression she wore while dancing?

"Ricky," he called, caressing the tingling injury, "come here, please."

Ricky swayed in, barefoot, grinning sloppily with half-lidded eyes. He unsteadily knelt next to the bathtub, and Daniel put his wet arm around the alcohol-vaporous boy and kissed him, tenderly, at the corner of his mouth.

"Eh," said Ricky, "that's a nasty bruise."

"Yeah," said Daniel. "It's a broken bone."

Ricky traced it gently with his rubbery, chilly fingertips. "Take some vikes," he advised, reaching into his pocket.

"Get in," said Daniel. "Kiss it better."

Flat white tablets scattered across the floor, loosed by

Ricky's limp fingers; he pulled his sweater and silk thermal T-shirt over his head and stepped out of the jeans, which collapsed floppily in on themselves where he had stood. His slight body sent a wave of water over the lip of the tub, melting the Vicodin tablets into a gummy powdery mess between the gray tiles. He covered Daniel's face and neck with kisses, weaving his head like a snake charmer, stroking Daniel's belly and crotch with his balls, blowing currents of cool air across Daniel's ears.

Daniel found the same spot on the boy's neck where he had bitten him so many dozens of times before, the tender column of pulsing tissue parting easily for his teeth, opening deep holes from which blood spurted dark onto livid skin, flowed brilliantly over Daniel's body and dispersed itself in the bathwater. Ricky barely moaned, but his limbs thrashed, splashing thin red solution onto the tiles and gold water taps; Daniel held him steady against himself, cock stiffening as it always did when he gulped so much fresh blood. He found and opened the boy's anus with his fingertips and forced himself inside.

"Mum," cried Ricky. His fingers found no purchase on the wet tile walls, and with an almost grateful sigh, the scrabbling eased to sliding, to slumping.

Ricky's thoughts blazed and sputtered rapidly—flashes of kisses on Glasgow dance floors and swellings of glory in Ibiza sunshine—fading down to swirling smokelike pleasure. He wanted to see his mother one more time, that was all, perhaps just smell the insides of her wrists as he had when he was a child . . . but this thoughtless ecstatic rush in Daniel's arms, with only the tiniest splinter of pain somewhere on the fringes, was not too bad . . .

It was gorgeous, a glory, to drink at last, for Daniel to give his body what it needed. It was all part of the same instinct, the perfection of being an animal; kill, eat, get high, fuck. He drank until he felt sick, paused for deep gulps of air, and as his head cleared he went back for the rest, gripping Ricky's limp hips with his hands until his fingernails pierced the flesh and his fingers tore muscle. He was not done yet. Ricky's heart fluttered, trying to force blood that wasn't there through its chambers; it staggered and seized, and Daniel was not yet finished.

Inevitable orgasm shot hot sparks through his groin, and Daniel let his head fall back onto the lip of the tub and quivered, holding the dead boy's body against his own. The bathwater, now frothy, diluted blood, remained warm, but not for long; the churning of their bodies had dispelled most of the heat. Orgasmic afterglow could not last for more than a minute, anyway. When he stood up, bloody water poured over his rosy, living skin and splashed the floor again. Ricky's eyes were open as he sank beneath the crimson waves.

Daniel left him there for the time being. As the bathwater dried, his hungry skin absorbed the blood from the water, leaving it very moist and warm and smooth; he shook himself in sections, like an animal, flecking the mirror and the walls with blood-lace, and ran wet fingers through his hair. He had plenty of time to go out, take down a few more victims, heal his body and his pride that much sooner. Something inside him was always ashamed when a woman surprised him, when a woman physically hurt him. He had ten times a man's strength and speed—how could she have done it?

Daniel rarely got severely hurt anymore; he was too good at playing the game, keeping others from seeing that it was simply an inconvenience for him to take a bullet. Far more dangerous, that, than just openly killing someone—that being, of course, an innate human characteristic.

He wondered at the mirror, "Am I getting soft?"

Scene Four: Supernova and Syncopation

"You just don't know how to take a hint, do you?" She said.

A smile this time; the gunmetal eyes blurry under a haze of liquor, she had come and sat next to him at the bar. One of her long rice-powdered arms stretched out across the Formica, picked up his drink, and brought it to her lips. They left a smudge of platinum shimmer on the rim of the glass. Daniel merely sat still and looked at her, silver tinsel bikini top, the waxed smoothness of the crease between her belly and her thigh, her scent of stage makeup.

"You should be dead right now," she continued in the same chipped-ice-and-whiskey voice, "or at least you should have figured out that you can stop coming here, so I'd like to know why I shouldn't call security. We got real nasty security here—bunch of Chinese guys, like to take parts of fingers off people."

"I came, as usual, to see you."

She swished the drink around inside her mouth for a while and said nothing. Her knees couldn't quite comfortably fit into the space between the bar stools and the bar, so she kept her legs semi-extended, with her platform-booted feet flat on the floor. Finally she swallowed and glanced away from Daniel. "I don't hustle," she said. "If that's what you think."

"I don't want a prostitute. That would be simple." He laughed, realizing how absurd that sounded even as he said it. "Would you like another drink?"

"No," she said. "Why aren't you dead?" She had shaved her eyebrows and replaced them with slim lines from a silver pencil. When she held her head at a certain angle, the silver line vanished into the general luminescence of her skin, and Daniel caught his breath, hallucinating the profile of the blond teenage boy he had rescued and treasured and loved in Hollywood, and who had escaped him forever without relinquishing that love.

"I don't know," Daniel said. "Sometimes I wish I were."

"That can be arranged, I'm sure." The dancer grinned. "I'd be more than happy to take that pesky life off your hands. That is, if you're offering."

Daniel instead offered her a cigarette from his plain steel cigarette case. She chose one with her fingertips, pointed and inquisitive at the ends of long, muscular fingers. Even the powder coating her couldn't completely cover the filth ringing her cuticles—multicolored oil paint ground to a mono mulch—or the tic-tac-toe patchwork of scars on her lower arms. Her nails were bitten to shit.

"Do you paint?" he asked.

"Yeah," she said.

"Did you cut *yourself?"*

Her forehead furrowed. "I wouldn't have it any other way," she said. The satin part of her silver miniskirt zinged across the vinyl of the bar stool, and her leg edged open the slit in her skirt wider. Visible at the slit, black mesh panty straps whispered into shadows. "You into cutting or something?"

"I've been known to be," Daniel admitted, lighting her cigarette. "But it's not my 'thing' or anything."

"What is your 'thing'?"

They stared at each other for several seconds. Daniel tried with all his might to break into her thoughts, grasping at any straw that might help him know what she thought, to tell her all of his *things* without wasting breath by speaking them aloud, but it was like trying to break through marble with a pair of school scissors. He gave up and sighed at his empty drink, and she gave a bright little quiver and sat up straighter.

"What are you trying to do?" she asked. "Did you just do something?"

"What do *you* think?" Daniel said, arching his eyebrow. "What did you just feel?"

She blinked. "Nothing," she said reflexively, as if in response to "What are you up to?" or "What'd you do in school today?" It was so obviously a lie, but there was no way for him to determine the truth. "Don't try to hurt me. You can't. You cannot hurt me." She said it with the same kind of intensity that he used when trying to hammer in the last hyper-mental suggestion, to make it stick. "You cannot do anything to hurt me, because I don't fear you. I don't fear pain. I don't fear death. You cannot frighten me, you cannot intimidate me, you cannot know the real me. So I can't imagine what you might think you can gain from me." She held up her arms and let them drop again. "I don't have any money, I won't give you a hand job, I—"

"I would like to see your paintings," he said.

"Well, I don't want to show 'em to you," she replied, frowning.

"To me, specifically, or to anyone?"

One of the momentous legs swung once and resettled. "I just don't," she evaded.

"You'll go far, with an attitude like that."

She sucked the inside of her cheek and looked away. "Do you paint? Looking for a model? I maybe could do that. For the right price. And as long as you promise not to touch me."

"I do paint," said Daniel. "I also make etchings and lithographs. I like doing figure studies."

"You want a model? A nude model?" She nodded.

"Hell, I'm naked all the time as it is." Daniel shrugged. "How much would you give me?"

"I can give you whatever you want," said Daniel.

"I doubt that," she said. "I don't think you could ever even know what I want."

"Be that as it may," he said. He withdrew a small parchment card from one side of another plain steel case and placed it on the bar between two puddles of condensation. "At any rate, since I've seen you perform so many times, why don't you come and see *my* show? It's usually sold out, and it's pretty good, if you ask me."

She cocked her head to read it, then put her finger on the card. " 'Featuring Daniel Blum as Frau Herr? The most devastatingly fierce revue on the East Coast'?" she read aloud with a slight laugh. "If you're such a superstar, how come I've never heard of you?"

"You have to be listening for me." He stood up and flicked a couple of creased bills onto the bar, making sure they landed in one of the puddles. "I'd like to see you there."

She sat still with her finger on the card as he put on his coat and walked through the club to the darkened, dogleg foyer. He never saw whether or not she even picked up the card.

He wandered the streets in a haze of misery, letting uneven speckles of rain hit him in the face without wiping them away. It was not like him to spend this much time pining over dead human lovers, but these wounds still felt new—he had not at all gotten his fill of the boy, Lovely, before Lovely was just gone, ripped out of existence, with so much more intense life still left in him.

Was it just childishness? During his dreadful last phone conversation with Ariane, his precious, adored, hellish, miserable vampire offspring, she accused him of pining for Lovely because Daniel wanted to be the one to kill him, and the laws of physics and inattentiveness got there first. "You lost a toy, and a toy you had already tossed aside for me, the next new, shiny toy, and you're just being a selfish little spoiled brat because you want to have it all. You have this grand romantic view of the way the world should turn out—you get all the sexy kids and then you either kill 'em when you get bored or you drag them down into the mud with you, lying to them about how fucking wonderful it is. Shut up! You *lied* to me! It's not fucking wonderful—it's a freakish lonesome hell on earth, kind of just like being a human being." On the phone she screamed so loud that the wires couldn't contain all her rage, her voice becoming a distorted bullhorn. She sobbed. She told him that she hated him, and then she hung up.

That phone call ended almost a year ago. A year since the wine of her voice turned to vinegar.

Daniel wondered what life would have been like if Lovely hadn't died, if there had never been a car accident—maybe everything would have been all right!—except that there was also Ariane, and how, according to her, he'd ruined her life. She wanted to be a vampire; she wanted a new life, she wanted to become other than human, better than human. He gave her what she wanted. But there were so many emotional and political machinations behind that, too, with Ricari and all the negative things that he'd said about Daniel to Ariane, and the hundreds of terrible things that he and Ricari had done to one another in the name of love and purity and freedom. And so on, back ad infinitum until he regretted having gone to art school in Zurich instead of staying in Berlin, and getting the apprenticeship at the shoemakers', as his father had wished. How pathetic! There was no way out except to keep going and hope there was a shining white light somewhere, with the voices of dead loved ones calling from inside it. And Daniel could not bring himself to believe in God or heaven or a misty illuminated afterlife—he had never known anyone who deserved it.

He chased his motivation into the psychotherapeutic rabbit hole; from the darkness, Dr. Sigmund winked and ashed his cigar and said, "Libido. It's simple. You're frustrated. You want the girl."

Abrupt hunger tunneled a headache through his skull.

On the wide half-circle of concrete underneath the Manhattan Bridge, on the Brooklyn side, he tore a john and a hooker apart from each other, the john's head smashing against the cobblestones and the hooker crushed into the space between the open car door and the chassis. Both were skinny, Asian, and in their thirties. Neither made more than a startled choking sound as the blow job was rudely terminated; the man died instantly, and the woman fell unconscious. Daniel tapped the vein in the woman's lean golden thigh and took a few swallows, but nothing more. He didn't need more, and didn't want more than the distorted Polaroid snapshot of her mind that he got. It was a methodical, joyless, thoughtless act, like visiting a convenience store in midday; no danger, no meaning.

Afterward he went home to rehearse his act; the difficult heifer probably wouldn't show, but in case she did . . . and anyway,there was no harm in sitting before the mirror, putting on makeup he didn't need, nuzzling a cheap and threadbare white fur collar up close under his chin, practicing languorous gestures with his long skeletal fingers, and singing his songs with only the melody. Without someone listening, there was no point in actually singing words that Daniel knew by heart.

She probably wouldn't attend.

But in case . . .

"We haven't heard from Ricky in a while—he has a paycheck to pick up and everything. Do you have any idea where he might have gone?"

"No," said Daniel. "I haven't seen him in more than two weeks. He took off in a huff—we had a falling out, and he said he wanted to see the country. He mentioned something about train-hopping . . . I apologize for not calling, but I've been very busy, taking care of my own business as I am right now."

"Oh, dear. We know he has an irresponsible streak—as I'm sure you know, too."

"Yes," said Daniel. "I do indeed."

"Ordinarily we do try to screen our applicants better—I do apologize for our track record—"

"Don't worry about it," said Daniel. "I would never

have imagined myself to be such a bad employer. Maybe I complain about New York too much and they take me seriously." He chuckled casually into the phone, pausing as he scrubbed soap into his faded black cotton T-shirt. Assistants, at least, were useful in that they did the laundry; in his case, a lot of it consisted of pre-treating troublesome protein stains. "But I do appreciate the efforts of the agency—"

"We are concerned, nevertheless, Daniel, and we would very much appreciate it if he contacts you if you could let us know—this is an issue with the INS and we'd like to keep things neat and tidy, if you know what I mean."

"I know exactly," said Daniel, startling at the sound of the door buzzer. "Now I really must go, there's someone at the door. Good night."

The laundry service had sent Daniel a new person—a man in his early fifties, thick-necked, tobacco-colored, a plush black mustache, heavy musculature stretching the bleached-white material of his uniform shirt. "Is Noor ever coming back?" Daniel asked ingenuously, handing over the black mesh bag.

"He is still in hospital," said the man gruffly. "He had operation, most of his spleen was removed."

"Oh, dear God, that's terrible. Excuse me, good-bye, thank you."

Daniel kicked the door closed behind him. Barely an hour left before he had to be at the club in Nolita, a good half-hour's drive away. And he wasn't yet dressed.

Being rushed would not help his glamour. He decided to put on makeup at the club, since he'd have a good hour of sitting around before he actually had to take the stage. He had his props and music already packed; his dress, gloves, shoes, stockings, and shawl already laid out on his bed ready to slip on. He glanced at the mirror in the foyer of the apartment; his hair was clean and full and sparkling today, only requiring the lightest touch of a curling iron to change it from a rock star shag into a soft mane of ebony waves. His eyebrows needed plucking.

This could be done. No reason for panic. It would not do to be nervous.

"Idiot," he said to himself, pulling his shirt over his head and unzipping his jeans, "you're ninety-seven. You've done more cabarets than she's had hot dinners."

He put on his dressing-up music.

The dress, ingeniously fitted so that he had no need for false breasts, a long narrow sheath of iridescent black silk taffeta; the stockings of colorless sheer nylon, fastening to soft rubber clasps of purple satin garters; black and silver stiletto-heeled pumps that had not worn out since he got them in 1933; long black satin gloves to cover his black-haired forearms and impossible hands; three yards of the finest black sheer sprinkled with silver flecks and edged with a thousand jet crystals to soften his jutting white shoulders and protect his pretty neck from the wind, spitting hard fragments of rain.

He seized a moment to enjoy the sight reflecting from the long mirror in his closet. That was half the satisfaction; and if the sight of himself did not make him nearly giddy with pleasure and excitement, he could hardly hope to bring about the same response in anyone else. He threw back his head, stripped off a glove, and, with his inch-long glossy black fingernails, touched the jut of his Adam's apple, prominent because of his thinness. Without the shawl, he could not come close to passing as a woman. Looking like a Real Girl had never been his desire; he wanted to look like a gorgeous man in a dress, just a little bit all wrong. Thrilling dissonance.

He poked at the bulge at the front of his dress. "This *certainly* won't help me look feminine," he said. "C'mon, Little Bastard, let's go fuck with people."

At the club (a restaurant called Remy's during the day, and either Gemini or Cuntbox at night, depending on who held the reins), Daniel marched in through the front door. Three men had already arrived, two of them drinking martinis and eating tapas and one of them dancing by himself at the edge of the stage. On stage, the Supreme Gina (also known as Gary Osterman) wrestled with a microphone stand that wouldn't extend any higher than crotch level. She shot a look of absolute poison at Daniel. "Are you too pretty-pretty to help me out here?"

Daniel stroked his ebony waves with one gloved hand. "If I tear this shawl, my darling, I'll have to kill everyone here."

"No big loss. Present company excepted, of course, and by present company, I mean me."

Daniel swept past through the kitchen. There was no point in trying to be pleasant to the Supreme Gina; if he told her that her dress was fantastic, she'd complain about how much it cost; if he apologized for being late, she'd remind him that he was late last time, too. In the past, Daniel had fun making the Supreme Gina trip over her skirt when going on stage, or belch in the middle of her showpiece lip-synch "Baby Love," but after a year of being Featuring Daniel Blum as Frau Herr, the game had gotten boring. Now he just let the Supreme Gina work herself into her little snits and did his show.

"Backstage," in the lavatories and kitchen-storage area, emergency eyelashes were replaced, lips were freshly glossed, and privates poked and taped and hoisted. "I'm getting this fucker *cut off!*" yelled Cindy Cameltoe, hopping on one foot as she pulled on a fresh pair of thick beige panty hose.

"Careful or you'll run your tights," Daniel advised mildly, dropping his makeup case into a bathroom sink and sucking in his cheeks at the mirror.

"Careful or your face will stick like that," said Cindy Cameltoe.

"It already has," said Daniel.

She kissed the air next to his face. Cindy Cameltoe was a big heavy trannie in her late twenties, tonight in a Wonder Woman miniskirt that nearly exposed the aforementioned fucker and a sequined bullet-bra bustier. Her breasts were huge and magnificent, purple Bettie Page wig immaculate, face glimmering with thick tan pancake makeup. It didn't quite hide the jail-pastime teardrop tattoo on her cheekbone. "Do I look all right?" she begged. "Jenny and I are up first. I'm not prepared at *all.*"

"You look wonderful," Daniel said. "Something new tonight?"

"Yeah, will you watch?"

"If I can," he promised.

"You look wonderful tonight," Cindy Cameltoe sighed, fingering the shawl. "This is so beautiful. Where'd you get it?"

"I've had it for so long I forgot." Daniel sighed and smiled. "I gotta put my face on. I'd like to see your thing . . ."

Jenny Juicemaster sidled up and put her arm around Cindy Cameltoe. "I've seen her thing, and it ain't much," she put in. Jenny was butcher, more rock 'n' roll, in studded leather corset and platinum-blonde mullet hair. Her tits were very fake and a little lopsided. Without Daniel having to say anything, she adjusted them. "Contents may shift during transit," she explained. "I gotta say, Frau Herr, you don't really look like you're dressed for a party good time tonight. This is more chichi elegant funeral wear."

"Wasn't it you who told me I look like a ghost, anyway?" Daniel patted on white powder.

Jenny shrugged. "Better go, honey," she sang to Cindy. "We have to do our Laverne and Shirley bit . . ."

" 'Schicmicl, schlmozcl,' " Cindy rcplicd with a laugh. "See you later, Danny boy."

"Make money," said Daniel.

"Make money! Girl . . . Is there even anybody here yet?"

"Couple of people," said Daniel. "Not a lot."

"Ohhhh boy," said Jenny. "The Supreme Miss Gina is gonna be on the warpath tonight. You'd think the bitch didn't have a day job."

Daniel didn't make money from his performances. If he made tips, he gave them to the other girls, knowing they needed the money far worse than he. When he was young, and human, he had performed for the money; the scraps of pocket change, enough to buy a meal, a drink, a few sniffs of cocaine, a book, a bauble for the next sexual conquest. But even then, he performed for those fleeting moments of pleasure in the eye contact with the audience, catching those delicious flutters of awe, desire revealed. He did it for love. Or the illusion of love. And was there a difference?

". . . Daniel, you're getting makeup on your scarf."

He glanced up; Antoine, spit-curls peeking from under a jaunty cream-colored beret, stood next to him, although the top of Antoine's head was at the level of Daniel's shoulder. Antoine was a Real Girl or, at least, the perfect simulacrum of such; dainty, olive-skinned, a dead ringer for Natalie Wood, post-op and quivering with the real and synthetic hormones that she gulped like handfuls of candy. Her voice sounded like wood flutes. Daniel hastily unwrapped the shawl from the sink and shook tiny golden particles off the fabric.

"You were really lost in there."

"Sometimes that happens when I'm looking at myself," Daniel confessed.

Antoine scoffed delicately. "I bet it does."

From the stage came the boom, thump, and wail of Diana Ross on tape. "Are there people out there?"

"Oh, I don't know. I can't bear to look until I'm there. If there's a lot of people, great! And if there's not, then there are fewer people to make fun of you if you fuck up."

"You're not gonna fuck up." Daniel chuckled.

"No, *I'm* not," said Antoine.

Daniel arched his eyebrow. "Is this your version of 'Break a leg,' little girl?"

Antoine shrugged and toyed with her little bone-handled pocketbook. "No . . ."

"Don't fuck with me when I'm nervous."

"Why are you nervous? You're always so . . . in command." Antoine rubbed one hand against the front of Daniel's dress, where there were no breasts to fill out the points at his bodice, and the Little Bastard had gone away.

"I invited someone who I really want to impress," Daniel said, finishing his eyes. "Tonight's very important to me. I'm doing an old song . . . I know I can do it, because I've done it before."

"I've never figured out why you still do these gigs," Antoine said. "Gina doesn't like you. You give away all your money."

"Why do you dress in vintage Chanel? Why the French manicure? I haven't figured out why you gave up . . ." He glanced at the smooth front of her skirt. ". . . All that."

" 'Cause it wasn't *me,*" Antoine retorted.

Daniel shrugged, as if to say, *so there.*

She made a tiny sound of concession and lowered her eyelashes. "Good luck, anyway," Antoine purred. "I hope you impress whoever it is that you want to impress."

"I usually do."

Antoine went away, humming, and Daniel returned to his face. At times it was difficult not to rip the throats out of every single person encountered in a day, particularly pretty little sadists like Antoine and her good-luck bullshit. He wondered if Antoine ever saw fangs behind the crimson lips; she was the sort who liked to court danger, anyway. She knew her life wouldn't be long or healthy, hips and lips plumped with silicone and forearms pimpled with needle tracks.

Daniel couldn't resist looking out into the house from behind the corner separating the kitchen from the rest of the place; more patrons had arrived, although tonight's show was far from standing room only. Only the usual suspects were there; transvestites from the sublime to the grotesque, cloudy-eyed career fag hags and their quivering alcoholic idols in cravats, boys in actual boy clothes but with gestures and accents all their own. Only half a house. Daniel sighed. But for the cut of the clothes, it might have been the same crowd from the Mikado Bar in 1930, after-hours, smoking bad cigarettes, gulping schnapps, picking each other up by glances across the room.

He caught sight of something creeping in the shadows at the very back; colorless in the dark, nearly bent double, a faint flash of pale face without eyebrows. He tried to burrow through the susurrus of minds in the club, most of them fortunately focused on Cindy Cameltoe and Jenny Juicemaster on stage playing patty-cake to "Dirty Deeds Done Dirt Cheap" and thus easy to ignore; but he couldn't find anything; the creeping creature, now huddled in a chair with the coat hood up, might as well have been made out of the wood of the chair.

Daniel rummaged quickly in his makeup case for his cards, wrapped his shawl around his neck and face, and rushed to the bar, where the Supreme Gina's on-again, off-again boyfriend Sammy filled his splashed tray with cocktail glasses. Daniel mentally tapped Sammy on the shoulder, and the man looked up, smiling when he saw who it was. "Oh, hey, how's it going?" Sammy whispered.

"I have a favor to ask you. Send this with a glass of champagne to the young lady in the far corner." From the folds in his shawl, he produced a card with the number of the cell phone with the red metallic faceplate; he used that phone the least frequently, which meant that it worked most reliably, and there was not a single living being left who had the number.

"Ooh, on the make?" Sammy deftly pinched the card between his fingertips and slipped it into the pocket on his apron. "No problem. And I think you're up next, aren't you?"

"She's a dealer," Daniel replied. "Now that Ricky took off, I need to make my own connections . . ." Gently, without touching, Daniel pushed him away.

"I'll talk to you about it later," Sammy said, and smoothly raised his tray above his head. "Time for you to go on—get back there!"

"Let's hear it again for the Titsome Twosome, Miss Jennifer Juicemaster and Miss Cindy Cameltoe!" The Supreme Gina shouted half to the house and half backstage. "Shit, I haven't seen that much jiggle since that Jell-O shot party on Halloween—oh, honey, I know *you* were there, I still have the stains on my dress! Fortunately the dress is white, too . . . Thank you for coming out to another glorious evening at Gemini. I am your splendid hostess, the Supreme Gina, and I am a Gemini. How many of you gorgeous people are lucky enough to be

Geminis? No, it's great! I have two *separate* walk-in closets." The Supreme Miss Gina toyed with the microphone cord, wrapping it around her shoulders as she stalked back and forth across the stage, squinting nearsightedly at the cheerful hecklers in the front row. Behind her, Cindy set up Daniel's props. "What was that, sweetie? Split personality? Yep, here's one, and here's two." She glanced down at the front of her sequined gown and whipped her hand out at the audience. "Don't look at me like that, you'll curdle my makeup. We're all beautiful here, aren't we, boys, girls, and otherwise? Yes, we're all beautiful, and just a little bit crazy, which helps us survive. Yes, child. Next up—shut up now! Next up, we have our featured performer. This is a very, very special creature; she's like nothing you've ever seen before. Even if you were here at Gemini last time. She's got multiple personalities worse than Sally Field. *Girl?* She will move you, she will freak you, she will terrify you, she will soothe you. . . . Ladies and gentlemen and whatever the fuck *that* thing is, I give you, tonight at Gemini, *sieg Heil*—Frau Herr!"

Daniel made his body into a whip, a long slim tightly wound riding crop, the metal heels of his shoes sinking gently into the low carpet on the stage and the beads edging the shawl clicking together. Daniel did not allow himself to notice the liquor-warm applause; he blocked out everything farther than the edge of the stage, any objects besides the microphone stand and tall four-legged stool next to it. If he listened to the audience, if he allowed himself into their minds, he would lose his concentration, let his voice slip out of control, stumble on the hem of his dress. None of these things had ever happened, but tonight would not be a good first time.

He reached his mark, stopped, and gazed up into the lights. He glanced over to where the drab lump squatted; her eyes were unreadable at this distance with the distraction of the stark white spotlight on his face. Enough, then, that she was there, with a glass of champagne in front of her. Time for him to sing.

Frau Herr's whole act was in German; it was simpler

than attempting to come up with saucy witticisms that could come close to the gleefully scatological words of the other performers. The spoken words weren't much, anyway; a good evening, an introduction, an explanation. Let the other trannies mouth the words to other divas' standards; he would sing his own song, and an original one, not something they'd ever heard. He nodded at the handsome young lesbian who ran the sound board and she nodded back, starting his tape. He had recorded his own music, as well—a slightly out-of-tune piano recorded in a Mafia bar uptown while the staff moved and worked around him without being able to see him, and guitar recorded in his study, mixed together just well enough to sound good through Gemini's mediocre P.A.

The microphone was just a prop. He didn't need it to amplify his voice, and if he sang at something even approximating full voice, there wouldn't be an unbloodied ear in the house. So many microphones had been destroyed by his proximity before he learned that they were unnecessary. It was his own mike, glamorous and classy and vintage, an Electro-Voice Cardyne 731 the size of two conjoined fists and gleaming immaculate chrome. Back when the mike worked, it transformed his voice into something dictatorial and faceted; too bad that was back in the Fifties, and that he'd since snapped its delicate ribbon innards.

With just a little extra breath and a tightening of the muscles in his throat . . .

"Synkopieren"; Eva had written the song for him in 1929, the end of their relationship; she was still in love with him, although his attention had wandered back across the gender divide and now Daniel wanted a man, a strange little Italian with eyes like ice-water, who spoke no German. Eva wrote songs the way others wrote in their journals. Gorgeous Eva, abandoned Eva, Eva who spent an hour patiently teaching a jazz song to her faithless lover and the next evening hanged herself in the lavatory of the Mikado. The bottom of her vocal range was almost exactly the same as the top of Daniel's. She played the guitar she'd learned in summer camp and smacked his hand when he became distracted. "Listen," she admonished, "I wrote this song just for you; the least you could do for me is try to remember it."

Syncopation . . . Originally the song was a faster one, jumpy and bouncing, with Eva's head full of Louis Armstrong; Daniel made it much slower, and it became disjointed. Originally the song was quirky, and Daniel delighted in making it achingly sad and odd. No one had killed Eva. She got rid of herself. And probably for the best.

He sang and remembered her warm green eyes, staring blankly ahead as she swung from the pipes in the ceiling.

The audience, prepared for an evening's giddy campy fun, squirmed uncomfortably in their seats, ordered several new rounds of drinks, lit cigarettes, disappeared into the toilets. All but one, really. One, the sullen army-drab lump, sat up straight, listening, galvanized.

In her direction, Daniel allowed himsclf a smile full of fangs.

All wrong; it destroyed the illusion of willowy melancholy, and it was awkward to switch back to it. From then on, his performance became camp by its very nature. Oh, look at her, isn't she *terribly* sad and gothic and miserable, isn't this a weird song. The audience began to talk amongst themselves and snicker behind smoke-shrouded hands. He wanted to get angry, but it was pointless; he'd blown it himself. Might as well finish in the right way. He hiked his skirt and straddled the stool and drew out his voice, cawing like a cross between Lotte Lenya and an ostrich in heat. He whipped the shawl around like a matador incensing a bull. The audience whistled and cheered and held up cocktail glasses; a few folded one-dollar bills fluttered to the stage at his feet.

When the song was over, amid brief and halfhearted applause, Daniel looked over into the corner again and the shadow was gone.

Scene Five: Fetish Objects

Daniel's studio occupied the penthouse of an office building in midtown. His staff of seven assistants met and worked there, and invited all their artist friends over to use the space; in exchange, Daniel sold and traded their artwork and designs, thus giving the young artists visibility, and making nice money from sales and commissions at the same time. Most of the transactions took place over the phone or by fax, and Daniel occasionally felt tempted to assign his own name to particularly audacious works—who'd be the wiser?—but his ego, masquerading as integrity, got in the way. If the bourgeois idiots who collected art hadn't yet recognized his talents, he had the time to wait and see if his recognition came at the end of a natural human life. Still, he had stalled; he had barely created anything since he escaped from Hollywood five years ago with only his life, his bank account numbers, and the clothes on his back.

He had not even visited his studio for eight months when he arrived on a bright Saturday afternoon, vibrating with tension, swinging a massive camera bag on one wrist.

At least thirty people stood around; artists, models,

scenesters, and young ruffians, blaring French *banlieue* rap music, drinking, and decidedly not making art. They all fell silent and rigid when Daniel walked off the elevator, Darth Vader–like in his long black leather coat, cowboy hat, gloves, and sunglasses. Ordinarily, Daniel came to the studio only after dark, and his assistant would call ahead and warn everyone, but such order had passed away with Ricky's mangled corpse in the bathtub.

"What the fuck is going on?" Daniel asked in a quiet, tightly controlled tone.

"Hey, hi, Daniel." Joachim, Daniel's head assistant, stood up from a beanbag chair and re-created himself as spokesperson. "Why'd'nt you have Ricky call? We weren't expecting you today."

"Ricky no longer works for me." Daniel took off the hat and sunglasses and scanned the party. Groups of apprehensive teenagers cowered on couches, unsure of whether or not to try to hide the drugs. Most of them had never seen him before. He decided to work the Vader angle, knowing the image resonated with these children more than the Devil himself, deepening his voice to the very bottom of its register and polishing up his usually hardly noticeable German accent. A little fascism was good for his soul! "I actually own this place; I don't see why I have to get permission to come here. I have something that I need to do today and time is short. Everyone here right now who is not actively involved in photography, film or digital, get out. Everyone here who *is* actively involved in photography, you will assist me in getting this place ready on the double. I am expecting someone in fifteen minutes."

She had called while he lay awake in bed, paralyzed with worry–insomnia, his body clenched as if waiting for a gunshot. "OK, I'm interested," came her disembodied voice through the telephone. "I need to know how much I'm going to be paid if I model for you."

"Like I said, I'm willing to give you whatever you ask for."

"OK, I need five hundred bucks." Her tone was flat and rushed.

Daniel chuckled to himself, feeling a new kind of tension in his body, infinitely preferable to that which had kept him from sleep. "It's yours. Why are you interested now? Did you get fired?"

"No, I did not. Huh. I wish. Anyway, I'm free today, so . . ."

"Let me give you the address of the studio."

Fifteen minutes of frenetic activity transformed the studio from a dope-smoky, way-after-hours party into a rough semblance of a workspace; umbrella lights, a black canvas backdrop, an upholstered antique chair, a long table set up with Daniel's three cameras and a menagerie of lenses and flashes, bottles of Cointreau and champagne and water. Joachim fussed over the arrangement of the empty glasses on the table, mumbling guiltily to Daniel. "Hey, sorry I didn't make it to the show last night . . . it was uh . . . Jo's birthday and we went to see *Les Miz* . . . y'know. But, hey, you're working today, huh? Is it somebody famous?" Joachim adjusted a tripod with blunt, stained hands.

"No," said Daniel. "It's just this girl I met."

The girl he met showed up precisely then, shuffling off the elevator in her aromatic coat, her hair vanished under a cheap stocking cap, no makeup. "This the place?" she called into the studio.

She took off her coat and hat and threw them on the floor; underneath, gray workmen's coveralls and her bristling shock of yellow-silver hair. Daniel watched her, smiling. "Did you like the show?" he asked.

She didn't reply, too involved in scratching her underarms and staring around the room.

"The least you could do is tell me your name," he said.

"You've heard my names," she replied. An assistant approached her with a lit cigarette, and she stared until it was withdrawn. "You have a variety of names to choose from. You have a couple yourself, don't you? I don't care what you call me."

"Your name," insisted Daniel. He held out a Lucite clipboard with a release form and pen attached. "Read this and sign it. So I can sell any pictures I take."

"Sybil," she muttered, scribbling, the pen cap in her mouth.

"That your name?"

"That's my name."

"Really?"

"In fact." She glanced at the antique chair under the lights, then turned and sat in one of the tattered beanbag chairs along the wall instead. Daniel scanned the release form, stroking her scrawly name drawn in so deep it dented the paper. Name *Sybil Morocco Drulli.* Date of birth *the beginning of the end.* But she'd actually put down a Social Security number; whether or not it was a real one was impossible to discern. She was smirking at him when he looked up, and she waved her arm in the direction of the elevator. "Tell those guys to go. We should be alone."

Daniel glanced around the room. "You heard her," he said.

The remaining assistants had again frozen in place in a stunned tableau, staring at the girl. It took a while for all of them to gather their things and head toward the elevator. "You're sure?" Joachim murmured to Daniel.

"I'm sure," Daniel replied. He was too anxious to sweeten the dismissal with a smile. Joachim wavered back and forth, balanced on the balls of his feet, and Daniel gave him a tiny mental push. "I said go and that means you, too. I'll call you later."

With a screaking of elevator gears, Daniel and Sybil were alone in the room.

"It's pronounced somewhere between 'drool' and 'dull,' " she said. "With an 'e' at the end." She turned away and scratched some more. "Smells green in here. I suppose they took all the grass with them?"

"Would you like a drink?" he asked, strolling toward the table with the cameras and beverages. He poured himself a glass of water. "Some coke? Vicodin? I don't have any marijuana. Sorry."

She arched the stubble of her eyebrows. "So you're some big-shot artist, huh? Do you sell those kids' stuff?

Must make a lot of money off it." She took out her own cigarette and lit it with a paper match.

"Some," said Daniel. "I make something like a living as an art dealer."

"But not as an artist?"

"No. I wish I did. I've never been able to quite make a living as an artist."

"You're not meant to," said Sybil, "it would be wrong. Art isn't a profession. It's a disease." She let out her breath in a sniff and pressed her lips together, the portrait of a child pleased to be naughty.

"Don't you want to sit over here?" Daniel stood by the antique chair, caressing the velveteen with his hand. "It's a lovely chair."

"Aren't you going to ask me to take my clothes off?"

He shrugged, thinking strongly *yes*. "I don't care if you do."

"Money," she said.

He reached into his pocket, began to unfurl bills from the roll restrained by a groaning plain steel clip. "Five hundred," he said, dropping the bills onto the chair. He unpeeled a few more. "Two hundred more if you sit in the chair."

"What's with the chair? Is it some kind of fetish object?" She stood up, though, and approached him, silent sneakered feet on the concrete floor, eyeing him curiously. "I can't figure you out," she confessed. "I've already told you I won't fuck you."

"You don't have to do anything," said Daniel. "I don't even really have to take pictures. That was a pretext. I just wanted to get you in the same room with me, without there being flashing lights and nipples and pubes and that whole strip-club vibe in the air. I'd like to form a separate association, think of you outside that context."

"I don't have a context," she said.

"Everyone does," he protested.

"I don't."

"You do. Before, you were in a stripper context. I always picture you naked."

"That's because I'm always naked." She smiled. She

bobbed her shoulders in groove to some song only she could hear. "Everybody's naked. I amuse myself by imagining what people look like without their clothes."

Daniel smirked and took off his coat, then his dress shirt and leather pants. She watched him incuriously, still half-dancing. He picked the bills off the chair and seated himself in it, arranging his cock and balls so that they lay on the velveteen, on display as if in a jeweler's shop window. "Is this what you imagined at all?" He met her shadowed, cool eyes. For a split second, he saw his own smug reflection.

"Have you ever been a stripper?" Sybil circled the chair, pausing to pick up the bottle of Cointreau, from which she sipped as she talked. "You carry yourself kind of like a dancer, some kind of circus acrobat or something."

"I was a stripper a very long time ago," he said. "I had a strip act that I did in full Marlene Dietrich drag and sang this Kurt Weill song, then took off all my clothes, and then I shook my johnson at the crowd. Very scandalous."

"I've seen that done," she scoffed. "This guy I saw in a bar in Chelsea does that drag act, that *Blue Angel* thing."

"I did it first," Daniel said archly.

"Yeah, right, like how long ago?"

"Long before you were born." He smiled and rearranged himself on the velveteen again, forming a different composition, balls to one side. "Back when it was still a new act."

"You can't be that old," Sybil said cozily, leaning over him and studying the jeweler's display more closely. "You can't be that much older than me."

"I'm older than both of your parents," he said.

"Yeah, right. You can't even be forty—I'd see the plastic surgery scars." She pulled his hair back from his temples, examining the skin behind his ears.

"I'm old," he assured her. "I've also been a mime, and an actor, and a model . . . they're all versions of the same thing. Being looked at. It's addictive after a while."

"It's also a pain in the ass," she scoffed.

"But I have a feeling you like it," said Daniel.

"I bet you do have a *feeling,"* she said, reaching out and touching his temple. He felt a fast flutter of pulse between his legs. "Your skin is like . . . softer than my skin. . . . You're probably like twenty-five or something, you can't be older. . . ." She ran her fingers over his temple and down his neck. Daniel caught his breath and sighed, parting his lips and looking up at her. Some unseen force stole his suave facade and replaced it with that of a slack-jawed, hormonal idiot.

She took a flinching step back. "Am I supposed to be getting turned on by this?" she demanded. "Am I supposed to be impressed?"

"No, I just want you in the room with me. I wanted to look at you, but if you want to look at me, that's fine, too."

"Fine. Because I'm not turned on." She picked up the smallest camera, a simple 35mm with autofocus, and took a photo of Daniel sitting naked in the chair. "You do have a good drag queen body," she admitted. "You take a pretty picture."

"Yeah, I've heard that, too," he said.

She moved in closer and focused directly on his genitals, harmless, soft, pale violet against the dark green velveteen. She took several snaps. "Can I have these when you develop them?" she asked distractedly.

"Of course."

"I collect photos of cocks."

"Do you have a lot?"

"Do *you* have a lot?" she mocked him. Her hand darted out and touched the head of his penis, retreating as it twitched up toward her, as if attracted by static electricity. "I thought so. You should make your cock hard. It's more interesting to look at that way."

Despite himself, he trembled, and goose pimples galloped across his body from neck to shins. "What're you, cold?" she teased, taking more pictures.

"I don't know," he said quietly.

"Make it harder. Do whatever you need to do." She

smiled as he took himself in hand, stroking himself slowly and firmly.

"You could always help out." His penis became bright pink immediately, warmed in his palm. He bent over and blew a stream of his own warm breath at it. It popped up, pointing straight at her. She shuddered, choking back giggles.

"Wow, are you *blowing* yourself? I always thought it would be more exciting." She was laughing openly now, biting her bottom lip to steady herself as she clicked the shutter. "Not to mention harder—um, I mean, more difficult." She stared into a corner of the room and spoke as if she were talking to God. "Penises are really stupid-looking."

He stared at her. "I think the idea of collecting photos of cocks is really . . . fantastic."

"Except that it's a lie," said Sybil.

"A lie?"

"You know, not true. I don't collect anything. I just wanted to see if I could get you to jack off in front of me." She unloaded the camera, slipped the film canister into one of the pockets of her huge coveralls, and tossed the camera onto the table. "You're an idiot."

"At least I got to jack off." He sighed and let his softening penis go. A lie. A lie he hadn't even felt a flicker of. It should have been painted on her face like dime-store lipstick, but he saw only her strong-boned pallid face with the superior smile and eyes that told him nothing. "Now take off your clothes so I can shoot you and you can earn that money you took from me."

She seemed amenable to the idea, even hummed as she unzipped the coverall and let the gray sack drop to her feet. Daniel stood up and offered her the velveteen chair. Under the intense silver-white light of the umbrellas, he saw the webbing of stretch marks that marked her all over, tits, shoulders, arms, hips, ass. Hence the powder she wore to dance. Compared to her, his skin was as poreless as paper, the fine black hair stark and obscene against it. He took up his favorite camera, a now-vintage Hasselblad, a replica of the first camera he had ever owned, and stared at her for a moment, trying to see a picture. "Do you want *me* to jack off?" she asked.

"You can if you want," he said.

"No," she decided, shrugging languorously. "You'd probably sell 'em."

"What's the matter with selling photos? They're my pictures and I have the right to do whatever I want with them."

"No, it's my body and pictures of me with my hand in my snatch."

"As if you don't take off your clothes in front of a hundred people every single night," said Daniel. He reached out and adjusted the right lamp so that her breasts cast a shadow against her belly and the single slight roll of extra flesh at her waist dissolved in the light. "As if those guys don't go home with an image of your body in their minds so they can masturbate or keep a hard-on long enough to fuck their wives."

"That's different," said Sybil with a smile. "I'm the one making money from that."

"You're making money now," said Daniel.

She sat quietly for a while, wrists trapped between her thighs, rocking slightly back and forth. "I don't get you," she confessed. "I can't figure out what you want."

"Neither can I," he said.

"Hmm. Well, this is boring."

"Modeling is boring. So talk," said Daniel. "About yourself."

"Like what, though?"

"Pretend you're on a talk show."

"Like a ravages-of-prostate-cancer-survivors talk show or a bitch-stole-my-man talk show?"

Daniel just laughed. "How old actually are you?"

"Eighteen," she said.

"Did you graduate from high school? Stretch out your legs, please."

"No," she said. She stretched out her scar-striped legs toward him. "I dropped out a couple of years ago."

"Why?"

"Hated it."

"So you became a stripper?"

"No," she said, "I came out here with my best friend. Then I killed her and stole all her money, which was a lot, to me anyway. But then I ran out of money and I needed something to do that would pay my bills. Exploiting men's sexual appetites seemed to be the easiest thing."

"You could have been a prostitute," Daniel suggested.

"I don't mind them looking, but I don't want to fuck them. If they're willing to pay me to look at me dancing around like a dumbass, awesome. But I don't let them touch me. There's a big fucking difference, and it doesn't surprise me to see that you don't know it."

"I know the difference," said Daniel. He paused for a moment to load another roll of film, a process that took a while because the film sprocket teeth were worn almost completely off. "You said you killed your best friend. Why would you kill your best friend?"

"Because she pissed me off," said Sybil off-handedly. "Haven't you ever just wanted to kill someone so bad . . ."

He finished the threading of the film and snapped the door closed, hands shaking. "Uh-huh."

"And then found yourself with exactly the right opportunity to do it?"

"Hmm, yes," said Daniel. "Where did you come from?"

"Colorado Springs. Ever been there?"

"No."

"Don't. Go, that is. There's no point."

"Colorado is beautiful," he said.

"Have you ever *been there,* or have you only seen it from airplanes?"

"Good point. How long ago did you leave?"

"Almost two years. I'm almost nineteen."

"Bravo. Plans for your birthday?"

"Try to survive, that's all. If I make it, I'll be happy."

He kept his back to her but smiled. "Are you afraid you're going to die?"

"I already said I'm not. Besides, I really don't care."

"I'm having a hard time believing you. How close have you been? Have you ever thought, 'This is it, I'm going to die now'? When you're truly close to death you're scared as fuck."

"I've been pretty close to death. Want to see?"

When he turned around she held out her wrists—thick seams of scar tissue stitched her skin from wrists to elbows. "I did that with a big butcher knife," she said with a naughty smile. "I was thirteen."

"Why?"

"I didn't want to find out what fourteen was like."

"Were you raped?"

"Why do you want to know? Will it answer questions you have about me? Like how I can resist your fabulous body and deep pockets?"

"Do you really think I have a fabulous body, or are you just making a very sarcastic statement to reinforce your point?"

She took her arms back. "I've never been successfully raped," she said. "Many have attempted it."

"Did you kill them?"

"Not good opportunity," she said, in a mock Charlie Chan accent. "Or so I thought at the time."

"Would you kill them now?"

"Absolutely," she said. "I made it my motto that 'the opportunity is always there.' You can kill a guy with a knife or a stick or a pen . . . or with your bare hands if you really mean to do it. You just gotta look around and—Why are you smiling?"

"Because it's so true," he said.

"You ever killed anybody?"

"Lots of people," Daniel mumbled.

"How many?"

"Ah—I've lost count." Daniel laughed awkwardly.

"My father killed a bunch of people in Vietnam and he remembers exactly how many. He killed some other guy in town, though, and now he's in jail. Will be for the next sixteen years, I think."

"Do you care?"

"Nope," she said. "So where'd you kill people?"

"Everywhere."

"Really?" She stared directly into his eyes. "Don't shit me."

"I will swear on any book, holy or unholy, you like."

"But like, where?"

"Everywhere I've ever lived."

"Are you a serial killer?" She asked in the same tone as she might ask, "Do you like oranges?"

Daniel shrugged. *In that I've killed many people, often conforming to a certain type, motivated by some obscure psychosis, and that I'll kill again? Right now feels like a good time to me.* "You should probably go home," he said.

"Why? I'm finally becoming interested. Are you a spy? Are you a hit man?"

"I don't think it's something glamorous for teenage girls," Daniel said, fumbling on the table for his lens cap. "I think it's dreadful."

"It is dreadful, that's why teenage girls are interested." She stood up and picked up her coverall. Almost immediately, she was dressed, pulling on her shoes.

"May I please see you again?" he burst out.

She eyed him, pulling on her stocking cap. "I have to work," she said. "You know, my glamorous day job?"

"If I give you enough money to live on, will you quit?"

"Yeah, sure," she said. "I was just about to quit and start my fabulous career as an investment banker."

"Instead, you're a kept woman."

She stared at him. "Excuse me. I'm a model. Or so I thought."

"You're a model. If that's what you want. This is all on your terms." Daniel sat in the chair and pulled his leather pants over his calves. "I'll meet you next week, then, and give you however much money you made at your best week working at the club. The week after that I'll do the same. All right?"

"I'll call you," said Sybil.

Scene Six: Looking Too Close

It was definitely raining now. A gray overbearing sky had threatened all day and had finally made good on the threat when evening fell. Daniel sat in his study looking over old photographs, listening to Brian Eno's "Music For Films." *It's regret music,* Daniel thought. He knew he shouldn't be listening to Eno, but the situation really demanded it, in all its overpuffed pathos. Sybil would imagine this scene and laugh her cruel, obnoxious laugh, the one that sounded like a boy's. That laugh never failed to strike his feet from underneath him, the bully's leg pushed out between rows of schoolroom desks.

In the end, was it worth it, really, for the illusion of love? The effort and agony and despair, for the simple fact that he couldn't stop that part of his soul that clung to people like a cocklebur? He knew that he had a simple, horrible, fatal weakness for beautiful figures, and that each new lover was a mere template of attractiveness for the age in question. Moth to flame. But why the despair? Some of the photographs were yellow and crackly stiff with age, but in all of them, he could see that allure that snared him in the first place, smiles, flawed and precious bodies, from Eva to Orfeo to Wolfgang to Gilda and Rachel and Steven . . . sunlight in Zurich, flashbulbs in Berlin, sunlight in California, f-stops, dilation, and measurement of desire.

And lovely Lovely . . . Only two pictures of him survived, one of him with Ariane at what had been planned as their vampire debut, all dark glances and tinsel, and one of Lovely alone, lounging about half-nude as usual, his slender girl's body marking a pale *V* on dark sheets. The boy had planned a series of letters formed out of his body, but he got to *E* and just couldn't figure out how to do it right, and Daniel had lost *L* and *O*. For years Daniel had carried the *V* Polaroid in the inner pocket of his leather jacket, and had caressed it so often with his finger that the emulsion had begun to rub off.

There was a Francis Bacon exhibit happening at the Met; Sybil called Daniel's red cell phone again, interrupting his angst session, and told him about it. "It starts tomorrow," came her voice, faint and crackly through the digital ether. "You wanna go? Are you into Bacon?"

"I love Bacon," he said.

"Four o'clock outside, OK?"

"Tomorrow?"

"Tomorrow."

The tiny plastic device was slippery in his sweaty palm. "I'll be there. And I have a membership, so you don't need to get in line."

"My best week, I made six hundred dollars in tips and got twelve free drinks."

"We'll make it seven hundred," said Daniel.

"OK."

When he arrived, she stood on the steps in front, smoking cigarettes with great absorption and intensity, shivering in tight faded black jeans and camouflage T-shirt stretched against her breasts and belly. Daniel attempted to sneak up behind her and approach her next cigarette with a lighter, but she turned and smiled at him. "You're late," she said.

"I believe the Bacon is still there," he grumbled.

She gestured at him with the unlit cigarette, so he produced fire. "You washed your hair," he noticed.

"Not deliberately," she replied. The clean bleached strands stood straight up, too finely seeded with free electrons to relax against her scalp. "I just kinda, like, *accidentally* got soap in it . . ."

"Have you ever for a moment considered trying to look good?" he asked.

"What's that supposed to mean?"

"OK, what I really meant was, do you want to dress well, have your hair done by a professional, get skin care, that sort of thing? I mean, you're a beautiful—you're a great-looking person; you're really tall . . . Did you ever even consider modeling?" He regretted saying that almost immediately, seeing her expression change to that hard, unfeeling mask that women wear when they are dealing with matters of their looks.

"I have the wrong body," she said. "I'm too fat."

"That is totally not true."

"C'mon, Daniel, how stupid are you? You know what models look like. Do I look like that? Do you think I even could? Because I don't want to. I don't eat enough as it is. I want to eat more. I'm always hungry. But I wear a size fourteen. You cannot be a model and wear size fourteen. And a size eleven shoe. And I have this face, which totally wouldn't work."

"Have you seen some of the dogs modeling these days? All you have to really do is be . . ." He ran out of steam.

She was smirking as she finished his sentence. "At least five-nine. Less than a hundred and twenty pounds. Willing to be treated like a clothes hanger made of meat."

"I think you're beautiful, that's all," said Daniel, huddling his face into the collar of his coat. "I don't think there's anything wrong with making money from your looks."

"That's your problem then, isn't it? I'm not right for it and I don't want to be. I wouldn't want to wear the kind of clothes that they'd want me to wear. And what's a professional going to do with my hair that I can't do myself? I mean, shit. Do you have your hair done professionally?" She flicked at the ponytail on the back of his head, gathered hair jagged as a bunch of black wires. Some strands escaped, stabbing into the air around his ears and above his head.

"Of course I do."

"What do they do? Sit you in a chair, suck your dick, attack your hair with scissors—even you have to admit you have fucked-up hair."

"I do not," said Daniel, trying not to smile. "I just want to give you, you know, a chance."

"Are you trying to Dr. Dolittle me?"

"What? Oh, you mean Professor Higgins. It was Eliza Dolittle."

"Whatever the fuck."

"I just can't stand to see people I care about living in poverty when they don't have to," he said. "I'm German. It hurts me personally. I was very poor for a long time."

"When was that?"

He almost said "In the Twenties, and I had to run to the store in the morning with pillowcases full of banknotes because my money would be worthless by evening," but took a deep breath and said, "When I was about your age."

"And did you care?"

"I wanted nice things," he said.

"And now that you have nice things, are you happier?"

"Finish your cigarette."

Inside the weighty warmth of the museum, Sybil paid for herself and he made no attempt to stop her; he had no desire for the kind of scene he knew she would make if he tried. "You're from Germany?" she asked.

"I'm from Berlin," he said.

"Are your parents American?"

"No, German." And dead a long time forever ago.

"You don't even have an accent," she said.

"I've been living in America so long that I hardly remember what living in Europe is like. Besides, it's all changed now." He hardly remembered the smell of pet dogs being cooked for food in the colorless bombed ruins, or how the old woman looked when she saw Daniel wearing the gold chain that had, earlier that day, been around the neck of her fifteen-year-old daughter, last seen buying horse meat on the side of the road. He hardly remembered the sharp tang of country cheese, or the rumbling of the trains on the Platz outside his window in the morning, or the scent and taste and feel of Swiss girls.

"You never told me how old *you* were," she said.

In the exhibit rooms, all voices dropped to a murmur.

"Why is it important?"

"I told you how old I was."

"When it's your age, that's important," said Daniel.

"I disagree, in my case."

Once inside the exhibit space they split up; he let her go off on her own so that he could attempt again to read her. Between them stood two young art students, intently studying a large single panel. The older of the two, with jet-black hair in a flippant bob, was touching her belly; a day in the museum with no money to get even a snack. Her name was far outside of her thoughts; her mind was not on the painting, but instead centered in her duodenum, where frustrated digestive acids gathered and burbled. She felt sick with hunger, but also trying to lose weight, so that she wouldn't look so fat compared to her friend, the other art student. The younger, Cynthia (her name and selfhood always the primary thing on her mind), a pencil-slim blonde, tired, thinking about how she would get home soon and change into her favorite orange satin pants, and do a few lines of crystal meth as she got dressed, and her boyfriend James (James, golden-brown skin, a silken stench of young manhood around him, big cock) would come and take her to a club, and they would dance and drink and then he would . . .

Sybil was visible, but for all the sense Daniel got of her mind, she might as well have not been there. If Daniel concentrated, he caught flickers of the minds of people passing outside the room; mostly they were thinking about dinner, money, clothing, pussy, embarrassment. Sybil turned in front of a triptych and smiled and waved Daniel over. He shuddered. It took a lot out of him to listen to other people the way he had just done, like going from relaxing in a chair to running a mile at top speed; he sweated, hungry and anxious himself.

"This is nice," said Sybil when he came to stand beside her. "I do some triptychs myself but this is fucking cool."

The outer two panels were your average everyday Francis Bacon—random flesh-colored forms that suggested human bodies after being stuffed into a bag and beaten with nightsticks for ten minutes or so—but the center depicted something like a bald middle-aged man, head and torso emerging from the shadows cast by a door. The shadow spilled out of the open door onto the ground in front of the man, twisting into an ineffable shape; it suggested a thousand horrible things: tentacles, pools of slowly spreading black blood, a dreadful creature with toothsome mouth gaping and claws outstretched. Daniel's bowels clenched and he looked away.

"Isn't that cool?" insisted Sybil.

"Yeah," Daniel mumbled.

"And check this one out. I could have done this myself. I wish I had." She pulled him by the wrist to another triptych and placed him in front of the center panel. "Inspired by T. S. Eliot's 'Sweeney Agonistes'—never read it. I hate Eliot. I bet this is what Francis Bacon feels like after reading Eliot because this is what I feel like after reading Eliot." A horribly bloodied and crumpled sheet draped itself over the back of a simple kitchen chair; a bright blue shade half-drawn against a featureless black night outside.

"Do you want to go get a drink or something?" Daniel said, his voice much too loud for a museum.

"Whassa matter? We just got here."

"I think I'm too weak for Bacon right now." The sight of the blood was just too much. The worst part of it was the night outside beyond the blue shade and the bright lamplight of the painting—it was not yet dark on the Manhattan streets, but Daniel felt that once they left there would be nothing outside, the world had been swept away, and all that was left was the cramped room, the bloody sheet. "I overestimated myself."

"Wow, you *are* sensitive. You have no stomach for Bacon. Ha, did you get it? I made a joke. You're supposed to laugh."

Daniel shook his head. "I really must go. Please come with me. Let's go get a drink."

"No. I think we should stay. Not only am I going to stay, you're going to stay with me and we're going to look at all the Bacon. Closely. I would hate to think you're such a pussy you can't even look at paintings without getting all freaked out." She put her hands on her hips and stood between him and the triptych. "I like seeing you freaked out, actually. Do you like horror movies at all?"

"You don't understand," he stammered, trying to laugh.

"Oh," said Sybil, "I think I do. I think I very much understand."

She pulled him to the next painting. "Why does this bother you so much?"

"It just does," said Daniel.

"You're so jumpy."

"I don't feel you believe the things I've told you."

"Why shouldn't I believe them? There's nothing I've seen that would lead me to think you're anything other than what you say you are—that is, except common sense. There are a lot of things about you that don't really add up, like why you keep wanting to hang around with me without asking for anything else."

"There are a lot of things about *you* that don't add up," countered Daniel, looking at her instead of the screaming faces of the painted figures surrounding him. "Like why you don't understand why I want to hang around with you."

"I do understand why. Because you're a pervert with a shitload of self-loathing. You seem to really dig abuse. Which I guess I can understand. I find that kind of disappointing." She leaned in close to examine the brushwork, almost touching the painting with her nose.

"Disappointing that you understand?"

"Shut up and look at the paintings."

"I want to go look at Max Beckmann," Daniel said. "He's much more my kind of shit."

"Shit is right. Francis Bacon is the master."

"How dare you dismiss a fine representative of Expressionism? That's where I came from."

"Oh, really? Well, if you want to look at limp-dick Max Beckmann, I suppose I should let you go. I'll be in here. Give me at least another hour, OK?"

"Compromise," Daniel suggested. "I'll leave you in this abattoir, but you have to come back to my place afterwards. I don't feel too much like being in public right now. And don't call Beckmann a limp-dick—he was a very vital force."

"OK," Sybil murmured distantly.

Daniel all but ran to the men's room, praying that there would be some slow old man that he could lull and sip from; but the lavatory was empty. He sat on a dry sink and looked at himself in the mirror, checking to make sure that he could still pass as human. Of course, he was pale, but his skin still held some color. He was not starving by a long shot. He was just greedy and addicted and spoiled, and had been so rich in blood for such a long time that even the slightest extra mental effort made him woozy and helpless. He wondered if perhaps Sybil had some kind of mutant ability to drain his essence and use it to nourish her own mind. Just because he'd never heard of such a thing didn't mean that it wasn't possible.

He wished there was someone he could ask about it.

After his hour of standing alone in front of Jasper Johns' "White Flag," Daniel found Sybil outside the exhibit room, and they left the museum. "I live across the street," he explained as they began to walk. "Lovely place. I bought it with cash, which is the only way to really do things—payments are for assholes. And of course I wanted to be close to the museum, so I can go in and fantasize about which of my paintings will go where. I know they never will. None of them."

"You're probably right," she said. "But what the hell. Museums are where they put paintings that are dead. I call 'em mausoleums. The Metropolitan Mausoleum of Art. I'm more interested in living art."

She followed him into the foyer of his apartment, and she stared at the architecture and the furniture and the Kurt Schwitters drawing above the entry telephone alcove. "That's pretty cool," she said.

"Do you like Dada?" He took her coat from her shrugging shoulders. Whenever she made the slightest movement, her breasts shook gently like crème brûlée. "I have several more reproductions and a couple of originals. Actually, I have a lot of originals, if you count my own stuff and the Schwitters material I don't keep here."

"Are you Dada?" She wore a precious smile as she said this.

"I was."

"You said you were an Expressionist."

"What I meant to say is that that's what I tried first," said Daniel. "Dada is so much less tortured. It's an entire movement devoted to saying 'Fuck it.' Of course, that's not all it is." He hung up his own coat in the closet and followed Sybil inside, running sweaty hands through his hair. The erection that sprung on him when he saw her breasts quivering had become painfully intense, and he needed to face away from her for a while. "That one on the wall there is one of mine. Drink?"

"What's the most alcoholic thing you have?" She approached the large collage on the wall and examined it closely.

"I have some double-distilled pear brandy," he said. "It's almost like Everclear. I can't drink it. My last assistant bought it. Ricky." Daniel ran his hands over the smooth, cool surface of the orange calf-leather chair. Ricky's skin was cool like that whenever Daniel drank Ricky's blood; he would rub one hand across Ricky's hairless belly and marvel at the flutter of the struggling heartbeat. "He always spent too much money on liquor."

"I'll have some of that. Ricky, huh? You say his name like he was your lover, not your employee."

"I fucked him a few times," said Daniel. "Nice kid."

"So, are you straight or are you gay?"

"Uh . . . I'm neither." He tried to disappear into the kitchen.

She followed very closely behind him, her breath gently caressing the exposed back of his neck. His skin was on fire. He paused in locating the brandy to pull the elastic out of his hair, but the touch of his own hair on the skin recently caressed by her breath drove him nearly mad. "Would you like to pour it yourself? I have to go to the toilet."

She didn't move out of his way. Her eyes flicked back and forth across his face. In the chill, conditioned air of the apartment, her nipples poked at her T-shirt like hard candies. "Do you really?"

"No, I really . . . um . . ."

"I might consider having sex with you," she said.

"When? Now? If it's not now, I'm afraid you'll have to let me go pee."

"There's something weird about you."

"There are a lot of weird things about me."

"Because you really ought to be dead right now."

"I know," he croaked.

"There's no reason why my being this close to you should have you shaking like that."

"There are plenty of reasons. I—look, I respect you, and it's obvious that you could kill me if you wanted to, so I'm not asking about sex. I'm not talking about it. I'm trying not to think about it. But the fact of the matter is that you're driving me insane and I really have to leave the room right now so I can . . . convince myself of another course of action."

She chuckled. "I am so drunk on power right now," she said.

"Why don't you get drunk on brandy and I'll be back in a minute." He put his hands on her shoulders and moved her aside as gently as he could. She stared after him as he left the kitchen.

He sat on the toilet in his bathroom for a while, then splashed his face repeatedly with cold water. His cheeks burned hibiscus red, eyes wide and frantic, staring back at him from the mirror. The empty bathtub behind him—

he saw it full of Ricky's blood and Ricky floating fucked and torn in it, pinpoint pupils in the golden irises of Ricky's eyes, Daniel shuddering in orgasm in the lukewarm blood-and-water suspension. Inside him, answering, his organs bickered, *Feed us. Soothe us. Release us.*

He stared at his wet, white hands, the thin skin stretched tightly over the bones, the black polish on his fingernails chipped at the edges, revealing the gunmetal sheen of the claws underneath. He had used those beautiful lacquered nails to disembowel women from inside, giggling at their screams. His own guts stirred. Fresh blood almost as runny through his fingers as water, guts softer than any silk, warmer than any kiss.

"Daniel."

Sybil stood in the open doorway, leaning against the jamb, a wineglass full of translucent brandy in her left hand. "What's happening?" she asked. "Are you OK?"

"Just some bad memories," Daniel said. He dried his hands and face on a silky-furry towel. "Francis Bacon does that to me."

"Nightmares?" She came into the bathroom and set down the wineglass. You could have used her brandy-soaked breath as a blowtorch. Daniel took her glass and drained it. It flickered in his belly and then dissolved ineffectively into his blood.

"It's all nightmares," he said.

"Did you pee?" She helped him out with half a smile.

He supplied the other half. "No, I never did. I guess I didn't have to after all."

"You're not much of a date," she said. "You totally skip out on the Bacon, which is the whole point of today, then you invite me in and you freak out and run to the john."

"I think you should probably leave," said Daniel. "I am freaked out. Let me get your money."

"Sure," she agreed, and followed him out to the coat rack, her eyes on him all the time. "Did you ever wonder if Francis Bacon ever killed anybody?" she asked. "Because it's so real, emotionally? Like he's seen some kind of truth with his own eyes that you can't possibly just make up?"

Daniel held out a thick short sandwich of folded bills, clamped between his oil-slick claws.

"You look like you're afraid of something happening," she said.

"If I tell you that I am, will you forgive me?" said Daniel.

"I never forgive anybody for anything," said Sybil. She snatched the money and leafed through it, counting and re-counting. Without another word or gesture, she put her coat back on, and Daniel held the door open for her. He watched her walk down the street, willing her to turn around and come back and fold herself into his arms—but must have been thinking of Ariane, so small and silky and pliable, or Lovely, who liked to curl up beside him and cuddle. Sybil was his height, and he couldn't imagine her making herself shorter to embrace him.

Scene Eight: The Creeping Awfuls

Daniel had started going to the Supernova Club in the first place because it was only a block away from his elderly European accountant, who would only see clients in person in his home office. Dr. Gestwirt had been a Berliner, a Birkenau survivor, and Daniel liked his sense of humor, not to mention his style—the old man often met Daniel in his ebony-paneled office wearing a gorgeous silk kimono—and his professional flexibility, not minding if they met at six in the morning or ten at night. Sometimes it was painful to lie to Gestwirt, for Daniel to pretend that he was just a young and avid scholar who had a very generous dead relative from Switzerland who had "picked up" his extensive knowledge of that time from listening to his relative's stories, from study, anything but the reality of it. Dr. Gestwirt had such a sparkle in his eyes that only dulled slightly when he had to mention Birkenau; Daniel never asked him about it, and the subject came up very rarely. Gestwirt had eleven grandchildren, and their pictures were everywhere, as a layer of emotional insulation.

Gestwirt stood up to shake Daniel's hand at the end of their evening appointment. "Any plans for the rest of the evening? Another journey to the wilds of Supernova All Nude Girls?" Gestwirt teased, black eyes glimmering under his fringe of white eyebrows like wet buttons in snow.

Daniel laughed politely. "No, I don't go there anymore."

"Why not? The girls are still nude—or they were last week."

"You old devil. No . . . the one who I liked the most doesn't dance there anymore."

"Which one was that?"

"Oh, what does it matter?" Daniel said lightly. "They're more or less the same, aren't they? You know, she was lovely, tall and young. And now that she's not there, I've lost interest in the club. You'll have to find a different place for my surprise party this year."

"Oh, what a shame. A healthy young man like you. Don't worry, you'll probably see her again sometime. I sense that you have that particular attraction that won't be easily shaken loose. Besides, she's a dancer; she'll be at some other club. She won't be hard to find."

"Probably not," said Daniel.

He went away with his feelings horribly mixed. The money was no problem; thanks to Gestwirt's sharp investment instincts, Daniel still had a lot of it. But he knew there was no more than a temporary escape from the thought of Sybil. He had hoped that at least with Gestwirt, he could be free for a while. But he'd forgotten Gestwirt's slightly perverse sense of humor about sex, something in the old man that enjoyed watching people squirm.

He went to the club again anyway, just out of ritual. Nothing seemed to have changed since the last time—the same cheap rope lights, the same perfumed artificial fog, the same Top 40 alternative hits and the waxed and powdered girls who gyrated to them, the same blank expressions on the faces of dancers, bartenders, and patrons alike. Daniel left his drink untouched and left.

Daniel found Sybil's tenement building by sense memory and stood on the sidewalk across the street, staring up at the rectangles of television lights across the side of the concrete. He saw movement in some of the windows; human beings in there, their brains buzzing a radio crackle of noise, ugly, complicated music.

A scattering of sharp popping sounds snapped him from his reverie; definitely gunshots hitting poured concrete walls. Daniel cursed the glaring paper whiteness of his face, melting himself backwards into the shadow cast by the condemned building at his back, all his muscles gathered to fight or run.

A dark form darted from the door opposite, sneaker soles sucking faintly on the wet pavement, and across the street. It brushed past him, loosing a bouquet of damp cannabis-girl-sweat scent, and a hissing came from it—"Walk."

He said nothing until they were in the Bowery subway station, down the stairs and facing the tracks. "How did you know I was there?" Daniel asked.

Sybil's face was stony under her moth-eaten stocking cap. "I could see you from my window," she said. "Looking up at me like a goon."

"What were the shots?" The smell of her stinky coat blocked out the clinging gum and newspaper and perfume and beer smell of the subway platform; that, and her still mind, comforted him. He began to relax.

"That motherfucker on the floor below mine. He's already killed one of his kids by accident, and that pretty much drove him directly to the land of not giving a fuck. I don't know why I get so freaked when I hear gunshots; I grew up with the sound of that shit all the time. My dad loves guns. They're his best friends. He's got names for all of them, he used to talk to them . . . hey, do you still have drugs and booze around? I need something to help me give up the notion that anything has to make sense ever."

She finally looked at him, eyes desperate, lips slightly parted to show her teeth. With effort, he managed a casual shrug, staring across the tracks at the red-and-white sign on the opposite wall—RECENTLY TREATED WITH

RAT-B-GONE. ASSOCIATED EXTERMINATORS OF MANHATTAN. "They're at my place," he said.

"That's fine," she said.

"Can we take a taxi? It'll be faster."

"Whatever." They stood and headed back for the steps to the world three flights above.

The taxicab smelled like fish, and Sybil said so as soon as she got inside. She asked if she could smoke in the cab, then she asked if she could smoke at Daniel's place, then she said she was hungry, then fell into a rigid, embarrassed silence. "I am just Sybil the Super-Wound-up," she explained. "I've been thinking way too much today. Sometimes I can't stop myself from thinking about shit."

"I dropped by the Supernova," Daniel said.

"Oh, really? Why?"

"I was in the neighborhood. I wanted to see if there was anything about it that I liked besides you. There isn't. I only started going there because it was convenient, and easy to pick up girls—I'm sure you know about it being this kind of prostitutes' break room."

Her laugh came out broken and folded, but at least it was a laugh. "Yeah, no shit. The guy who owns the place pimps, and he's always trying to recruit from the ranks of the dancers—get the assholes excited by watching someone dance for a few weeks, then tell 'em she's available for a hundred an hour. Working girls versus working girls. The only real difference is that the dancers don't get free AIDS tests."

"You never had to fuck anybody at your job," Daniel pointed out. ". . . Did you?"

"No," she agreed. "Even though people tried it a lot." She shuddered. "No, I don't want to think about that, either. I don't want to think about anything. There's a great quote from my favorite comic book that says, 'I wish someone could just switch me off and fix me.' I try not to live in that state, but sometimes it just creeps up on me and I can't shake it."

"I never pegged you as being a person who suffers from the Creeping Awfuls," said Daniel.

"I am the Creeping Awfuls," she muttered.

"Ssh . . . don't think," he said.

In Daniel's apartment, he fetched her a water pipe and Ricky's tiny stash box of hashish, poured a glass of the plum brandy, and spilled a miniature Mount Fuji of powder cocaine onto a flat black porcelain plate. She hit the hash in the pipe, gulped the brandy, and lit a cigarette, but shook her head when Daniel began to razor the coke into lines. "No, fuck coke. I don't want any right now. Do you do a lot of coke?"

"No," said Daniel. "I haven't for years. I don't really take drugs; these are for guests."

"Well, you're a rockin' host." She refilled her glass and pulled off her sneakers and damp socks. Daniel relaxed on his side of the couch, watching her pouring the alcohol down her throat, a second glass and a third. She paused with a gasp and wiped her mouth. "Whoa. I sure do like this brandy. It kicks like a mule. Makes me feel like talking. Want to listen to me talk about what's bothering me?"

"I would like nothing more," said Daniel. "Let's go into the back room—the furniture is more comfortable. Do you want me to bring the coke?"

"No, leave it. If I take cocaine right now I'll completely spaz. I don't like being tense. Tension makes your muscles fragile. The successful warrior is a supple warrior. And I like to be . . . Sybil the Supple." Already, her voice sounded smudged.

They meandered into the study, and Daniel lit a single twenty-watt lamp, little more than a tall night-light, near the floor. She sat in one of the two deep plush blue chairs. "This is a nice carpet," she said, sinking her toes into it.

"It's hand-woven." And the chair where she sat covered a crispy, dark stain. You could not clean a hand-woven Kashmir carpet, and only a small part of it was ruined.

"Goddamn, you're fuckin' rich."

He smiled. "It's just a reaction; I bought a lot of nice objects when I moved in here. I lost everything not too long ago, and I think I probably overcompensated on material goods." Daniel sat on the floor beside her chair and took one of her feet into his hands, the skin burning hot against his blood-starved palms. "Talk," he said.

She resisted concentration on herself, instead fascinating herself with his hands. "You have the weirdest hands I've ever seen. I mean, this is like, freak. And what is up with your nails, dude? I usually only see nails like that on Jersey girls who work at the phone company."

Daniel looked at them. "I admit, I've considered putting silver glitter stripes on them and making them into L.A. Raiders fingernails. Oh, and little team logo decals. Little helmets with the Jolly Roger. But enough about my manicure. Talk to me. What's the matter?"

Sybil's bright and grinning face clouded, mascara-stained brown eyelashes obscuring her eyes. "My best friend's name," she began with a sigh, "was Ruth. Everybody in school called her Sonic Ruth. Big eyes, big hair, big tits, big mouth, never shut up. Never fucking shut up for a second. Rich, too. Probably her parents were almost as rich as you are. She was really into coke, and speed, *and* heroin, and . . . pot . . . and acid . . . fuck, I don't know of any drugs that she didn't do on a regular basis. I did a lot of drugs with her because there was pretty much nothing else to do, get fucked up and go to the park. . . . She used to pick fights with people and then make me defend her, and that pissed me off so much. Still, I did it because I liked having an excuse to fight. We drank a lot, too, vodka and beers, vodka because it's easy to water it back so her folks didn't notice as much. Beers we would get from the frat jerks at the college; they'd buy Sonic Ruth beer and then she'd give them blow jobs or fuck them and their friends. And she used to try to convince me that I should get fucked by a guy and become a huge-ass frat-ho slut like she was, because she loved it *sooo* much and she wanted to, like, share it with me. She was really into sharing. She had all this . . . *shit,* she'd take a bunch of cocaine and go on shopping binges, and she'd get bored with it and give it to me. Like, she'd give me her clothes, and she's like this tiny little freak, like five feet one, with a fucking giant head. And like, I couldn't fit into any of the shit, so I'd just go sell it."

"Did you have a good time with her?" asked Daniel,

caressing the satiny moist arch of her foot, smelly from her sneakers but in a pleasant way, like baking bread. He almost laughed at himself—*Even the stench of her dirty feet is like perfume to me.*

"No," spat Sybil. "She was a fucking bitch. I hated her."

"But she was your best friend," Daniel continued, filling in the space where her voice had paused for too long.

"She was the only friend. And not even that. She was the only person who even kind of pretended. She was the closest thing to a friend I had," Sybil admitted.

"Have you had any friends since then?"

"No," said Sybil. "You're probably the closest thing to it since Sonic Ruth. I dunno, I don't really want any friends."

"Well, for God's sake, if that's the way you think of friendship, I can't say I blame you. But you know, it isn't always like that."

"Isn't it?" Sybil said, poking him in the chest with her foot, almost forcefully enough to be a kick. "It is for me. I don't give a fuck about the way other people live their lives, this is me."

"I'm glad you think of me as your friend," said Daniel humbly.

"I don't," said Sybil.

He didn't look up, but sighed heavily. "Just a lie, huh?"

"No, you're just the closest thing to a friend I have. That doesn't mean I consider you to be my friend. I'm doing friendly things with you, going to museums, telling you shit . . . letting you play with my feet . . . which is a seriously ill thing to do, if you don't mind me saying."

"Tell me about killing Ruth," said Daniel.

"Like what?" Her voice barely emerged from the shimmery white noise of the lightbulb, the electric hum of appliances, the sounds of cars outside.

"How did you do it?"

"I . . ." It was plain that she'd never spoken of it before. Her face transformed in the shadows, drew some of the ambient misery out of the air and gave it flesh. "I pushed her in front of the subway. The train, I mean."

Daniel blinked. "Deliberately?"

"Yeah," she said.

"Nobody noticed?"

"Well, the driver noticed there was something really getting in the way of his train . . . but . . . nobody else was there on the subway platform and . . . it was really late. . . . It was an express train and our train wasn't going to be along for fifteen more minutes and she was . . . standing on the edge where they have the bumpy rubber and talking, talk talk talk talk talking—"

"About what?"

Sybil's eyes darted toward him. "What makes you think I remember?"

Daniel smiled. "Because I know."

They exchanged a glance, and Daniel shrugged. "She was . . . talking . . . about . . . Sonic Youth," Sybil said, drawing out the words in a long, draggy, reluctant mumble. "That's all she talked about when we were here. That's why we came here. She was going to stalk Sonic Youth. She had this fantasy that she would become their drug dealer and then she would steal Thurston away from Kim, and then *she* would get to be the bass player in Sonic Youth—I mean, she had all this shit planned out like the fucking psychotic she was. Of course I didn't believe her, but I came out here with her anyway, because at least she had the most interesting fantasy life of anybody else I'd ever met. I guess I'm attracted to the insane . . ." Sybil scratched her hair. "Because sane people are intensely boring."

"Yeah," Daniel agreed quietly.

"So the express train was coming, and she was standing right on the edge . . . so I went up behind her and gave her a good hard shove, and she fell off, and then the train came." Sybil threw up her hands briskly. "That's it."

"Did you see the blood?"

"Only afterwards."

"You waited until the train went by?" He gripped her ankles tightly.

"I . . . I was kind of nuts myself. . . . I wanted to make sure she wouldn't just get up. . . . I could picture her just wedging herself down between the rails and then popping up after the train had gone, still talking about fucking bootlegs, and I couldn't even deal with that idea so . . ."

"Was she there?" Daniel asked.

"She was gone. Well, not all of her. Like her hands and—" She fell abruptly silent, and Daniel realized that she had gagged. "This is fucking sick, I don't know why I'm talking to you about this. This is the kind of shit that gives people nightmares."

"Like I said, my whole life is a nightmare," Daniel said, releasing her ankles. His fingers had left welts in her flesh. "If you had any idea of the things I've done . . . you must know I appreciate how . . . wasteful and upsetting . . . You'll have more nights where you just can't think."

"I don't care," she said. "I don't care. I'd do it again today if I had to. She just gets in my head sometimes and I can't get her out. I lived in her world. A prisoner."

"It must be agony to kill your only friend," he murmured.

"Actually I felt pretty good afterwards," she confessed. "I had to puke, but after that I felt pretty good. I felt . . . liberated. I felt really free for the first time in my life. I didn't have any friends or family anymore—I didn't need to be human, I didn't need to interact or listen to or be with *anybody*. I could just deal with my own shit. I didn't have to do anything except what *I* wanted to do, forever."

"There's no forever."

"You would know," she said softly, resting her hand on Daniel's shoulder and caressing the side of his neck, toying with loose strands of his coarse, shiny dark hair. "Wouldn't you?"

"I do know," he said plainly. "I do know for a fact. There is no forever. There's just now."

"Have you ever killed a friend?" she asked.

"Yeah," he said. "A bunch of times."

"And how did you feel afterwards?"

"Sad and sick and horrible."

"Yeah," she said, "me, too. But better, somehow."

In the silence, she finished off the pipe and loaded it

again, sitting very still in her curling rising cloud of sweet smoke, transcendently grim, like an oracle. "Where did you get your name?" Daniel asked.

"Oh, Jesus. It's a whole other story." A wide grin split the sacred illusion with two rows of glistening, crooked teeth.

"Well, I don't meet women your age named Sybil."

"My mother saw it on TV," Sybil said, coughing and laughing. "She saw the movie about the woman who was insane and abused by her mother and had multiple personalities and she thought 'Oh, wouldn't that be a nice name?' Of course what my mother doesn't realize is that *she's* crazy." Sybil, squinting through the smoke, kept laughing, but bleak and harsh, like chains on a metal fence. "The bitch is crazy. And I don't mean what a lovable, daffy, wacky old lady. I mean that she's drunk a bottle of vodka every single day for years to keep herself from doing the things the voices in her head tell her to do. And I've seen what happens when she does those things, and it's so much better when she's just drunk. Meds don't really work; they don't make meds for what's wrong with her. She'll be dead soon; her liver's fucked, ulcers. . . ." Sybil drained her glass again, grimaced, and shuddered as the gulps of brandy went down. "Tell me about your mother, Daniel," she said abruptly. "What was *she* like? Now that we're sharing."

Daniel cleared his suddenly thick and lumpy throat. "My mother," he said. "Um, nice, typical German mother."

"Nice. Typical. Those adjectives mean nothing to me."

"She was five and a half feet tall and had dark hair and pale blue eyes, and she had a bit of a mustache that annoyed her, that she bleached every day, and it left a rash. She had a rash mustache." He smirked, and Sybil laughed. "Wow. I never thought of it that way. In German it's *Ausschlagschnurrbart*—doesn't have the same ring to it. But, you know, she made cabbage a lot, she would yell at me to finish my milk at the breakfast table because poor boys didn't have milk, yada yada yada. It's nothing. She wasn't interesting." Neither of his parents were interesting in and of themselves; it was the decisions that they made that were interesting. His nice atheist mother married his nice atheist father, not caring that, in the eyes of the state, he was still a Jew and she a Christian. Eventually, too late, they would both care very much.

"I'm stoned," confessed Sybil ruefully. "Could we get some food?"

"You want me to order out? I don't really keep much food in the house."

"Do you keep much blood in the house?"

"What?" said Daniel, staring at her.

She stared back at him, widening her eyes slightly in challenge. Daniel looked away, letting go of her foot.

"Can I just ask you a question?" Sybil slid the foot into his lap, edging her toes toward his hands, poking at his wrist. "Are you planning to kill me?"

"No," said Daniel.

"Why not?"

"Do you want me to?" he asked wearily.

"I just want to know what's going on."

"I'm trying to get you into bed, to be honest."

She laughed quietly, and poked his belly with her big toe. Daniel lifted her foot and placed a kiss on the white curved arch. "I don't fuck," she said.

"At all? Or just me."

"At all," she said, but her voice was soft and distant.

"Saving your virgin power?"

"Maybe that's all I have."

"Oh, come on."

"Maybe I don't want to be like the rest of the sexually active normal people. Maybe I don't want to know how great it is. Maybe it's like crack—so dangerous I want to stay away from it."

"It's not like crack," said Daniel, standing up. "You are stronger than sex is. It's not going to change you instantaneously. But it does change you." He pulled her up from the chair. "Come on, stoner girl."

"Where are we going?" she asked slackly, pretending to be drunker than she was; her body retained plenty of its strength, resilience, and balance. "Are you going to throw me into your bed?"

Daniel smiled at her. "No, you're going to go take a shower. You need it. You stink and your skin is cold."

"No, a bath, I want a bath," she cried. "I haven't had a bath in forever."

"You may have a bath. I have a wonderful tub," said Daniel. He playfully pushed her into the bathroom, closed the door behind her, and leaned against it from the other side. "Bathe," he called to her, mad cackles echoing off the bathroom tiles. "Don't come out until you smell excellent. When you come out there'll be food."

"Pizza!" she bellowed.

"No fucking pizza."

"What the hell do you care? You just drink blood."

Daniel massaged his temples.

"Or does the garlic get to you?"

"No, actually, vampires are repelled by mozzarella cheese."

"Har! *Har!* So you admit it!" She screamed in triumph, screaming over the muted whoosh of water filling up the tub. Daniel kept massaging his temples, imagining her indelicate struggle to undress reflected in the gold water taps, distorted and cubist, a sudden blob of eye, a nipple brilliantly defined. "I knew it! I fucking knew it!"

"Good for you," Daniel said quietly.

Suddenly subdued, "So you're not going to kill me?"

"No," said Daniel. He faced the door, his hands against it searching for the warmth of hers, and pressed his lips against the door. "I want you alive. I need you."

"Why?"

Her hands made ovals of radiance against the wood.

"Because I need someone to love," he whispered, too quietly for her to hear. "I need someone to give me a reason to live."

No sound came from behind the door for several seconds, then the spots of warmth were gone and her voice came softly. "That's fucked."

Scene Nine: Transmission

When Sybil came out of the bathroom, the scent of lavender soap followed her like a drifting, invisible veil, trailing at the edge of the bath towel she held around her moist, clean body. "You know what," came her voice from the hallway, "I seem to smell pizza."

Daniel stood next to the dining table, an empty glass held loosely between his fingers. "They're calzones," he said. "But I was going to show you just how much garlic terrifies me." He waved the dish of crushed raw garlic under her nose, then dished up a spoonful and crunched it down. The violent piquancy made him shudder and tears run from his eyes, but that was all.

"Wow, hard core." She chuckled and rolled her eyes at him.

"I got one with sausage and one vegetarian—I didn't want to take any chances in case you're a vegetarian."

"I'm too poor to be a fucking vegetarian. When you're poor enough, you'll eat your own leg." She sat down and seized the nearest calzone, the sausage one. "When you're hungry you don't give a damn where the food comes from."

Daniel smiled at her. "How come you didn't get dressed?"

She shrugged and paused to finish chewing and swallowing before she spoke. "I figured it was a waste of time."

"Why?"

"I thought we were gonna have sex," she said, taking another huge bite.

Daniel blinked. "We were?" He filled his own glass with the last of the brandy and took a swallow. "But I thought you didn't fuck."

"I changed my mind," she said, not waiting to swallow before speaking this time.

He bent down to kiss her naked shoulder, but she edged away from him. "I need to eat," she said. "Go to the other room or something if you can't leave me alone when I'm eating when I'm hungry like this."

Instead, he sat still as she consumed both calzones, not looking at him, but instead staring at her plate. As soon as she had swallowed the last bite, he asked her, "So how do you want it?"

"I don't know," she said.

"All right, then," he replied. "You lead."

In his bedroom, he passed a hand over a switch to kill the lights, but she said, "No, leave them on, I need to be able to see." In compromise, he turned on the lamps at either side of his bed. She sat in the precise center of his bed, rigid, the towel bunched at her armpits, her eyes unfocused. She didn't watch him undress this time.

He knelt behind her and rubbed his hands together to warm them, and began to briskly massage her shoulders. His touch was firm, almost rough, steadying himself as well as her. "Sybil," he said darkly, "is Sonic Ruth still in your head?"

"Yes," was her terse reply.

Careful not to scrape her with his claws, he changed the rhythm of his hands on her, turning to long, deep muscle strokes down over her shoulder blades and back over her smooth, warm arms, and leaned in close so that she could feel his breath against her skin. "I want her out," he said, "I want it to just be you. I want it to just be you."

Slowly, she arched her back, and the towel slipped down a few inches until it hung suspended at the peaks of her breasts. He could hear her eyelashes clicking together. "I want it to just be you," he repeated again, glancingly close to her ear; the fine hairs on the back of her neck stood up and goose pimples raced across her skin. The locked sinews had begun to melt.

His voice trimmed to a whisper. "Where are you, Sybil? Who are you? Are you there?"

He dared to brush his lips against her cheek, and she turned her face at the same time until their lips met. They shared the fire of the garlic on their tongues, and when Daniel opened his eyes, she was lying on top of him, with the towel open and half cast aside. Her nipples tickled his ribs.

There was a moment where they just stared at each other; then Daniel pulled the towel from between them and tossed it onto the floor. "I lead," she said distantly, as if she were speaking from a dream. He nodded and caressed her bare bottom and pulled her more securely over him, simultaneously opening his legs so that she slid between them and against his tense and throbbing groin. Her response was a startled, "Ah," but she arched against him, too rough, uncoordinated, delicious. He caught his breath and grimaced.

Sybil smiled. "You like that," she said, her hands slipping between them and down, tugging on his long, coarse black pubic hairs until he squirmed, the blood rushing from his limbs into his penis and thighs. "Hmm," she continued, and slid half aside so that she could see her fingers pulling scoops of hair until the skin tented in a thousand places. "I bet you get big," she said.

"Not too big," he protested. "Then again, we'll see, maybe."

She explored the rest of his body with her hands, pulling the hair under his arms and the hair that ringed his red-grape–colored nipples and cupping the thick base of his cock in her palm. He had to close his eyes when she bent her face toward it, and clenched his hands on the bedspread when he felt her lips brush the shaft just below the head. How could she have known? Her touch was maddeningly sure . . . or perhaps it was just the culmination of what he had wanted for so long, those rough and bitten teenage hands, softened by the bath, her whole body scented like a bed of lavender.

After a blissful eternity of being touched, Sybil's hands stopped, and Daniel opened his eyes. "OK, I'm bored," she said, and he prepared himself for the long process of gentling her again until she added, "your turn."

He was careful, but not gentle; his fingertips bit into her round breasts only just so far; he suckled and tested his teeth against her nipples, and his hands smoothed and spread her thighs. Her expression tried to be disinterested, but her eyelashes moth-flickered and her lips twisted and she writhed her hips in slow circles. He lay only a brief kiss on the cleft of her shaven pubis, then pulled her up and around and sat her in his lap with her back to him. He thought that she would like it, being able to feel his whole body without having to look at him; her thighs spread over one of his, and he felt the dampness of sweat between her legs.

"Now I want you to jack off," he said. "I want you to show me how you do it, so I'll know what you like."

Her response was a quiet laugh deep in her throat. "You can't do it, 'cause you have long nails," she told him.

"I can do it, if you show me," he said.

She splayed the lips of her vulva with her first and third fingers, while the middle one stroked rapidly, expertly, up from the folded entrance to her vagina to her clitoris. Daniel crushed kisses into her shoulder. "I just want you to get off," he said against the back of her skull, the blond-tipped hair soft and clean and still moist from the bath. "We don't have to fuck. I just want you to get off with me holding you. That's all I want."

"Lie," she breathed.

"OK," he conceded, touching the tip of his tongue to her earlobe, "lie."

With her back still to him, she rose up onto her spread

knees, pulling her vulva still wider, and he gripped his penis in one hand and rubbed the head of it between her nether lips. She shuddered and gasped, "Oh, shit, wow, that's really good," throwing out one hand to catch herself on the bed, and a glorious rush of runny moisture oozed between them, at the fragile point of contact. He didn't know if it was from her or him, but he took the advantage and tried to force his cockhead into her. She was so tight she would have barely admitted a finger. He tried a finger, the "pinky," with the shortest nail; her cunt twitched, let it in, gripping it and letting it go.

After a moment he inserted his forefinger, then his middle finger, then the two of them together. "This can be done," Daniel said. "If you want it. You have to want it. I'm not going to fight you. If I fight you, we both lose."

Her hips shifted from side to side, then up and down on his fingers. "What do *you* want?"

"*I* want to fuck."

Her face was slack, eyes half-lidded. When he took his fingers out and sucked them, she sighed and made a soft complaining noise in her throat. "Do you have a rubber?" she mumbled distantly.

"No," said Daniel, holding his cock in one hand and her left hip in the other and trying again, this time with some small success; he passed the tight ring of muscle that held her vagina together and the head of his cock found a tense, hotter spot in the midst of her insides. She bit off a bizarre yelp of pain, and Daniel had to bite his own tongue to keep from coming. "I can't get you pregnant. I'm sterile."

She froze a little, but it was too late; she wanted it too much now, and her hips made tiny motions of trying to get him deeper inside. "But . . . what about . . . everything else?"

He couldn't help laughing, and he slipped out a little bit. Her inner muscles rippled around him, forcing him the rest of the way out. He swept his tongue against the side of her neck. "I'm immune to everything. I've never given anyone a disease my entire life. My blood is poison; everything that comes into contact with it dies," he said, rubbing the full length of his thrumming cock against her wet channel, asshole to clit, back and forth and again. "My spunk is poison. But a different kind—it'll only make *you* stronger."

"Such bullshit," Sybil said, but she didn't resist as he slipped in again, and deeper this time, the knob of the head entirely inside her, slippery fluids running down over his pubic bone. When he pulled her down closer, forcing, she cried out, a mad combination of pain and desire. "It's too fucking big," she whispered.

"What?"

"It's too big!"

"It's not; it's perfect. It's the perfect cock. For your perfect pussy."

"This is gonna take forever."

"Then let it take forever."

With every tentative thrust, she gasped like her heart was being torn out, and her cunt opened up a little bit more. "Are you in all the way?" she kept asking, as if afraid of the answer, as if she already knew that he was not and there was so much more left. "Are you in all the way?"

"Does it hurt?" he whispered. Pause and thrust and drink in her anguished sounds.

After a second, she responded softly, "Yes."

"Good." Slow, spiraling pressure, and this time a shuddery moan. "Do you like it?"

"Yes."

"Good." Slow again, long out, long deep *in*. "Are you ashamed of yourself?"

"Yes."

"Do you hate yourself for loving it?" He curled his damp fingers across the ridged box of her throat and pressed in, just a touch.

She did not answer this time, and he kissed the edge of her jaw, as close to her lips as he could reach.

Her nipples were rigid under his fingertips, her belly as tight as a board. Her breath became shallow and rapid. He could not fuck her as savagely as he wanted while in this position, but the contact between them was fantastic, slick and tight as a fist. He wanted to slide out of her cunt and take her anus, shove into it brutally until pleasure shattered him and the sodomy transmuted her soul. But there'd be time for that; there'd be time to teach her new forms of surrender, different faces of astonishment and ecstasy. Instead he put his arms around her and rested his cheek against her back, the bones of her spine digging into his skull, and agitated her clitoris with the side of his hand. Inside, her vagina spasmed and tightened as if to rip him to pieces, and she yelped and gasped and cried out, her fingertips clenching the skin of his thighs until the bitten fingernails punched in violet parentheses. While she was coming, he fucked her seriously, using her hips as handles to slam her body down onto his. "I'm in all the way," he told her, "I'm in all the way. It's not too big. I'm in you all the way to the balls . . . all the way . . ."

Ah.

She rose herself off him in time to see his glossy, purpled cock emit the last oily spurts of opalescent semen onto his own belly, and she stretched out floppily alongside him, running her fingers through the semen spread over his crotch. Daniel lay back onto the ice-cold sheets, trembling, his heart half exploded with joy, but . . . hungry; the restraint took so much out of him. Sybil experimentally licked her fingers. "It doesn't *taste* like poison," she said. "Tastes like zinc."

"Eat it all up; it's good for you," he said. He didn't expect her to do it, but she sucked her fingers clean and smiled at him, returning the dare.

She then curled up and touched her fingers to the sticky mess between her legs. "Sybil the Slippery. Sybil the Slobbery. Mmmm, I actually came," she said dreamily, "I came *hard.*"

"You did," he said. "You were very brave."

"Like it's that scary," she scoffed.

"Sex is terrifying," Daniel said sternly. "It's the pain and the violation and the fear of the unknown. I know you won't admit it, but you were afraid. And it's hard work. I'm glad you liked it the first time. I think you deserve it."

"It's like a cool secret that the world spoils before you find out for yourself," she said. Her eyes were fatigue-glazed now. Daniel caressed the crisp blond hair at her temple and wondered if sharing his semen was going to do the trick this time, if it would unlock her mind to his, give him control of her affections as it did with all other humans. At the moment, her thoughts were as closed to him as ever, and only the clammy rose-petal texture of her skin gave him any information as to her pleasure. There wasn't even any way to know if she had really had an orgasm, or if she'd faked it. He gazed deep into her eyes but saw only his reflection.

He tumbled out of bed away from her. "I have to go do something," he said, putting on a pair of socks.

"What?"

"Um . . . eat," he said.

"You mean drink blood."

He didn't feel it was necessary to answer that. She sat up in bed and watched him putting on trousers over his naked behind, tucking his tender, still-engorged penis into the fly and buttoning it closed. "Where?"

"Somewhere. A bar, probably."

"You're going to go kill someone in a bar?"

"That's right," said Daniel, smiling and then letting the smile drain away.

"I want to go," she said.

"Oh, come on. You're drunk and you're high. You're in no shape. I have to be very careful. I'm not doing this for kicks; I do it to survive."

Sybil's eyes glittered. "I won't get in the way." She ran to the bathroom and came out with her armload of clothes. "Look at this. I practically disappear. You think I don't know what's at stake?"

He watched her get dressed, hardly fumbling at all, and sighed. "We're in this together, then," he said.

"Of course we're in this together," she huffed. "Why else do you think I fucked you?"

"Maybe because you wanted me."

"What I want . . ." She ran out of words, gave up, and shook her head. "How else am I supposed to believe you about anything? I believe you now, but how much of that is just wanting to believe it's true, just because it would make everything different? Everything in the whole world, different?"

"Fine," he said. "I'm running low on time."

They drove into Newark, and Daniel chose a middle-class dance club with a prominent bar attached, the parking lot and surrounding street choked with cars. He walked ahead of her into the club, not looking behind him or seeking out her hand with his. Neither doorman nor bouncer acknowledged their presence, even though she stuck out her tongue and waved her hand in the doorman's face. "Hey, dude!" she shouted into his sweating face, but he might have been blind and deaf for all his reaction.

"Don't," Daniel said to her over his shoulder. "I'm hiding us, but don't fuck with it. I don't have as much strength as I would like. If it comes down to it, you're coming out, not me."

She retained her coy smile but again fell silent and looked away. Daniel had run out of time for idle chat; once his mind and body seized on the idea of killing, of consuming, it was impossible to argue. They surrounded him, fountains of satisfaction waiting to be consumed, soft easy skins with heat and warmth and goodness inside them. Newark was not the place for a quick snack; Newark meant life-taking, gluttony, a real feed after weeks of nibbles and tastes. The hour had struck when everyone in the bar was drunk, and the place smelled boozy and sweaty, a vicious, decadent air trapping the bodies like insects in honey. He let the swaying Sybil go and brushed through an obstacle course of drunk people, headed for the bathroom. He paused at the door and looked behind him; Sybil had followed close behind, watching him. "I said I wanted to go with you," she told his ear.

"I'm going into the gents," Daniel said.

Her tone was clipped and firm. "I want. To watch."

He gave up and went in, Sybil following behind him. Daniel stood still for a second and concentrated; every bastard in the room had to be tricked stupid. It would take the last of his strength.

Sybil stood next to the doorway, statuesque, supple, freshly fucked, and very female, and the men in the john pissed and zipped and checked their hair and walked right past without noticing her. Daniel took a look around, chose the smallest one, let the man zip up and look at himself in the mirror. Ordinary looks, around forty, dot-com company polo shirt and Dockers; guy's name was Mike. *Come right this way, Mike.* Daniel closed one hand around his shoulder and guided him into the largest of the three stalls. They were designed for minimum privacy, a sadly inadequate defense against drug use, and the doors only covered a four-foot section, leaving almost three feet at the bottom and three at the top that could be seen. Daniel wanted to look at Sybil and wink, but his body didn't let him. He pressed the yielding Mike against the wall beside the toilet and put his teeth against the side of his victim's neck. The punctured carotid artery spurted into Daniel's mouth faster than he could swallow, and blood smeared all around his mouth and ran down his neck and Mike's neck. Mike had almost no thoughts as he died—his eyes and mind were full of the soothing repetition of the soundproof ceiling tiles, his eyes finally seeing the patterns in the random dots that had earlier confused him. His blood; bitter-sour tang of alcohol, sweet-turpentine taste of cigarette additives, nerve-numbing Prozac. Job; friend; drink; no partner and no pets. Middle management. And to all a good night.

Click and flash, the information sparked like a flashbulb and faded softly at the edges. A portrait of a tranquilized brain.

Daniel stood back and caught his breath, sitting the dead man on the toilet and wiping his own face with his hand. Presently, he looked over at Sybil standing with her back to the door, standing up straight, staring at him. He couldn't stop himself from grinning the stupid grin of the satisfied baby, the junkie's ecstasy, the everything's-all-right-forever bliss of every cell in his whole body flipping over themselves and dancing with joy. His hands and feet and belly and face felt fat, and he knew he looked very pink.

He came out of the stall and went to a sink and washed his hands and face with liquid soap from a large plastic dispenser bolted to the wall, the diaphanous curls of dissolving blood foaming the water pink. He wasn't perfectly clean but it would do; the bar outside the bathroom was dimly lit, and no one would stare. "Thank God for black T-shirts," Daniel said out loud. Sybil held the door for him. They drifted through the bar crowd like leaves on a stream and went out the front door past the doorman, who did not so much as glance at them.

Daniel paid twenty dollars for six minutes of parking. Sybil fished through the pile of compact disks in the glove compartment, picked one, and fed it into the obedient, caressing slot in the dashboard. *Daydream Nation.* She flopped back against the seat. "I see you found the Sonic Youth," Daniel murmured, glancing back over his shoulder at the traffic glittering on the street. "Why do you still listen to it?"

"Because I actually really like Sonic Youth," Sybil replied, just as softly. "I had to understand where she was coming from. And I do. I did. I kind of understand it."

"It reminds me of someone I loved," Daniel said, "that's why I bought it. He liked it a lot."

"Is he dead?" Sybil asked.

"Yes, he's dead."

"Did you kill him?"

"No." Daniel shook his head and smiled. "He died in a car accident. Listening to David Bowie."

"You fall in love with guys a lot," said Sybil.

"Yes," he admitted.

"Try to say something to my mind now," she said.

He sighed, and felt that he desired her madly. She chuckled instantly. "We'll be in bed soon," she said.

"You *can* hear me," he said. He bit his lip and smiled.

"I have to be listening," said Sybil, stretching her arm

up along the underside of the roof of the car, sleepily like a cat, then suddenly twitching and jerking a little in time to the music. Instantly, she became a child in his eyes. "I block everything out. It's just easier that way." She lit a cigarette and stared out the window. "How far is your reach? How much power do you actually have?"

He was, from Mike's blood, probably a little too drunk to be driving. "About a room," he said. "A small room. Twenty people tops—and that'll nearly kill me. Proximity helps. Being full of blood helps."

"Do you like the way it tastes?"

"Blood? I can't help but like it. Cocaine addicts like the taste of cocaine; they like the way it makes their tongue and gums numb. But it's worse than that, it's worse than an addiction. It's an addiction like you're addicted to air. You could quit, but you would die. As simple as that."

"That was really very elegant," she said. "It doesn't even look like you hurt him."

"I didn't. It didn't hurt him at all—well, maybe for a second. He slipped away."

Back at Daniel's apartment, he coaxed her back into bed with him, first with her clothes on, then, after a moment of lying against the smooth naked furnace of his body, she wriggled out of her clothes. "That's better," she whispered, pressing her breasts against his chest. "You're actually hot now. You were really kinda inhumanly cold before."

"You really only fucked me because I'm not human?" he asked.

"Is that how you see it? Not human?"

"I'm not human. And you know it."

"If you want to look at it that way."

"What other way is there, Sybil?"

"I dunno . . ." She pinched one of his nipples, then caressed the tingling apex with her fingertip. "You could try some stupid positivity shit and think of it like . . . I fucked you because you're not like anyone else I've ever met. But I don't think I would have fucked you if you weren't a vampire. Because I would have just dismissed it. Because if you weren't a vampire, you'd be a different person, and probably not someone I'd be interested in wasting my time with."

"Because I'm the only person you've ever met who could understand why you'd want to kill your best friend?"

"No, that I *did* do it. Everybody wants to kill their best friend at some point. Don't they? But they don't do it almost ever. You're supposed to be safe if you're someone's best friend—nobody kills their best friend. Do they?"

He stopped her mouth with a kiss, and the kiss lingered, and her fingers slipped into his and they lay softly linked for a long time. He felt her gradually relaxing, like chocolate softening in his mouth, and he raised his head and looked at her, and realized that she'd fallen asleep. He lay there and gazed at her for a long time, now that he could without fear of being mocked or injured by her. Upon closer inspection, she had a face that was only beautiful, not pretty—the bridge of her nose was a shade too strong, one eyebrow higher than the other, her muscular jaw suggesting butchness; but her mouth was delicious, and the skin of her eyelids like the bloom on a plum, supernaturally fine blond down on her cheeks thickening to dishwater hair at the temples. He kissed her again while she slept, whispering, "Sybil Morocco . . . please . . . listen to me, Sybil Morocco . . . let me in."

Scene Ten: Shattering

Daniel awoke to the sound of shattering glass.

He had fallen asleep in the study, looking at books of collected snapshots from Hollywood, stalled on another picture of Ariane, and thinking loving and bitter thoughts to her, wherever she was (still in Oregon, no doubt, being scientific and cataloguing her every thought . . . she was too far away for him to reach). He woke naked and chilled, the cashmere blanket having slipped off his body long ago, and started up from the chair and out of the door.

One of the windows in the living room had been shattered, thick splinters of glass glittering on the wood floor. Sybil skittered through the kitchen, tearing open drawers and cupboard doors, dressed and wearing one of his best cold-weather leather parkas. "What the hell are you doing?" Daniel shouted.

She whirled, spraying glass diamonds from the elbow of the parka. "How the fuck do I get out of here?" she shouted back at him.

"Why couldn't you wait until I woke up?"

"I didn't know where the fuck you were. I want to get out of here. Alive. Need a crowbar or something. Fucking bars on the windows." She weaved back and forth in a trance, like an excited cobra, clenching her hands into intermittent fists. Looking for something to grab. "Something heavy . . ."

"It's Manhattan," Daniel explained. "You need a key code to get out as well as get in. Security, right? Forget it, you can't get out without my help."

"I don't like this!" she screamed.

"Why are you afraid?" Daniel spoke calmly and pleasantly. The sight of her, even in her agitation, soothed him. He picked up scattered silverware and napkins and returned them to their drawers. "I'm not going to hurt you. That's the last thing I want. I thought we had an understanding. Sybil. C'mon. You're panicking. I didn't think you were capable of panic."

"I'm a human; humans panic," she said, calming, returning to herself. "Let me out of here. This is not cool."

"Sudden attack of conscience?" asked Daniel.

"No," she shot back. "Look, we're even. I saw you kill a guy last night. You know I killed Ruth. Blackmail would be pointless. So don't even try it."

"I'd like to see your paintings today," he said.

"You can't." She wouldn't look at him. "They don't exist."

"What do you mean?"

"I throw them out. I mean, I take them out and leave them places. I don't keep them—that's not the point—besides they're not very—forget it, OK?"

"Sybil," Daniel said slowly, "it's nine o'clock in the morning, I'm tired, and you're probably really hung over. Why don't we go back to bed and I'll order in some breakfast? Are you hungry?"

"What do you want from me?" she demanded.

"Just this," he said quietly. "Just . . . being here with you, in the same room, trying to communicate with you. Remembering last night."

"You're the first."

"I know," he replied, "I could tell." She stared at the floor, her mouth working against her teeth, licking her lips with a dry tongue. Daniel sighed. "Are you that frightened?"

"I woke up, I'm alone in this strange place, and I stepped on your shirt. It's like bloody and wet . . . and . . . I just want to get out of here."

He cautiously approached her, put out his hand and touched the puffy leather of the parka, and took her icy, trembling hand. "We can get out of here if you want," he promised. "But let me come with you. We'll go wherever you want to go. I mean it. Wherever. If you say you want to go to Bangkok, we can go to Bangkok. I mean it, Sybil. Just let me come with you."

She blinked at him suspiciously for a few seconds, then frowned at nothing, heavy dark circles carved out of the dough-pale flesh under her eyes. "OK . . . I just . . . want something to eat."

"Wherever you want to go," he said. "It's all right."

He got dressed, maximum coverage for morning sunlight, and let them both out, sighing at the broken window. Sybil started walking intensely, hands crammed into the pockets of the parka, and he skipped hastily into step behind her.

They took the subway downtown. Together, they stood at the very edge of the platform, Sybil kicking at the filthy nubs of beige plastic an inch from the abyss. She stared down at the tracks; he put his arms around her, side-on, her shoulder against his chest. "Which station was it?" he whispered against the collar of the parka.

"In Brooklyn somewhere," she said dismissively.

She led him to a greasy spoon in her neighborhood, the menu in translucent red plastic letters on a lighted board above the bar. Sybil sat down heavily on a bar stool. Daniel shrugged out of his motorcycle jacket and spread it on the stool before he sat down. At this hour, they had the place to themselves, except for a grimy old woman mumbling to herself over a stack of equally grimy pancakes.

"Coffee," Sybil grunted to the waitress, "potato knish, sour cream, please."

"And for you?" The waitress, not so much old as affected by a stronger gravitational force that weighed down her face, mottled arms, and stained dark-red uniform, regarded Daniel through grease-spattered half-glasses.

He couldn't even speak for a few seconds, wondering what her blood would taste like—rich and creamy, swirling with undigested lard. "Just coffee," he half-whispered. The waitress didn't move. "Coffee," he said louder. "Please."

"Manners," the waitress grumbled.

Sybil spilled a packet of artificial sweetener onto the counter and began to chop it into lines.

"You come here often?" Daniel grimaced at the shuffling bulk of the retreating waitress.

Sybil shrugged. "It's near my house," she said, "and they're open twenty-one hours a day."

"Your house," he repeated with a grin, watching her losing some of the sweetener in the cracked varnish on top of the bar. "It's hardly a house."

"Sorry, I'm from the Midwest. My apartment." She looked up at him. "My shithole apartment."

"Can I see your place? Now that you've seen mine?"

"Why? So you can feel better about not living in poverty?"

"Call it morbid curiosity," he said. "Call it me walking you home. Whatever. Can I come over?"

She shrugged.

In the apartment building, the ammonia of the urine of several species, not all of them mammalian, became an entirely new physical sensation—encapsulating scent, but also pain, and a ringing in the ears. Most of the overhead lights were broken, the glass still scattered on the bare linoleum floor, and the walls wore layers of graffiti tags, some of them excellent but generally idiotic marker scrawling. Sybil hesitated in the ground-floor hall and stared. "I like to see how this changes every day," she said. "Like here, that's Manny, this ten-year-old who lives across the street. He writes something every day—here's a couple of new ones—'Sickness spreads.' 'NYC die today.' 'It feels good when I touch myself'—that was the first one I ever saw. It was there when I moved in here. He probably wrote that when he was like eight years old."

She wrestled a series of keys into locks and knobs on her door, criscrossed with flat bars of wood sloppily hammered into place; visible below them, the door panels were horribly splintered. "And how long have you lived here?" Daniel spoke up at last. She had managed to get the door open, lifting it up on rusted hinges to get the door to clear the frame. Her apartment consisted of a single room, half the size of his living room, with a small sink against the far wall; a large, scuffed picnic cooler sat on the floor beside the exposed pipes of the sink, and a battered, holey twin mattress covered with worn thermal blankets and a collection of cardboard boxes and milk crates did duty as furniture. The walls were ringed several rows high with drawings, watercolor paintings, and scribblings on cheap lined notebook paper.

"A little less than a year. Rent's not bad—eight hundred a month."

Daniel scoffed. "I'm sorry, that's just wrong," he said. "This is not living. This is barely subsistence. I wouldn't pay eight dollars for this dump."

"I could keep it up better, but what would be the point? Somebody's meth lab might blow the whole building to kingdom come tomorrow. It's not like I'm in love with this place. There's rats the size of wolverines here. They come out at night and chew on my cooler and I have to throw things at them. Sometimes I hit 'em. And then I have this dead rat to deal with. I throw 'em out the window and the other rats probably eat 'em." She laughed and turned on the water in the sink and began washing her hands with a huge cake of heavily perfumed soap. "Jesus. And I used to kind of like rats. Bathroom's down the hall, but I usually just piss in the sink."

"I'm surprised that you don't squat," he said. He sat down on the mattress—attack springs leapt out of it—and regarded one of the watercolor paintings. Underneath the washes of mixed brown grime, he could just make out the grim faces of two girls in crayon, both with crazy yellow hair and huge eyes in layered black. One of them had red lips and cheeks and the other didn't.

"Squatting requires a collective to really work," Sybil said, scrubbing her face in the sink. She wiped her eyes with a colorless towel and looked at Daniel, grimacing at the picture. "Oh, that. Ruth did that."

"This is really terrible," he said.

"Trust you to go straight to the piece of shit. It's got sentimental value, OK? It's not like she's an artist or anything. Was."

"Did you do all the rest of these?"

"Not all. Some of them are Ruth's. That's the only picture she ever did of the two of us. She only drew when she was tweaking. I have some of her writings up there, too—you can tell because her handwriting is totally psychotic. Imagine that."

Daniel stretched out on the mattress, his eyes closing again. He would have liked to get more sleep, but if he had been awake enough to hear the glass breaking in his flat that morning, his body had committed to consciousness. "I want to get you out of here," he said.

"What, now?" She bounced onto the mattress beside him, miraculously avoiding the freed spikes of mattress spring stabbing up through the cover. "I just got home."

"No, permanently," he said. "This isn't you. I don't feel your soul in here. This place has about as much feeling as a mall."

Sybil giggled. The dark circles had receded somewhat from her eyes, and droplets of water sparkled on her hair, her eyelashes a moist, rich tangle. "What, you want me to move in with you?"

"Not into my place, no," he said. "I've got too many valuable *tchotchkes*. I think you'd destroy everything."

"It's what I do best." She fumbled in the pocket of her jeans and produced another cigarette. "I could move into your studio," she suggested.

"Do you really want to?"

"If you want me to move . . ."

"I don't want you living here anymore," he said. "If you want to move into my studio, you can live there."

"What about all your little munchkins?" she asked, still

giggling. "Where are they going to have their little party?"

"They'll figure it out," said Daniel.

"Ya got a shower there?"

"Yep."

"Let's roll," said Sybil.

Eyes still closed, he pulled the green cell phone from his pocket and hit the code to call Joachim.

Daniel's "munchkins" moved all of Sybil's things out of the apartment by noon and installed them into a sad, small heap in one corner of Daniel's studio by 1:30. Sybil insisted that they handle the crates carefully. "Don't jostle them too much or you'll get a big nasty surprise." When everything was out, she locked her apartment door behind her and then threw the keys one by one down the hall into pungent darkness.

In the studio, she sat on the floor smoking and drinking a glass of champagne, watching the assistants scurrying about, fractionating themselves off into subsets that moved things, told other people to move things, or stood around talking and staring at her. "OK, you guys," said Daniel, clapping his gloved hands, "nobody fuck with Sybil, you got it? She lives here for right now. Treat her with the same respect that you treat me. And the city is crawling with kids who would circumcise themselves for your jobs. So act accordingly."

The assistants answered in a gym-class grumble.

Joachim stood next to Daniel, eyeing everything nervously. "Is she your new personal assistant?" he asked, chewing one of his fingernails.

"No," said Daniel, "she just needs a place to crash. And she's an artist."

Sybil looked up and smiled when he said this. She got up and walked toward the bathroom on the side of the room.

Joachim watched her go in and slam the door, then shook his head. "I dunno, man," he said. "I don't feel right about this."

"Life is change, my child," Daniel replied, patting Joachim on the top of his head. "You're too young to realize that. But you have to get comfortable with it. Embrace change. Chase after it and embrace it. Kiss it all over its ugly face. You know what I'm talking about?"

"But—" Joachim's best feature was his wide-eyed, innocent stare, and he turned it on Daniel full blast, like a painting of a betrayed child clown asking *why*. "Are we still going ahead with Toby's installation?" he asked.

"Of course. It's done, right?"

"Yes, but—"

"Then we are. And tell Cindy at Loop that Gerold Major is still on for Friday, and—"

"But how are we supposed to *work* with her living here?" Joachim hissed urgently.

"Work *around* Sybil," said Daniel. "I haven't seen anybody doing anything for ages. If there's no work getting done, why come here? There's gotta be someplace for these people to go. This is a huge money sink, and you all hang around here all day not producing anything I can sell so I can afford to keep this place, and frankly I'm getting bored with paying for you all to waste your art school educations."

"Daniel, that's not fair," said Joachim. He was still paying off an MFA from the Rhode Island School of Design.

Daniel collected himself, softening his voice. Diplomacy. "You want to know what's not fair? It's not fair that this girl is now homeless because of me, and I just want to make sure she's got a warm place to sleep. I just want her to be safe and I know you can help take care of that, for a little while. C'mon. It's just a little while. A little while." Daniel took off his sunglasses and folded them in his hand, and met Joachim's glance with his naked eyes, emanating waves of reasonable gentleness. "OK? Do we have an understanding? It's not forever. Not forever." Joachim gave an extended sigh and rolled his shoulders, then waved helplessly with his hands and shrugged. Daniel squeezed his shoulder and smiled.

By two o'clock, Sybil and Daniel sat down to lunch at his favorite dark, obscure grill. It had just enough regular business to keep it open, but it was never full, and he never recognized anyone there; the main patrons were traveling northern European businessmen who favored the Swedish-owned hotel across the street. In the basement, Daniel was far out of the reaches of the milky, anemic sunlight which, nonetheless, had scraped at the exposed parts of his skin like knives. Daniel took off his coat, gloves, and hat, and unfastened the top two buttons of his shirt, rubbing gently at his tender chin and jaw. Sybil, showered and hairbrushed and changed but still swaddled in his leather parka, bemusedly watched his preening display. "You actually are really attractive," she said with a grudging laugh. "In a kind of generic Dracula kind of way."

"Oh, what's that supposed to mean?" He shook out a wine list.

"It means, damn, could you maybe dress a little bit less like a fucking vampire? How obvious do you want to make it? Have you ever considered like a football team T-shirt and a pair of jeans or something? What is it with all the leather?"

It was a common question. "I dress like this because I can afford it," Daniel said, "and because it looks good on me."

"I see," said Sybil. "And why do you paint your fingernails?"

"Because if I don't, they look really scary and obvious. They look like claws."

"They look like claws anyway."

"Yes, but they look more like human fingernails." He stretched out his bare hands on the table and held them in the glow of the glass-globed candle. The warm golden light could humanize his porcelain skin but not soften the grotesque span of his fingers. "Look at that," he whispered, fascinated all over again. "You can see . . ."

"It's ugly," she said matter-of-factly. "I um . . . I think you should leave me alone now."

"What?" said Daniel.

"Thanks for giving me a different place to live, it *is* a vast improvement, but I would really like it if I didn't see you for a while. Just leave me totally alone for at least two weeks. I might take off. You can understand why I'm a little bit freaked out. I mean, shit, I just lost my virginity. To something that's not even supposed to exist . . . *And* it really hurt." Daniel raised his eyebrows, looked down at the table, and said nothing. "And this is a whole new fuckin' situation and I need some time by myself to figure out what the hell is going on. So whaddya say, is it a deal? Do you think you can actually handle that?"

"Yes," said Daniel, "if I have to." He didn't look at her, but only because he'd burn his blood trying to convince her otherwise. If he wasn't looking at her, he could pretend that she, or he, was far away. Europe, perhaps. Or dead.

"Because if you really care about me, you'll leave me alone for a while."

"Yes."

"All right?"

"Do you still want to have lunch?"

"Well, yeah," she said, shrugging. "I'm hungry and you're paying."

She ate smoked cod, potatoes, salad, and a trembling slab of lemon cream cake, and drank three glasses of blond sherry, smoking unceasingly. Daniel toyed with his food and smiled as he watched her eat. As soon as her plates were clean—she scoured them with her fingertip and then sucked herself clean—she ducked under the hood of the parka and bolted for the stairs, the door.

Scene Eleven: Phone Calls and Photographs

"Who is this?" is how Daniel usually answered the phone. He was halfway through "is" before he knew that such a statement was redundant. No amount of subterfuge would fool this person. That someone on the other line *knew* it was him, knew in some deep and significant way. Daniel did not believe in precognition, but he knew, by now, the sensation of being on the telephone with someone whose brain worked the same way his did. Perhaps it had to do with the vague electrical current in the phone lines, setting up a field of transmission, static that briefly coalesced into the image of a beloved face and then scattered into chaos again.

"Hello?" said the voice on the line, female, baffled. "Who did I just call?"

"You know who it is," Daniel said softly.

"I—I didn't mean to call *you,*" stammered Ariane sincerely.

"I know you didn't," Daniel said, "but I've been thinking for the last hour solid that I wanted you to call me.

See, it does still work, whether or not you think I'm the biggest asshole in the whole world."

He had the photographs arranged on his desk blotter in a pattern reminiscent of a tarot spread; a parking lot in the sunset, a dim mess of darkness with a candlelit staircase slashing diagonally through, Ariane and Lovely, Ariane by herself, asleep in his bed with her hand grasping the black pillowcase. And he'd thought how much he wanted to feel her touch again, grasping his flesh like that, asleep next to him.

She laughed comfortably. "Oh, OK," Ariane said slowly, "it's like that, is it?"

"I am only going on the last thing I heard from you. Plus, you never call me. I don't know if you're still where you used to be, or what."

"Have you ever stopped to consider the fact that I might be busy? That I actually have a job? I know the whole concept is foreign to you."

"Busy nothing. You can't spare a call for your dearest dada? It's only ten cents a minute on Sundays." He listened to her laughing, and, as an accompaniment, the silken chords of jazz coming through the phone. "Are you listening to Miles Davis?"

"Oh, my God, this album. I've been listening to it on repeat for the last couple of hours. I just can't stop listening to it. I've owned it for years, but it never really sounded like this before. I never really *heard* it before."

"You'll get over it," Daniel promised. "If you're quite careful, you can hear every jazz record ever recorded. I have. Or had; actually there's some new stuff out, but it's nowhere near as good as I want it to be."

"You're talking like an old man," said Ariane.

"I am old," said Daniel. "I'm ninety-seven."

There was an awkward silence, soundtracked by "In a Silent Way" on vibraphone and trumpet and congas. "So, um, I was thinking about taking a little trip to Portland to sell some art," Daniel led in casually.

"Really? Portland, the thriving art metropolis?"

"There are some very respectable galleries in your town. And a lot of computer people with money who need something to put in the dining room. There is one gallery called Arclight that has been asking me to send a bunch of my work there. My work, not the student fumblings I sell. Mine. A very nice lady named . . ." Daniel consulted his Filofax, old-fashioned but still more reliable than a digital device, which always got sat on or magnetized somehow. "Jackie Cundera. At the Arclight Gallery. Fourteen-eighteen Northwest Everett Avenue."

"That's in my area of town," Ariane said. "In the same quadrant, anyway. Are you thinking of staying with me? You, in this uncivilized burg? What'll you do if you can't hail a taxi?"

"I drive." Daniel chuckled.

"I don't know how you can," she said.

Everything stopped short.

"That has nothing to do with it," he whispered hotly. "You have to learn to get on with your life."

"Oh," said Ariane airily. "So I'm . . . obsessed with the past."

"You're obsessed with blaming me for it."

"I never said anything about that, Daniel. I was just expressing surprise. I think you're making way too much out of an innocent comment."

Daniel bit his lip with his left upper fang, a typical grimace for him. Lovely used to call it his "hillbilly face," back in the days when Lovely was alive, before that day when Daniel really should have been driving himself, since Lovely was always stoned, and not a very good driver at the best of times. Daniel swallowed back a reflux of angry retorts and said, "Right. I'm sorry."

"No, I'm sorry."

"I wasn't actually thinking of staying with you, Ariane. I can get a hotel in the area. Since we're spontaneously on the phone, can you recommend one?"

Through the phone he could hear her raking her fingernails through her hair, faint ticks of static electricity, the crunch of the curls being pulled tight, her wrist against the phone receiver. "Um. There's a nice one called the Entr'Acte that's not too yuppie scum. Unless you want yuppie scum, in which case there's the Benson.

Or the Hyatt downtown; though you're getting kind of far from the gallery. But I guess you're renting a car or something."

"I'll have to," said Daniel, "I have to move some paintings about. She wants eight of them, so I'll bring five and have the other three shipped in a week or so. She assures me that they'll sell."

"Oh, Daniel, you sound so cute when you're insecure."

"That's not funny, Ariane." He laughed.

"Damn, I miss you," she said softly, possibly not meaning for it to be heard; but surely she knew better.

"I'd love to see you, if that's all right with you. We can, you know, go somewhere, have a drink."

"The Entr'Acte has a great bar," said Ariane. "When will you be here?"

"Friday, early afternoon," said Daniel.

"Jesus, that's soon. Meet me in the Entr'Acte Hotel bar Friday at seven o'clock."

"My heart belongs to you," he said out of reflex. For a moment he considered this and wished he could take it back, but he was several years too late.

"I'll rip it out if you're late."

"I know you would," said Daniel.

Scene Twelve: Oxygen Drunk

Daniel never really liked being on airplanes.

He enjoyed airports; their particular airlessness, their brilliant neon shopping-mall micro-stores, the duty-free shops, newsstands heavily stocked with business papers, bottled water, and bad local souvenirs, excitement thrumming through the air. Sometimes, though, it would all be too intense, and Daniel would panic, have to leave the airport, reschedule his flight. When people were really agitated—late for a flight, lost luggage, family tragedy—their minds screamed their private anxiety, and Daniel had a difficult time shutting it out. They prayed. They called out to God, whether they knew it or not, to deliver them from this place, to get them on their planes and far away. They didn't know anyone in the room was listening. The entire airport became a chapel of fervent zealots. He wanted to cry out, "Shut up! I can hear you! I am not God; I cannot deliver you!" Except that, of course, he could deliver them. No more arguments, no more embarrassments, no more airline food.

And on the plane itself—even in the arid cool of First Class, the chairs so soft they clasped your ass like a big caressing hand—it was even worse. Even some of the most staid flyers spent most of their flight edgily leafing through glossy thoughtless magazines or heavy sharp-edged airport bestsellers, or drinking themselves daft, giggling nervously through turbulence, trying actively not to think about how close death was. Fortunately for Daniel, they had no idea exactly how close—many an older passenger on his flights suffered a mysterious heart attack in a lavatory built for one.

On this nonstop flight to PDX, nobody died. Daniel took care of that before he left; a work-shift change at a nice Indian restaurant in the Village provided him with a rather romantic dance with a bleached-blond Hindi teenager, who would probably live, as someone would have to throw out the vegetable scraps and spot their fallen sister, settled sleepily among the milk crates and Hefty bags.

Daniel refused both in-flight meals and every beverage cart; he spent the hours sketching in a small, worn notebook that had lain ignored for almost ten years. Most of the drawings from the previous decade were unfinished; the new addition, an impression of Sybil's naked haunch from memory, stood as complete as it would ever be.

Daniel had asked for the largest car available at the rental agency; he was led to a vast dark-red minivan, menacingly shiny, bullying the town cars and sedans in the adjoining parking spaces. Daniel stood there and giggled at it for a few seconds. "I guess this will do," he said to the airport lackeys, wrestling his mounted canvases, wrapped in layers of burlap and felt padding, from wheeled carts and into the gaping maw of the van. "Please be careful with that—it's terribly expensive . . ." He withdrew his blue cell phone and Filofax card with the number of the Arclight Gallery on it.

"Arclight Fine Arts?"

"Jackie Cundera, please," said Daniel.

A moment of indistinct staticky murmuring passed, then a different woman spoke. "Is this Daniel?" came an excited voice.

"Jackie. How are things?"

"I can barely hear you, darling." Her words wore a halo of distortion.

"It's my cell phone—it's always difficult." And Portland seemed to be making it worse.

Long pause. "Did you (blank) all right? Are you (crackle blank) the airport?"

"I'm just about to set out now, actually. I have this insane spaceship car."

"Wonderful. I'll make sure someone (zeet) can find parking—it's monstrous around here at this time of (blank). The goddamn students think the world is their parking lot—no, not you, Andrea. So you'll be here soon, OK? Do you want lunch or a drink or anything?"

"I'd be happy with whatever you've got there. I just want these things off my hands and then we can think about hanging."

"This is great. I'm so excited. You're in the last First Thursday opening of the millennium. Who knows, it might be the very last one ever!"

"Don't tell me you're superstitious," Daniel said, cradling the phone between his head and shoulder and checking the seat belts cinching the canvases into the back compartment.

"Oh, superstition has (blank) it. This is Oregon—some survivalist nut might (crackle) in the middle of the night and decide to take me as one of his wives. I mean, there are things worse than death, right?"

Daniel laughed a stage laugh. "Absolutely."

"Do you know how to get here?"

"I have a map of some kind."

"All right. Call me if you get lost. It can be kind of tangly."

"I will."

Once Daniel figured out that the minivan drove more like a sports car than a Humvee, everything was delightful. He found a radio station playing Beethoven's *Ninth*, and his heart swelled as he swept out of the airport and saw the sloping green hills that bounded the roads.

In New York, he hadn't seen anything growing green for months; here, in the pouring rain, the lawns and trees dripped, soaking, rotting green. The chilly air, dense with oxygen and humidity, breathed thick and syrupy. Daniel shook with a case of helpless oxygen-drunk giggles and missed his highway exit.

Tangly indeed; he lost thirty minutes scrambling around the overpasses and flybys and side streets, completely baffled and mixed up. A minute ago he was on an Interstate; now he was on some street called Front, and there was nothing but rain-soupy train yards and warehouses. He shifted the van into neutral and fished out his cell phone. "Jackie, what the hell is going on with this stupid town?"

"Where are you?"

"I have no fucking idea."

"Look at a street sign, darling."

"Uh . . . Vaughn Street," he said. A car nearly sideswiped him, the driver audibly yelling as he went past. "Northwest Vaughn Street."

"OK, you're almost here. What's the cross street?"

"Nineteenth it looks like."

"OK, in that case go up to Twenty-first, if you can, I know there's some construction there, and turn left. Go down Twenty-first until you get to Flanders. And then—"

Somehow, miraculously, he drove up behind a nondescript cube of dirty-gray concrete and saw a woman in a purple raincoat waving frantically at him with a red umbrella.

The Arclight space was disappointingly small, and the gallery assistants of ordinary beauty and sternness, but Jackie Cundera herself was a vivid spark with a loud, encouraging voice and wide sweeping arm gestures that seemed to caress the walls of the gallery and the metal-framed photographs currently upon them. "This is the exhibit we have on now," she said to Daniel as she led him in, "an amazing young woman from Montana named Emily Green. They're selling like hotcakes—I only have two silver prints left. Do you collect? I have some of her photo-emulsion transfers that will send chills up your spine."

"I do collect," said Daniel. "Unfortunately for you, I

only collect Dada and Surrealist, old stuff. If you would give me a catalogue, though, I know a couple back East who would probably be very interested."

"Oh, I don't mean to treat you like a broker." Jackie Cundera laughed, her hand up to her mouth, and then reached out to touch his chest. "Here, you are the artist." When her fingertips made contact with his polyester shirt, a visible spark jumped between the cloth and her skin. "Wow! You are *electric!*"

"Yeah, I love to shock people."

"And I thought I couldn't be shocked anymore." They shared an embarrassed laugh. "Anyway, where's *your* work? I know you brought me five and I'm tracking the other three online."

"In the minivan of death," said Daniel. "We should probably get some help getting them out. They're all pretty heavy." Daniel could move them by himself, but it wouldn't do to let anyone see that he could; most men his size couldn't safely lift six hundred pounds of Lucite without assistance.

"I can't wait to see them in person at last. They're amazing in reproduction."

After two hours of moving the pieces and having his ego massaged, Daniel checked his watch. "I'm sorry, Jackie dear, but I really have to run off," he gasped. "I'm meeting an old lover for drinks downtown in fifteen minutes."

"An old lover? Well." Jackie looked at him a little hungrily over the rims of her glasses. "Have fun, then. Want to meet for breakfast tomorrow? Shall I call you?"

"I don't yet know—I'll call you. We'll maybe eat something tomorrow."

"Take care, Daniel." She spoke to the back of his coat, going out the door.

The Entr'Acte Hotel lay mere blocks away, but the thick Friday evening traffic, in the pouring rain turning to sleet, limped along. Daniel considered abandoning the minivan and making a run for it, but the weather outside was too nasty even for him. He decided to take his chances on the road. Ariane, Ariane . . . he could feel her already, drawing him in like the thought of home. Traffic opened up after a freeway entrance, and he seized the opportunity to gun the minivan's eager engine.

The Entr'Acte had been built in the earlier, simpler part of the century, with a quiet, restrained elegance. It was very much the kind of thing that Ariane would love, would find exotic; she adored old things. He wrestled the enormous vehicle into a parking space a block away, locked the doors with the remote-control keychain, and checked his watch. He had two minutes before seven—no time to fuss with an umbrella. In the rain, the deserted pavements reflected amber streetlights and multicolored neon signs. Daniel skipped for the pleasure of the sounds of his Italian shoes on the water. He knew Ariane was close; no emotions or thoughts yet, just her physical presence, a locus of magnetic warmth.

Daniel climbed past wrought-iron spikes in a side stairwell to the tiny, dark hotel bar, about half the size of his living room in Manhattan. Ariane, seated calmly at a booth in back, reflected a hundred times in the beveled-mirrored wall. How perfect—a thousand Arianes gazing up at him, on the edge of her seat, the only thing that had ever mattered, how much he wanted her.

Why did he chase so vehemently after the ones who were so difficult?

She looked quite different than the last time he'd seen her, miserable and strung-out in San Francisco, spitting obscenities in his direction as he walked out the door of a room in a different hotel. Her wildly curly dark red hair had been tamed somehow into an elegant Art Nouveau curve that rested heavily on one shoulder; she wore a gleaming white dress that draped gently in a wide *U* over her breasts. Her skin would never be pure white the way his was. Once it had been a yellow-golden café-au-lait with hundreds of cinnamon freckles; now it was the color of cappuccino foam, the freckles almost gone. Her eyes remained pools of reflective dark, but not shiny like Joachim's eyes; Ariane's eyes suggested velvet, rumpled waves of darkest black-coffee-colored velvet. He sat down opposite her, his breath catching in his throat. Was this what Ricari felt when he looked at Daniel, his sacred and profane offspring; did he feel this painful desire to be physically joined, like a part of him was missing? And yet, fear, distaste at the mindless intensity of the emotion? No wonder Ricari, inclined toward mildness and peace, felt the need to damn and escape.

"Ariane," said Daniel, "your hair—"

"You're late," she said. Like a slap.

He gulped, all the hairs on his body standing up. *Oh no oh please oh don't be angry at me my darling how terrible how sorry I am oh I'm so sorry.* A drop of rain fell off his hair, into his collar, and sliced icy down his spine. "But—"

Without speaking she pointed at a digital beer-company clock on the wall; the big red numerals screamed out 7:02. He stared at her, mouth open. "But—" he started again. "I—it wasn't my fault. My watch says—"

"I said be here at seven," said Ariane. "I don't like being made to wait."

Daniel put his head down on the table, sick with despair. And from there, he felt her smile. He looked up—the impish smirk, the single dimple that made her right cheek so special, so kissable. She put out her hand and stroked his wet black hair. And the *spark!* How—her fingers in his wet hair—the current poured through him, and for once, he was complete. Perfection. He grabbed her hand, kissed her wrist, her bare arm.

They knocked over two glasses on the table when they kissed. Daniel's leather sleeve swept through spilled mineral water and ice. She pulled him closer; he rose from his chair and into the booth next to her without their mouths separating for an instant. Tongues. He pricked his tongue on her sharp fangs, and she sucked hungrily at his spit and blood until he bit her tongue, too. They relaxed and feasted together on the fluids.

Suddenly she pushed him away. "You're fucking up my hair," she said, trying to pat the curve back into place on her shoulder. "I spent about half an hour with a blow-dryer trying to get it to do this."

He held up a dark-auburn lock and kissed it.

She leaned against him. "Oh well," she sighed, "with this humidity, it'll probably only last about another ten minutes anyway."

"I was going to say your hair looked spectacular," Daniel said, kissing it again. "When you interrupted me with your petty lateness bullshit."

"Oh, hell. I just like to watch you squirm. Besides, I figured you'd be early; I mean, how long has it been?" She ran a fingertip over his cheek and kissed him quickly again.

The bartender trudged over with a rag to mop up the spilled drinks. "Can I get you something?" he asked in a voice strained with the effort to be pleasant.

"I'd like a bottle of whatever is the most expensive champagne you have," said Daniel. "I'm going to be checking into the hotel so we can just put that on my bill."

"Oh-kay," said the bartender. Daniel and Ariane were gazing at each other so intently, he knew there was nothing more to be said, and he shared a bemused glance with the people sitting at the table opposite and went away.

"It's been five years," said Daniel to Ariane.

She sighed deeply. "Yeah," she agreed.

They said nothing more. The fingers entwined and they continued their conversation without speaking aloud. Experiences, thoughts, and emotions flashed through them and to each other.

You look beautiful too. This weather! This oxygen! I don't even need to drink when the champagne is in the air itself! And sometimes I don't even let myself think about you because it's just too painful. Ricari. Ricari. Yes, isn't he beautiful? And such a great fuck? He's like a shy little girl. We watched the sunlight crawl over the floor and almost let it touch us, but then we chickened out and closed the curtain. We drank blood together, an entire floor of old people, they were dying in a, that pink high-rise just across the street; we climbed in through the fire escape and put the nurses to sleep and took them all in their beds and they were so blissful in those last moments. Those blond hills in California where I lived and killed the sheep and drank their lanolin blood and my clothes were rags—Out in rain?—Not like this. I was a wild creature for years after you. I couldn't face anyone. Do you understand how much I can hate myself? Understand. My lover John. My lover John doesn't live with me, I won't let him, or he won't let himself, he's gone, it's been months, he's completely wild. Ah yes, John, cute, I found him very stiff, very English. Those dark eyes! That incredible skin! And that look on his face when I loomed over him, I did a kind of Nosferatu thing and went "Boo!" before I bit down on his throat. I get the giggles remembering! You fucking bastard, don't even think about him, you think you hate yourself, but I'll never be able to express how much I hate you. . . . But it's never quite that simple, never quite that cut and dried, how I wish love was like science. John and me never did get married. I guess there's no point now. I can see your nipples through that dress. How is it that I can understand German when I'm with you?—Lovely and his pierced. Lovely!—Lovely!—Do you ever go mad-sick-wild with missing him? Our precious boychild hustler. I've got a girl—she doesn't seem to have a name, does she? Not a real one anyway, does she?—Sometimes when I look at her I see Lovely, but she's not at all like—I didn't mean what I said. No, I didn't mean. No, regretting is hopeless and horrible when you're here and you're smiling like that. I see myself in your eyes. How do you cope? Do you ever . . . Feel . . . Horribly . . . Alone. Even together.

But they weren't alone, not right now.

She let go of his hand, breaking them into individuals again, and picked up her glass of champagne.

"Here's to forgetting," she said.

He picked up his own glass and chimed it against hers. "I'm getting pretty good at it," he said, taking a swallow.

"Really?" Ariane raised her eyebrows, slender wing-arcs the color of dried blood across her pale forehead. "I can't. I didn't think we could forget anything."

"Maybe it's just years of denial." Daniel sighed. He took off his coat at last and draped it across a chair.

"You're pretty good at that, too," she said.

Daniel laughed. "You're such a bitch."

"Thank you."

"I'll go get a room now," he said.

"I'll be here," she replied.

In a painless, quick transaction, he got a single room instead of a suite, giving one of the credit cards he'd most recently acquired from a victim, thankful he didn't need a drivers' license to verify it. He accompanied a valet back to the minivan—outside the wind had picked up, sleet piling up in the gutters like diamond shavings—and they got his things out of the passenger seat. "That's a big van," said the valet, squinting into the wind. "You got kids?"

"In a way," said Daniel with a laugh. "I'm trying to sell them."

When Daniel returned to the bar, Ariane was emptying the champagne bottle into her glass. "You drank all that?" Daniel gaped.

"I was bored," she said. Her burnt-sugar New Orleans accent had gotten stronger—an alcoholic placebo effect. "And it pisses me off that I can't feel it. I want to get champagne tipsy." As she had said, her hair was already springing back into spirals, which she twisted idly with her finger.

"You can, you know," he said. "It's as simple as a little nip and tuck."

"But where?"

Daniel glanced toward the ceiling.

"Oh, come on! Not here, not at your own hotel," she admonished. "And it's really yucky outside."

"Oh, for heaven's sake, it's tropical out there. You're spoiled! And besides, it's your town. Surely you know someplace where we can grab a bite."

"That's a terrible pun, Dan."

"Oh, God, don't call me Dan. It sounds ugly coming from you. I like the way you say 'Dayne-yel.' " He imitated her accent badly. "Come, come. I'm hungry. And I bet you are, too."

Her eyes searched his face. "I'm always hungry," she said.

"Let's go. How long has it been since you killed someone?"

She said nothing. He already knew the answer to that, read from her mind like a wallpaper pattern in the background. Ariane didn't like to kill; that's why she was always hungry. She had not drunk her fill for more than a year, and when she had, she felt so sick afterward that she hadn't left her house for a week. Ricari had taught her well, but she was still so young; she was a baby still, only a vampire for five years, and needed ten times the blood Daniel did just to survive. "It's too early," she mumbled.

"It's never too early."

"That sounds like something you would say."

"Let's not fight. Take your aggressions out on someone else."

She sighed and stood up. Her dress, falling just below the knee, emphasized the full, easy curves of her body. She was a walking bonbon. He admired the view for a few seconds before joining her at the coatroom at the front of the bar, and while she was distracted getting her sheepskin-lined coat from the hanger, he grabbed one fruitlike curve of her ass. "My God, I almost forgot what a fantastic behind you've got. So *säftig!*"

She slapped his hand, leaving a purple welt. "Goddammit, Daniel, you're such a pig."

He sulkily sucked his knuckles, but the bruise hadn't lasted more than a few seconds. "Oh, come on, surely you know that that's what men see in you. You turn round and then nothing you've ever said or done means anything. All they can think about is all the unspeakable things they want to do to you."

"Oh, thanks. You *really* know how to make me feel good about myself as a person. Jerk." Her adorable coat had a hood with bright-red ribbon trim. "You're an old decrepit bastard from the days before you idiots woke up and figured out which half of the human race actually got shit done, so I'm gonna let it slide. But I'm warning you; for every sexist comment you make, I'm going to make you hurt." He wanted to take her hand and apologize, but she put her hands into her pockets.

"Sweetness, I was only joking," Daniel murmured.

"I know," she squirmed; she didn't resist when he put his hands alongside hers in her pockets. She frowned as he kissed her eyebrows. "I'm just not used to it anymore. I'm not used to *you* anymore."

"Were you *ever* 'used to me'?" he whispered, millimeters away from her moist, red champagne lips. "Honestly?"

She didn't have to speak aloud; the information passed between their skins, the answer to his spoken question and the ones he didn't say.

She broke off the kiss and gave his hands back to him. "Cut it out," she said, her voice a thick, husky grumble. "Let me be myself for just a little while. You're in my head as it is. And you're way too intense for me right now. Give me a minute." She smiled a little bit, awkwardly, the way she used to. "I'll be with you in a little while. Meet me out back, on the light-rail tracks."

Ariane bolted almost silently, invisibly fast to the far-too-ignorant human eyes of the people checking in, her toes barely making contact with the floor, through the lobby and out the glass front doors. Daniel watched her go, as choked up with pride as a new father, then went up to his room.

In the dark he changed his coat from a short black motorcycle cut to a long brown wool as slight and fluttery as silk. He thought to himself as he opened his window, *I ought to be neat tonight, I'd like to keep this coat,* eased himself outside, and squatting, balanced precariously on the ledge, closing it again but for a crack. The street was clear, except for Ariane, a creamy smudge on the dark slate of the parking lot. He gauged it; forty feet down. Piece of cake.

Daniel always loved letting go.

Hard skill to perfect; it was so logical, but the fear of heights was hard to eliminate entirely and there were panicked urges to curl up or straighten out. No; curl slightly, knees slightly bent, feet straight down, like a kid jumping out of a tree. Daniel broke both legs twice in his first year as a vampire, and learned the unique agony of having bones set when no anaesthetic is possible. Whenever he jumped, he always thought of Ricari tapping and wrenching his legs, screeching at him like a bitter wife, "Jump off of small things first, you idiot!"

The painful tang of the asphalt contacting the soles of his feet; the rebound launching him three feet in the air. He threw out his arms and the coat and came to an expert rest on the balls of both feet. Ariane clapped her puffy sleeves, then turned on her heel and sprinted away.

He followed the pale streak of her coat and the flashing heels of her shoes; she cut across moving traffic and across the hoods of cars in parking lots like the little daredevil she was. Daniel hadn't engaged in such antics in a long time—not such risky ones, anyway—and he got so excited that he lost her around a corner with a sign sputtering a blue neon skin on the half-cobblestone street. Only the mental link they shared helped him to locate her—she thought *ART! your stuff will look good here the girls are cute reminds me of*—she had paused in front of the Arclight Gallery and peered into the glass-walled front entrance at the photographs, art patrons, and assistants. Ariane glanced back at him, watching her from the corner, and stuck out her tongue. The mist abruptly curled around the empty place where she had been.

She began leading him into bars, one after another; they would enter, she would either scan the crowds inside, or pass through them; her head held up, enough to smell the room. Daniel wondered what she was about; she flashed him the tiniest smile across the scratched and pitted wood of an ale-dizzy Irish pub. Champagne. She still wanted champagne.

In a large club on a glittering street, Ariane found what she was looking for. Most of the patrons were drinking beer, but a group of seven women occupied a long booth across from a rack of pinball machines, four empty bottles and two half-full ones on their table. They were shrieking with laughter and making a huge mess of cigarette ash and napkins on the table. Ariane shot one long glance to Daniel, who still stood uncertainly in the doorway, nonplussed by the television above the bar showing a basketball game, and the glance read *Might as well come in.*

He shook his head slowly. *We're not together.*

An angle of her head and she looked away. *Understood. Hope you like cold.*

He brushed past her. *Fuck that, I'm playing pinball. I have four quarters; I bet you'll be done first.*

Fucking showoff . . .

A bachelorette party. The bride-to-be wore a necklace made of four strands of immense fake pearls, a red stretchy top with plunging neckline, and tinsel-streamer barrettes in her hair. A younger bride surrounded by older, mostly already married friends, all of them drinking fervently for individual reasons. Ariane glanced over them, wrinkled her forehead for a moment, then shambled over to the bar, exaggerating the sway in her walk.

Daniel settled into the game, but he didn't know the table and it was all far too flashy for him. When was the last time he'd played pinball—ten years ago? His reflexes kept the ball on the table, but he got bored, trying to listen for Ariane's voice through seventy others and a basketball game. He didn't hear it, and he wondered if she was savoring her drink, watching the Frexinet fertility ritual. He deliberately took his fingers off the flipper buttons and watched a round silver streak run down the garish circus pattern of the table.

"Jessie!"

Ariane's voice, pitched about an octave higher than normal, sounded behind Daniel, and he looked over his shoulder to see Ariane standing with a drink held out in one hand and a featherbrained grin on her face, staring at one of the women at the table. The chosen one, a plump brunette in a hot-pink sweater, stared at Ariane, first widening her eyes, then squinting, her mouth open. "Hello?" she slurred.

"Jessie?" Ariane leaned closer and made eye contact

with the woman, who squinted and shook her head, put her hand to her forehead. Ariane rocked back onto her heels and put both hands over her mouth. "Oh, my God, I thought you were my friend Jessie," she gasped, voice frayed with shame. An innocent, gawky shrug. "Sorry!"

Game over, Dan.

I know what I'm doing, my love. You first.

"Guess I need to get new contacts," Ariane said, giggling, letting her eyes play over every woman at the table, and then hurrying away. They would each remember her differently, if at all. Daniel balanced the ball delicately on one flipper, sending her his extra concentration.

Ariane had gone to the bar and put down her empty drink. She said a soft good night to the bartender, and when she had gone, the bartender poured himself a shot of scotch on ice to fill the sudden hole in his mind.

The bachelorettes were more subdued now. The brunette in the sweater gave a heavy sigh and urged her friends to move. "I'm going to get going home," she explained, which was followed by her hugging every single one of them, and sitting hugs would not do; they all got up out of the booth and hugged her as if they knew something. "I don't want to be hung over tomorrow; I'll see you there, and don't forget to pick up your corsages, everybody!"

The bride gave her an extra-long hug. "Honey, are you OK to drive? Oh, you're getting a taxi home, aren't you? Oh, good. . . ."

He gave the table a subtle jerk, just enough. Tilt. Third ball. He cursed peremptorily, hitched his coat over his shoulders, and left the bar. All right, a taxi, not quite something in his plan, but somehow they'd manage. . . .

But no, she wasn't going to take a taxi; the silly drunk walked up a side street, veering from a straight line by several degrees in both directions and fumbling out a set of car keys from her pocket. Ariane was already waiting on the passenger side of a pale-colored, painfully new Korean-import car. Daniel swiftly caught up, pleased at her strategy.

"Unlock all four doors," Ariane said.

The woman pressed a button on her keychain. Her car replied with a subtle chirp.

The three of them slid into a womb of petrochemical perfume and nubbly-soft upholstery. The woman reached over to her seat belt, but it was too much effort, and she flopped back in her seat. "Way too drunk to drive," she mumbled. "Should prob'ly take a nap first . . ."

"Yeah, just a little one," Ariane said. "You'll be much better."

"Yeah," said the woman.

"Quickly," Daniel whispered from the back seat, his eyes scanning the empty street. The leaves on the trees drooped under the weight of ice. No one, just the freezing mist and the midnight bells lowing from a nearby church.

Ariane rolled up the woman's coat and sweater sleeves, exposing a forearm glossed with an unseasonable tan, waxed smooth and gleaming. Ariane almost winced with hunger looking at it before she lowered her head and took a bite.

And then a deeper one.

The bachelorette's head wobbled. Daniel reached around the seat and worked the plastic latch to lower it back, toward him; her body stretched and relaxed. He wanted to mention the woman's excellent breasts, but then remembered the rule and the hurting. Right now it wasn't worth it, watching Ariane suck down blood and knowing that if he didn't hop to it, there'd be nothing left for him. After letting her drag him all around town so she could have champagne, he needed a little something to keep him going. He felt like he'd been awake for days.

And it was *Teri* and she wanted some sleep right now. She felt unconsciousness floating her away, thinking, *Finally, thank God.*

Ariane lifted her head and gulped the air. "I'm hot," she said in a small voice. Her teeth glistened red between reddened lips.

"She's not dead yet," said Daniel, holding his thumb over the new wound under her chin. "Finish her. Don't waste it."

"No," she whispered. "I'm done. Go for it."

"You're too kind."

There wasn't much left. Her lips and fingernails were colorless. Daniel sat back, too; pointless to be desperate, he'd gotten his swallows, and it would be enough until tomorrow, if he got some sleep. Across the infinity of the car interior, across the finite slack body of Teri Haddock, Ariane smirked, eyes glimmering. "I always forget how good it is. *And* a bottle of champagne . . . my God."

"Let's go," Daniel whispered.

They ran back together, both much sloppier now from the alcohol, but still fast enough to keep them from too much trouble. Daniel ran smack into a man walking out of a pub or restaurant that poured out the scent of spiced wine and hot toddy whiskey with its human flotsam; Ariane caught up, spun the drunk guy around so that he was facing the opposite direction, and by the time he came to his senses, they had both vanished.

The standing jump to Daniel's window was impossible, even for him, but there was a fire escape on the opposite side of the hotel that went all the way to the roof. And from there climbing down was unpleasant but possible. Daniel had to tie the loose flaps of his coat, so pretty jumping down, around his waist to keep them out of the way, and was very glad that she was wearing incredibly sensible, ultra-modern light-gray sneakers with her glamour-girl dress. But then, that was Ariane.

In the room, she tore off her coat and threw it onto the floor, took off her shoes with her toes, and flung herself into a chair. Daniel didn't stop with his coat; all of his clothes ended up on the floor or tossed onto the other chair. Very slowly, she stood up and slid her dress up over her torso and arms and shoulders, baring herself, the quivering hem skimming over her nipples.

See what I can do, Daddy.

She stood there for a moment in her white fishnet panty hose, staring at him, her body full and warm and glistening slightly with sweat, and Daniel came closer and pushed her savagely onto the bed. She almost smiled then, but managed to keep a straight face; she had not stopped trembling. He stood at the foot of the bed and pulled off the fishnets, sliding them off, ripping them slightly with his black fingernails, then pulled her legs until she slid on her behind across the gray-blue-and-dusty-rose bedspread. When her lower legs hung far enough over the edge, he pushed her knees apart and stared at her. She then fully smiled, and cupped her breasts with her hands. Her fingernails had been painted with pearl-colored polish; her nipples gleamed like soft flesh jewels in a setting of mother-of-pearl. Fiercely she clenched her fingers, then let them relax, showing him the dark pink welts she left on her skin.

"I'm going to eat you," said Daniel.

"I'd like to see you try," said Ariane.

Extraordinary creature! And as many dozens of times as he'd made love to her human body, he had never experienced her like this, and wanting him. It had been so long since Daniel had made love to another vampire—decades in fact—and again he had forgotten what it was like, from the rich flavor of her burning-hot cunt to the fact that he could, actually, stab his fingers deep inside her, slashing her tissues and making her bleed, and though she cried out in pain, she made no move to stop him. He sucked eagerly at it, and held up one of his fingers for her to lick, but by the time his fingertip reached her mouth, the blood had already dried hard and tight and dark to his flesh. She licked it anyway, but pulled his shoulder with her extraordinary strength, something that would have torn a human's arm from its socket and reduced the muscles to shredded ribbons, and gripped his penis with her right hand to rub it against her pubic hair, already slick with her juices and his saliva and her blood mixed together.

He pulled her upright and balanced her thighs across his hips before he began to fuck her. With his fingers and the head of his penis he found her opening and shoved himself all the way in, all at once, up to the sweat-moist tendons that held his balls on. Once upon a time, she had nearly howled with pain when he did this, but now she just closed her eyes and rocked herself hard against him, riding him, rubbing her nipples across his chest. The transformed pain coursed through her to him, vertiginous, crunching and then melting through her nerves. He grew dizzy and pulled her over so that his back was to the bedspread and her legs went in impossible directions, knees settling in his armpits. She was beyond waking thought.

"Look at me," he said. "Look at me when you're fucking me. Look into my eyes."

"I can't," she mumbled.

He pumped his hips up, holding her steady. "Liar. Look at me. Let's go. Let's go there."

He almost regretted it when she did look at him; he felt falling and spinning, his stomach actually spasmed, motion-panicked, as his selfhood dissolved into hers through the portal of her pupils. Barely visible in the dark brown irises, her pupils were huge and drinking, and he could see his soul disappearing—and though he doubted the existence of souls, he knew what it felt like when his was lost, sucked right out of him. But not really gone, just transformed beyond his ability to comprehend. He laughed the giddy, hysterical giggle of a madman confronting the reality of his actions. He had *made her.* He was responsible for making her into this, for giving her these powers, for changing them both forever, making it impossible for either of them to feel truly alive except in this embrace. And he felt for a panicked second that they had lost contact with each other—he felt nothing from her—but he realized that their thoughts mirrored perfectly, no longer separate minds, not thee and me, only this: all thoughts and sensations pooled.

Let me be just myself for a little while. Before forever goes by and I'm still in you.

He tore away from the gaze to hold her body tightly to his, and he was back at Daniel, back at what he alone felt, back to the feeling of his cock jerking into her, her claws tearing at the skin of his back. The bedcover beneath them was damp in the middle and crunchy on the edges. Both of their bodies ran with sweat; how long since he first penetrated her? Autonomous for a moment, she changed the position to the one they had before, both of them sitting up, one of her legs across his hip and the other forcing his leg open, neither with the advantage of balance, neither able to relax. She threw back her head and drew in her breath, as if it were her last on her deathbed. He thrusted his best and last, then pulled away from her. He jerked her upright and slid again into her eyes.

A rat will happily die for such ecstasy in a drug.

Falling.

Like brain being ripped apart, cell by cell. Very much like how it felt to be made into a vampire in the first place—when the whole body literally fell to pieces and was rebuilt in the same pattern of tissues—but instead of the agony of the nerve cells shattering, it was the helpless terror of pleasure, the simultaneous collapsing and transcending. If one could harness this energy—if one could only hang on to it forever—

They held each other, locked, coming.

Time stopped.

Nothing else had ever existed.

Only

this.

Scene Thirteen: Coming down

Daniel broke them apart.

He had gotten only the last taste of Teri; and he first felt the pangs of hunger in his body and the desire for more blood that superseded everything else, even the madness of bliss, holy joy, perfect communion. He remembered again why he didn't believe in God—if God's benevolence was real, He would have taken Daniel's soul at the perfect moment of ecstasy and gotten him off the accursed wheel of meat, but hunger was stronger than any religion. If God existed, He would sweep Daniel's brow clear of fatigue and not chain him to this steadily mounting exhaustion. The pleasure of the orgasm faded away almost instantly—there was no afterglow here, not when his body felt like the husk of a coconut. He pushed Ariane onto her back and withdrew his shrunken and wrinkled penis.

She blinked at him in confusion, and he swept his arm to indicate the window, dawn rising sickly gray over the now-bland concrete of the wet city. "Oh, hell," she said, and rubbed her temples. "I didn't know about this part.

I should have known about this part. It's the bad comedown section. Oh, I see. Now I get it."

Daniel scrubbed his hands over his face. "I feel like shit," he muttered.

"I'm sure you do." She relaxed and curled up and smiled. "My God, I bet it's fucking addictive, isn't it? That was hours, just hours . . ." She blinked at him. "I'm surprised you don't fuck other vampires more often. You're the one always trying to make your orgasm more freaky or more intense. This was . . . That was . . ." She gestured emptily.

"It's not like that with everyone," Daniel said. "Only the ones to whom you are linked by blood. Your progenitor, or your offspring. And you have to come at the same time."

"Oh. That would explain it," she said. "No wonder Ricari only made you," said Ariane. "I can't imagine he likes getting that close to God without prayer. And I'm not surprised that you're always trying. But how could you let Ricari go, knowing this—*doing* this?"

"It's so hard on me." He sighed. "If you had *any* idea."

"Of course it's hard. Dumbass. I just said I know how you feel. I'm going through the same thing. You'll live."

"My whole body hurts. I'm gonna have to do something unreasonable." His glittering eyes glanced madly around the room.

"I'd rather you didn't. I have some blood at the lab. I want to go back home and check on something first." She slid off the bed, put her ripped tights back on, and reached for her dress on the floor. "Geez, you've got a hangover. When was the last time you had a hangover?" she muttered.

Daniel curled his lip. "What's it, cold? Out of the fridge? Or animal blood? I don't want to drink dog blood again, Ariane, I've come too far for that."

"Oh, really? Then go inconvenience yourself. Go get caught and crucified. It's not dog blood, it's human blood. It's actually OK—I put this anticoagulant in it. It kind of tastes like aspirin, but you get used to it, and it's great in a pinch. Besides, it was *me* that drank the dog blood, remember?" She stood before him dressed, smoothing her curls hopelessly.

"I've drunk dog blood, and I drank a lot of it, trying to recover from you. Don't forget, my dearest, you destroyed my life, too."

She scrunched her eyes tightly and rubbed her fingertips over a tender forehead. "Please. Don't. Come on. I can help you. And I have a lot of really interesting stuff to tell you, stuff that I've found out."

"Shit," said Daniel after a pause, and it was as good as an agreement. He got dressed, trying to ignore the pain in his limbs and his face, and they went out through the kitchen service entrance, around a sleepy teenage chef prepping onions for breakfast who never even glanced up.

Last night's sleet had transformed into a chilly drizzle. Ariane's car, a jaunty little Japanese thing about twelve years old with old towels on the seats, waited on the street three blocks from the hotel, tiny puddles of rain in every rusted dent. She watched him fold himself in agonizingly slow stages into the small passenger seat and collapse there, breathing hard and fluttering the muscles in his eyelids. He glanced at her, then away, his mouth sinking into a thin line of bitterness. She twisted her hair into a bun and skewered it with one of the pens on the dashboard, then asked with raspy, forced cheer, "Do you like the towels? The nice thing about them is that I can pull 'em up and throw them into the washing machine. I've had many a struggle in this car."

"Smart idea," grunted Daniel. "I might have to use that. Maybe you could make little towel slipcovers, easy on"—here he paused to yawn—"easy off."

"I've toyed with the idea of starting a mail-order company for vampire conveniences," she continued, gunning the little car's engine to proceed up a steep, slick hill. "You know, stuff to make our lives easier. Like full-sized incinerators for bodies and evidence. Anticoagulant that doesn't taste like aspirin—tastes like, oh, I don't know, a stiff gin, maybe. Bulk discounts on protein-dissolving laundry soap. Stuff like that. I'd make a bucketload of money."

He couldn't help laughing, albeit halfheartedly. "You're such an American."

"Except of course that I know that there isn't much of a market for that sort of thing. . . . I mean, how many vampires are there in the world? How many do you reckon? Are there a lot of vampires in New York?"

"If there are, they haven't introduced themselves to me," said Daniel miserably. He looked at his emaciated hands with dismay. All this trouble, just for the best orgasm in the world? He supposed he should try to look at it as a hangover, since it wouldn't last long; but then again, he had whined about hangovers even when he had them every day, when he was young and drinking terrible homemade wine in cellars and schoolyards.

"That's odd . . . you're such a public figure."

"In New York? Whatever. The place is lousy with public figures. And I'm not, really. No more than any other wealthy but not very successful dilettante artist. There are thousands of them in the Hamptons every summer."

"Pity party. It could be worse. You could be famous, and then you'd have a hell of a time getting rid of bodies."

"Are there many vampires in Portland?" he asked, trying to change the subject.

"Besides John?"

Daniel shrugged and stared out the window.

She twitched her nose, focusing straight ahead on the road. "They haven't exactly given me a big debutante ball," she said. "I'm pretty sure they're here. I've just never seen them. Or felt them. Or heard them . . ."

They said nothing for a little while, not talking about John, avoiding the subject of John altogether. Ariane turned on the radio, set to a jazz station playing a jittery piece by Herbie Hancock, completely inappropriate to a hangover at seven on a Saturday morning, and rolled down the window. These Portland people seemed to be some strain of bizarre masochists.

"So tell me about this Sybil," she said. "You kind of

didn't want to go there when we were . . . um . . . you know."

"I don't know what I can tell you about her." He sighed. "She's difficult as hell. She's an artist—she used to be a stripper, but I made her stop. She wasn't dancing because she liked it. I don't think. Except that it's obvious that she really loves to dance, it's just the getting paid aspect of it that she doesn't like. Except, of course, that's why she does it. I can't figure out almost anything about her, actually. When I think of her . . . I don't know what to think."

"I think you're in love with her," said Ariane.

"I'd say that's obvious," he replied. He laughed shortly. "It's shitty."

"You fucked her," she pointed out.

"Yeah, whatever. It doesn't seem to mean anything. She's angry at me because of it. I'm the only—she's never fucked before. She hadn't. Anyway, that's what she told me."

"Is it true?"

"I don't know. It did take me ten minutes to get my little finger in." He smiled, nibbled his lip with a fang.

"How can you not tell? You *fucked* her, didn't you?"

"There's no way to tell," he said. "Girls don't have hymens these days. Or at least Sybil wouldn't. She'd have busted her own cherry a long time ago."

"Hymen, schmymen. You didn't—read her?"

"I can't," he admitted.

Ariane furrowed her forehead. "What do you mean, you can't?"

"I mean I can't. I can talk *to* her. If she wants to listen. But only then. And she doesn't tell me—she doesn't give me anything. I can't read her." Daniel sighed again. "It's driving me crazy."

"Extraordinary," she agreed. "I've never heard of such a thing. Not even from Ricari. I mean, I don't see why it's not possible . . . any more possible than we could do what we did last night and—"

He smiled weakly at her, but he didn't want to remember touching her right now. He never wanted to touch anyone ever again. His flesh felt like old dry newsprint in a landfill.

She lived in the hills west of town, near enough to smell the cemeteries nearby, soaked through with rain; a distinctive scent of rotting wood and shellac, rusting metal, the tang of slowly decomposing and softening human flesh. She owned a charming house, brown brick and wood with white-painted shutters and, in the yard, a large marble bath with a stone-swan–crowned fountain, choked with fallen leaves and overflowing in a frozen curve onto a frozen puddle on the grass. As they passed it, Ariane put out her bare hand and caressed the smooth icy lip of the pool.

The warm, dark house smelled sleepily of cinnamon and vanilla. Daniel collapsed heavily on a velvet sofa, only to spring up again and pace the floor, wiping his hand across his mouth. Ariane wordlessly turned on a lamp and disappeared through a doorway. Daniel went to the kitchen for a glass, then crushed it between his hands and licked at his own blood when it came, an instinctive action like a hungry child sucking its own tongue. He spat a shard of glass, tinkling into the sink.

She reemerged in more usual Ariane garb—a dark-gray hoodie over a black turtleneck and jeans and sturdy cold-weather boots—and put her coat back on. "Good for you for not snooping—what did you break that for?"

"I just wanted to see blood," said Daniel.

She grimaced. "Big baby . . . OK, let's go."

Another interminable car ride in the Japanese rattletrap took them through the hills and past cemeteries, dark-wood houses, hundreds upon thousands of immense trees. Ariane had brought out a tape for the car stereo—more hangover-inappropriate music, this time bass-heavy techno. Daniel tried not to groan, but he didn't quite succeed. All at once, the curtain of trees opened up before them as they gunned down a smooth concrete drive, between more concrete cubes stacked into buildings, bordered with white-painted steel tube fences. "This is my home away from home," Ariane said, "the best medical research institute in the Pacific Northwest. And no, I'm not asking you to care, so you can just keep your nasty little thoughts to yourself."

"Like I have any control what I think," Daniel muttered.

"There's a wonderful little thing you may have read about called meditation. Or, in other words, if you can't think anything nice, don't think anything at all."

He glanced over at her and chuckled, even though it made the top of his head pound. "I do love you, you know," he said.

"I know you do." She kept her eyes focused on the parking lot in front of her, descending underground into a lightless gloom. "And you know I love you." Unspoken, *whether I want to or not.*

With that, she turned her thoughts inward, into odd analogies and symbols Daniel knew nothing about and thus could not interpret. There was something else bothering her at the moment besides his own presence, but either she didn't know what it was or it was important enough to try to keep from him. Until he got some blood back in his body, wrestling with the latter was far too much effort.

Daniel followed her into one of the concrete cubes, into fluorescent-lit, Saturday-empty hallways lined with felt message boards, heavily plastered with fliers advertising grant information and environmental consciousness. He licked his hand again, but the palm had scarred over, coated with a chilly sweat. In an elevator, Ariane stroked Daniel's chest through his shirt. "Don't worry," she assured him again. "I know you don't mean to be such a prick." Her formerly peachy golden skin looked like chewing gum with the flavor chewed out of it. She held her hand still over his heart, searching for a pulse, then shifted her fingers left and right and up and down, finally taking her hand back and putting it into her pocket. Daniel allowed himself a vague smirk.

"Look how dead I can get and still be standing."

"Sweetie . . ." Ariane slipped a key card into a slot next to a featureless door and let Daniel inside a completely dark room that flickered into life as she palmed a fat light switch. "You're pretty far from dead. You're more dead when you sleep. But if we don't feed you soon, it'll be pretty nasty trying to wake up."

"I know." He sighed, "I've been there. More times than I care to admit."

"Small talk, damn you, small talk." Her eyes flashed a warning. He nodded and looked away.

One room of her office contained a couch, a desk, an ergonomic chair, and a school chair in front of a half-wall window of smoky glass. In the other room, a vintage dentist's chair rested with its lowered head pointed at the glass. A fist-thick bundle of cables connected the two rooms, the chair's head terminating in several slender black wires; the others led to a big console next to the school chair, a rack of silent and blind computer screens resting on top. A third tiny room, hardly more than a closet, held racks of bottles of chemicals, a small black-rubber–topped table, a sink, boxes, and piles of obscure equipment that made no sense to him whatsoever. Taking up most of the closet, two large industrial refrigerators loomed, their pallid yellow vinyl skins reflecting as if wet. Daniel had to touch one to make sure. He opened the one on the right—only more chemicals, and half-finished six-packs of generic fruit soda. Ariane opened the left one, solidly hung and packed with IV bags full of blood, dated and labeled with alien numbers. She took out three IV bags of dark crimson fluid. "Here you are," she said, handing him one. "I assure you that it's perfectly safe—I drink it every day."

"Where do you get it?" he asked, carefully popping off the seal on the bag. He took a deep swallow—a toxic flavor like industrial cleanser filled his mouth with the blood, and it was bitter cold, but he drank it anyway. His mouth absorbed half of it before he could swallow, and it gave him a raging ice cream headache.

"I work at a research hospital, Daniel. And there are a lot of student volunteers who are used to giving quantities of blood, both for live-saving purposes"—she handed him another bag—"and for research in the hematology lab. I just ask for them to give us way more than we need, that's all."

Daniel wiped his mouth on his sleeve and tossed the empty slab of damp plastic into the sink next to the refrigerators. "Tastes like shit," he muttered.

"Yeah, but you'll be all right now. It's better than killing people all the time." She sat in a chair opposite him and shrugged out of her coat. "Poor Daniel. Nothing's ever good enough for you, is it?"

He didn't respond. He did feel better, but the horrible taste in his mouth spread all through his body, and he ached trying to metabolize it. He sat in the dentist's chair and stared at the tiles in the ceiling—the same tiles as on the bathroom ceiling in Newark, where he'd swallowed down a man's life so that he'd be warm for Sybil.

Ariane sprawled in the ergonomic chair, drinking her IV bag into flat vacuum. "I wish Sybil loved you, too," she said. "Love is good."

"Love . . ." He smiled at her. "We had some Hollywood laughs, didn't we? We had a California rockin' good time?"

"Yeah, we did. Freak." She laughed.

"Yeah, right, I'm a freak. Look at you. You're such a brain—man, dig your mad scientist secret bat cave!"

She blushed and smiled at the floor, like he'd just given her flowers. "It's just some shit I threw together for when I can't deal with going upstairs. Like today; there's no way I'm going upstairs today."

"Today? You're not doing work today!"

"Well, no, I guess . . ."

"C'mon, I'm visiting from out of town. How could you even think of working? You can't even slow down, can you?"

"I can't slow down now," she protested. "Look what I've got. Am I the first scientist to ever know about the existence of what we are? I mean, yes, we're vampires, but how did it happen? How long have we existed? How many are there now? How long do we actually live? Everything. The cool thing is"—she rose up from her sprawl and began to gesture with the empty bag—"I've started figuring out some stuff. It's not a whole lot, but it's something. Tell me, do you have a cell phone?"

"Yeah—I left it at the hotel, why?"

"Does it work?"

"Well, only sometimes. They're damn fun, though."

"Do you have a computer?"

Daniel peaked his eyebrows. "No, I don't. I've tried . . . but they just break."

"Ever wonder why?" She stood up and tossed her empty bag in the sink. "It's the electrical charge that we give off. You hit sparks off people all the time, don't you? I know I do. I measured the level of charge on my skin, and it's about forty times higher than a human's. Electricity is magnetism. The magnetic field that we produce is higher than really delicate electronic devices are shielded against. I went through three cell phones before I figured it out. I can use these computers, but only if I'm grounded." She held up a paper wrist strap with an exposed copper wire running the length of it. "Ever notice that your cell phone works better when you're touching, like, a metal street sign? Or you're standing in a puddle? Grounding. It's very useful. Unfortunately, grounding doesn't always help."

"So I should throw away my phones?" Daniel pouted. "But they're so pretty. They're my little babies."

"Daniel, sometimes you're so *gay* it blows my mind. Keep the stupid things if you want to; they'll just die and you'll get new ones. In Japan, they're working on disposable ones anyway. I dunno, you'd probably fry the shielding in one of those babies as soon as you looked at it." She was edging around the room, trying to disguise the fact that she was approaching him. He watched her, bemused, for a moment. "I spent a lot of time in that chair hooked up to the machine," she added.

"Stop pacing and come here," he said. She completed the distance and put her arms around him, but flinched a little when he lowered his lips to her forehead. "I want to get naked with you again, at least once more before I go," he said softly into the warm flesh of her neck.

She clenched her fists at her sides, meeting his lips

with hers, and slowly relaxed again. One hand crept under the loose hem of his shirt. "Why am I even touching you?" she mused aloud.

"Yeah, I know, you can't help it, either. I have that effect on you. That's your power over me, Ariane—I can't be in the same room with you without wanting to tear your clothes off and fuck your little brains out."

"*Not* little," she said, kissing the corner of his mouth.

He chuckled. "Well then, it'll take a lot of fucking, won't it?"

She pulled away from him and leaned against the sink, a silly, embarrassed smile on her face. "I need to get some sleep," she said.

Daniel sighed in agreement. "Yeah," he acknowledged. "Me, too. Worse than you; I've been awake for a really long time. I'm surprised I didn't just crumple up hours ago."

"Like I said, you were far, far from dead—with as much blood as you drink, you could stay up some more. But I think I should take you back to your hotel so we can get some sleep."

He trapped her between his body and the sink, holding her arms down at her sides and kissing her cheeks. "You know what *I* think?" he said. "I think that you should come and sleep with me, to make it up to me for making me wait. Yeah, I know what you were doing. You weren't suffering, and you wanted to twist the screws, watch me squirm. Yeah, I know you. I know you want to wake up and see me beside you."

Her eyes were unfathomable, her mind like a glossy black pearl, with the truth hidden at the center. Nonetheless, her mouth was smiling, and she went to the refrigerator again and grabbed a handful of blood bags.

In the car, Daniel turned the stereo off. Ariane drove on autopilot, her eyes half-lidded and her fingers slack on the wheel at ten o'clock and two o'clock. Daniel tried to be more alert, but there was only so much he could do, his mind attempting to crawl away, curl up, darken into peace. The world around him came and went in mosaic fragments. The whoosh of cars going past outside.

A green highway sign, directing the world to Salem. Yellowish buildings and—"Is that where they burn the witches?" His voice came out unforgivably slurred.

Several seconds passed before she replied. "No . . . different Salem," she said. "The real one's on the East Coast."

"Oh."

Soft, charcoal wool, surrounding him.

"It's your lucky day, Herr Blum." Her voice slipped through the fabric. "I'm not gonna make it home."

"No, you're not." Through his eyelashes, the parking lot that he'd jumped into the night before, the gray ground steaming.

"Your mind keeps putting me to sleep."

He was standing outside the car, next to her. He squinted up at his window, beige tail of curtain protruding a few inches. "Think you can jump it?" he teased.

"No. Fucking. Way."

They entered through the side door, the one that led to the bar, and he kissed her hand as they walked past the spiked iron railing. He knew she wasn't mentally present, felt her startle as she returned to full consciousness and felt the buzzing of his lips on her skin.

Elevator. Whir. Gravity hum and musical chime.

In his room, he took off coat, shoes, pants. Ariane just flopped down, still wearing everything, but she began to squirm on top of the churned and filthy sheets and sat up to untie her boots. He joined her on the bed, pulled off her boots for her, helped her out of her clothes. She groaned theatrically, settling back on the bed, pulling the bedcovers over them both. Daniel laughed at her and shifted around, pulling his shirt over his head. "Ugh! God, look at us. We're like two old drug friends just come back from a rough night of partying on the town."

"We kind of are," she said, kissing his bare shoulder.

That was the last thing he felt before falling unconscious.

Scene Fourteen: Lest We Forget

When Daniel woke up, Ariane still slept, lying curled and stiff and gray-fleshed, her mouth sunken over her teeth so that the two points of her upper fangs poked out onto her dry and purpled lips. He knew he looked as bad when he slept—someone in Hollywood had once taken a snapshot and showed it to him—but he never wanted to think about it. Ariane looked like a corpse, and not an embalmed and undertaken corpse, but a neglected corpse on the side of the road, dead three days.

It was dark again. He got up and took a stretch, wondering where she'd stashed the blood, if it was still safe to drink; his hotel room was pleasing enough, but it wasn't so nice as to have a refrigerator. He paused for a moment before the bathroom mirror, just in case, make sure he hadn't woken up looking like a fresh zombie. All was well. His eyebrows needed some attention, and he had more stubble than he particularly liked, but it was his face, his beloved, familiar, unchanging face.

He remembered Ariane stuffing the blood bags into her backpack and sat in a chair next to the window with the backpack on his lap, ready to dig in. The blood was still cold, still liquid, still effective. He tried to taste a personality in it, but age, blending, refrigeration, and the anticoagulant rendered it generic. He found himself staring at the window, opening the curtains somewhat, opening the window farther to let in the wet, cold evening air. He stared at the opening between the pane of glass and the wooden sill, examining the gap, measuring the space again and again with his eyes.

Energized by the blood, Daniel gathered some things from his carry-on bag, returned to the bed, and sat next to Ariane, willing her to wake up. He dared to touch her wrinkled forehead, but her consciousness lay trapped inside, and, at first, he felt nothing underneath the cold clay skin. But, as if in response to his touch, he felt a faint sizzling sensation under his fingertips as she returned to wakefulness and life.

He grinned in response to her wicked, sleepy smile. "Breakfast in bed?" he whispered, waving an IV bag in front of her.

"And a little more . . . ?" she purred.

"Oh, God, yes."

Before she'd even finished the blood, he had her legs over his shoulders. She hissed at him. "What makes you think I'd want to fuck you? After you were such a shithead to me this morning?" Her voice came out more silk than steel.

"I want to make it up to you. Besides . . ." He reached over to the bedside table and waved a jar of coconut oil under her nose. "I didn't fuck your sweet ass last night."

She raised one eyebrow. "Oh, that'll definitely make it up to me, baby."

Daniel didn't need to be told twice. He caressed her body just out of habit, but it wasn't necessary for him; he had been partially erect since he first awoke, and the sound of her voice brought him even closer to perfection. Ariane writhed, twisted, and moaned, grasped his buttocks with her fingers until her claws cut into the flesh. "Oh, c'mon, I'm ready," she wheedled softly. "You don't have to wait for me."

The cry she gave when he penetrated her lashed orgasm instantly from inside him. Daniel quivered, moaning and helpless in her arms, and she burst into peals of vicious laughter. "You are so predictable," she chortled. "Your mind really is subordinate to your dick, isn't it? Get off me."

"What?" Daniel shifted aside, following Ariane's line of sight. A red flag of consciousness unfurled. He had been set up.

John had returned.

The other vampire stood, his mud-smudged, tattered coat reeking of blood, gazing down at them, his mind invading Daniel's like a barbed arrow, broken glass in a wound. The smell of the cemetery clung to him; that sweet, rotting, melancholy odor, grass, old soaked flowers, turned earth.

Daniel violently remembered that handsome face, exceptional cheekbones and funny square jaw vaguely softened by a week's growth of dark brown beard, but his eyes, portals to his soul, had changed; once they had been brilliant, if terrified. Now John didn't focus on anything, continually distracted by the torn chaos of his mind.

Daniel stared at Ariane. "I should have—how did you—"

Ariane slid off the bed and pulled her underwear back on. "You're strong, my love," she said, wrestling the sports bra over her head and positioning her breasts in it, "but you're not as strong as the two of us. All you can think about is fucking, so that's all you did think about."

"How'd he get in here?" Daniel whispered.

John's eyes were very dark. He looked over his shoulder at the open window. "I jumped," he said.

"But you *can't,*" Daniel said.

"I can," said John matter-of-factly.

Ariane glanced at Daniel, sending him, *He can.*

John smiled a little, and his eyes clicked into alarming focus on Daniel. He struggled to speak aloud. "Daniel-you-trouble-shouldn't-bloody." John's smile vanished. "Fuck!"

Solid hatred emerged from the mental chaos. Daniel actually lost his purchase on the bedsheets and collapsed into a sloppy heap, clutching his temples. He had been hated before, but it was never like this; this was like being punched in the nose over and over again. "Good old John," grunted Daniel wearily. "I always forget you exist."

"I didn't fuck *your* sweet ass last night," John recited, no struggle, no hesitation whatsoever.

"What? You want some of this?" Daniel sprang off the bed. A voice inside him—perhaps Ariane's, perhaps even his own—told him that he sounded ridiculous, that he should shut his face now before the fur flew. But his rage controlled him now. "Why don't you come here, you sad little bitch, we'll see who gets fucked?"

In the darkness, everything was a muddle. Ariane darted to the wall, slipping into her clothes. John kicked over the chair by the window and wrenched one of the legs loose. Daniel threw the dead cell phone at the spot where John had been; when it hit the wall, it left a dent two inches deep and flecked with blue plastic fragments. John stood and stared at the dent, helplessly fascinated, and Daniel went for John's throat with claws outstretched. John stepped out of Daniel's way; the older vampire's claws added further rips to the shoulder of John's filthy old coat.

"I don't see any fucking," Ariane commented. "Where's the fucking, Daniel?"

Daniel's attention snapped to Ariane as if yanked by a string. "How could you do this to me?" he cried. "I didn't think you had it in you."

"You *put* it in me." She shrugged.

The chair leg punched a ragged hole in Daniel's belly. And then John twisted it.

"*That's* from Ricari," said John.

Agony blinded Daniel, mixed with remorse, a devastating gush of blood and memories. In a candlelit, frigid room, almost seventy years past, he had committed this same violence against the vampire that had given him a new life. He wanted rid of Ricari. And Ricari, helping

Ariane, had also given John a new life, and a love letter to deliver to Daniel.

But the memory didn't end there—it could help Daniel now. What had Ricari done? So hard to think through the pain . . . Ariane also remembered, a story told her by Ricari . . . She tried to yank the thought back, but Daniel caught it. *That's right!* Ricari had kicked Daniel in the crotch with his booted foot, dropping Daniel in his tracks. *Thanks, baby. Now we're even.*

Daniel swept his bare foot off the floor and up, and the force of his kick sent John's head banging into the ceiling.

John landed, retching, and crumpled to the floor. Daniel felt the urge to kick him again, in the ribs or in the face, for the indignity, to teach him a lesson; but with Ariane's litany of "Jesus fuck, Jesus fuck," her hands over her mouth, he couldn't do it. Daniel pulled the wood out of his belly and put a hand over the hole to stop the gushing blood. His head swam, and he could barely see Ariane creeping slowly up to Daniel, her head bowed, face invisible under the heavy mane of auburn curls.

"Daniel . . ." she whimpered quietly. "I wish you hadn't . . . done that."

She flashed at him with her palms out, shoving his chest, and the vertigo of pain snapped into the vertigo of falling.

He corrected his fall just enough to keep from breaking his legs, but he lost his balance on impact and, flailing helplessly, landed on his backside. Something in him was glad that he had a deep gut wound, so that the shredding of the skin on his ass and the cracking of his tailbone seemed minor in comparison. He stared at the open window four stories up to see Ariane throwing down his clothes, his luggage, the pieces of his broken cell phone. "See?" she sneered. "I'm really nice after all!"

Daniel gingerly stood up, and only then did he notice a handful of spectators gaping at him, naked and bleeding, in the parking lot. Daniel found his coat in the scattering of his luggage and wrapped it around himself.

"What the fuck are you looking at!" he shouted, and the onlookers hurried away.

Daniel gathered as many clothes as he could carry and hobbled back up to his room, racking his pain-taxed and blood-starved brain of some way that he could kill them both, preferably taking their blood as well (when he walked, the stabbing of his tailbone overwhelmed the stake wound), but how to humiliate them as well . . . ? He found the door hanging open, and Ariane and John gone. Yes, Ariane was really nice after all; she'd left a note on the bloodstain where John had lain with his gonads ruptured.

Leave town tonight, or next time, I'll hold you down.
All the love I have left,
Ariane

Scene Fifteen: What's Wrong with Art Today

Daniel went straight from the airport to the studio when he returned to New York.

Snow had fallen, making the city beautiful again, if only for today, before everything half-melted into gray goop. He was glad to see it after the oppressive green everything of the Northwest, glad to be off the oxygen high, to be able to think straight again.

He had sat in his Seattle hotel room for ten days, staring out at a theater across the street, watching the miniaturized people streaming in, pouring out, clotting on the street in front. He only left his room to follow other solitary hotel guests into their rooms, leaving them drained and lifeless; the hotel staff, convinced of food poisoning, performed a cover-up worthy of Stalinist Russia. Daniel also talked to Jackie Cundera on the phone in his room every few hours as she came up with more questions. She had been exceptionally understanding when he called her from Seattle; he explained that his cell phone had gotten destroyed in the same altercation that convinced him to relocate. "Sometimes those meeting with old lovers can be kind of rough," she'd said. "You never know what kind of old grudges can come out." He told her she didn't know the half of it.

But it was best to put it all behind him; he had to get back to Sybil and find out if she was still there. If she was gone, he didn't know what he was going to do. He had spent a lot of time in Seattle going over all the ways that he knew to kill vampires, and the options came up sparse: complete dismemberment, cut off the head and keep it separate from the body until death occurred from blood loss and shock, destroy the body completely by burning, a day's exposure to direct sunlight (though he wasn't sure about the last one). Not much he, or anyone else, could do. He would stay alive.

He walked off the freight elevator into a radically altered studio space; the furniture had been shifted against the walls, and two-thirds of the floor had been taken up by a crazed structure of steel pipes welded together in a half-dome fifteen feet high, some of the polygonal spaces blocked with multicolored drip paintings on glued scraps of canvas. A dozen theater spotlights with pink and blue gels lit the whole structure, still being busily built by several of his assistants and their friends, laughing, playing loud rap music. On the edges of the room, safely away from the welding equipment, other kids smoked marijuana and drank green bottles of beer.

One of the welders turned off its blowtorch, swept back the faceguard and rushed toward Daniel, standing stunned in front of the elevator doors. Sybil, wearing a ripped and stained blue chiffon ball gown underneath an industrial canvas jacket, jumped at him, threw her arms around him, and gave him a rough, dirty kiss on the cheek. "Hey! You're back! Look what I built!"

"Sybil . . . my studio . . ."

"Oh, whatever. Isn't this nice? It's just how I pictured it—I was sitting around drawing with crayons on the day you left, and I drew this, brought it in here, and said 'Can I build this?' and they said 'Yeah.' " She bounced back and gave him a good look. "You look different somehow."

Daniel blinked. "What are you wearing? Is that a Galliano?"

"I don't know." She shrugged. "I found it in a Dumpster downtown."

"This is incredible," he said, staring at the structure again. "Did you do this all yourself?"

"Well, no, folks helped me out. And they're getting me really fucked up," she added, accepting a cigar-tobacco–wrapped spliff. She took several rapid shallow puffs. "Eh?" She offered it to him, face shrouded in smoke.

"No, thanks, blunts make me crazy." He walked closer to the installation, looking at the sloppy joins in the metal, the gentle creaking as artists glued on more canvas panels. "Wow. I . . . really like it."

She scratched her temple. "Yeah . . . at the same time I'm really kind of over this, now that it's almost done."

"What do you mean, you're over it? Can I show it to people? What's it called?"

"I don't care," she said. "You can call it whatever you want. It's just a kind of freaky weird jungle gym. I like making things, not finishing things. . . . But no, what I'm thinking about doing now is on a much larger scale, something a lot more important, and I don't care if anybody ever sees it. And I want *you* to help me with it."

"What do you mean?"

" 'Whaddyuh mean?' " she mocked him. She plunked down on a couch. Daniel sat next to her, suddenly desperate for her to kiss him again. She pulled off her face-guard and riffled her fingers through static-spiky, platinum hair—she had bleached it again, and it stood in stark contrast to her light-brown stubble eyebrows. "Isn't it pretty?" she asked.

"Whaddyuh mean?" Daniel mocked back. She laughed, a belly laugh, real. Amused by him. He felt as though his heart, his head, his crotch, would burst.

Joachim severed himself from the group of working assistants and sat down next to Daniel. "Hey, how'd Portland go?" He gave a friendly smile.

"Fine," said Daniel. "Without a hitch. I have every confidence that I'll sell the lot. How were things here?"

"Sybil kept us busy," Joachim said. "And I got a lot of other work done, too."

"Yeah, I kept him busy especially." Sybil grinned.

"Oh?" said Daniel.

"Yeah, I fucked him," said Sybil starkly.

Daniel stared at the smirk on Sybil's face. "Really?" he asked, arching his eyebrow. He looked back at Joachim. Quivers of fear and embarrassment washed over the RISD boy's face. "You won't even try to deny it, will you? I did tell you to embrace change, didn't I?" Daniel admitted with a wry smile. "And kiss it all over its ugly face."

Joachim jerked to his feet and walked away. Sybil laughed, watching him go with sparkling eyes.

"He's got a cute little dick," she said. "It didn't hurt a bit."

"Did you like it?" Daniel asked her quietly.

"Yeah," she said. "I liked it a lot. So did he. I fucked a girl, too. But I didn't like it as much."

"As him?"

"No, you," she said.

Daniel sighed. "Can we go somewhere else? Do you want to come to my place? I haven't gone home yet and I have the urge to change my clothes."

"Sure," she said. "But let me finish this one weld—if I don't secure it, we can't put up another light. I'll only be another couple of minutes. Maybe you should check your messages or something."

She got up and left him, so he did what she said. Mostly, the mail consisted of invitations to parties and openings and raves, the phone messages from his connections in the art world, talking about the same parties and openings and raves. He erased them all after listening to the first two, weary of it, weary of other personalities and the empty machinations of the social life. He wanted to go home, take a long hot bath, and think.

Out on the street, Daniel attempted to hail a recalcitrant taxi, and Sybil played with the train of her dress, caked with paint and filth and snow. "You went to Portland?" she asked him. He nodded. "Oregon? Why?"

"I'm showing some pieces at a gallery there," Daniel said, "I'm sharing a show with some Japanese installation artist in December. And . . . I went to see an old lover who lives there now."

"Really? Who?"

Daniel arched his eyebrows askingly at her as a taxi finally pulled over and accepted them, but Sybil remained staring brightly as they got in, silently demanding an answer to her questions. "Her name's Ariane Dempsey." Daniel sighed. "She's a biologist. She's studying what make us, us."

"Us? She's . . . one, too?"

"Yes," said Daniel.

Sybil scratched her head again. "Hmm," she said.

"I told her about you," Daniel added.

"Really? What did she say?"

"She said that she thought I was in love with you." Daniel stared at the gutters rushing past.

"And you told her . . . ?"

"I told her that she was right."

Sybil went back to picking at a loose thread in her dress. "So what else did you do?" she asked.

"I had some drinks," he said. "Sat around. Boring, really."

"So do you want to hear my ideas?" she asked.

"Can they wait until I'm at home and in the bath?"

She snorted softly, then shrugged. "Fine. But you have to promise to really listen, and you have to promise to assist me."

"How can I assist you when I don't even know what I'll be doing?"

"You'll want to be a part of it when I describe it to you. It'll just be you and me—nobody else can know what this is all about or that ruins it. There must be an impenetrable veil of secrecy." She said this while staring straight ahead between the two front seats at the wiper blades whisking snow off the windshield. With each swipe, her eyes changed from gray in shadow to green in reflected light. Her tongue worried at the moist dent in her lower lip. "Now, will you promise?"

"Anything, Sybil," Daniel said. He picked up her hand and kissed it. "Anything."

"So in the meantime, tell me about this Ariane Dempsey," she said.

Daniel wished he hadn't brought it up. "I can't really start from the beginning because that would take too long."

"Well, start with the basics. Where did you two meet and all that. Did she answer a personal ad that started 'Horny undead stud seeks willing submistress'?"

"No, silly." He poked her playfully with his elbow, and she reached into the lapels of his jacket, roughly pinching one of his nipples with her fingertips. A slow smile spread across his face, and he pulled her hand back out, kissing the pinching fingers. "When I first saw her she was covered in blood. Well, not all covered, just her whole torso. The skin over her tits had been sliced open."

"Shit," said Sybil.

"Ricari did that. With his fingernails, apparently, while they were fighting."

"Who's Ricari?"

"He's the one that made me." He gestured with one hand to clarify what he meant.

She immediately seemed to understand that relationship, and more. "Did you make her?"

"Yes, but not until later."

"Why did you make her?"

"Because I could tell that that's what she really wanted," Daniel said. "Just like it's what I wanted. But for a different reason. I don't really know what her reasons were."

"I think it's probably like letting yourself get caught up by your most kinkiest desires," said Sybil. "Those people who can't stop thinking about getting smacked on the ass with a ruler by their third-grade teacher. Or those people who hang from hooks through their nipples. Or fuck little kids because they've always been turned on by them. I mean, it's not really crazy to think about that stuff—as far as I know, everybody does. But only some people are extreme enough to really live it—to really go to the other side. It's like, basically, a kind of soul transformation."

"You make it sound so chic." Daniel laughed.

"Oh, God, no, that has nothing to do with fashion. And the whole concept of it being in *fashion* is totally dead now. Piercing is totally normal, pedophile chic is totally normal . . . No, I think it's something that's really part of the way people think—it's hard-wired into the human brain. Since day one. That urge to be more than just the sum total of your flesh, to get out of it."

"Transcendence," said Daniel.

"Absolutely. Transcendence of the self. Escape from the cage of selfhood." Sybil fidgeted with her hair yet again. "My fucking scalp itches like hell. I used this insane peroxide shit and didn't rinse it off until I felt like screaming. I wanted it white. I guess this is as close as I'm gonna get, huh?"

"It is pretty."

"I was kidding. I wasn't actually trying to be pretty."

"You can't help it. And you look smashing in that Galliano."

"It's a size eight," she said, "according to the tag. I ripped it open in the back so I could fit into it. I kinda like it with the jacket. What's a Galliano?"

"He's a designer," Daniel explained. "He's really good."

"I kind of like it, but it's basically just something fucked up to wear. It doesn't keep me warm or anything. Do you have anything I can change into at your place?"

"I might have something that fits you," said Daniel. "If nothing else, I bet you can fit into my clothes."

"Something like that," replied Sybil.

"Will you help me with my luggage?"

They went into the flat together, garment bags slung over shoulders. After setting down his bags on the patent-leather sofa, Daniel went straight into the bathroom, stopped the tub, and turned on the bathtub's hot faucet. Sybil went to the kitchen and poured herself some Scotch, returning to the bathroom to find Daniel naked and lowering himself by inches into the hot running water. She sat on the floor next to the tub and waited until he had settled in, and said, "So my project . . ."

He poured handfuls of water onto his hair. "Yes, tell me about this world-changing top-secret project."

"Don't be patronizing. First of all, tell me what's wrong with art today."

He laughed and waved a puff of steam at her. "What's wrong with art? Haven't millions of volumes been written about that already?"

"I want you to tell me about what *you* think is wrong with art."

He sat a while and thought about that for a second, dunking his nipples below the water line, rising out to let them cool and stiffen in the air. "What I think is wrong with art is . . . that it doesn't have enough power to really change society . . . that it's not immediate enough . . . that not enough people are really paying attention to the . . . transformative properties of artistic expression?"

"Exactly," said Sybil. "Not enough people are being directly touched by art. Not enough people these days are really faced with the immediate nature of art being created. How many people hear 'art' and immediately picture the 'Mona Lisa'? They think about art that's dead. Not enough people are touched by living art." She settled back onto her heels with a bright smile on her face.

"And you propose to change this how?"

"And why do you think that reality-based TV is so popular now? People enjoy watching the spectacle of public, but recorded and played-back and edited, embarrassment and horror and aggression. They set up some poor sucker, or a group of them, and let chaos take its course. They're sick of the predictability of a script. They like to watch a person who's just found out they just fucked their own mother, and they wonder what it's possible to feel in that situation. They wonder what it's like to be under the surgeon's knife. They wonder what it's like to be on TV while the cops are cuffing you and beating your face into the hood of a car. They imagine that because they're watching it thousands of miles away on TV, that they're safe. What I propose . . . is to erase that distinction between the passive audience . . . and the exposed nerve. I want to shove that feeling of terror and the unexpected into their faces. I want to see real fear and revulsion in the faces of people—not audiences, not taxpayers, not the folks at home plugged into their Nielsen ratings dehumanizing machines. I want to make art a real living spectacle."

"It's been done," sighed Daniel. "Over and over again. I did it."

"To what purpose? Why did you do it? And aren't those reasons still valid—right now, more valid than they've ever been?" She leaned toward him, her face shrouded in steam. "We're—I learned this from you, even though I feel like I already knew this—we're sitting on top of a huge compost pile of repressed feelings, repressed reflexes of the subconscious. These people around us don't feel and they don't care, and it's not often that they feel fear for their lives or their sanity—real fear. Uncut adrenaline. Fear of the unknown."

Daniel stared at her. "And . . . what do you mean in concrete terms? Where do I come in, besides regurgitating Dadaist rhetoric?"

"You perform with me," she said. "Or you provide backup. Or you sketch the scene like a court reporter and we then analyze it later to provide more material for our performances. What I propose is a series of lightning strikes on comfortable normal American consciousnesses. We go out there, in the street, and make a spectacle. Then we get the fuck out of there and nobody's the wiser. The way we make this work is to perform only stunts that will cause such humiliation or terror or confusion or lunacy to the mark, or to the spectators, that they would never want to speak of such things to anyone. It's really easy. People have so many societal hang-ups about what to do in really weird situations, and those hang-ups are very, very easy to exploit."

There was silence for several moments, which Daniel shattered by laughing again. "You are *so high,*" he said.

Her response was an eye roll and a sigh. "Think about it," she said. "Think about it outside of your limited framework of being famous and making bucketloads of money. Think about what the creation of true art forms means to you—think about the transcendence." She stood up and yanked the blue dress over her head, then pulled off the thermal long johns under it and climbed nimbly into the tub with him. Her breasts were noticeably fuller, heavier, and what had been a suggestion of extra flesh at her middle had become now definite. Less dancing, more eating. He touched her skin without meaning to, imagining sinking his teeth into it, to see if she tasted as creamy as she looked. She slid across him and dunked her head under the water, coming up with furious bubbling and a gasp and raking her hands through her wet thin hair. "I'll do it with or without you. But we can do so much more damage if there's two of us. And you're like the master of disguise—you can totally pass for a woman if you really try. You'd have to tape your wee-wee down a little better—I could totally see it. And plus, y'know, in the confusion, it shouldn't be too hard to find somebody to bite . . . ?" She slid forward to him again and puckered her wet lips against his chin.

He put his arms around her and kissed her mouth and pressed his body against hers. She was no longer stiff in his arms, but rather supple and warm, her skin stippled lightly with indentations from the thermals. His fingers played against the welt bitten into her skin at the waist from the elastic, and she slid her fingers over his spine and into the cleft of his buttocks.

Daniel spoke against the skin at the sounding board of her skull, just below the ear. "You know . . . last time I was in this bathtub, I killed Ricky," he murmured. "And then I fucked him. I fucked him as I was killing him."

"Did you fuck him in the ass, you queer?" she murmured affectionately.

"Yes," he confirmed. "And I tore him open. And I drank all his blood. And he died happy because he loved me."

"You didn't love him," she added sleepily.

"No, I didn't love him."

The pain of the world seemed so far away, holding the beautiful girl in his arms and kissing her lips, listening to the tight squeaking sound of her legs on the sides of the tub, the splashes she made riding his thighs. He wondered that he wasn't consumed with the urge to kill her as well, just get her over with, suck her impermeable blood and ditch her body in the park; but he only wanted to hold her, draw out this luscious, drowsy tension for the rest of time. "Write me a proposal—a scenario—and I'll help you," he said to her between kisses, smoothing her hair off her ears. It would probably only be one time. The obnoxious public spectacles of Dada theater were long, long dead, and for good reason—after a while, shocking people became so boring.

But not really.

Scene Sixteen: Daddy Spank

It never ceased to amaze him, after decades of making love to women, how incredibly soft and smooth, at once delicate and resilient, was the flesh of the inner folds of the labia. It was only mucous membranes, after all; but those words never seemed right to describe the ecstatic journey along those silken coral slopes, how infinite a few square inches of bare pink flesh could seem. Orchids and sunlight and melted butter . . . he could never run out of ways to describe it, and none of them was ever quite accurate. This was transcendence, this was the private art of ecstasy that she sought. . . . Sybil was still new to having her pussy eaten, still trying to work out what she should do when half of the blood in her body had concentrated between her legs, and Daniel held her open with the fingers of one hand, while the other arm flung across her belly kept her body still. She lay diagonally across his bed, almost relaxed but for a rigid tremor that swept across her body over and over again.

He wished that he knew how she felt, that she could know how he felt. Under normal circumstances, the pleasure of the experience was shared; humans couldn't help transmitting their thoughts and sensations to him while he touched them, and he could easily use the same connection to give it back to them. But there was almost none of that with Sybil. All he had to go on was the moisture of her vagina going from sticky to slick, and the trembling of her arms and legs. He could almost feel her, and he lapped at her desperately, craving more of her soul, wishing she would bleed so that he could get inside her mind. There was so much glory in her unknowable flesh, her fingertips repetitively massaging his scalp, and the freckles on the tops of her thighs.

"I want something inside of me," she groaned after an eternity of near silence.

Daniel propped himself up on one elbow and smiled at her. "Too bad," he said. "I'm going to leave you wanting it." He didn't feel like adding, *Just like you leave me.*

"You fucker," she replied with only slight hostility. She sighed, arched her back, rolled onto her side facing him, and rubbed the long scars on her arms.

"I'll make it up to you," he promised, recalling suddenly one of the invitations he'd gotten while he was away. He picked up the telephone beside the bed, fed a number into its keypad, and rested the receiver against his white cheek. "It's midnight; want to come out and play with me?"

She smiled back. "What does that entail?"

"I know this really interesting club . . ." He bent over and ran his tongue along the scars. She quivered and giggled—a most unlikely sound, one she obviously didn't make very often, an odd, rusty burbling with sparkles. ". . . Where we can be naughty. Very . . . naughty." He circled his tongue in the crook of her elbow. On the telephone, a voice spoke, and Daniel said his address and hung up.

Her lips quirked in a comma of skepticism. "Like how naughty?"

"I'll show you. Don't be a 'fraidy cat."

"What*ever,*" she retorted, sliding off the bed. "Sure, show me the way to be . . . naughty, or whatever." A more usual laugh from her, a kind of hissing snigger. "I can't imagine what you think naughty is."

"Do you want to look at some of my clothes? I think that almost any of them will fit you except maybe the Very Tightest Leather Pants, and I'm going to wear those myself."

She laughed and followed him into his closet. After a few minutes of pawing through hangers of material and stitching, she turned to look at him standing in the doorway to the bathroom, rubbing cornstarch powder on his legs. "This is all dresses," she said, whining, rhetorical. "Why do you have so many dresses, Daniel?"

"Because I look fucking fabulous in them," he grunted, lying on the floor and pulling the Very Tightest Leather Pants over his feet. He had to get into them in a series of wiggles and shimmies—a laborious process, but worth it. "Because I'm a crossdressing faggot fairy queen. Why do you ask?"

"Just wondering." She grabbed a pair of dull gunmetal leathers off its hanger and compared their length to the outside of her leg. She stepped into them and zipped up the sides while Daniel wriggled and grunted on the floor. "Can I wear anything from here?"

"Anything you want," he said. Only a few more inches. Usually the pants were too much bother, but he wanted to go out of his way tonight. With effort he forced the blood out of his erection so that his penis would fit into the pants—it took some tucking to accomplish.

Sybil chose a fishnet top that squished against her ample breasts and scored her nipples like screwheads.

Daniel stood up and tugged gently on the crotch of the pants. Nice thing about the VTLPs—his balls always sorted themselves out somehow. Sybil stared at him. "Well, OK," she said admiringly.

"Like them?" Daniel turned around and rubbed a powdery palm across his slick behind. "As long as I don't try to move too much, they're not too bad."

"Your legs are so long."

"Yes, they are," Daniel said.

"It looks good on you," she told him.

He came over and kissed her quick and sweet on the mouth, then put on a more substantial shirt himself.

"There's a car coming to pick us up," he said, hastily applying black-red lipstick and checking himself in the mirror. "This is not a night for driving if I can do anything about it."

In Midtown, on the sixty-fourth and ultimate floor of a business high-rise, a wealthy married couple ran a ridiculously exclusive monthly fetish club called Daddy Spank. Daniel had first been invited because the couple had been passionate fans of his drag cabaret act, singing Lotte Lenya, and Daniel had accepted because he approved of the design and typography of their invitation. Unfortunately, the very best thing about Daddy Spank was the design of their invitations, but Daniel returned to it occasionally with a kind of masochistic glee. He loved hating it.

There were occasional genuine fetishists there—one of the regulars was a shoe designer who had never sexually touched a human being but who brought his favorite shoes with him in a special fur-lined bag and caressed their surfaces all night and wouldn't let anyone else touch them, and the electricity fiends always got their AC/DC kicks there—but mostly instead of Freudian fetishes, the club's attendees were strictly there to put on their own personal dress-up dramas in multi-thousand-dollar rubber hot pants and skin coddled by spas and milk. A low crawl of sex-o-rific bass thrummed from the sound system, only a bare fraction more interesting than the featureless, chirpy pop music at the Supernova Gentleman's Club.

He loved the place in all its trying-too-hardness—didn't they know that a dank basement with a set of restraints hanging by a chain in the ceiling would do just as well? The windows were draped with thousands of yards of red gossamer, which trailed onto the black-plastic–wrapped floor, dented here and there with marks from stiletto heels. Clouds of frankincense smoke thickened the air, mingling with the scent of sweating human bodies and the fluids produced by their arousal. The whole room smelled horny, like a church, home to wild visions of bleeding martyrs. And yet there was such a sense of control, such decorum, such a sense of restraining the very pleasure they were there to exult. A girl in a white dress, desperately gulping red wine poured into her mouth by her unsmiling corseted mistress, was as close to a feeling of bacchanal as it got. He wondered that there was not more acting out, no temper tantrums—he wanted to someday see a slave rise up and strike his master across the face, screaming, "I've been the bitch long enough, motherfucker!" But it had not happened yet.

Daniel had imagined that Sybil would be interested in seeing it. She held her drink close to her fishnetted body and leaned against the floating bar in the center of the room, glancing around herself casually, touching the plastic rim of the cup to her lips without drinking. "This is kinda boring," she said, her eyes settling on a huge buxom woman forcing a happily cowering man on a leash to lick the spiked vinyl heel of her boot. "This is just a disco where nobody's dancing."

"You think so?" Daniel asked, sipping his own drink. Tonight there was only wine; the owners of Daddy Spank disapproved of alcohol and drugs, and only provided (and tolerated) them grudgingly. "I just kinda like the atmosphere. It's fascinating what expressions people here have on their faces."

"I always wanted to go to one of these when I was a kid," Sybil said. "But this isn't what I pictured."

"A kid."

"You know, like fourteen."

"And what did you picture?"

"I dunno," she admitted. "Something more Hieronymous Bosch-y. I thought there'd be more sex."

"No, it's all foreplay." Daniel laughed. "Actually, if you play your cards right, and exercise a lot of patience, there'll be actual sex eventually. Fucking's not what this place is all about, but some folks just can't help themselves—although sometimes I wonder why they bother getting all dressed up, if that's all they want."

"That's obviously not *all* they want," Sybil pointed out.

The shoe fetishist smiled in her general direction, stroking a pair of feather-covered pumps.

Daniel nuzzled the edge of Sybil's neck under her ear, and she leaned into him for a second in acknowledgment, but only for a second. "Like that guy over there licking the boot," she said. She stuck out her own tongue and curled it into a tube, as if to demonstrate. "Do you think he's wanted to do that all his life, or is he putting on a show for somebody?"

"Does it matter?"

"I dunno," she said again. "It's all so . . . abstracted here. Like this is all just a reenactment that they can store up and use to jack off with later."

"Well, yeah," Daniel agreed, "isn't that what any erotic experience is supposed to be? They're putting on a show, sure. For you, or me, or anybody else who's watching. Most of all, for themselves."

"That seems kinda sad to me. All these people come together to this place and show off how twisted they are and then they go home and they're alone and all they can do is live off of what they remember."

Daniel grunted impatiently. "God, Sybil, you're such a fascist. Have you ever thought that maybe that's what it is to you, but not to them? Maybe this is the actual experience, and they're not thinking about being alone? Or maybe they're not alone. Maybe some folks are together and this is how they make love to each other. In front of other people. Surely you must understand that."

She laughed softly. "What, are you upset? Or are you just frustrated because you didn't fuck me like I asked you to?"

He bit down gently on her shoulder, stopping just short of breaking the skin. He gathered his strength and thought to her, *I want your blood.* She grabbed his jaw and squeezed it tightly in her fingers, as if to crush it, but it just pursed his lips out. "You look really stupid," she said, letting him go.

"That's what your pussy looks like," he retorted.

She laughed softly to herself. "My pussy is beautiful," she said. She rubbed some of his lipstick off and rubbed it onto her own lips. "It looks better than your face."

He chuckled grudgingly. "It's true," he said.

She cocked her head slightly, rubbing her lips together so that the smudge of color spread over her broad, diamond-shaped mouth. He touched her hair, wet from melting snow, then licked his fingertips. Sybil smiled. "Hmmm . . . watch this. *I'm* going to put on a show."

She walked away from him, toward a section of chain-link fence ten feet high where a young woman, perhaps a few years older than Sybil, straight fibers of long black hair sliding across her nude back, stretched and gyrated out, her wrists in metal handcuffs, latched to the fence. A graying man, who looked more like a high-school English teacher than a devotee of de Sade, stood over her, occasionally flicking at her hindquarters with a cat-o'-nine-tails; grinning as the woman writhed and moaned in response. Sybil took the man's arm and leaned over his shoulder, and Daniel heard her say, "Can I try?"

"Sure," said the man, handing her the whip. He even sounded like an English teacher. "Her safe word is *not now*—otherwise you can go for it."

"What, she's not 'yours'?" Sybil asked archly.

"She's anybody's. She's a fucking slut for pain," said a tall, gym-buffed, dog-collared spectator, standing to one side while his boy lover tongued circles around his pierced ear. "She'll let you whip her all night."

"Mmm-hmm," acknowledged Sybil.

She raised the whip and brought it down smartly on the brunette's buttocks. The brunette gasped and looked over her shoulder at the new assailant, Sybil standing over her and tossing the whip from hand to hand. Gently Sybil stroked the newly slapped flesh with the ends of the tails, then brought it down again.

"Oh!" cried the brunette. "That hurt!"

The watchers laughed. Sybil brought the whip down again, and the lashes hit flat across the skin. The brunette let out a throaty groan, a smile spreading across her face. The smile vanished on the third stroke, this time cutting into her pale buttocks.

"I think I'm getting the hang of it," said Sybil. "You

have to snap it back at the last minute so that the tails"—*whap*—"take the velocity of the hit and—you *snap* it!"

"Ow! Jesus!"

"Shut up, stupid," Sybil shouted, balancing her boot against the brunette's thighs. "You're the one who cuffed yourself to this stupid fence."

The brunette choked back a response.

Sybil struck again, more firmly, but adding the snap. The brunette's fair thighs now bore stripes of angry red, her neck bright with sweat, biting her lips. Daniel took a step closer, gulping his glass of wine and grinning. Again and again Sybil brought the lash down. "I mean, what kind of stupid fuckup would—huh!—voluntarily chain herself up—huh!—and let any old sleazy fuck—huh!—hit her with a—huh!—cat-o'-fucking-nine-tails!" With that last comment, Sybil bit her own lip and began the thrashing in earnest. A small crowd of observers had gathered round, attracted by the sounds of thwacking and screaming. At last—something genuine.

"Ow! Christ! Stop!" howled the brunette. The whip came down again, slick with blood, painting fresh lines across the soft skin at the back of her thighs. "Not now! Not now! Safe word, safe word—Goddamn it!"

"Hey, that's not cool," said the English teacher in a timid voice. "She's giving you the safe word."

"What the fuck does that mean? Why do you keep saying that?" Sybil shouted.

Daniel came forth out of the background and took the whip from Sybil's white-knuckled hand. "That means stop doing what you're doing," he said.

One of the owners of the club, Madam Miranda Martin, ultra-top and an internationally successful professional dominatrix, strode forward in her embroidered silk robe and marabou mules. "Young lady, you are violating house rules," Madame Martin said coldly. "I'm going to have to ask you to leave."

"She's my guest," said Daniel, still holding Sybil's trembling arm. Sybil panted, her face rosecea red.

"Mr. Blum, it's been a while, hasn't it?" said Madame Martin, arching an eyebrow. She was a stunning fifty-year-old, having nothing on her conscience and enough money to pay the best spas and plastic surgeons in Manhattan. "Your guest has violated house rules. When a willing participant in a scenario gives a safe word, all activity stops. You know that."

"Forgive me, Miranda," said Daniel.

Doors within hallways. So many doors. So many codes and links. But not really, not with Miranda Martin, that pampered tigress, who always got her own way. Her doors were clearly marked PRIDE, AVARICE, LUST. It was easy to find the way in. And once there, so easy for him to rearrange the room to his liking.

He smiled his handsomest smile and kissed the back of Sybil's hand.

"I will make an exception," said Madame Martin. She drew herself up even more severely, head thrown almost completely back, attempting to look down her nose at people six inches taller than herself. "Enjoy yourselves."

The brunette's companion had uncuffed her from the fence and grimaced over the cuts made by the whip, while the brunette quivered and chewed on her hair and stole glances at Daniel and Sybil.

Daniel smiled at the brunette. She, in her fragile state of mind, was also simple to unravel and reweave. She gave him a weak but genuine smile. "Sorry," she said.

"No, that's perfectly all right, Laura," said Daniel, smiling back. "That's perfectly all right, Laura." He backed away slowly, herding Sybil to the farthest corner of the room.

Once there, he turned a tight smile on her. "Nicely done," he said. "But yeah, that's what a safe word is, just for your information."

"You learn something new every day." Sybil shrugged.

From the opposite corner came yowls and hisses from the electric nipple clamp machine people.

"Did you enjoy that?" He wiped a drop of sweat from her temple.

"Yes," said Sybil. "I did."

"You looked good doing it," he told her. "Maybe you need a slave."

"Maybe you need to . . ." She looked over her shoulder and smiled out at the club. As if loosed by Sybil's outburst, the atmosphere had changed from posing to genuine pursuit and role-play, and the music got faster and more insistent. "Looks like I had a good effect, though."

"It's all about pushing the limits of what people expect," Daniel agreed.

"So tell me," she said, "what it is that you actually do find naughty. Because I can tell that this is not it."

Daniel shrugged. "I like this place, and I wanted to see your reaction."

"Now you've seen it," Sybil declared. "C'mon. Really out there."

"I think about the orgies I went to when I was young."

"Oh, really. When you were young. When was this?"

"In Berlin, with Ricari," he said. "In the thirties. Early thirties, mostly."

"They had orgies in the nineteen-thirties?" she asked, alarmed.

"They had orgies in the Roman Empire, darling. Hell, the Trojan Empire, and probably in caves, too. What the hell *do* you kids learn in school these days? So, of course, Berlin was the same. There were incredible orgies in my neighborhood. I lived near Haus Vaterland, which was this huge multiple restaurant cabaret thing, in one of the most beautiful buildings in the world. . . . I watched it get really good, then lame, then really good again, and then it was gone. I remember the bomb." He put his hands on her hips and swayed with her in time to the music, moving every other beat. "I worked there, for God's sake," he remembered with an abrupt laugh. "I worked in one of the restaurants. And I was really bad at it. I got fired six times, but I always managed to get work there again. Anyway, um, Haus Vaterland was a very popular spot for prostitutes and amateur sex-mad freaks, from countries all over the world, so orgies happened fairly regularly. I used to drag Ricari with me to these because they were the best way to feed without having to kill anybody and get laid at the same time, if you wanted to. I thought I was doing him a favor. I'd hear about an orgy going on in so-and-so's back parlor, and then we'd make sure to show up a little late so everyone would already be doing it. So, y'know, we'd just . . . join in. I bet you can't imagine."

"I can *too* imagine," she said. "I don't know, but I can imagine. A bunch of naked, fucking people, getting bitten by vampires."

"Naked, fucking *German* people," he corrected.

"Y'know, I'm German," she said, angling her chin upward in parody of Madame Martin.

"You are?" He looked her over, and thought that she would have been considered a success of the Nazi pure-Aryan breeding project, or else a popular receptacle for SS seed, and hopes for a taller, blonder Germany, in the bedrooms of the *Lebensborn*.

"At least partly. My last name's German, so I should be at least kind of German."

"Unless you're adopted," Daniel pointed out, wagging his finger. "Maybe you're actually a Communist Filipino Jew."

"Oh, shit, there goes my application for the Aryan Nation." She let her head relax and roll forward to touch his chest. "Tell me about the orgies," she said with her lips against his shirt. "What was it like? Give me specifics."

He caressed the side of her neck with his black claws. "The fucking? Monumental." The claws slid over her throat and found one of her straining nipples, tore a hole through two cells of the fishnet, then touched her with his fingertips. She drew in a breath through pursed, quivering lips. "Imagine being buried under a pile of breasts and buttocks and legs, with a cock in your ass, another one in your mouth, and your cock off somewhere fucking some hole and you don't even know what hole it is. Imagine . . . seeing a perfectly normal and reasonable and serious librarian, still wearing her spectacles, getting fucked donkey style right in front of your face, then the next day, she's distributing Nazi propaganda and he's vanished without a trace. They didn't want to know about any of that at the orgies. Not anywhere, really.

That whole kind of . . . not wanting to know was the real basis of Berlin. It was an unspoken agreement. You came to orgies to fuck, not to be who you were, not to be part of your family or your party or your religion. Although, of course, circumcised cocks were a dead giveaway."

"Didn't anybody care about getting bitten? Didn't anybody notice *fangs?*"

"It was dark." Daniel shrugged. "I mean, I could see, of course. And when everyone was good and sexed-up, I'd just lean over, take someone in my arms, and kiss them, kiss their necks, their thighs, anywhere the blood was near the surface."

"Anywhere?"

"Anywhere," Daniel agreed.

She bent her head to look at his fingers on her breast. "So why did your friend have a problem with it?" she asked.

"He's a Catholic," said Daniel.

"He's a *Catholic?*" Sybil echoed. "How could he be a vampire?"

"Oh, it's all too easy. He's been drinking the blood of Christ for two hundred years. Funny how it hasn't saved his ass."

"Two hundred years!?"

"As far as I know. I assume he's still alive. I think I'd know if he were dead." For a moment his fingers paused.

Sybil took his hands and rubbed them against her. "How did he let you take him to orgies in the first place?"

"Ricari . . . had problems saying no to me," Daniel said. "And it was an easy way to feed. You know that when a vampire bites someone, unless they make a mess out of it, the person tends to enjoy it."

"I find that hard to believe," Sybil said. "I've lost blood. It's not the most pleasant sensation in the world, let alone having it sucked out of your body."

"You should try it and see," said Daniel. "You might change your mind."

Sybil backed away, out of his reach. Her nipple jutted out of the hole in the fishnet. "I don't think so," she said indignantly.

Daniel put his hands on his hips. "Oh! Tremble before the great Sybil Morocco, who doesn't fear death and doesn't fear pain and . . . is just the ultimate bad-ass!"

"That has nothing to do with it," she said, shaking her head and smiling. "It's just that I *don't* have a problem saying no to you."

A glorious melange of conflicting desires reduced his face to slightly slack-jawed jumbled angles. Instead of replying, instead of grabbing her and crushing their bodies together, Daniel turned away and scanned the fetish club's patrons until he saw a likely candidate for a small bloodletting. In fact, Laura, the recently flogged, looked perfect for his purposes. She had already been roughed up enough; eyes closed, lost in endorphins, she swayed between her English teacher's hands, which occasionally snaked around her slight body to pull on the rings that pierced her nipples. Her, yes. Daniel muttered to Sybil, "Stay here and listen," pointing to his left temple just behind the eye. "And watch. I'll show you how it's done; how they don't notice."

Laura had wide dark brown eyes under Bettie Page bangs, and a beautifully willing and drowsy expression. The English teacher frowned at Daniel but didn't say anything or make any moves to stop him. Daniel leaned forward and kissed Laura's hair. "I seem to keep finding you," he murmured. "You're beautiful."

"Your girlfriend hurt me," Laura whispered huskily.

"Did you like it?" Daniel whispered back.

"No," she said, her naked flesh shimmering suddenly with goose pimples. "She hits too hard."

"I told her to be nicer next time . . . but she probably won't. . . ." Daniel leaned in and let his breath play against the hollow of her throat. A vein leaped there as she swallowed. "She's a bitch. She never listens to me."

The black hair sweeping across her shoulders provided a convenient veil for his teeth, and he caught a mouthful of it as he bit down, piercing the warm, smooth, scented skin just deep enough. Laura gasped faintly, the same sound as she would make when just feeling a penis penetrate her, when she had been anticipating it for what seemed like lifetimes, but that always, every time, came as a surprise. His body screamed at him to suck her dry, but he took his teeth away immediately and licked at the four neat punctures that oozed warm crimson. Her arms, which had been hanging slack at her sides, rose up and slid around Daniel's waist.

"Ah," she said.

He kissed her with blood-moistened lips, then nicked at her bottom lip from inside and swept his tongue along her lower teeth. Her tongue filled his mouth, pushing more blood into him, and with it a terrible crush of thoughts/emotions/memory/chemicals, all the things she was on (a dizzying cocktail of amyl nitrate, some kind of amphetamine, the first time she had ever let a boy put his tongue into her mouth, the sizzling sensation of the cuts on her back and thighs, alcohol and sugar, and a reflection of the rocketing transmission of Daniel's lust into her brain).

Daniel pushed her gently away, back into the arms of the English teacher, who was her uncle and had a tidy business in selling videos of the two of them fucking. "They're right," Daniel said to him, wiping his mouth with his fingertips, "she is a slut for pain, isn't she?"

"Come on, baby," said the uncle to the near-orgasmic Laura. "We're going home."

"Oh, Daddy, please, please, can't we stay?" She sank to her knees on the floor and began to kiss the tops of her uncle's boots. He sighed and rolled his eyes impatiently.

Sybil smirk-grinned when he returned. "Thank you for the show," she said.

"That wasn't a show," said Daniel, rinsing his mouth with wine, "that was life."

"You must be very hungry."

"I'm fine," Daniel said. "But I'm bored. Done with this. Let's go."

"All right by me," said Sybil.

"I'm almost sorry I picked her," he said, walking past the compliant Laura being pulled up by one arm, her chin sunk guiltily to her chest. "She's had enough excitement for one night."

Sybil looked over her shoulder at them. "If I was that guy, I'd smack the bitch into next Thursday."

"That's your answer to everything, isn't it?" Daniel said, guiding Sybil to the coat check, his arm around her shoulders. "So, to finish my naughty story, you know why Ricari and I stopped going to orgies?"

" 'Cause of the war?" she guessed.

"No, because that didn't really happen until about two years later. Not that there weren't orgies during the war, but that's something entirely different."

"Well, why?"

"Well, as I said, Ricari was a Catholic. A quite devout Catholic. When I think *Ricari,* I think *guilt,* especially sexual guilt. And one night . . . after being a willing participant in this for . . . oh, I don't know, months at least, it's very easy to lose track of time, he stands up while everyone else is still doing it . . . I mean I was so close to coming and I was trying to concentrate. Just starts screaming in Italian. I mean screaming. He had a sudden vision—"

"Maybe it was a burning bush," said Sybil.

Daniel didn't react for a few seconds, restrained himself to merely smiling, and continued. "Anyway, he lost it. Freaked out. And in Italian, which I didn't understand then and I don't understand now, but I could hear him in my mind from across the room, just blistering with horror; he saw tentacles, he saw the lake of fire, he saw all the holes in the human body as being shortcuts to the void. And a whole room full of naked, fucked-up people panicked. So I panicked. We were going to wake the neighbors, and that was also very dangerous—you'd be amazed, but even with all that screwing going on, they were really very quiet because they had to be. Having orgies is always very risky, unless you're in the middle of nowhere, and we weren't—we were in Berlin. So I had to kill everybody."

"All of them?"

"Every last one. By myself. Without Ricari's help—I had to shut him up, he was doing Hail Marys, or whatever it is—like I said, I don't understand Italian, but it sounded something like that. I hit him in the mouth.

Broke his teeth. Burst his lips. And I had to kill about eight people in the room, plus two who had gotten out and had run out into the street—it took me about two minutes. It was actually kind of fun."

"I bet Ricari felt pretty healthy after that."

"Oh, yeah, that was the beginning of the end, really. Or the middle of the end. From then on, we were enemies who still depended on each other as lovers. Or something more bizarre than that."

"Ten people," Sybil whispered, running her fingertips across the racks of leather and fur and glittery-vinyl coats. The coat-check girl, in Jean-Paul Gaultier's rubber couture, had fallen asleep, sprawled in her plush pony-skin chair. "How many of them were women?"

"Ummm . . . how many women?" He rubbed his fingertips over his face, then looked down at his long and skeletal hands. "Three. One on the street."

"OK," Sybil said. She shook her head and grinned into space. "Bloodsucking Catholic Italian sex freakout." She laughed. "That's what I'm talking about when I ask you to tell me stories." She let him put the leather parka over her shoulders and fluff out the synthetic fur hood, as yielding and preoccupied as a child, already, in her mind, outside playing with the others. He took the opportunity to kiss her forehead and the tip of her nose; she looked right through him. In the elevator, though, her reverie broke, and she fixed him with her eyes. "Why did you call me Sybil Morocco?"

"That's your name, isn't it?" he said, staring out the glass walls of the elevator, snow coasting down in thumb-sized flakes from a pink and windless sky.

"Well, yeah, but I never thought about it—nobody's ever called me that." She sighed at his reflection in the glass. The elevator came to a halt with a muted thump. "It sounds really nice when you say it."

A large black sedan, part of Daddy Spank's private car service, received them on the sidewalk outside. Daniel had already prepared himself to direct thought into the driver to take him home, but Sybil said in a loud clear voice, "West Forty-sixth and Seventh." The driver glanced back at them, as if they'd just spoken at once. "West Forty-sixth," Sybil reinforced.

Daniel stared at her. "Why are you going back to the studio?" he demanded.

"Because it's where I live," she replied, deadpan. "I don't like your place. I can't think in there."

"Maybe it's me," said Daniel.

"It's not you," she said, shaking her head. "I can think right now. I can think when I'm around you. Just . . . I don't know how to describe it. It just makes me uncomfortable. I like living in the studio, actually." She slid her hands between her thighs to warm them, and Daniel immediately pulled them out and put them inside his coat, under his arms. She gave him a slight smile and left them there, even digging her fingers into his ribs in some hostile form of appreciation. "Actually, no, maybe it *is* that I can't think straight when I'm around you."

"I can't think straight when I'm around *you,*" he confessed. "It's been driving me a little crazy."

"Oh, whatever. No, that has nothing to do with anything. I just don't feel like sleeping at your place tonight. I'm kinda through with you tonight, Daniel, no offense."

"No offense," he echoed, nodding. She dug her fingers in deeper, and he flinched—when agitated, he was ticklish. "OK. If you say so."

She pulled him toward her and kissed him violently on the lips, sliding her hands around inside his sleeves to cup his shoulders. At first, he relaxed into it and gave his best efforts to the kiss, but then she poked him in the ribs again, and he flinched again, harder this time.

And he bit her tongue.

She jerked away and pressed herself against the car door, yelping in surprise. "Ow! You fucker!" she shouted.

"I'm sorry—I didn't mean to, I swear." He wanted to say a lot of other things, too, about *dumb little sluts who kiss too fucking hard and stick their tongues into dangerous places,* but decided that none of the above judgments were true, settling for shaking his head convulsively. "You tickled me! I didn't mean to. It was an accident. Look, haven't you ever bitten your own tongue?" *When eating something so delicious you forgot where or who you were?* "I mean, did you mean to do that? No. This is the same thing. I would never hurt you. Never."

Her fingers closed over the door handle, then opened again, and her shoulders went limp. "Oh, for Chrissake." Experimentally, she touched a finger to her tongue, and it came away with a vague orange stain. "Did you get any?"

A lot more sarcastic replies backed up in his throat, and he swallowed them down and ran his tongue across the ripples of his palate. "I think I must have," he said. "I can taste it. And I'm starting to think like you."

"And what do I think like?"

He smiled. "Like a nasty, evil bitch who's constantly holding herself back from telling every fucking idiot on the face of the planet exactly what she thinks of them."

Her transformation was truly remarkable—from an openmouthed stance of outrage, she passed through defiance, then a moment of truly elegant, shining pride, settling on a sloppy, you-got-me grin. "Oh," was all she said at the end of this. "Well, that's true of everybody, isn't it?"

"If you kiss me again," Daniel said, "and I promise I won't bite you again, it won't hurt any more."

"You won't sap my will, will you?" she said, wagging her finger at him. "At the first sign of will-sapping, I cut your fucking head off."

"It's a deal," he agreed.

They spent the next thirty seconds in a less painful kiss. He had tasted so little blood—so much less than even a mouthful—that the click-and-flash was more just afterimage, floating and dimming but never quite gone. He could taste that she was still a little stoned from earlier in the day, the wine, the excitement. And she wanted him; the world blurry from desire, her lips swollen with it. Her name, as he had said it, flowed through her mind, skipping and repeating, a fugue counterpointed with her own mind's voice, much more beautiful than the one her throat produced: *Sybil Morocco. Me, a name I call myself. A good punishing, destroying, film noir goddess name.* But more than the pride and the lust, she wanted to be back in that studio. She felt that like a cramp. She needed to make something. *Sybil Morocco. It's* mine. *It's who I am, only he said it first . . . sybil morocco . . .*

When the car stopped, she gazed and shrugged at him apologetically. "Bye," she said, opening the car door and putting one foot into a gutter full of fresh snow. "I'm glad you're back . . . and . . . everything."

"I'll see you soon," said Daniel.

Scene Seventeen: Caught in a Storm

Daniel slept for sixteen hours.

He bolted upright when he awoke; he expected the clock to read somewhere between noon and two, his usual, and when it told him 7:18, he had a wild terror that he had died in his sleep and that it was now a different year. He jumped out of bed and pulled on the clothes nearest him and bolted out the door and into the street. He had seen the final orgy again—dying, nude bodies in a wriggling pile; the slashed tracheas, eyes cooling to a glassy jelly, Ricari's emaciated white figure hunched in the corner, rocking back and forth, still litanizing through his destroyed mouth.

The old woman at the newsstand a block down jumped back at the sight of the white-faced, wild-haired apparition in stained white T-shirt, black vinyl pants, and poison-green Italian suede loafers, demanding to know: "What day is this?"

"It's Saturday," she stammered.

"What day, I said?"

"Saturday, the Thirtieth," she added, handing over, by

her gloved fingertips, an evening edition of the *Post*.

Daniel skimmed the masthead until he found the date—it was, indeed, the same year that he had fallen asleep, the year the world was supposed to end, or a new era of enlightenment would begin, depending on whom you believed. He handed back the paper and dropped his shoulders, rubbing his forehead.

"You should prob'ly put on a coat," added the woman, "it's only twenty-two degrees out here! Are you high on cocaine or someth'n?"

He was amused, and aware enough to smile at her. "No, nothing like that. I panicked. I just woke up."

"Still. It's pretty cold out here. You got a place to go to?" She glanced back down at the eight-hundred-dollar loafers, squishing in the gravel-choked slush at the base of the newsstand. "You want a cup of coffee? You need me to call somebody?"

"No, that's all right, thanks."

"Storm comin', supposedly," she called to his back. "You should probably stay at home tonight."

He began trudging back, wishing it was still snowing. Falling snow was innocent and clean.

Ricari had warned him that the sleep, and the terrors, would happen more frequently as he got older—Ricari had sometimes woken up in a panic and couldn't remember any language except Italian, or French; he imagined himself in a monastery in Switzerland, or a burning house in Paris. Once in his life, Ricari had fallen asleep for two weeks, and when he woke up, he was in a pine box, on a cart, on his way to the pauper's graveyard. Daniel knew that deathlike sleep could strike him any day, and to all appearances he'd be dead. Undertakers would try to empty his clotted blood into a drain and replace it with chemicals, and that wouldn't work, and they'd just give up and bury him anyway. And one day he would have to crawl out of that grave. He knew he could do it. He had been buried alive before, caught in the collapsed building on Karlsbergstrasse; and though the effort nearly burst his heart, he got himself out, claws, teeth, screaming, and all. When he emerged, there was no living thing as far as the eye could see, when just ten minutes before there were dogs and old women and children and an officer shouting to everyone to head for the shelters, but the warning had come too late. . . .

He paused in the foyer of his apartment to whisper, "Let me never die in my sleep. On my feet—in a flash—eyes open—"

He pulled off the wet loafers and changed into a sturdier pair of boots, and added a shocking-blue ski sweater that Ricky had bought him; it reflected blue light onto Daniel's face from underneath and carved electricity-colored shadows into his cheeks. He couldn't bear to wear it without putting on something to make his lips redder. He looked ghastly, blood-starved, artificial, and petulantly emphasized it by crunching styling wax into his hair to make it stand on end. On top he added one of his cheap, flimsy dark plastic raincoats. A nice convergence—mongrelized Swiss ski mod and Potsdamerplatz deathrock speed freak. The mirror beckoned, *stay and be fascinated,* but Daniel flipped his middle finger at it and went out again.

Daniel drove to the studio through drifts of half-melted snow. Tonight it would freeze, and there would be death on the roads. A frozen death, in a car, drunk on a Saturday night, a pile of metal and broken-glass amethysts and coolant and blood. This would be another night when it would be handy to be able to fly. He imagined himself as a satellite, monitoring the city for fresh death, then settling down upon it with a soft flutter of crows' wings and a smile. The radio spoke about a massive snowstorm the day before, the suffering in rural Ohio, where people had been without power for three days. Flakes of half-tuned crackle FM words slid across his mind without sticking. He felt barely conscious. The car seemed to drive itself.

She's calling me, he thought. *I'm her somnambulist.*

The studio space shuddered with candlelight and the flickering of light from a single, scraped 200-watt bulb, screwed into a spindly metal lamp on the floor. Sybil, in a worn translucent T-shirt and panties, knelt on the floor in front of a canvas as long as she was, worrying at its surface with a rag, her arms and legs smudged with color like she was using herself as a palette surface to mix paint. The stereo played an early Mudhoney song at speaking volume.

"So what is it?" Daniel asked, walking over but keeping a safe distance.

"It's the orgy," she said, without looking behind her. "Do you see it? Look, there's you." She indicated a whitish smudge to the left of center, and when he leaned in closer to the canvas, he found his features hastily but accurately scraped out of the white paint to reveal the black charcoal underneath. "I don't know what Ricari looks like, so I put me there instead." Dead center of the canvas, a thin stretched white figure with white curvy flames for hair, teeth bared in a scream. "These are the people you already killed, and these two are making a break for it."

"Jesus, Sybil, you did all this? How long have you been working on it?"

"Since you last saw me," she said with a satisfied smile. The whites of her eyes crackled with red capillaries, making her road-slush–colored irises seem to protrude from them. "It's done, just about. I could probably use some sleep soon."

"I just woke up about an hour ago," he told her. "I was hoping I'd get to spend some time with you." *And sodomize you until you scream.*

"Oh, that's nice," she murmured. "I guess I can stay up for a little bit longer. My drugs have kinda worn off, but I won't be able to get to sleep for a while." She took one last dab at the painting with her rag, then relaxed until she was lying on the floor. By stages she stood up, stretching and tottering unsteadily around the studio. "Mmmmm. Ugh. Shit. Legs asleep. What time is it?"

"It's about eight-thirty."

She came to a stop in front of him. "You look cute," she remarked. "You look dead."

"Thanks. Want to come hunting with me? I need blood." He wanted to put out his hand and touch her, but he felt a strange fear, a reticence to put his hand through her caul of visionary exhaustion. He knew this state—it was sacred, and his taking her away from it at all was a sacrilege of the highest order. But she nodded.

"Yeah, let me take a shower and put some clothes on," she said. "I'm all painty." A corner of the room had been rigged up as her sleeping area with a couple of ripped Japanese paper screens, one of the couches, and her crates of belongings. She moved behind the screens and rummaged in a box of clothing. "So where are we going? More exciting men's rooms in dumb Top Forty dance clubs? Or have you got another fetish party lined up?"

"No," said Daniel, "this is the real deal. Find a person. Kill him. Dispose of the body."

She stood up and looked at him through a tear in the screen. She opened her mouth as if to speak, but then closed it again and went back to picking at clothes. "You sure you want to show me all of this?" she murmured casually.

"You know I'm sure," he said. "You want to see it."

She snaked out, holding up some garment that shimmered in the flickering golden candlelight, moving sinuously, all wrong, to the music. "You're right, I do. I just wonder how you know."

"Me, too," said Daniel.

In silence they drove through Manhattan, neon lights flashing across the brilliantly slick charcoal streets. In front of them, a car slid between lanes and skidded into the curb with a resounding thump. Sybil half-rose out of her seat, but Daniel smoothly edged around the accident and kept driving. "She asked me, 'How can you drive?' " he mused, his claws biting into the flesh of his palms as he gripped the steering wheel. "She had the nerve to ask me."

"Who?" said Sybil, back in her seat, pushing the junctures of her fingers into knit acrylic gloves.

"Ariane."

"Your old lover? In Portland?"

"Yeah. We had a lover who died in a car accident because he was driving, and not me or her."

"Is that really because?"

"Well—"

"Or was it an accident? As in, you can't see the future?" She frowned at him. "You can't see the future, can you?"

"No," he said.

"Oh, good. I can't even keep track of all your psychic powers."

Daniel chuckled. "I wish I could see the future. Whatever it is that gives me whatever power I have, didn't give me that."

"If I could see the future, I'd know where the hell we're going."

"Brooklyn," said Daniel. "I don't go there very often. Good place to make somebody disappear."

"I made somebody disappear in Brooklyn," said Sybil wistfully.

"Yes, you told me."

"I wonder what her parents thought," she went on. "Sonic Ruth's parents never cared about her—it was weird. She was adopted, and I saw her baby pictures—she's like a baby out of a catalogue, she's totally adorable and blond and Gerber. And then she grows up and turns into this hateful, ugly little bitch."

"Aren't friends grand?"

"They just threw money at her," said Sybil, shaking her head. "Like that would make her into a better person. Like they could make her shrinky-dink back into that baby they got at the Perfect Baby Store."

"And *your* parents?" Daniel had just enough time to spare her a meaningful glance before they got onto the Brooklyn Bridge. Icicles by the tens of thousands hung off the massive cables suspending the bridge, glittering and trembling as they passed. Another car gaily fishtailed in the other lane, four car lengths ahead. A passing car scraped it, and then everything went on again as usual.

"What about them?" asked Sybil.

"To be perfectly honest, as you pretend to be, I'm sick of hearing about Sonic Ruth. She's dead. I want to know about you."

"I just didn't exist until after she was dead." Sybil shrugged.

"Really, or metaphorically? And I know it wasn't really, because you told me about having to beat people up to get Ruth out of trouble. But did you ever fight for you? Just for pleasure? For Christ's sake, what were you like before you met her?"

"I was a kid. Without any friends." She sat there pouting until it became clear that Daniel was waiting for more. "A tall ugly kid who everybody hated. I suppose you were wildly popular as a child and can't possibly understand what I'm talking about."

He had been, unfortunately. "I do understand what you mean. I know what it's like to not have any friends. I don't really have any friends now. I mean, you haven't exactly seen me wiping clean my social calendar recently."

"Who sends you all that stuff in the mail? Who are all those kids who hang around in the studio?"

"Those people," said Daniel coolly, "are using me. They want my money, or they want to have a good time at someone else's expense. It's perfectly natural and I don't fault them for doing it. But friends? C'mon, Sybil. Are you so alienated from the world of friendship that you can't tell the difference?"

It was her turn to fall resentfully silent, and Daniel bit his lip, despairing of having gone too far. But no—let her know what it was to test limits of emotional nakedness, so she could decide for herself if she wished to remain that way. "I haven't had a friend since I left Los Angeles. And when I lived in L.A., I had . . . a lot of friends. I had a couple of good friends, some chums, and some of them were vampires, too. And a lot of subjects." He caught his breath and blinked away the stinging in his eyes. "I guess I need to live in adoration."

"It must suck to be you," she said.

"Since you're so concerned, yes, it does." He stared at the road. Brooklyn seemed exceptionally dark. "It means that when I lose even one friend, it's devastating."

"So you think I was wrong to get rid of Ruth?" she said.

"I didn't say that. I just think it's a shame, that's all."

"No it's not," she said, and that was the end of the conversation.

Daniel parked about four blocks from the off ramp of the bridge itself, alongside its humming pylons, and they began walking into Brooklyn, breaking through thin crusts of ice on top of slush-pooled gutters. Daniel felt the cold, agitated wind slapping at his cheeks, but it was a sensation of secondary importance. Instead of cursing the wind, he lifted his nose into it, trying to read the scents of the area. With the wind chasing its own tail in small eddies, he could only smell himself and occasionally Sybil, walking along ahead of him and holding out her arms wide for balance. It would have to be eyes and ears tonight. Right then, he didn't see anyone else on the street—the weather kept most people inside.

They turned onto a typical neighborhood corner—restaurant west, video store north, florist south, grocery east, apartments above all, thin trees choking and frozen. Only the video store was still open, and even they were shutting off the neon sign and flipping the sign on the door. Two men stood out on the sidewalk, sharing a cigarette and dancing to keep warm.

Sybil strode right up to them, gleaming like an oil slick in her dark, skintight velour leggings and giant parka. "Oh, man, is the video store closed?" she wailed.

"It is now," said the younger of the two men, pointing with the lit end of the cigarette.

"Oh, hell. Well . . ." Sybil swung her arms aimlessly for a moment. "Do you have a cigarette?"

"No," said the older man with a note of sincerity in his voice. "This was my last one, that's why we're sharing it."

Sybil swung her arms some more. "I was really hoping to get a video." She sighed. "I was going to rent a porno and watch it with my honey." She pointed at Daniel, who waved and smiled. "Do you two ever do that?"

"What?" said Younger.

"You two are . . . together, right?" Sybil waggled her hand back and forth.

The men exchanged nervous glances. "No," said

Younger, huffing through his lips. "No way."

"Oh . . . that's funny . . ." said Sybil. "Do you know that guy who's working now?"

"Who, Andrew? Yeah, we're waiting to pick him up," said Older.

Sybil stared longingly at the sparkling faces of movie stars on posters, trapped forever in two dimensions. "Could you maybe . . . just talk him into letting me go in and get something? I know exactly which one I want. Or you can send my honey in. He's got the money anyway."

Daniel caught her look and nodded. Behind his closed lips, his fangs ached and he felt like they were ready to fly out and embed themselves in someone's neck. He looked into the eyes of both men and gave them a gentle push in the right direction.

"Oh, yeah, totally." The younger man all but took Daniel's arm as he led him to the door. The man knocked cautiously on the glass, and Andrew inside opened the door a crack. "Hey, Andy? Could you let this guy come in and grab a movie? He'll only be a second."

"Dude, I'm fucking closing, OK? I need to get home before hell freezes over." Andrew looked at Daniel's face peering in through the crack. "What video do you want?"

"I don't remember what it's called," Daniel said, "but I've been here before and I know exactly where it is on the shelf. Please. Let me in, Andrew."

Hey. I'm your buddy.

The door opened just enough to let Daniel in. Andrew stood with his hands on his hips, glaring at him. "Now hurry up and get it so I can turn the computers off," he snapped.

Daniel sighed. "Go ahead and turn them off. I'm not renting anything."

"Oh, *c'mon!*"

"Go tell your buddies that you're taking a cab home—I'm giving you enough money so you can go in a taxi. Just as a tip. To say thanks." He circled the video store clerk, who kept the same skeptical expression on his face until Daniel stared full into his eyes and slammed him with his thoughts. Andrew crumpled immediately, catching himself on the counter with one hand, but only barely. Daniel wiped his brow. When he was hungry, it was much harder to be subtle. "Go on. Tell them. And then remember, come out to the alley when you're done. Remember—you need to get to the alley."

Andrew staggered to the door, stuck his face out, and relayed the message. Halfway through, Daniel shouldered his way out of the store, turning around with a swirl of his coat and a jaunty, "Thanks. We really appreciate it."

Younger and Older were staring at Sybil, who grinned at them with all her teeth. Daniel took her arm. "I got it, sweetycakes," he said. "Now let's go."

They walked to the alleyway, enclosed with a gate, and waited. "Sweetycakes?" Sybil demanded.

"Your honey?"

"OK, that was lame. It worked, though," she said. "And this can be the first demonstration of my art project. Street theater witnessed only by innocent bystanders. Nobody asks to be in any of our pieces—chaos brings them in!"

"Ssh, he's coming," said Daniel.

The two friends had gotten into their car and driven away, blasting Abba, and now the gate in the alley rattled and the quarry Andrew yawned his way in, wrapping a long blue acrylic scarf around his neck and muttering "I'll never get out of here on time as long as I live. . . ."

Sybil stepped in front of him. "Hi!" she sang.

"Who are you?—Oh, shit." Andrew did a double take of Sybil's manic grin, Daniel's gentle and sinister smile.

Sybil closed and latched the gate behind him, stood against it, leering. Andrew tried to scramble over a pile of plastic trash cans, but Sybil grabbed him by the collar of his puffy down coat and swung him down onto his knees. "Oh, Jesus! Oh, shit! Don't kill me! Please, please don't kill me," he begged, gagging for breath as Sybil tightened the blue scarf around his throat. "Take the money—please—"

"What? What? Can't hear you."

"Please don't—I uh—I got a new baby!"

"You beg, you bargain, *and* you lie," Sybil snapped.

Somehow he managed to twist and struggle free from the scarf and broke into a run, heading toward the smooth brick facade of the building that bordered the alley on the third side, away from the gate. He slapped his hands and squeaked the toes of his sneakers against the brick, trying to climb.

Sybil bent and rummaged in the trash bins until she found an empty beer bottle, and Andrew whirled to face them, his eyes glassy with panic. Daniel rocked back on his heels and smiled all throughout his soul; watching her was glorious, watching the grandiose curve her arm made as she broke off the end of the bottle against the brick and drew the jagged scythe edge across Andrew's throat from ear to ear. In motion she seemed smaller, younger, fluid. At the end of her stroke she came back to rest on the balls of her feet, and for a moment, Daniel hardly recognized her.

"Ooh, you've made a hell of a mess," Daniel whispered to her. He held Andrew up and opened his mouth under the spurting carotid. "Never cut the whole throat," he paused just long enough to say. Andrew, consciousness snapping off in his brain, slumped and fell forward onto the ground when Daniel let him go. "See, look at all this. This is sloppy."

Click and flash! A whole life! But even Andrew had grasped that last moment of beauty as the girl danced the broken glass toward him. Andrew thought *Whoa! So it does happen in real life. Just like in the movies.* Nothing about any baby. Not a moment about what he had or hadn't done with his life. Just awe at the way her down-slashing arm had cut through the steam of his breath.

Sybil delicately stepped out of the way of the slowly spreading pool of blood. "OK, Sybil the Sloppy. But was it all right? Did it look OK?"

"It was gorgeous," he admitted. "Even he thought so."

"You are *covered* in blood," she said. "It's on your boots."

"This is a fucking mess." Daniel looked up at the sky, a thin strip of starless puce between the buildings, and saw what looked like gray birds circling above. With alarming speed, thick white flakes fell and kept falling. "We'll have to hope for the best."

They couldn't just pitch Andrew's body into the Dumpster—plastic garbage bags had to be rearranged, spilled beer and rotting fruit forming a soupy ichor at the bottom. "Get his wallet," Daniel said to Sybil. "You might as well make a living." He grumbled at the video store clerk's unseeing, slack face as he covered it with garbage, adding his soaked gloves, his coat. "This is *not* how I would have done it, my friend. But nobody gets to choose how they go . . . and at least it was pretty, wasn't it?"

As soon as they had left the alley, Daniel plunged toward the ice in the gutter, crunching and splashing until he was soaked and freezing to the bone, but his boots were clean. "Fresh snowfall, good," he said. "If we get inside soon, nobody can track us."

The wind had found new direction and now blew east with a keen determination, bringing smaller, denser, and icier snowflakes with it. "This is shitty," said Sybil with a note of grim joy. "This happens in Colorado." She let Andrew's wallet, divested of thirty-one dollars and five credit cards, slip from her fingers into the slush. "Blizzard conditions. I haven't ever seen it do this here."

Two police cruisers bookended Daniel's car, lights scintillating. An officer bent a black man in a puffy down coat over the hood of Daniel's car, trying to cuff the struggling, cursing man. The perp wiggled out of the cop's grasp and scrambled over the hood of the car, and the cop shouted and went for his gun. Sybil snatched for Daniel's hand; together, they turned the corner onto the next block and headed away from the scene. "Holy shit, what's up with that?" Sybil muttered.

"I wonder if he was trying to steal it," Daniel mused.

They heard gunfire echo off the underside of the bridge, more shouting.

"Jesus . . . we have to get inside. Now." She squinted up at the sky, flakes impaling themselves on her eyelashes. "You've got blood on your pretty sweater."

At times it seemed impossible that the wet knife slicing off the river toward them was only moving air with frozen water suspended in it. An ambulance siren's wail floated there, too, rising and falling, harmonizing with another of its kind in bent Doppler-effect counterpoint, and then soloing, but never fading completely. The bridge, looming very black against the anemic night sky, hummed along with its subsonic grumble. Daniel paced his footsteps to find a rhythm in it.

"Let's try one of these warehouses," she hissed.

Nearly under the bridge, within view of the oily black river, the structures tended toward a roughly cubic shape—huge buildings, a whole block each, as if they had grown out of the broken cobblestones like mushrooms, their ubiquitous Dumpsters clustered around them. Sybil ran to the side of a building, its ground floor windowless, with a garage door made of a single huge sheet of corrugated metal. She examined the lock on the door with a frown of deep concentration. "Nope," she said. "We'll have to try a window. How well do you climb?"

Daniel scrambled up onto a Dumpster, found the row of windows upstairs unboarded and already partially broken. He set his teeth and pushed his hand through a pane of glass, tearing the wooden frames between panes with hands slippery with blood. In less than a minute, he opened a hole wide enough to fit his skinny body through. "I'll see you at the front door," he stage-whispered to Sybil.

It was a long drop inside to the floor, at least ten feet straight down and onto an inch of filthy water on concrete and broken glass. Daniel, who had landed on his feet, searched around the room with his eyes, making out mostly broken glass but also some large twisted hulks of machinery that might have been paint mixers or restaurant equipment or torture devices. He walked through the devastation to the door, wrestled a rusty dead bolt open, and twisted the lock on the doorknob. Sybil, shaking water and glass off the palms of her cheap gloves, gazed into the dark, immense space. "Shit," she decided, jingling her keys and flicking on the flashlight attached to them; a thin beam of light picked out the edges of the machinery, gouged and piled along the far wall. "Good thing you didn't try to come in on that side."

A tiny sliver of glass had healed inside Daniel's hand.

"There's stairs," said Sybil.

On the second level, the ground was dry, and about three-quarters filled with rotting and filthy office furniture, piled as haphazardly as the machinery downstairs. "Hello, ratsie," Sybil called fondly to a scurrying form, startled by the light of her flashlight. "Look, Daniel, built-in pets."

Daniel pulled a chair from the pile and sat on it. The glass would grow out by morning, but in the meantime, it itched like the devil. "Sybil, have you got a knife?" he asked.

"Yeah."

"I thought you might." He smiled at her chasing the rats with the flashlight's beam. "Let me see it. I got some glass in my hand."

She came over to him, aiming the flashlight at his feet and then at his outstretched hand. The glass splinter wasn't visible on the surface, but the purple angry flesh around it, and the niggling pain, told him exactly where it was. "Jesus," she said, taking a folding knife from her pocket. "Does it hurt?"

The tiny blade of the knife was dull. "Not as much as this does," Daniel murmured, sliding the point well into the flesh. "This is the mount of Mars," he continued, "and as you can see, it's extra meaty . . . which means that I have great warlike passions." He only cut skin away, but an inch of epidermis, oozing plum-colored blood, looked and felt like acres. Daniel dropped the already dry and crackling skin onto the floor, raising a cloud of microscopic dust.

Sybil looked at it, and poked at it with her toe. The skin crumbled into dark flakes.

"Trust you to run away from civilization," he grunted to her, licking the raw meat on his palm with just the tip of his tongue. "Nice place you got here."

She squeezed into the chair with him and curled against his warmth, shivering. "You know what, I'm going to sleep now," she said.

"Is that so? Don't you want to try going back to the car?"

"I wouldn't trust it. Those cops are gonna be there a while. If they shot that guy, expect even more cops." She gazed adoringly at his wound, sealing itself over with a gleaming film of dark blood. "Can I kiss it better?"

"No," he said. "You can't. Don't ever touch my blood unless you feel like becoming a vampire. Whatever you do, don't ever let it touch your mouth or your eyes or anything else where there's no skin. It'll eat your skin away, too, but it's not too bad when your skin gets a scar. It's not so nice when it's your eye."

"Good to know," she said. "I'm glad your sperm isn't like that." She put her arms around him and rested her face against the dry place under his arm.

With his good hand, he stroked her crackly bleached hair. "You just killed an innocent man in cold blood," he whispered.

"Yes, I did," she said. She snuggled closer to him, breathing down the neck of his coat.

"You realize you're in it now. There's no going back. There's no un-killing. And you'll probably have to keep doing it."

"Yes, I do."

"You'll think about it for the rest of your life."

"I feel better about Sonic Ruth, though," she said.

"You do?"

"It doesn't make me sick to think about it anymore. That was so much at a distance. I didn't kill her, the train did; I just made it possible for the train to kill her."

"So are you saying you didn't kill Andrew? That the bottle killed him?"

"No," she said with a faint laugh. "No, I killed him. I killed him for you." She hugged him tighter.

"You didn't have to do that," Daniel said, kissing her forehead. "I can kill people all by myself."

"I wanted to," she said. "I'm glad it helped you, but that wasn't it."

He sighed and shook his head.

"I saw her face," she said. "Sonic Ruth's. Instead of his. Made it easier. I could kill her over and over again and not feel anything."

Her body swelled and warmed for a second, shivering, then relaxed and collapsed back in on itself. "This place is perfect. We're going to die here," she murmured sleepily.

Daniel laughed faintly. "We aren't going to die here," he said. "We're not going to die. I'm not, anyway."

Her eyes opened a fraction, then closed again. "You're not going to die at all," she said.

"No, I'm not going to die at all," he agreed.

Scene Eighteen: The Beautiful Warehouse That Burned

Daniel woke to a strong smell of butane and Sybil's astonished face, ten inches away from his eyes. He stretched stiffly for a moment before he realized with a shock what she had been looking at. She had seen him asleep, withered and hideous; she had seen his flesh become sentient again, going back to the same features as on the day he ceased to be human, one cell at a time perfectly recalling an April night in 1930. Something like a genuine miracle. He sprung to the opposite end of the moth-eaten chaise longue from where she sat, facing him on the floor, and now shaking her head.

"Oh, my God. I can't believe it," she said. "You came back to life. I watched you come back to life. 'Cos, dude, you were dead. I would swear it. I mean . . ."

Pain gnashed his foot, first dully, then with a stabbing, tearing intensity. He brought it out from underneath him to find his left-most toe missing, and a spurting stump in its place, twitching as the muscles of his foot tried to wiggle flesh that was no longer there. He stared up accusingly at Sybil. She shrugged.

"I thought you were dead," she said. "I did that at least an hour ago. You didn't breathe, you didn't move. . . . You didn't even bleed." She stared interestedly at the wound. "Is your blood really *black*"

Daniel applied pressure, clasping both hands around the end of his foot. Immediately the cascade of blood stopped. "Great; now I can't walk for hours," he grumbled, secretly grateful that she had stopped with a toe.

He had set his sweater aside, draping it over a chair to dry before falling asleep, he remembered that; but where had the sweater gone? He could handle cold without ill effects, but that didn't mean he liked being cold. All the heat in his body seemed to be concentrated in the phantom where his toe was supposed to be, all but sizzling as blood rushed to it and grew upon itself. He felt the thick slimy clot wriggling between his palms.

Sybil went on, cheerful and oblivious. "That's fine. We're fine in here. You don't have to go anywhere. The snow is getting totally deep, but there's almost no wind coming in. We get some space heaters up in this shit, we are set."

Daniel glanced around him at the blanketing gloom, then risked a glance at his watch. It was three in the afternoon, though by the light, it might have been three in the morning. "Set for what?" he demanded. "Are you abandoning the studio so soon? And I thought you were so comfortable there."

Sybil stood up and put her hands on her hips. She wore a different set of leggings—white and thickly woven. "Why do you even pretend to understand me? The studio is good in that I don't feel like I'm going to get shot and I can work there, but this is—this is a *place.*" She went to the railing of the stairs leading down to the ground level and leaned over it like a long movie cruise-ship farewell, one booted foot held daintily off the floor. "We can work on this without distractions."

"We?" said Daniel.

"Yeah, we," she said, looking over her shoulder. The daintily raised combat boot flopped back onto the floor with a faint puff of dust. "You're inspiration. You're subject." She gazed back down at her repulsive palace. "You come back from the dead."

"I do it every day," said Daniel.

She put her head between her hands, crushing her snowflake hair. "You don't know how amazing that is. You've totally forgotten."

Daniel, putting his weight on his right foot, half-hopped, half-hobbled over to her. "I can buy it, I suppose," he mused, taking one of her wrists in his blood-blackened hand.

"Nobody can know," she said to the room. She turned toward him and kissed the corners of his mouth, her eyes mostly closed and dreamy. "Secret. Like everything. It's easier."

"Easier for you, maybe," he said. He changed the kiss.

"Sorry about your toe," she said. "I've got it around here somewhere—can you maybe just stick it back on?"

"I have to grow a new one. Sorry. But thanks." The scent of her unwashed ears generated something within him that made the pain melt away.

"You grow new ones? Like a lizard?!"

"Sort of like," he said.

"Sweet! Can I cut off your head?"

"I'm fairly sure that kills the patient."

She arched her eyebrow at him, then spun away from him down the crumbling concrete steps, some of them still showing traces of blackened linoleum. "Once upon a time, there was a beautiful warehouse, full of hopes and dreams and money." Her voice rose up as she descended. "A lady with cat-eye glasses answered the newfangled telephone machine, and big tough guys named . . . um . . . Jett and Rhett and Vinnie . . . moved furniture in and out, in and out, every day except for Sunday, and on Sunday, Vinnie and the lady with the cat-eye glasses come to the beautiful warehouse to fuck each other, because they're married to other people. The lady likes the guy named Vinnie because he reminds her of her father. The little girl sits on Daddy's lap and he gives her a little ride." At the landing at the base of the stairs, she turned back to Daniel and smiled. "And every time, after they fuck, they share a cigarette. Because it's traditional—no, ritualistic. And one day . . . they fall asleep."

To one side of the room rested a pile made up of Daniel's boots, his sweater, Sybil's gloves, and the velour leggings, glinting attractively from underneath. Sybil approached the pile and lit a match. "And the place goes up," she declared, flinging the match and covering her face with the other arm.

The pile ruptured into flames, but not as violently as Daniel had expected, watching her hide her eyes like that. He couldn't imagine that a blaze existed that Sybil wouldn't stare full into. She staggered back and crowed happily, clapped her hands, pumped her fist in the air.

"Why are you burning my sweater?" Daniel asked.

"It's bloody," she called up. "Your boots are bloody. My legs got bloody. I'm burning the shit. I bring a bottle of butane with me everywhere I go, just in case I need to set something on fire. Y'know, get rid of it. Permanently."

"Oh, suddenly you've got the instincts of a seasoned killer." Daniel rested back on the chaise, holding his foot above the level of his heart. Already the toe was closing up and itching as new skin cells remembered themselves into being. "Perhaps you should have thought of that before slitting a man's throat in an alley."

Sybil stomped back to the second level, her cheeks almost orange with fury. "What the fuck are you talking about? What other way to kill is there?"

Daniel sighed. "Subtlety," he said. "Subtlety, my child. It saves a lot of time."

"Don't fucking call me your child, I'm not anybody's child. You do it your way, I'll do it mine."

"Do you particularly want to go to jail?" he asked. "You're heading there at a breakneck pace, *liebschen.*"

"And how do you stay out of trouble? And just how would you have handled last night?"

"I stay out of trouble by confusing people's minds," Daniel said. "I encourage them to forget. My secret super powers, remember? And if I'm going to kill someone and make a mess, I do it someplace where I can damned well wash up afterwards. I can't go losing sweaters every single night just because it's too much trouble to get a fucking room."

He paused and winced as the new, stiff toe-phalange cut through the thin tissues still growing over it. How can such a tiny bone cause so much pain? "Ow, Jesus fuck—Sybil, this is too dangerous. I don't want either one of us to get caught."

"Then why'd you toss Andrew in the Dumpster?" she countered. "You know they'll find him."

Daniel paused for a moment to compose his thoughts. "It was the only thing to do, in that situation," he said. "With his throat cut, he'd be terribly messy and obvious to move."

"But would you?" Downstairs, the fire spat, perhaps a button snapping. The flames gave off a wretched smell of cooking leather and melting acrylic. "Would you have moved the body, if you could?" When Sybil stood closer, her legs at eye level with Daniel and backlit by the fire-glow, he could see that what he had thought to be white leggings were, in reality, long-john underwear. They held the scent of her genitals, the sweat from her pubis, the faint tang of moisture from her vagina itself. Daniel closed his eyes and opened his mouth, to improve his smell by tasting the air along with it.

"Yes, I would have moved him," he said softly. "I would have found him somewhere else, farther away. I wouldn't have done him in public; I would have followed him home, which was my original plan, and told him a little good-night bedtime story and sent him off to sleep. Then again, I don't know. Sometimes I'm sick of being wise and discreet."

"This neighborhood gives me a feeling like corpses," said Sybil. "Probably because I've left so many here."

"What, all two of them?"

She laughed dismissively out of the side of her mouth.

"I brought a body to this neighborhood," he continued, relaxing completely so that his blood, his energy, would be used making that toe. "The first night I ever saw you."

Sybil blinked. "Really?"

"She was a whore. Remember Angelika? Or maybe Jane?"

"Oh . . . so *that's* what happened to her. She was so annoying."

"It was an accident. If she hadn't been so stupid, she'd still be alive."

"What did she do?"

"She bit me," said Daniel, not without some satisfaction, only compounded by the way Sybil dropped her eyes to the ground and shuffled her boots. "So when can we get out of here?"

"You want to walk it? Snow's about eighteen inches deep and I bet there's ice under that."

Daniel frowned.

"I didn't think so. So in that case, we wait for the snowplows. I heard them a couple of streets over a little while ago. Once they've gone past here, I say you use that precious little cell phone of yours and call us a taxi. Have the taxi meet *me* outside the subway station. I come over here and pick you up on the next block over—sorry, but you will have to walk that far."

"Can't it wait? Right now the flesh on it is like jelly."

"All right, I'll take the taxi to the studio. I get out of the taxi, then get another taxi to come and get you."

Daniel sighed.

"Look, I have some spare socks you can have. If you're careful, nobody will even notice you don't have any shoes on." She shook a plump black ball out of a pocket of her coat and shook out two approximations of human feet. He slid one sock on to his right foot, and it left a centimeter of white skin visible at his leather hem. "Or," Sybil pointed out, bisecting another of his sighs, "you can just stay here and feel crappy until the sun goes nova. I know you really want a bath and to shave your legs or whatever. But I *have* to get back to the studio so I can get all my stuff."

"You're serious about living here?"

"I have never been so serious in all my life," she said. "Don't you feel it?"

He tried to lift his head, but with half the blood in his

body down below his left ankle, it was just too much effort. "I'm sorry—all I feel right now is how much my foot hurts. Please don't cut off any more toes or fingers, and don't stab me, or stake me—it doesn't kill me; all it does is either make me angry or make me whine. I just got staked not too long ago . . ."

"No shit! When?"

"In Portland."

"For real? You ran into vampire hunters?"

Daniel smiled. "It's a really long story," he said.

She fluttered her eyelashes, coming across less as a femme fatale than someone in the grip of a mild epileptic seizure, and licked her smiling lips. "Well, I don't hear the snowplows yet." She came back and straddled him where he lay, gently gripping his waist with her thighs. "Get telling, Niner."

Scene Nineteen: Curiosity/ Jealousy

Daniel got back to his flat in a taxi, had a bath, and shaved his legs. His toe grew back, albeit stunted and sore and without the thick curved claw that ended every other one. A twenty-seven-year-old dot-com delivery service boy died of a stroke, slumped over the steering wheel of his van on his way back to the shipping warehouse. Daniel sent six more home with nothing more than a general sensation of light-headedness, which might have been attributed to the wicked joints with which Mr. Blum tipped. He was a popular customer.

The car hadn't been damaged by police or criminals any more than a few head-sized dents and scratches on the paint job; if there had been bloodshed, the snow hid or washed it away.

Jackie Cundera called from Portland to tell him about the opening of the show. Mostly she gushed about the Japanese man's installations—walk-in freezers full of beaded mannequins—but when he asked if any of his pieces had sold, she gently reminded him that the show would be going on until February. "Portland art consumers are a cautious bunch," she said. "It's like they comparison-shop . . . they come in and look, and only later do they make the investment. You could always consider lowering your prices."

Sybil and the assistants finished the evil jungle gym and then threw a party underneath it, the club kids and art queens gathered in a throbbing, shouting mass. Daniel watched impassively from one end of the room, and Sybil the other. At some point in the evening, someone tried to light a pipe and caught the nearest canvas triangle, heavy with tempera and oil, aflame. Instantly, the bobbing of dancing and conversation became the boiling of panic; the drunk people forgot which end you could crawl out of and crushed themselves away from the smoker and his flaming arm and collar. Joachim, dashing out of the bathroom with his baggy pants falling around his knees, fumbled with a chemical fire extinguisher; after five precious seconds of struggle, he ejaculated a thick white plume of anti-incendiary powder over the fire and metal tubes and coruscating disco lights and sparkling, shrieking disco people. As the chaos cooled itself, you could hear Sybil bellowing laughter, galloping down the stairs.

After that, Daniel's assistants couldn't get Sybil out of the studio fast enough.

Two evenings after the party, Daniel climbed out of a taxi in front of a chic little créperie a few blocks away from the newly adopted warehouse. The restaurant stood in polished incongruity in the general desolation of this little slice of Brooklyn, locally known as DUMBO (its absurdly twee name an anagram of its geophysical being, Down Under Manhattan Bridge Overpass). DUMBO could be called a "neighborhood," but that word implies the presence of neighbors, humanity strangely lacking in this colorless, industrial-warehouse limbo. The créperie's only tidy new companion, a brilliantly gleaming bank tower with an emerald-green clock at its apex, rose inappropriately a few blocks of mangled concrete away. The fact that the clock was always on time dismayed Daniel. The time of day had no place here; it should be stuck in an imaginary time, always 4:12 perhaps, a slo-mo landscape under the unseeing Cyclops eye of a senile colossus who has forgotten how or what to count.

Daniel had to admit that this part of New York was suited to him. A large part of why he loved Hollywood so much was its atmosphere of decay, how the wind scoured the bones of dreams, how there was just *nobody* around. DUMBO felt the same, only far more intensely. Ten streets away, or four thousand feet across the river, hundreds of groceries, delicatessens, movie theaters, and shoe shops brought New York's mass of humanity again, but here (even the créperie seemed a very realistic painting of an empty restaurant with the waitresses sprawled napping), he heard only his own footsteps.

This impression increased as he approached the warehouse. Nothing had been touched, it seemed, since the snowplows went through a week earlier. Hard ravines of sooty, gravel-choked solid-frozen snow grew on every street and peaked into plowed drifts at Daniel's eye level. At the warehouse, dark footprints danced around the rutted tracks of a shopping cart.

Daniel knocked on the locked door. A liquid rustling came from inside, and the mailbox lid lifted a few inches. A scarred white hand, with a pistol gripped in its fingers, thrust out. "Go the fuck away." A white thumb with paint-stained, stunted nail cocked the hammer.

"Go ahead and shoot," Daniel grunted impatiently. "It's cold out here."

The hand and gun withdrew, and through the mailbox slit Daniel saw a strip of dirty face and two suspicious gray eyes. "Coast clear?"

"There's nobody."

The dead bolt screeched, and the door opened a crack.

Daniel slid inside, catching a curtain of heavy black polyvinyl tarp on his shoulder. He shut and locked the door behind him. "So how am I supposed to get in when you're not here? Are there keys?" Daniel called, lifting the tarp over his head. "You should make a peephole in the—God in heaven, Sybil!"

The smell of burning plastic remained but had been

joined by a miasma of different kinds of incense—frankincense bullying the others onto the edges of his perception. Most of the ruined furniture from the upper level, cushions ripped off, had been moved down to the ground floor. In the middle of the warehouse floor, two long tables formed a *V*. The chair frames, arranged in a semicircle around the twisted studio lamp with the 200-watt bulb, served as easels for a score of canvases in various stages of completion, but fairly well sketched out in charcoal or pastel or crayon. The broken window had been covered with more black polyvinyl, nailed tightly in place. All the broken glass and chunks of burnt and ripped wood had been swept into a terrible pile against the wall under the window where he'd first entered, just out of reach of a glowing industrial space heater, looming behind a ratty old box fan. A massive boom box played frenetic punk music. Dozens of lit, scented candles addled Daniel's senses even more. Sybil walked around the edges of her palace, dressed in baggy olive-drab cutoffs that came past her knees, white long underwear, and several layers of sweatshirts, swinging a brass censer foaming with heavy, funereal smoke.

"So when are you moving in?" she asked.

Daniel sat on the second-to-last step leading upstairs. Just perceptible underneath the clobbering frankincense, her smell intrigued him, made his thoughts tangle, and his response come only after a long, strange pause. "I, uh, inquired about the building since I saw you last," he said, running his hand through his hair. "It's zoned for development next year. Most likely the city will demolish it and put up something else."

"Does anybody own it?" She kept walking around the perimeter away from him.

"Not at the moment. They want ten million dollars for it."

"What? C'mon!"

"I told you, it's zoned for development. Next month that price will be double. All of this is going away." He waved his arm.

"Don't you *have* ten million dollars?" she groused.

"Yes, I *have* about ten million dollars." He sighed. "And I can't get to more than a couple of hundred thousand at a time. It's all tied up in investments."

"Investments? What, for your *retirement* plan?" She swung the censer in a vicious loop beside her. "So when you get old, you can buy an RV and move to Florida to spend the rest of your mature years in sunshine and diapers? What the hell is wrong with you? Fuck, dude, spend it. Who the fuck knows whether or not you'll still be alive next year or in six months or tomorrow?" The censer seemed to gasp for breath, then, as it came to a halt at her side, belched out a cloud of white fleecy smoke. "Anyway."

Daniel rolled his eyes to indicate a change of subject. "Checked out any videos lately?" he asked.

She stood still, smiled and laughed faintly. "They found the guy."

"Oh?"

"He was already in the garbage truck at that point. There were two cop cars and an ambulance. Nobody saw me."

"So that's all right then," said Daniel. "Now we pray that the gods of hairs and fibers are on our side. And what's with the gun? I thought you hated guns."

Sybil looked at the gun tucked into the waistband of her shorts. "It's a prop gun. It's not even loaded with blanks. Your photo assistant Josephine gave it to me. She used to use it to freak out muggers, except one day some crackhead called her bluff, mugged her, and beat her up. Now she's got a real one. Y'know, I suggest you don't try to bite *her*."

"Well, there goes my weekend."

"I want to do it again," said Sybil.

He didn't need to ask her what *it* meant. His heart constricted sharply with lust and hunger, remembering the thin crimson fan that spread from Andrew's neck, steaming into the cold alley air. "My way, this time, please? I hate cops."

She snapped her tongue dismissively. "I've seen it your way."

"I have many ways." Daniel walked forward into the crescent of canvases. "What are you working on?"

"I can't tell you. I don't know. I just keep . . . starting over." She resumed her circuit, swinging. "I can't figure it out. I'm kind of almost blocked. I'm too busy thinking about those people out there."

"Don't think about them," said Daniel. "I don't."

"Are you making anything right now?"

"I'm sketching, same as you." But not at all the same things—while Daniel drew Sybil's hips and toes and her oddly placed teeth, hers were unrecognizable shadows of things, the angles shattering the laws of good composition. "I think about you naked to keep myself company."

"Oh, poor guy. Don't tell me you're doing without."

"I haven't wanted anyone else," he said to himself, then cleared his throat and more forcefully clarified, "I never thought of it. But now that you mention it, Josephine *is* a really attractive girl."

"She's not a girl. She's thirty."

"You're all girls; I'm ninety-seven."

"Have you ever been whipped with an incense burner?" Sybil swung the censer on its chain again, letting it skip across her fingers and blur a golden barrier across her face and chest. "One that's still burning?"

"Why did you sleep with Joachim while I was away?" he demanded flatly.

"It wasn't sleep, and it's not like he was the only one."

"Yes, but why? Why Joachim?"

"Because he's cute, and he was into it. Why does anybody fuck anybody? Besides, you fucked someone else within, like, forty-eight hours of taking my virginity—why do you wanna know? What does it mean to you?"

"Curiosity. Jealousy." He shook his head, shrugged, smiled. "The great problem of mankind—wanting to have your cake and eat it, too."

"Why don't you ask them why *they* had sex with *me*," she said. "When they knew they were risking pissing you off, losing their jobs, or worse—they knew how you feel about me. And if you think they don't know what you are, you're sadly, sadly mistaken."

"What?"

"They know. They just can't put a word to it. They can't say it. I was like 'vuh-vuh-c'mon, you can do it' . . ." She laughed.

"*Scheisse—!* Why? Do you want me exposed? Do you want me killed?" Daniel flashed to her and tore the censer from her hand, sending it skittering and smoking into the corner. Her eyes widened and she blocked off her face with hands blade-curved, ready to chop or gouge. Daniel noted her stance and forced himself to relax and open out his hands. *Diplomacy,* he thought.

"Who wants who killed?" she bit out, taking a step back but keeping her hands hard. "I was just trying to find some things out. I have the right to do that. And I found out that they know pretty much exactly what you are, but they just can't say it. It's literally like their tongues get paralyzed when they try to say 'vampire.' Like their minds go blank. So whatever you did to them, it works, kind of. They know and they just don't worry and they just kind of take it for granted. It's just not really happening in the foreground. It's like something they saw on TV."

She fell silent, picked up a stub of broken crayon, and added a few strokes to one of the canvases.

Daniel glancingly kissed the nape of her neck. "Don't talk to them about me," he whispered.

"You're not even real," she murmured. "You're a . . . an empty set of clothes. You're a myth. You don't even exist."

"I am real," he insisted. "I'm real to you, aren't I?"

She shook her head slightly and frowned. On the canvas, a set of curved triangles emerged, sails, blades . . . teeth, perhaps. She rubbed at the lines with the side of her hand. "Nothing is real to me," she said.

"Do you want me to leave you alone?" He pressed his teeth against the heavy padding of sweatshirts over her shoulder. "I wanted to spend time with you."

Instead of replying, she reached behind herself with her left hand and grasped his bony hip, pressing him into the plush shelf of her full buttocks. She barely paused in sketching when his chilly hand traversed yards of jersey knit to cup her breast, tugging and straining with the movements of her crayon. "You're cold," she pointed out. "You feel to me like you need blood."

"My way," he repeated.

Sybil stepped away from the canvas (the sails and fangs transformed into a peculiar mongoloid face), away from Daniel. "All right, your way," she agreed. "Let me see how it's done properly, O Mr. Subtlety."

"Come home with me," he said. "You have to change clothes."

Sybil groaned. "Can't we just go someplace cheap?"

"My way."

The woman breathed a faint, sensual sigh as Daniel punctured the tender skin over the crook of her elbow, her heavy head sliding across the frayed leatherette of the backseat, dropping onto Sybil's shoulder. Sybil kissed the woman's open lips, her fingers skimming the pockets of the woman's coat. Daniel opened his eyes, pink with excited capillaries, and shook his head at Sybil. Sybil met his eyes and smiled, holding up a slim billfold with her fingertips.

Daniel let Sybil rob, continuing his meal with the kind of leisure that was so often denied him by his own impatience. He was in no rush to kill the woman, charmed into sharing a taxicab from the airport; he had already brought an older man to the point of cardiac failure on the way there. Sybil had been angry at him for killing the man and sending his dead body back home in the same taxi; the slack smile on the man's face had done nothing for her needs. Sybil wanted to be actively involved.

She gave the glassy-eyed, thought-stilled driver the address of a large parking garage downtown, and she and Daniel and the semiconscious woman got into an elevator to the penultimate floor. "I know this garage well," Sybil said during the lift, staring up into the sputtering overhead light in the fiberglass box. "Sonic Ruth and I came up here on our first day in New York to do drugs.

She sat in that far corner—right there—and shot up a speedball."

The woman glanced around her at the blank, gray, mostly empty floor, eyes unfocused and lids heavy, and said plaintively, "Where am I? What's going on?"

Daniel ran his fingertips over the woman's temples, across pale brown hair darkening and thickening to walnut heat-cured curls. Her eyes bore the faintest suggestions of crow's feet. "Don't be afraid," he said to her, and he knew the knowledge that he was lying would be transmitted to her. The woman let her head droop forward, too tired, too tired to do anything right now . . . but her bladder tight with anxiety.

"She wanted to do one to me, too, but I wouldn't let her." Sybil skipped to the corner in question, then jumped up and down on it.

"Why not?" asked Daniel. "You love drugs."

Sybil pressed her hands against the sides of her head—at the temples, where Daniel had just sent waves of patently false comfort to the woman—tearing at her hair with her fingers. Little clumps of fried blond hair fell fluttering across the toes of her boots. "Because—I knew that if she ever tried to put a needle in my vein, she'd end up breaking it off in there—I just knew she'd do it—I mean, I could see it, I could see it right there—!" Her words cut off into an anguished howl as she stared in panic at her arms, the crook of the elbow where Daniel had just taken blood from the woman.

"Sybil—"

"Do you see her? Do you see her *right fucking there!* With the *needle!* With the *needle!*"

"Sybil, no! There's nothing! I don't see—"

But even as Daniel spoke up, Sybil ran back and ripped the woman from Daniel's arms, holding the sides of the woman's head between her forearms, and threw her to the ground with an almost invisible, vicious twisting. Sybil's feet left the ground, twisting, flying. "Fucking bitch! Fucking bitch!" Her screams sent flecks of spittle flying onto the concrete and her hands had ripped out great chunks of the soft brown hair. She came to a stop on the balls of her feet, gasping, a yard away from where she'd thrown the body.

Daniel crouched at the woman's side. Her mouth and eyes remained open, but her neck flopped broken, and a few last breaths gurgled and bubbled in her throat. Daniel closed her up, dropped a kiss onto her warm hand, where a gold-plated band trapped a finger, already beginning to swell. He lingered on the kiss, puncturing the skin over a prominent vein. She was still good, still warm, and her heart beat gamely on, keeping the circulating blood fresh.

"Don't fucking kiss her!" Sybil yelled, a shrill, tearful wreck.

"You don't know her," Daniel said, folding the limp arm across her chest. He sidestepped over to one of the four cars on the entire floor and leapt up onto its hood, as lightly as a spider, crouching and swaying. His fingers stroked the strings of invisible harps. "I do. She deserves a kiss. She deserves another day."

Sybil stared at the floor, ravaging her fingernails with her teeth. "Leaving. Now."

They ran silently down flights of stairs. Outside, the night city continued on as usual—cars passed and honked, blinking cranes bent over buildings, sparse foot traffic hurried along. "She's a teacher for young children," Daniel said.

Sybil tossed her head. "She's dead." Her voice came out thin and sharp.

"She's married and has two children of her own."

"She's dead. Fuck her."

"Her name is—"

"I said, fuck her. I killed her. She's dead. You didn't give me the autobiography of that asshole we gave a free ride to the airport."

"You mean Arthur Lewbinski," said Daniel.

"Yeah, fuck Arthur Lewbinski. I don't give a fuck about his job or his kids or his dog, and neither does he." Then, "I feel filthy. Let's go walk in the street."

At first there wasn't much of a problem, as a center median gave them something to walk on, but the median vanished after four blocks, and the two of them, Sybil first and then Daniel, ritualistically toed the double yellow line. The blaring of warning car horns wove a constant backdrop, and Daniel swayed slightly, his ears finding a stark beauty in the atonal, arrhythmic sound that penetrated his flesh and ricocheted from his bones.

In front of him, a clumsy car fender clipped Sybil's leg and ripped the hem of the borrowed black cocktail dress. Daniel had to look behind him to see Sybil tearing down the road after the car, flinging herself onto the back, hammering the fiberglass trunk with her fists.

The car skidded sideways to a halt. Sybil slid off onto the street. Daniel rushed to where she sprawled, and a car approaching in the other lane bumped Daniel in the thighs and shins as it didn't brake quite soon enough.

Sybil picked herself up and kicked the license plate until she had left a good solid impression of the steel toe of her boot, screaming obscenities. Daniel clasped his arms around her waist and ran, carrying her, through two more lanes of swerving oncoming traffic, to the curb, across an alley, to the next street. He propped Sybil against a building and bent over to gulp some oxygen to feed his aching muscles.

Sybil laughed as soon as she had her breath back. "Did you see what that asshole did to your dress?"

"You're bleeding," Daniel said.

She lifted the ragged hem and glanced at her leg, the black stocking ripped, a great nasty tear marring the skin of her calf. "Holy shit. It didn't feel like it was that bad."

"Do you want to go to the hospital? I think that could use some stitches." Recovering, he stood between the row of parked cars to hail a taxi.

"No, I don't want to go to the hospital. They'd want to know how I got it. Got any Super Glue at home?"

In Daniel's bathroom, Daniel irrigated the wound with a needleless syringe full of expensive European drinking water, then carefully held the edges of the torn skin together, surreptitiously licking his fingers before and after he did so. He didn't trust Super Glue's healing powers, but he knew what even a little of his saliva on a wound could do. Sybil paused in gulping down Valium tablets long enough to say, "Now I feel clean."

"You're dangerously insane," said Daniel. He wrapped clean gauze around her leg, fastening it with an inch of black electrical tape. "I won't save you next time."

"I didn't ask you to save me this time." She set down her water glass, slid off the edge of the bathtub, and gingerly slid on her baggy shorts. "Don't save me. I won't save you. God, Daniel, *live* a little once in a while, would you?"

"Live?" he echoed, chuckling mirthlessly. Daniel cut off another, longer strip of electrical tape and wrapped it across his wrist in a bracelet. "Was that the first of your performances?" he asked.

"Far from it," she said. "Far from the first." She caressed the purplish-green bruises on his legs, already several shades improved just in the last few minutes. "Just the first one with you."

"Just let me know next time, OK?"

"No, I won't let you know. You have to be with me. We have to think together as a single aesthetic mind."

"And how are we supposed to do that, when you don't let me have access to yours?"

"The same way musicians have since the dawn of fuckin' time, man . . . instinct. Pure instinct. And knowledge. And intuition. You're cheating. You've been cheating all along. Regular normal human people can do what you do without having any damn super powers. Why don't you learn to know me without having everything instantaneously spelled out for you?"

"I can't," he said. "You're too obscure."

"I'm not," she defied, shaking her head. "I'm not. I think you can do it. And if you can't . . . huh . . . well, I'm sorry I wasted your time."

"You'd never be sorry to waste anyone's time, let alone mine." Daniel stood up and tore away from her soft fingertips on his throbbing injuries. "You're an evil little bitch who wants more than anything else to see me destroyed. I'm going to have to keep an eye on you to make sure you don't strap explosives onto me while I sleep.

You're like the worst kind of immoral little boy, pulling the wings off flies . . . being cruel to kittens."

Sybil sat quiet. Daniel had expected any other response than that, and he chewed his bottom lip with his fang. When she finally spoke, she said, "Would it make you happy to drink my blood?"

"I never asked to drink your blood."

"You don't have to ask."

"Why do you want me to be happy?"

"I didn't say I did."

"But you do."

Sybil again made no reply.

Daniel sighed. "I'm in love with you," he said ruefully, not looking at her. "When I'm with you, I don't feel happy. I feel really confused. I should hate you. I should want you killed. But when I'm not with you, I feel like some part of my body has been shut off. But I know you hate me."

"I hate everything." She shrugged. "I hate everything that's real, let's put it that way. But you don't really exist, so I can't hate you." She took his hand and squeezed his palm between her thumb and forefinger. "C'mon back to the warehouse with me. Bring as much stuff as you can carry. *I* want you to be there."

She kissed him. He thought of his immense soft bed, the linens washed with essence of lily of the valley, the slice of soft yellow-green light from the fixture under the bedside table, his plush chairs in the study; and he caressed the satiny slopes of her ribs and belly under five layers of sweatshirt, felt dizzy, bound by her rich, intricate scent and the pillows of her lips.

A fourth taxi for the evening returned them to the vicinity of the warehouse. Sybil ran for the shopping cart to transport Daniel's suitcases and heavy wad of lily-scented bedcovers. Daniel stood and waited for the clattering sound of her return, and stared into the crêperie, just now closing for the night at 1 A.M., the sleek waitress covering her yawns with the back of her hand. The late-night dishwasher, an equally stunning young man, came out front to joke with the young woman, and their faces stretched in silent laughter. They couldn't see Daniel out on the road with a seventy-pound suitcase full of leather and his bedclothes bundled over his shoulder like an obese, floppy corpse, staring in like a starving waif at their carefree, beautiful, French young lives. Their lives had no aspect of terror or self-loathing or immobilizing depression; they were youthful, sexy, and in New York, America's nexus of possibilities. They didn't even have to work, it seemed; they didn't seem perturbed by their perennial lack of patrons. Under simple and tasteful clothes, their buttocks and backs shifted like pert dunes. Perhaps they were only waiting.

He thought of it again—*a suit of empty clothes.*

In the warehouse, Sybil lit more incense and candles around the perimeters of the room, put dub reggae music on the boom box at low volume, and carried the bundle of blankets upstairs. What she had been sleeping on, apparently, were cast-off futons and mattresses, these in substantially better condition than the one she'd had before, up a few inches from the floor on industrial wooden pallets and covered with piles of her clothes and a sleeping bag. She kicked the clothes onto the floor and spread the sheets and the goosedown comforter over the mattresses, then added the sleeping bag. "That might be warm enough," she said. There was another space heater on the second level, and Sybil turned it up full blast. "You think it's cold at midnight, you just wait till five in the morning. . . ."

At five in the morning, they were still fucking, albeit without quite as much intensity as that which had taken place in previous hours, and had long since shifted aside the sleeping bag. Sybil lay in prayer position, kneeling with her face over the side and her knees tucked under her arms, and Daniel, behind her, kept up the regular hip-and-back tempo, inhaling in, exhaling out, that had hypnotized him and brought a comfortable peace of not-thinking. He felt invigorated rather than tired, but he could tell that she was fading beneath him; full of pills, her formerly tense arms lay softly relaxed at her sides, her breath coming in slow deep moans. At once she clenched her back muscles and grunted. "Daniel . . . stop now, please," she whispered; he sighed heavily, put-upon, and did as she commanded.

"Are you *well* done?" he asked, lying next to her on his belly. He rubbed his slickened penis against the sheets until the skin hurt. Sweat poured from the hollows of his back and armpits, rolling ticklish over his ribs.

"Can't you tell?" She rolled over onto her back and slid her hands down her torso and between her legs. "I'm sore." Her fingers searched among the heavy, ravaged petals of flesh and came away with a dark stain. "Fuck. That's what I thought. I'm surprised you couldn't smell it."

Daniel involuntarily licked his dry lips. "Oh, I could," he said. "I was going to fuck you first, though."

She sighed languorously. "Have at it," she murmured, too tired even to snicker. "I'm gonna go to sleep."

"Good luck," said Daniel.

He lay beside her and stroked her belly with the tips of his claws, breathing on her swollen and glistening vulva, and she let her legs relax, unbent and slightly open. For a while she ran her fingers over his scalp. "I hope it helps you," she whispered.

With a few minute twitches of her legs, she slipped out of consciousness. Daniel pulled himself forward a few inches and slipped her sex a tentative French kiss.

She had fallen asleep thinking of the first orgasm she had ever had, trying to remember exactly what it felt like, if it was anything like the ones she had with Daniel. Exactly two people in the history of mankind had brought Sybil to orgasm—Daniel and herself. But her first one—the guy—what was his name?—who had tried to rape her when she was passed out drunk at a party in Sonic Ruth's parents' den, and the look on his face after she'd cracked his skull, as precious to her as any lover's astonished, post-ecstasy expression. At first she hadn't known what was going on, with his hands all over her and his sticky beer lips on her face, and her body responded the only way a wildly hormonal fifteen-year-old's could; her panties got wet underneath the stupid plaid skirt that was too small for her. But the jerk had taken it a step too far by sticking his fingers into her slippery, tight crevice, hurting enough to break her out of her stupor and take a good look at the stoner creep, with his sleazy downy mustache and a tooth that had gone bad in his grimace. He was wearing a Grateful Dead T-shirt and Sybil yelled "Is this what you assholes *do* at Dead shows?" And the abrupt gasp of pleasure that went through her as she slammed his head backward into an oak-veneer entertainment center—she didn't even know what it was, that feeling, splitting her wide open like a slaughtered cow, but one filled with iridescent glitter sprinkles that streamed out and seemed to bring the universe joy.

Daniel wiped his tears across her thighs, and in her sleep, Sybil shifted and spoke a nonsense syllable.

She'd spoken to Ruth about it. Everyone knew that she'd sent the guy (his name might have been Dane or Zane or something) to the hospital, but nobody knew what happened to her at the point when she felt bone give way and watched blood gush out and soak the collar of the tie-dyed shirt.

Not like she could tell her mother. Her mother sat at the table in the kitchen at the front of the apartment, sometimes with the blinds cracked or even drawn up, but mostly just sitting there, watching dust collect on the slats and taking pulls on the ever-present bottle of bargain vodka that Sybil's father brought home by the dozen. And then after Dad had gone to jail . . . she had to get out. . . .

Ruth would know. Sonic Ruth knew every disgusting thing about sex there was to know. Sybil decided not to mention that she felt it when she broke that guy's head open, but she described the physical sensation to Ruth in a halting voice.

Ruth became urbane, an imaginary cigarette holder extending her painkiller-languid gestures. "Oh, you had an *orgasm,*" was her reply. "Don't you *masturbate?*" Sybil told her, the words blocking her throat like stones, but determined to be frank, that of course she touched herself, but *that* never happened. "You're doing it wrong," was Ruth's opinion. She took it upon herself to show Sybil how to do it right. After school, still sunlit, early fall, while Sybil was still going to almost every class almost every day, in Ruth's bedroom with the *Goo* poster above Ruth's bed. A line of coke apiece to start. The two of them toyed with their vulvas while looking at each other, and Sonic Ruth provided directions. "Watch this. Do it like this. No, Big Stupid, you're doing it wrong. Jesus, loosen up, do another line." Sybil couldn't come with the sharp pale bird eyes stabbing at her, and the sight of the other girl's dirty little fingers agitating her own genitals, her reddish, fuzzy, and viciously trimmed pubes, made Sybil feel jumbled up and queasy. Sybil snatched her pants and underwear off the floor and sprinted from the room, the dusty mirror, the poster, zipping up as she paused on the second landing down. Ruth had the time it took Sybil to get home timed and memorized; the phone was ringing when Sybil ran panting and sick into the kitchen, past her mom immobile at the table, and on the phone, Ruth yelled that they had to get rid of Sybil's Big Stupid cherry, "But Matt says he wants a threesome, so I told him you would—c'mon back, we're already naked. . . ."

And Sybil threw up in the kitchen sink.

She had fucked Joachim to see if he could make her come. And the next day Sybil had a threesome with Joachim and Josephine, his girlfriend, just to make sure that it was Ruth's pussy that she hated, and not pussy in general, to see if maybe she was just queer and no man would ever work for her. Making out with Josephine while Joachim rubbed massage oil into both of them had been very nice. The two women adored each other's scars, shared long slow champagne-flavored kisses, teased Joachim when he came tumbling and turgid into bed with them. She made Josephine come, she was fairly sure of that; Sybil humming against Josephine's tiny clit, while Joachim wiggled his fingers inside her, seemed to be plenty enough to make her writhe and yell and make terrible faces. And of course Joachim came, repeatedly, making a pile of scummy blond condoms on a towel beside the bed. But Sybil herself was unshaken. It had been a delicious waste of an afternoon and evening; they went out for a late dinner, then stayed up even later smoking pot and making dumb things out of plasticine. Sybil wasn't used to fun with people. It was much easier when the fun was purely sexual, so that conversation wasn't expected. She didn't want to bond with people. She was afraid that she had bonded with Josephine, what with the sex and the gun and all.

Daniel wanted to wake her and remind her of the fire at the studio, of how many of Josephine's friends had had their eyebrows singed off, and female bonding probably wasn't something she should worry about. He let her sleep, rubbing his tongue savoringly against her pink folds, his cheek against the softening stubble growing on her mons.

He had, of course, brought his Hasselblad along in the suitcase full of leather pants, and he sat naked on his heels loading film, studying her position. He decided on a sidelong view, so that she would look, her arms folded slack across her belly and her mouth open to snore, like a freshly washed corpse lying in state.

Scene Twenty: "It Ends in Your Hands"

Daniel awoke every afternoon to the sight of Sybil on the ground floor, bopping around the perimeter of the warehouse, trickling smoke through her nostrils and lips clenched around a cigarette or a joint, or else simply dancing by herself in the huge space, throwing herself about like she had a fever and her body alternately tormented and delighted her. Occasionally she worked on three of the canvases, having viciously destroyed the others, or created potentially lethal sculptures out of wire hangers. Her sculptures were extraordinary, hammered and twisted into and out of shape, occasionally tree- or animal-like but more often the ineffable, each one containing the transmogrified bodies of dozens of hangers. As soon as he was conscious enough to sit up, she would be there, throwing her arms around him, kissing him with her corrosive mouth.

One day he woke up to find her hair light blue.

Daniel's things had been trucked over on the second night; he brought only the important things, leaving most of the furniture, including the leather chairs that

Ricky drove himself to froth over, to the next owner of the flat. His library came in its entirety; mostly, his books were valuable and rare, as well as being books he still cared about and read regularly; first-edition printings of the works of Artaud, Cocteau, Gertrude Stein, Raymond Chandler. Naturally, most of the clothes came as well; the art went into the same storage as he kept his own paintings. Sybil respected all those decisions, especially the clothes—almost everything he owned fit her, but for a few pairs of trousers that were too tight for her muscle-plump thighs. However, she preferred to wear her own things.

Every day the warehouse gained some new addition; a big blue E from the lighted sign from a demolished hotel, a medical blowtorch with portable propane tank, bolts of ugly fabric, stacks of carpet squares, a broken motorized adjustable bed stuck into a knees-to-chest configuration. He could never figure out how she managed to find or retrieve such large objects, and he never asked. The shopping cart outside had bent and warped from the weight of carrying far more than it had been designed to bear.

Immediately upon awakening, Daniel was hungry. Rush hour provided them both with ample opportunities to satisfy themselves. They took the subway into Manhattan, and sometimes Sybil couldn't wait to get there; she stabbed a teenage hood, reeking of Newport smoke, in the kidney with a pen as they stood on a crowded train platform, then pushed him down onto the concrete floor with a nasty snarl of "Don't touch me, you piece of shit!" She lifted up her shirt so that Daniel could fondle her breast in front of a group of fascinated schoolkids in uniform. She put up Ruth's crayon drawings over the advertising placards in the trains with strips of duct tape.

Once across the river, an infinity of possibility awaited them. Sybil demanded food; Daniel demanded style. He spent a lot of blood energy confusing restaurant hosts into finding Sybil elegant and well-heeled as she scratched her pubes through her pants and pulled out broken strands of sky-blue hair.

"I used to be shaved all over," she said to the Japanese maître d', who arched his eyebrows enquiringly. "Sybil the Shaven. I'm not used to having hair."

"Yes? Smoking or non?" the maître d' repeated, smiling.

After the closing of the restaurant, the maître d' wore the same smile as he lay on the floor with Daniel on top of him, holding up his vicious claws. Instead of striking him, Daniel bent his head and bit the man's neck. The maître d's gasp bordered on the orgasmic.

Sybil stood over them, frowning and shaking her head. "That's bullshit," she said.

Daniel paused in drinking to look up at her. "What are you talking about?" He turned back to the Japanese man, eyes rolled back and sighing, murmuring his wife's name. His blood was crisp and smooth, shimmering with the alcohol and scent of expensive Irish whiskey.

"I just disagree with the way you did that," Sybil continued, watching Daniel finish him off. Daniel sat back on his heels and moaned himself, licking his chops like a dog after eating a stick of butter. The maître d' gave one last sigh, his body relaxing limp. "I mean, this guy's Japanese, he's got a strong sense of honor and bravery . . . and you just put him to sleep practically. That's not honor. He should have been spitting in your face."

Sybil helped Daniel to stand, then poked at the corpse with her toe. "I mean, don't you ever want to know what they're actually thinking when they're aware of being killed by a vampire? Don't you ever want any kind of truth?"

Daniel leaned against the front counter and shrugged. "This is truth," he said. "Why should he suffer?"

"He's going to *die,* that's why."

"You insist on violent deaths that hurt, huh?" Daniel tossed her the leather parka.

"Yes," she insisted. "You don't see me putting people to sleep."

Daniel clenched his fists so hard, his claws bent like bamboo in his palms. "People suffer all the time. And I've had more of what people were thinking while being killed by a vampire than you can ever, in your tiny little short life, imagine. You have no idea the things I've seen. At best, you've seen it on TV, and you can't smell what it smells like when hundreds of people die all at the same time. On top of you and surrounding you. All of their bodies being crushed and ripped apart. Nothing is worse than the smell. Fuck honor."

He bolted from the restaurant, rushing home, but he wasn't sure where that could possibly be. The calm, delicate, carnal thoughts of the maître d' in his last moments on earth (the wedding party in the hotel ballroom, the view of Fujiyama, even that singer's bad Frank Sinatra impersonation wonderful, dancing with Yuko, his arm around her waist, the fresh cherry blossoms on her veil falling apart, showering his face with petals; her soft mouth on his neck, her hard sharp gentle teeth on his skin) evaporated before the heat of Daniel's panic.

What could be home now? A safe place, away from Sybil? Home is where you hide.

Daniel ducked into an all-night coffee shop to have some time to think. The place was well-populated at midnight, mostly full of off-duty waiters and the theater crew. Daniel sat at a tiny corner booth, took a paper napkin from the dispenser and etched its arid whitish surface with the point of a toothpick. He had lost track of how many killings they'd done in the last two weeks, and she had the nerve to criticize the way he did it? Like his life was an exam and he could do it incorrectly?

Suffering . . . Terror, certainly; terror was simply delicious, a flavor on his tongue, but torture was not his style . . . or it hadn't been since he was much younger. But suffering . . . how much suffering had he insisted on? When he was a child, he'd held a smaller boy's head under water in a muddy puddle on the edge of the schoolyard, in a deep pit cratered from the last war's bombing, until the boy stopped moving. The boy had called Daniel's father a filthy Christ-killing Jew, and Daniel had laughed it off until he noticed that nobody else was laughing, that all the other boys were standing staring at him or staring at snow and rocks on the ground.

"Hey, Daniel."

Daniel glanced up from the napkin-littered tabletop to see Joachim standing there, awkwardly twisting on the toes of the handsome cowboy boots that Daniel had bought him for a birthday present. "Joachim." Daniel smiled, voice thick with gratitude. "Please, sit down."

"No, I-I can't. I'm here with some friends of mine." He glanced over his shoulder at a black-clad gaggle of pretty girls—fashion students, no doubt. "I was wondering how you were."

Daniel shrugged, not smiling anymore.

"I guess you moved—your old home phone number doesn't work at all now."

"Yeah," said Daniel.

Joachim blinked slowly, waiting for further elaboration, and when none came shoved his hands into the pockets of his baggy fleece jacket. "So, uh, where's your new place?"

Daniel smiled slightly, looked into Joachim's eyes, and stroked the back of his neck under his loose black hair. Joachim laughed, embarrassed but reassured. Daniel said, "How is the studio?"

"It's almost back to normal. The fire wasn't too bad."

"I'm selling it," Daniel said.

Joachim's eyebrows shot up. "What? When? What are we going to do?"

"I don't need it anymore . . . my work has changed direction. It will be sold as soon as a buyer is found. I'm going to contact my broker after the first of the year." Daniel slowly tore another napkin in half, then in half again. "And what *you're* going to do is get other jobs."

"I can't get another job," Joachim blustered.

Daniel arched his eyebrow indignantly. "Excuse me, what? Why don't you take up some of those offers you turned down when you were working for me? Gilbert and Waite would cream their jeans to get you on some of their campaigns. Not to mention the fact that you still want to work with Jeff Koons. My God. You'll be fine."

"What happened?" Joachim slid into the other side of

the booth, as Daniel had wanted him to in the first place. "This is all about Sybil, isn't it?"

Daniel curled his lip. "It's *all* all about Sybil."

"I never meant to hurt you," said Joachim grimly.

"Oh, now—"

"No, really. She swore up and down that you two weren't . . . and she was just . . ."

"No, no, no." Daniel shook his head. "No. That's not what I mean. I don't care—you can fuck Sybil tomorrow if you want to. If she'd let you—"

"I never should have; but Josie—"

"Joachim, shut up. I just told you that isn't the issue. But I guess it is, as far as you're concerned, isn't it?" Daniel tossed the napkin fragments into the air. "Oh, Joachim. You're a *good* person."

"No, I'm not; really, I'm not." Joachim nervously patted his coat, looked up to see the cigarette that Daniel offered. Once the cigarette was lit, Joachim used its smoke as a shield. "I really miss you. We all really miss you. I miss your—your—ability to inspire people. I miss the way you get things done and you stay true to your own vision and you don't stoop to compromise—"

"Joachim, please."

Joachim held up his hand. "No, this is honest, really. I've never met anyone like you. I feel very lucky to work with you. I have so much more to learn from you that I could never, never get if I stayed at RISD for a hundred years."

Joachim bit his lip and looked away.

"Joachim," said Daniel slowly, poking an invisible finger between Joachim's averted eyes, "what do you think I am?"

"You're . . . a visionary," said Joachim.

"No, what am I? You, for example, are a human being. What kind of creature am *I?*"

Joachim said nothing, but he looked up, and Daniel saw himself reflected in the dark pools of his eyes, lips bright pink under smudged red-black lipstick. Joachim knew. But he didn't know. But he had to know how Daniel lived, what he lived on, if he knew. . . .

Joachim looked back at the girls sitting at the bar, now glancing down into the coffee shop looking for him. He gazed at Daniel desperately, his mind begging, *Please let me go. You have what you wanted to know.* Like a violent headache, Joachim felt pressure in his ears, fingertips crushing into his skull.

"What are you doing for New Year's?" he asked, his voice light and rational.

"Times Square, of course," said Daniel, glancing away. Across from him, Joachim relaxed. "Why? Are you having a party in the bomb shelter in case the aliens come?"

"That would be too cool," said Joachim with a grin. "No, I am going to a party underground, but we've having dinner and dancing in an old abandoned subway station—Amarantha's setting it up. That's her, right there." He pointed at a scarecrow-y wraith with whitewashed skin and a waterfall of black wavy hair down her back. She waved to Joachim impatiently.

Daniel raised his eyebrows and smiled to himself. "Let me know where you're going to be—perhaps I'll join you for dancing when the Times Square chaos gets to be too much."

"That's fine," said Joachim. "I don't know where it is exactly, but if you have your cell phone, I'll call you when we get there, give you directions. OK?"

"Yes, I'd like that," said Daniel.

"Well, I'd better get back. It's good to see you."

"You'll be fine," Daniel said.

Daniel sipped black coffee. Joachim and the ladies left. Joachim made no attempt to introduce him to the women. Daniel made a nest out of the napkin confetti and stared at it until he decided that a drop of red blood in its center would complete the composition. He tried with a drop of his own blood, but it came out a gloomy purple and dried black as soon as it touched the paper.

"You shouldn't bite yourself."

Sybil slid into the opposite seat, her breath deep from exercise. "How'd you find me?" Daniel asked, cursing whatever part of him that gave him that prickle of happiness when she was nearby.

"Patience," she said. "Legwork."

He sighed. "What did you do with the body?" he asked.

She smiled back at him, her cheeks bright with exertion and cold. "I didn't put him in the Dumpster," she said.

"Was it honorable?" His voice razored quiet and efficient.

"Fuck honor," she replied, yawning and stretching. "It's a corpse. Corpses don't have honor." She rested her warm hand against Daniel's pallid cheek. "Home, darling?"

On the adjustable bed in the warehouse, Sybil stretched out with her arms over the jacked-up edge, watching Daniel pace through her collection of mysterious and significant trash. "What are you doing for New Year's Eve?" he asked her abruptly. "It's soon."

"When is Christmas?"

"Day after tomorrow."

"What are you gonna get me?"

Daniel stared at her coldly. "I've already given you everything," he said.

Her answering smile chilled him with its guilelessness. "Not quite everything," she replied. She pulled at a loose thread on the mattress stitching. Yellow foam poked out in porous carbuncles from several spots where she'd worried it. "I am spending New Year's Eve here," she said, looking up at him again. "Waiting."

"For the aliens?"

"Bring me the bottle of whiskey from upstairs, wouldja?" She sat up and waited for him to return with the bottle. She took it from his outstretched hand delicately, unscrewed the plastic cap, and swallowed a mouthful. "Waiting for the destruction to start," she said. "It'll happen. Sooner or later. A whole world full of people expecting the world to end, for the nukes to come, for the powers that be to screw up in some total and cataclysmic way. Apparently all the computers are going to crash at midnight because they're too stupid to count."

"Why wait here for it?" said Daniel. "Why not meet it head on, in the street? With the rest of the whole world full of people?"

She drank silently for a long while and Daniel, despairing of an answer, began to walk away. When her voice came, it was smaller and scratchier, less certain, less polished. "I want to be alone," she said. "I want to be here . . . creating something."

"Scared?" Daniel accused, but softly.

Her eyes told him what he wanted to know.

"I'm not," he said, lifting his head, addressing the sooty gods of the abandoned warehouse. "It would be ideal, if you ask me. I need to die a violent death. My eyes open. Staring it in the face. Not fighting against it, but rushing toward it, rushing to—embrace it."

"Not put to sleep by some helpful guy," Sybil said.

"No," said Daniel. He sighed. "I *would* want it to be that way. But I know it can't be. Nobody can put *me* to sleep. Nobody can soothe my pain or strip my terror away. You're lucky—humans are lucky. . . ."

"Bullshit," she said. "You wouldn't be a vampire if you believed that."

"I didn't use to believe that," he said, "until I knew for myself. Nobody can tell you what it's really like to have the luxury of the palliative taken away. I don't think I ever really believed for a second that I couldn't just . . . I don't know, take an aspirin. I thought that by becoming a vampire, I could just avoid pain. I could just skirt around it. But no. I can never avoid pain. Humans, at least, can mask it."

"And yet you made your girlfriend Ariane into a vampire," Sybil pointed out. "If you knew that, and you cared about her—"

"I wanted to hurt somebody," Daniel confessed. "I wanted to hurt somebody that I love in the same way that I hurt." And she'd gotten him back for it, but good.

"You perpetuate violence," said Sybil, "just like a shitty parent."

"Just like every thinking and feeling creature," said Daniel. "That's what sentience really is—the desire to take it out on someone else, who you know hurts just as badly as you do. And don't give me that rhetoric pop-psych bullshit. You take your problems out on everyone else. I've seen you."

"That's—that's Sonic Ruth," Sybil stammered. "That's not me. She started it."

"It doesn't matter where it started," said Daniel wearily. "It's where it ends. It ends in your hands."

She laughed a low, hollow laugh. "Far be it from me to change the course of sentient beings," she said. "And careful where you cast stones, honey. You're in the same house as me and I can see right through the walls."

Sybil had taken a wealthy woman too distracted by the last-minute shopping rush to notice a husky teenager with a brick in her hand coming up behind her. Sybil brought home the multiple bags of toys, candles, expensive terra-cotta planters, the woman's dark brown fur car jacket, and her wallet. Daniel watched bemusedly from bed as Sybil arranged her acquisitions in a shrinelike pile along the upstairs wall. "Christmas already?" he yawned.

Sybil didn't respond. She straightened out all the receipts and taped each one to its corresponding object, then sat on the floor, wiping blood off the back of the fur.

Daniel swung his legs over the side of the bed. "I didn't know you liked fur."

"I don't," she said. "I hate it. It's seal. It's so soft. Poor seal . . ."

Her hand with the damp, pinkened, caressing sponge trembled.

"Why do you care about a stupid seal?"

"Fuck you, Daniel."

"Why keep the receipts?" he asked, changing the subject. Her face had a raw look, as if she'd been crying all day. "Are you going to return the stuff and take the money?"

"No, I don't need to. I'm keeping everything."

He wanted to take a bath, but in the warehouse the only running water was what thawed on the roof and trickled down one corner of the building. There was a nice bathhouse in Manhattan not too far from his old place, but it was bound to be closed on a holiday. "So when are you going to install plumbing in here?" he quipped.

"Fuck you, Daniel."

She sniffed and kept wiping the coat. He sighed heavily and gave up, pulling on yesterday's clothes and brushing his hair. "Enjoy your goodies," he said, pulling his coat off the railing. "I'll leave the phone here, and if I need you, I'll call."

She remained sullen and silent as he let himself out through the black plastic curtain. He gave the door a good slam behind him. As he flitted at high speed through the silent, snowy streets, he thought about dropping a dime on her, going to a pay phone and calling the police with a tip on last night's murder of a rich lady rushing home to give, give, give, to her family or friends or clients or whatever, a tip on a squatter, on a dangerous and ruthless murderess. There would be other women, ones who were happy to see him every day, women who appreciated quality, women without scars.

He sped all the way to Queens, sat on a bench opposite a movie theater showing the season's popular children's film, and watched the families and fragments of families come and go. They wore big puffy coats, stocking caps, galoshes, the children miniatures of the adults; one tiny girl, no more than three, wearing skintight leopard-print leggings and pierced ears, mouth glossy with Vaseline, a terrifyingly perfect replica of a Times Square whore of thirty years previous. They rushed inside and they rushed back out again after sitting still for ninety minutes, bustling to dinner, bustling to play with new toys and new scented soap, bustling to watch a television program. No one seemed to be worshipping Christ. A charity Santa Claus with bucket disconsolately rang his bell, eyes mostly closed, listlessly thanking the splash of change or the near-silent whisper of a folded dollar bill.

When full night had closed over the city, Daniel got up and took the subway back to DUMBO. The trains were fairly well deserted at eight in the evening on Christmas Day. Daniel walked through until he found a train empty but for a single person, a hollow-eyed, sexless addict with hair like paper straw. Daniel sat next to the junkie, picked up one cold, hard hand and rubbed it between his own.

The junkie glanced up, pinprick pupils centered in vivid indigo irises, and smiled vaguely. Male, heroin and methadone and liquid cold medicine, a metal-sugar tang on his breath, he said to Daniel, "Spare any change?"

"You don't need money," Daniel replied. "You need a home."

"I got a home," said the junkie sadly.

"Then it's me that needs a home." Daniel held the cold hand against his cheek, then pressed his naked lips against the skin. The junkie shifted a little in his seat but stayed where he was, enveloped in two layers of artificial well-being. Daniel continued, "I'm in love with someone who hates everybody. I haven't got a chance with her."

"Don't try to understand women," said the junkie, hazy eyes sharpening. "Gets you nowhere."

"Having a good Christmas?" asked Daniel.

His companion smirked. "Scored," he said. "Coming back home with a little more for tomorrow to tide me over."

"Going back tomorrow?"

The junkie nodded.

"Don't go back," said Daniel.

The train car rocked gently as they curved underground, lights flickering but never going out entirely. Daniel brought the cool, bony wrist up to his mouth. The junkie idly stroked Daniel's hair as he bit into the unfeeling flesh, gladly pouring his blood out into Daniel's mouth and belly, and when Daniel raised his head again, they shared the same silly opiate grin, lopsided and blissful.

"That feels good," mumbled the junkie.

Phillip.

"Phillip," said Daniel, taking a deep breath into lungs that felt compressed, massaged by the drug now pouring sweetness and light into his own body, "have you ever kissed a man?"

"Yeah, I did, and now I'm dying," said Phillip.

Daniel kissed him on dry leather lips, tasting still of an artificial mint, an herb analogue reminiscent of Austrian monastery liqueur poured over a box of bullets. Phillip's tongue eagerly sought out the tiny pockets of blood left in Daniel's gums—*anything better than the taste of generic Nyquil,* thought Phillip, a soft laugh rippling through his wasted body. Daniel kissed him again briefly and embraced him.

"I'm dying," Phillip repeated. "You're kissing a dead man."

"It wouldn't be the first time," Daniel said.

He stood up and walked to the other side of the train car, awkward as a newborn foal, unsteady on his legs. He hadn't had heroin for a long time, let alone in that particular mixture—it was devastating. Phillip, behind him, laughed knowingly. "What are you doing on the subway at Christmas, kissing men?" he asked, his eyes closing and stretching out on the seat. "Are you a hustler? I can't give you any money, man."

"I told you," said Daniel, "trying to find a home. . . . It's not you."

Phillip looked at his wrist, held out in front of him into the aisle. There were no marks that his leaden eyes could make out in the flickering light. "It's not?"

"No," said Daniel. He breathed deeply and slowly, and his blood got control over the drugs and broke them down. Now he could stand steadily without having to hold on to straps or walls, and he balanced himself with his arms held out like a surfer in the middle of the car. He took deep breaths and his body warmed.

"I wish it was," Phillip said with a sigh.

"Where are you getting off?"

"Fulton Street."

Daniel had to transfer there onto a different train to get closer to the warehouse. Again, he was returning to Sybil, but he had cast away everything else. He looked over at Phillip, who struggled to keep his eyes open. "I'll make sure you make your stop," said Daniel.

A new wound, a few more gulps of the druggy mixture, a good-bye to Phillip, and Daniel swayed off the train at Fulton Street, collapsing on the stairs up to the next platform. A passing man cursed him for falling to his knees and blocking the way; Daniel put out a hand to beg for assistance, but his claws only scored the damp material at the hem of the man's pants, struggling past.

Daniel remained where he was for a while. The concrete, tile, and steel poking into him, deforming his abdomen, was preferable to moving, attempting to shift the anvil weight of gravity from his joints, defy it, an irrefutable law of physics—who was he to rebel against gravity? No one else commented. It wasn't the most uncommon sight in the world—a man in leather pants and jacket, sprawled on the steps between subway platforms, off his face on drugs. He couldn't help laughing at their expressionless faces and their absurd athletic shoes, the laces encrusted with melting snow, the soft molded plastic soles besmirched by filth and gravel. These beautiful expensive objects, meant to make mankind fly, instead standing on grimy underground platforms and leaking in snow, some of them with red jelly plugs like clots built into their soles. Daniel scraped his face against the floor, knowing himself to be no better, no less absurd, no less of a waste.

When finally he dragged himself back to the warehouse, Sybil stood next to a huge tin washtub, large enough to sit in, full of water with silver steam rising from its surface. Daniel shed his clothes and stepped in, finding the hot stones at the bottom and avoiding them, and crouched, huddled, weeping, while Sybil washed dirt and cigarette butts and gum from his hair with a soft old flannel and kissed each inch of skin she made clean.

Scene Twenty-one: Idiotically Dangerous Animals

Sybil wouldn't be budged from the rack of giant televisions, her hands clasped lovingly at her chest, her eyes drinking in the flashy images. "Sybil, we have to go," Daniel urged, hand on her shoulder, "the taxi's waiting."

"I *have to* see men bitten by sharks," she protested, her breath a long sigh of desire. "*Have* to."

On television grid, six-by-six screens wide, an underwater cameraman in a black rubber suit thrashed away from a dead-eyed, furious, flashing blade of fish, seeking purchase with rows of jagged teeth. Sybil's body rocked with each blow. When the segment was over, she drooped into Daniel's arms.

An announcer's voice blasted so sharply that Sybil jolted in Daniel's arms—"Coming up, Steve encounters the Wyoming wolverine—next on 'Idiotically Dangerous Animals'!"

Sybil gazed at Daniel, the downy skin of her sparkleglam cheeks bright red. "Does television ever make you feel like the end times already happened, and we're now living in the manifestation of hell on earth?"

"At least my generation wasn't raised by it," Daniel said.

"No, yours was by the fucking Nazis."

He kissed her. Her teeth chattered behind closed lips.

"OK, I'm ready," she mumbled, eyes glazed, mouth ripely grinning. "Let's go."

In the taxi, she sang as she delightedly played with her new videocamera, feeding batteries into its backside and spreading the paper manual across her lap. Daniel watched her bemusedly. "I've long ago learned I shouldn't ask you why you do the things you do."

"That's smart," she agreed. "What next, Mr. Post-Christmas Sale?"

"What do you want?" he asked.

"I want another kiss," she said.

He leaned over and put his mouth out to hers. Her kisses had changed; now, they tasted instead of biting, her lips only gently aggressive. Sybil broke off and rubbed her cheek against his cashmere scarf, worn at her request. "Do you think the world's going to end?" she asked.

Their fingers played together, stroking each other, in Sybil's lap. "I don't know," he said to her. "I don't think so. Not this week."

"Yeah," she decided, flicking the camera on and bringing it up from her thighs to point at their faces. "I don't think so either. I used to think so. I read a lot about Nostradamus when I was a little kid and got scared shitless. But now I think that if there's going to be an apocalypse—and there will be, sooner or later—that it's already started, and it's just sort of a long, downhill slide."

"Do you really think so?" asked Daniel comfortably.

"Don't you?"

"I think it pays to be optimistic."

"Sometimes I don't try to understand you, either. How can you say that, having lived through the twentieth century? And seen the worst of it?"

"I didn't see the worst of it," Daniel said. "I didn't get shipped to Poland." He reached over her and switched the camera off. "And you know as well as I do that the worst of it is everywhere, and that it's always existed."

Sybil made the guileless face she wore whenever she was actually listening. "Hmm," she commented, switching the camera on again and pointing it at her window. "Are you going to go to Joachim's party?"

"Well, it's not really his, he's just going to be there." Daniel rubbed the end of the scarf against the back of Sybil's neck, where millimeters of dishwater-blond rooted her aquamarine hair. He saw her smile, but she didn't move at all. "I think it might be charming. It might also be dull, but I find ways to enliven parties."

"A great way to do it is with drugs!" She chittered out a restless laugh.

"I'm sure there'll be drugs there already."

"Drugs! Man, I love drugs! Let's go buy some more drugs! Do drug dealers have post-Christmas sales, do you think?"

"I don't think they have problems with excess inventory."

Giggling, she panned the camera around the cab and focused the lens on him. "Pout," she commanded, and Daniel obliged. "You are such a hottie. Hey, you know what, I never showed you the pictures I took of you naked."

"No, you never did."

"They're kind of fucked up."

"Oh, I'm sure they're good—everything you do is good."

"No, they're really not very good. I wasn't concentrating. Maybe I'll paint them, though."

"You should."

"Christ, stop indulging me. You're making me sick."

"Nonsense, look at yourself, you're smiling." He touched her moist, high-colored cheeks, each with a dot of silver glitter sparkling in the streetlight, propped up with an architectural smile. "I refuse to let you stop me indulging you from now on. It's not fair you've made me wait this long."

"I just never want anything," she complained.

"You're just so used to telling yourself no that you've

forgotten how to hope for or want anything."

"Not true, not true . . . Hey, Daniel. I have an idea. Let's go somewhere."

In a tiny fourth-floor dance club, hardly more than a decorated and amplified living room, Sybil sat on a tall thin stool, her long, muscled legs crossed at the ankles, videotaping Daniel. He danced with a lithe young man about his same height and build, obviously a professional dancer; after a few minutes of careful observation and determined listening, Daniel danced perfectly in sync with him, mirroring his steps and flourishes. The other people on the dance floor stood back to give them room, pressing themselves against the walls, watching the photo negative of Daniel, white face in black, against the dancer's pale synthetic trousers and vest and the sweat-glinting umber of his sleek shaven head and malleable arms. The dancer pushed Daniel to greater and greater effort, spins and kicks, subtle shimmies and jazz-hands, racing through styles, his mouth open in a wide grin, gasping, with his tongue sticking out and to the side. Daniel smiled. The dancer was falling in love.

Finally the dancer stopped and half collapsed into a crouch on the floor. The spectators applauded, then, cautiously, returned to dancing. "Amazing! Who did you study with?" he panted, dropping his head briefly between his knees and standing up again, accepting Daniel's hand up.

"Only you," said Daniel, not out of breath.

"You should audition for Lee—he's my choreographer—he'd be crazy about you!"

"No, I'm certain . . . I shouldn't . . ."

Hours later, after convincing the dancer that Daniel was not actually in the business and did not want to join any companies nor take on students, Daniel searched for Sybil in the club, still pulsing full of bodies. Her steel-lockbox mind was not among theirs. He turned around and around, disoriented in the smothering of solid beats and minds that twined around it, brilliant flowing strands of rhythm- and movement-induced peace, pressuring his mind to join its twirling helix. He shook it off, the hunger to be next to the girl burning in his gut, edging himself around the walls.

Behind one of them, a mind flashed full of the brilliant image of Sybil, and he pushed through a door in the direction from which it came. Behind the door, on a love seat in a candlelit bathroom, Sybil lay with her stretchy dress unzipped to the waist; a slim girl with a coral-colored Bettie Page wig, hanging askew over short black curls, rode herself on Sybil's thigh. One hand agitated Sybil's bare breast, the other pressed between her legs under the hem of a denim miniskirt. The videocamera sat propped on Sybil's backpack, pointed up at them.

Daniel overcame his initial sensation of shock, his reflex of jealous anger, instead resting with his back to the door, watching them. Neither of them had their eyes open and the music was so overwhelming—shaking the floor and walls even with the door closed—they couldn't have heard him. After a brief twitch, transmitted to her muscles from Daniel's mental alarm, the strange woman continued, pinching Sybil's nipple and grinding her hips. Sybil groaned feverishly, but it wasn't her orgasm that was at stake. She gently pushed the other woman back a little, slipping her hand between the bare thighs, pushing fingers in. "C'mon," Sybil urged softly. "C'mon. Oh, yeah, that's it. There you go."

Definitely a strong one. Her whole body twisted with the spasm and she screamed through gritted teeth, then relaxed, thoughtlessly, moaning, "Ohhhh . . ." Daniel stepped up quickly and caught the woman in his arms as she fell backward; she jerked up in panic when she touched him. "What the fuck?" she cried out, her voice thick and husky still.

She tore away clumsily and pressed herself into a corner of the room next to the garbage can, yanking her dress as far down her thighs as it would go (barely six inches from the branching of her crotch). Daniel leaned over and kissed Sybil, and she put her arms around him and kissed the sandpaper stubble on his chin. "Ready to go home now, E-Girl?" he said in her ear.

"Yeah, I'm all done." She zipped up and picked up her

videocamera, touched a button on its flank, and stuffed it into her backpack. She and Daniel walked out of the toilet without glancing back at the hyperventilating woman trying in vain to find her discarded panties.

"What was that?" Daniel asked.

"What did it look like?" Sybil was glistening and smug. Most of her glitter had been rubbed off, and the ten or so remaining fragments sparkled on her cheeks and chin as they came out onto the street. "Did you like watching?"

"Not as much as doing," said Daniel. He unfolded his mobile phone and dialed a car service number. "So what's the tape for?"

"Part of an installation."

"Did you get her to sign a release form? Ah, yes, West Sixteenth Street, between Sixth and Seventh. Yeah, sure, I'll hang on."

Sybil arched her eyebrow. "You're kidding, right?"

"Of course I'm kidding." It was easier not to look at her, vibrating and incandescent, unreasonably aroused. "Transgression, right?"

"I really want you to make *me* come. I get to come sometimes, too, don't I? You wanna fuck?" Her bare leg, stockings discarded, curved and stroked up the side of his, snagging her knee on a ripple in the leather. "You do, huh? I can feel it; you're hard already." Daniel tried to turn away to concentrate on the scratchy voice in the plastic divot of the phone, but her breath shushed out in a brittle whisper into his other ear and he lost his train of thought, their location, everything except for the heat steaming off her lips and the sweet stench of her genital sweat. "No, really good. You're really good."

In the service car, sweeping over the Manhattan Bridge, he knuckled her melting clitoris, nibbled and sucked her earlobe. He wanted to press his teeth straight through the tender loop of decorative flesh, swallow it, absorb its sweat-salty sweetness into his own body. "How was your boy?" she murmured, then laughed.

He wondered that she didn't taste the aspirin tang of semen in his mouth. He licked her eyebrow, all grown back now, sleek coarse hair over skin and bone. "I let him go with a peck on the cheek," said Daniel.

"Did you ask him if the world would end?" Her tongue stretched out of her mouth, pointed, seeking his.

"Only you know that, little girl." He dug his knuckle in, twisted it about.

"Damn straight." She laughed again, then her fingers tightened on the lapel of his coat and her eyes rolled back. "Oh, Dan—it's happening—"

Her orgasms continued in staggered ripples until Daniel removed his hand to pay the driver with crisp new hundreds, dampened with the scented milk that wet her when she came. The driver didn't seem to mind; he would only remember the money, and that it smelled like pussy.

Sybil had bolted for the warehouse as soon as Daniel's hand left her. By the time he got inside, she had already lit candles and fired up the space heaters and stood in front of her slash-and-smudge paintings, wriggling out of her dress. Daniel pulled the polyethylene curtain around his face like a cloak. "You're in danger, my naked lesbian friend," he growled, thickening his accent. "Your attacker vaits yust outside."

"Well, then, my dangerous attacker should come inside and get his ass kicked," she replied, tossing the dress into the pile of burnt clothes. "I think I can show him a thing or two."

He picked her up, tossed her over his shoulder, and jumped over to the broken Craftmatic. She was on the bed, in the valley at the center, before she'd had the chance to take another breath. "Oh my God, that's so fun!" she yelled. Daniel began to strip. "Would you do that again?"

"Tomorrow," he said. "I've got plans right now."

The other woman had left tiny bruises on Sybil's tits. He brushed his claw tips against them to watch her writhe and murmur in an endless golden loop. He took a moment to just look at her, willing and naked and eager to the point of impatience, when mere days before she wouldn't even look at him. The memory of that ebbed away, growing dimmer with each thick pulse of the heavy blood in his groin. Her eyes were glazed and bright and the lids fluttered now and then, as if even her eyes could orgasm.

Conversation ceased. He did not ask her permission before he prodded his penis into her mouth or took her cunt roughly from behind; he didn't warn her before he ejaculated copiously both inside her and against the shadowed divide between her buttocks, and said nothing as he used the flat of his thumb to work the semen into her anus. Again, there was blood; their shared cells would make some kind of communion. In his arms, across his thighs relaxing, her body stayed limp, unprotesting, murmuring quietly to herself, her eyes closed. Daniel was grateful to be free of their brilliance even for a short while; the intensity of her gaze dissected him, demanded things from him that he wasn't sure he knew how to give. Once upon a time, with other people, sex had been enough. He gazed at her still face, smudged obscenely with his black lipstick, and wondered when that had changed.

Do you hear me? he asked through his skin, his thumb in her anus. *Can you feel me?*

With her mouth she whispered, "Yes."

Do you love me? Will you belong to me?

"Yes."

Do you promise not to leave me? The claw on the thumb gently eased in, experimenting, careful not to cut her.

"I can't promise that," she said.

"Don't leave me," said Daniel's tongue.

"Don't ask me dumb questions." The slice of her eyes went through him again; she kicked away his sodomizing hand and sat up. "God! Don't you know anything yet? How could you be such an immature child and you're so old? Don't you ever learn?"

"No," he replied sadly. "I don't ever learn. And you can ask Ariane about that. And you can ask Ricari about that. And you could have asked Lovely about that, except that he's dead."

Her eyes lowered and her drug-drawn face was beautiful again, an ivory-and-charcoal cameo instead of a weapon. She lay her palms flat against his chest, then slowly moved them around his ribs until they rested together in an embrace. "It's always better to just kill the ones you love, so they can't be taken from you or leave you," she said against the hair sheeting his ear, like a black wing. "But . . . don't get any funny ideas."

Scene Twenty-two: New Year's Eve

"What should I wear?"

"Whatever you want, but follow festival logic and wear sensible shoes. Hopefully you won't be up to your pits in mud like we were at Reading." Joachim grinned at the memory of the summer before, when Daniel had given him a "grant" to go to the legendary British festival. Indeed, the atmosphere of barely controlled chaos and the constant flow of excellent music and drugs had inspired him, and his next paintings sold very well. "I don't think that'll happen. The organizers really know what they're doing. They've been doing this for a few years and they wouldn't plan a party anywhere that water would be a problem."

Daniel raked his hands through his hair. He had accepted Joachim's invitation to lunch (a late lunch, of course) with a kind of achy reluctance to leave Sybil. He knew that she would want him to go; he was learning her rhythms, trying to give her space. It was like learning to exercise a hopelessly atrophied muscle that he'd never used. He'd never had to give anyone space before. He hadn't even told her; he went while she was still asleep, frowning in it, the duvet clenched in her fingers and bunched around her body. He saw her form echoed in the swirl on the surface of their dish of olive oil and his own curled hand on the tablecloth and the whorls in the weave of the tablecloth . . .

Joachim was staring at him.

Daniel shook himself and sat up straight. "Were you saying something?" he asked politely.

"Is Sybil coming?" said Joachim, his mouth going tight.

Daniel shook his head. "No," he said. "She says she's going to stay in and 'create.' " He laughed to give Joachim permission to laugh. "It doesn't matter."

"I was kind of afraid you'd bring her today," Joachim confessed, all loose after his laugh. He took another big swallow from his glass of wine and pried an olive from its pit. "I don't know, no offense, but . . . Daniel, that woman is up to no good. I think she's just trying to rip you off, blackmail you or something. She's a thug, a little thief."

"Did she steal from you, too?"

"Hell, yeah, she did. She took my live Future Sound of London CD. She fucked me, she fucked my girlfriend, and then she stole from me, and *then* she nearly got a bunch of my friends killed. It's kind of hard for me to tolerate her presence."

Daniel raised his eyebrows. "Joachim, that fire was an accident," he remarked.

"I don't know if it was, man." Joachim shook his head at the dish of olives. "I'm sorry, Daniel," he said. "I know she must mean something to you, but . . . but I have to be honest. Speaking as a friend, even if it drives you away, I have to tell you to get out of this before it's too late."

"Too late?" Daniel smiled. "Before I die alone and old?"

"I didn't mean that," said Joachim hastily. "I meant . . ."

Silence at the table, broken only by the sound of Joachim's foot tapping at a leg of the chair. Daniel made a faint excuse for a chuckle. "I know," he said. "I wish I didn't, but I know."

"Why are you even seeing her?"

"Because she's extraordinary."

"She's insane. She needs to be locked up."

"Once upon a time you were a big fan of outsider art," Daniel said pleasantly. "I see now that it only refers to junkies and retards."

"Daniel—"

"No, never mind. She's not coming. You don't ever have to see her again. Nor me, if you like."

"That's not what I want at all. I miss you. I invited you to lunch, didn't I? I'm more surprised that you came."

"But I love this place," said Daniel, gesturing at the interior of the smoky Spanish café. "I miss the food. I miss the smells. I miss coming here with you. I miss *you.*"

They smiled at each other.

"I'm glad you're going to stop by the party," said Joachim. "It's gonna be great. Wear what you usually wear."

"I'll see what I can do."

When he got back to the warehouse, Sybil had gone, having stripped her paintings from their easels. He supposed that she had finished with them and was preparing to do whatever she did with her work. Her wire structures remained, though, in a row on one of the long tables she'd salvaged from upstairs, the pitted, peeling veneer surface already rimed with paint, glue, and candlewax. Daniel picked up his two favorites, a structurally complex but symmetrical ball with two halves linked with twisted hooks in the center and a missile or tower that rested on four tightly coiled feet. He passed them between his hands, unable to choose one, then put both of them into a large leather satchel with his change of shoes and Hasselblad and film. His car keys weren't on the crates shoved next to the bed.

He went onto the street and saw that his car was gone. By this time, Daniel knew that he'd have to wait hours to get a taxi or a car. Across the river, Manhattan was on fire. Seemingly every electric light in the city blazed; the various sounds of sirens sliced and faded in the air. Fortunately, Worth Street Station wasn't a terribly long walk; he need only cross the Brooklyn Bridge toward City Hall.

The civic neighborhood was largely deserted, even of police; he imagined that half the police force was surrounding and infiltrating Times Square. Joachim had given Daniel instructions about entering the station, madly detailed things about the doors, the tunnel entrance through a dank, lightless stairwell too deserted even to smell of piss. "Worth Street Station closed in 1964. My friends have been trying for ages to find a way to get in and take a look around before the city demolishes it completely. Only recently," Joachim had said, "did they break the lock on that door and find this method of getting into the station. It was maybe a month ago. The city'll probably brick it up pretty soon after the first of the year, so this is your first and last chance to experience it. It's supposedly really beautiful."

On the first landing, before the stairs went down, sat a basket of small flashlights. Daniel lit one, and the light painfully flooded his dilated eyes, thrusting light into the shadows of the stairwell. The light wasn't quite strong enough to show him the bottom of the stairs. It did illuminate the sheets of paper taped to the walls that read NO SMOKING OR OPEN FLAMES PLEASE. AIR QUALITY STILL UNKNOWN. PLEASE WATCH YOUR STEP GOING DOWN. Piles of shattered wood and broken concrete had been shoved against the walls on the sides of the stairwell, but the stairs remained cluttered and hazardous.

On the second landing was a huge basket full of white roses and hairclips. "On your way down, take and use one of everything you find," Joachim had said. "That way we'll know you're one of us. There are two guys doing security, and supposedly they have rubber-bullet guns."

The third landing had a huge box of multicolored plastic sticks that gave off an insistent glow when bent and shaken. Daniel held his lightstick up to his eyes, watching the gentle swirling of light inside it, and thought about Ricky, buying cases of them for parties. Daniel had seen them but had never held one before, surprised that it gave off no heat.

On the fourth landing were tinseled, velvet-patterned paper party hats. Daniel paused again, listening to the faint strains of chamber music coming from below his feet, finally deciding on the silver hat with curly tinfoil ram's horns; Sybil; the curls; the silver. He wondered if she was thinking of him, wherever she was, if she was thinking about the imminent end of the world, due in exactly two hours by the estimations of Nostradamus. No hellfire or brimstone had been sighted all day, and the throngs already cheek-to-cheek in Times Square, shoving each other for a chance to be broadcast on television, seemed desperate for some form of violent revelation, their screams of excitement more motivated by thinly repressed terror than the hedonistic glee that usually ushered in every January. This would be different, they thought; a new number in their checkbooks, and the satellites and servers might come crashing down first thing in the morning, plunging the world into a confused and threadbare stone age. They had packed away their canned beef stew and batteries and now it was time to meet their destinies head on, drunk and making as much noise as possible.

For a moment, Daniel turned back the way he'd come, but thought of Joachim; the decrepit station. He would visit for a while, then go on his way.

Behind the door of the fifth landing, a tall chocolate-brown man greeted Daniel with a silly grin on his face. "All right then?" he shouted at Daniel in an ingratiating Brixton bellow. He opened his coat slightly to display an ostentatious holster.

Daniel fluttered his lightstick and smirked harmlessly. *Hi, I'm your buddy. Don't mind me.*

"Hat on, please? Brilliant. In you go. Enjoy, and remember, no smoking!"

Inside, down a long tiled hallway hung with lightsticks in mirrored lanterns, Daniel found the party. The flashlights and lightsticks borne by eighty or ninety people, almost all of them young and dressed in black or in costume or both, madly distracted and unsettled Daniel's eyes. The guests avidly snacked from a thirty-foot table spread with catered food, and helped themselves to the countless bottles of champagne bristling from tin troughs around the table. The shattered ticket booth and turnstiles had been hung with silver tinsel garlands. And indeed, there was a real string quartet, merrily hacking through Haydn in C major. The rumble of a passing train, just behind the wall, shook the floor.

Joachim found him right away, face shiny with amphetamine sweat. "What do you think?" he said to Daniel, shifting from foot to foot and swinging his flashlight on the end of a cord. His hat was a red bowler with red tinsel wings. "Cool-E-cool, eh?"

Daniel embraced him. "It's quite beautiful. As beautiful as you. *Love* the hats."

"So glad you're here. I was gonna be so upset if you didn't show up. Let me introduce you to our hosts. I never did introduce you to Amarantha."

Amarantha, the witchy girl from the coffee shop, had a husband who was bald, severe, scientific, and Danish; he did not speak when introduced, only nodded crisply and kept staring out at the flickering lights and varied faces. Daniel examined him for a few seconds, long enough to read the pattern of his shifting, muted emotions. Mr. Klein did not feel anything in particular about anything, unlike Joachim, who shot out sparks of nervous excitement and pleasure as he danced in place next to them. "Do you often trespass for fun and profit?" Daniel asked Klein.

"Not profit," said Klein. "Adventure."

"Ah; I understand," said Daniel. "Joachim, would you get me something to drink?"

"Sure, Daniel," Joachim agreed, dancing away.

"The city is built upon deception and death," Amarantha put in, her voice like the bottom-most key of an out-of-tune piano. "The decay underneath the city is what interests Amstel."

"We charge fifty dollars per person for each adventure," Klein went on, "to cover the cost of a taxi to the hospital should anyone get hurt in the process. We trust everyone not to get hurt. No one has ever gotten hurt on our expeditions. This party has been financed by all the money paid by our attendees this year."

"That's marvelous," said Daniel. "I could have done that in Berlin . . . if anyone wanted to go, that is."

"Berlin is mostly in pieces now," said Klein. "They build it with blocks like children."

"I haven't been back for decades," said Daniel.

"It is a very different Europe," said Klein.

"Decades?" asked Amarantha, looking Daniel up and down; Daniel wore a puffy silver parka, fishnet blouse, leather pants, his unlined face dusted with white shimmer powder.

Daniel threw back his head and laughed a stage laugh; in the presence of people as artificial as these two, it would hardly be remarkable. "Did I say decades? Sorry, sometimes my English isn't the greatest. I think I meant to say 'ages.' I haven't been back there for ages. Correct?" He turned dazzling smiles on them both, proudly displaying fangs, and watched them blink glassy eyes and nod.

Joachim returned from the food table with two overflowing glasses of sparkling wine. "Daniel, don't dominate them," he chastised. "Come over here and tell everyone what you've been doing with yourself."

There they were. Everyone. Assistants and friends and gallery contacts, fifteen of them, wildly excited to see him. He leapt into them like a warm shower, a wave of hysterical curiosity and a sense that, for each one of them, a feeling that a lack of something in their souls had been abruptly satisfied. They loved him, by God, they loved him, wrapping him in layers of gauze adoration. He remembered this telepathic glory—the delicious joy of being wanted so hard from every direction—with the same shock of pleasure as his presence caused in them.

He forgot about Times Square and Nostradamus.

Closer to midnight, tipsy on the secondhand champagne that he'd sipped from countless necks and wrists, Daniel asked the youngest of his assistants, Alexandra, barely seventeen, "Why do you love me so much?" His arm slid around her velveteen shoulders, leaning up against her, his words blurry. His hat on its rubber-band strap had slipped to one side of his head.

Alexandra had a tiny cleft in her chin, and dimples, and a thick mass of wavy golden hair. Her body reminded him painfully of Ariane's. The girl had been taking painting lessons, combined with theories on artistic living, from one of Daniel's former assistants, Clarkie, and when Clarkie had gone off to teach at the Savannah College of Art and Design, Alexandra remained a fixture of Daniel's studio. "Why do you love me and I haven't even *slept* with you yet?" he asked her.

She giggled, twisted her ankle fetchingly, tossed her scented hair. "You know," she said. "I just do. I just love working with you."

Daniel gently stroked the furrow in her chin with an outstretched claw. "You are *so* my type, little woman."

"And you already know how gorgeous I think you are. Too bad you're *way* too old for me," she said, her voice throaty with the force of her flirting. Only young girls can get away with doing this without coming to the harm of intimacy; a woman of twenty-five speaking in the same manner doesn't expect to still be standing vertically at the end of the hour.

Daniel arched his eyebrows, grunting, "Yeah, that's true . . ."

"But you know. We don't all love you for your *face,*" she explained. "We love you for being you. You aren't like anybody else. I don't know—" She threw up her hands and giggled again, the same pattern of sounds like a bird-call; three peaks, then four, then two. "There's just something so special about you. Like how you always understand what I'm trying to say, even when I'm too tongue-tied to say it myself."

Daniel smiled and put his hand to her cheek. She clasped it with her hand and drew it closer. Daniel lifted her chin with his finger and kissed her on the lips.

When she opened her eyes, her expression hovered between bliss and agonizing uncertainty. "Like it's like you can read my mind," she murmured.

"I'm glad you can't read mine," he said, "I think you'd be pretty embarrassed to see some of the things there."

"I can imagine," said Alexandra.

Danger, little girl. You should go home.

To her, it seemed very sudden. The moment, him bending so far down to kiss her, not wanting to stop kissing her, her eyes close to panic, had become unbearably awkward, and they broke apart, seeking safer conversation elsewhere.

Alexandra sought the company of her chaperone father, a weathered old beatnik smashed on champagne and coming onto the repulsed Amarantha. Daniel talked business with a gallery owner, who hounded him for more work from assistants. "Man, those collages from what's-his-name—oh, yeah, Bastard Son—sold out like beer at a Yankees game. Extraordinary. I cleaned up on those, even with your fees."

"That's what I use to pay 'em," said Daniel. "It's fairly cool if a new artist gets at least a percentage of his gallery price."

"And how much do you take?" The owner had a chummy leer and breath so minty it burned Daniel's nose from two feet away.

"Only what's necessary for my labor," said Daniel. "I'm not interested in ripping anybody off. I have plenty of money."

"Yeah, where'd your money come from, anyway? I know you had plenty of it before you started shopping art around. What'd you, marry into it or something?"

"I inherited it," said Daniel vaguely. This line of conversation had also gotten boring. He barely needed to interfere at all to derail it.

Immediately, from within, the man was contrite. "Oh, my God, I'm so sorry, I can't imagine how I ever said anything like that, that's not like me."

"No, that's all right," Daniel soothed. "I'm over it. So are you."

"Yeah, yeah, I'll try to move on. You know, I'm drunk and high on coke. Don't take it personal."

"I wouldn't dream of it. Please. Excuse me."

Daniel stood in front of a big sheet of silver Mylar, quivering with the air strokes given off by the string quartet, now playing along with a mean-spirited breakbeat being mixed by a DJ from equal parts "Miami Vice Theme" and recorded chainsaw. He watched his face undulate and distort in the Mylar reflection, his asymmetrical features repulsive to him when before, in the still candlelit silence of the warehouse before the mirror, they had been distinctive, seductive, an Art Deco turn-on.

"Hey! It's time! It's time!" A dozen voices in cacophony; at once they settled into counting down, and Daniel counted himself down, *vier, drei, zwei, ein . . . please complete this* . . . Here, at the end of the world, he was ugly. He shut his eyes and prayed that they would never open again.

And the world ended, for him and everyone else, with a swell of sound.

Scene Twenty-three: New Year's Day

People screamed, acres and acres of them all crying out at once. Five stories underground, the voice coming from the street twisted funneled and broken from the stairwell, pitch-shifted to a low lion's roar. Daniel felt lips against his chin, his cheeks, his hair, his ears. He closed his eyes even harder. *Earth, swallow your most wretched product! STOP LETTING ME LIVE!*

But no.

A blare of saxophone opened Daniel's eyes; a sample of an old song by a one-hit wonder; the phrase "move fast in the tunnels of the underground," and the DJ flipped and repeated it, chopping the beats into thirty-seconds and bringing in a different rhythm. No conflagration, no panicked violence, only dancing and pouring and guzzling yet more champagne. What alcohol Daniel had gleaned from the blood of the partygoers had already worn off, leaving him feeling queasy and irritable. None of this made any sense. How stupid that it was just another hour, another day, another lifetime. Nobody seemed bothered by it. There was something that just made sense about everything ending, or at least changing, at that stroke of midnight; surely it was not just a number, but the structure that had driven western civilization for several hundred years?

"Nostradamus was full of shit," Daniel muttered.

"C'mon, Dan old man," said Alexandra, hooking her arm through his, "let's go dance."

"Nothing better to do," he conceded.

He let it take him away this time. He let himself be lost in the fractal infinity of music and movement, floating along in a wave of minds deeply relaxed, more relaxed than they had been all year.

Good. Enough. Perhaps.

For a little while; then Daniel found himself bored with the same beat continuing on and on, only gaining tempo every ten minutes, and he stopped dancing and began to observe Worth Street Station. The station itself was attractive enough, beautiful tiles lining painted brick walls and iridescent shards of glass hanging from former light fixtures, but the real beauty of the place was the darkness, the shadows, and the intermittent, inappropriate glittering of the tinsel decorations. The trains kept going past, not bothered by the holiday or the apocalypse, and with each pass, the tinsel quivered.

He went to the farthest edge of the station, where the tunnel was exposed, the air still sharp with ozone from the passing train, and trained his flashlight into the gap, staring down at the tracks. They looked the same as subway tracks everywhere. He wondered how the tracks had looked after the passing of Sonic Ruth, whether gore rimed their dull metal sheen or was whisked clean by the slicing wheels. It would be easy to jump down, wait, and find out for himself. Or find someone else . . .

Daniel felt a sudden violent urgency from the direction of the party and instantly focused on it, like a startling noise. The sensation came from Joachim, a moment ago dancing, shirtless and holding a sloshing champagne glass in front of him, in the center of the crowd. Joachim transmitted only a panic, the sweat rolling over his ribs suddenly icy. He never thought a name; but it was panic in a very particular shape and set of associations, a combination of remembered lust, pervasive distaste, and, more than anything, fear.

Daniel followed Joachim's stare to find her. At first he didn't see Sybil; Joachim's eyes were locked in hostility on a grinning little blond teenager in a short pink dress with pink cotton balls in her hair. She wasn't wearing one of the absurd hats, or carrying a lightstick or flashlight, and Daniel didn't recognize her. Nonetheless, he rushed back into the station, pushing dancing people aside, and there was Sybil, right in Joachim's gaze, and the little blond in pink was nowhere to be seen.

She was very drunk or high, dressed in her gray coveralls and the leather parka and a blue velvet propeller beanie, arguing with Klein about something, gesturing wildly with a green lightstick. She leaned forward to make a point and stumbled against Klein's chest, her hand sloppily seeking purchase on his sharkskin torso. Klein plucked her away from him with the tips of his fingers, wrinkling his nose and edging his face away. As Daniel's curiosity swam across a current of chemical fog and perfume, he found her scent, her usual hypnotic mixture accompanied by the tang of human excrement and blood. He couldn't be positive, but neither was hers, or at least not all of it was. He would need to smell her somewhere in which there was less interference. And, his heart nearly strangling him with happiness, he wanted nothing more in the world.

Daniel took the girl from Klein's grasp and plunged his nose into the hair at her temple, drinking in the smell of her dirty scalp. The parka's fur hood was encrusted with ill-smelling mud. Sybil threw her arms around Daniel and squeezed him breathless. Klein glared at them both with heatwaves of distaste arcing from the waxy bald dome of his head.

Across the room, Joachim threw down his glass and disappeared into the crowd.

"This person was not invited," Klein shouted above the music.

"She's a friend of mine," said Daniel. "Allow her."

"No," Sybil mumbled against Daniel's collar. "Fuck 'em. Let's get outta here. I came to pick you up."

"Pick me up? Oh, you've got the car, don't you."

"Let's go," she begged, tugging at his jacket.

"Let me say good-bye to Joachim," Daniel protested, trying to disengage her fingers. They clamped the fabric like wire staples.

Her forehead gleamed wet and feverish, and she shook her head. "No. He's gone. Fuck him. Let's go."

Daniel quickly scanned the faces in the crowd and listened for hidden voices; indeed, Joachim was gone. "I wonder if he's gone to get the cops," Daniel mused. Sybil tugged at him again, and he indulged, "Yes, yes, we're leaving now."

She leaned on him out the door and up the steps. "What have you been up to?" Daniel murmured. "I thought you were going to stay home, darling."

"I was beginning a beautiful conceptual piece," she slurred, tongue thick in her mouth like a prizefighter's. "You know . . . getting raw materials."

"And how did you find out where the party was?"

Her smile glittered on the edges of his vision. "I called Joachim and pretended to be Josephine. They broke up, apparently, but not so much that he wouldn't tell her where he would be for the night. What a nice boy." She turned to face him. "Oh, shit." She stopped short in the middle of the last flight, swaying a little. Her skin reflected green glowstick glow.

"Are you gonna throw up?" Daniel asked warily.

"No," she said. "I left my bag downstairs. It's got my camera in it. Go on, I'll be right back. Unless one of your slick hip friends has already sold it to buy Vicodin."

"You have sixty seconds," he agreed, kissing her mouth and letting go. "Fifty-nine. Fifty-eight."

She let her fingers trail across his cheek as she went down. "Happy New Year . . ."

Daniel skipped up the remaining stairs and spun on one toe. The air was beautifully cold and crisp and clear, the streets deserted. He danced a little more, just for the hell of it, indulged his Gene Kelly musical fantasies, skipped up and down the curb, a pirouette, a cartwheel using only one hand. "You *are* a gorgeous bitch, after all," he told himself. "Who would have guessed?"

When Sybil made it out, he grabbed her and whirled her off her feet. She had lit a cigarette, and her outstretched arm painted a trail of tiger sparks that winked out before they touched the wet and trembling ground.

He had not quite settled her, laughing and breathless, back on her feet when the pavement shook itself in one rough snap like a sneeze; Sybil lost her footing and sprawled into the gutter. Car alarms for two blocks wailed and beeped into the night, an electronic solo on top of the muted human noise from Times Square. Daniel stared at the concrete; when he was spinning on it, the cracks were fine and lined with rotting dead moss; now they gaped open, sand trickling from the edges of the gashes in the ground.

Sybil grabbed Daniel's arm with her pincer fingers, reeking of lighter fluid. Her hand left traces of blood on his jacket. "Look, I brought the car," she said, pointing to the low dark double-parked vehicle, the front bumper dented and spattered with mud. She had to flail to stay upright. "Let's go before the cops get here. Get in—I'll drive."

"You're drunk; I'll drive," said Daniel.

She sprawled in the passenger seat and laughed until she couldn't breathe. Daniel fastened his seat belt and started the engine, which sounded wet and unhealthy. Sybil scatted nonsense to herself, touching the window glass with her filthy fingertips.

"What the hell was that?" he said quietly.

She said nothing; she grabbed a disc off the floor and slid it into the dashboard. She rolled her head across the fur collar, muddying her hair, scatting in perfect sync with the music. She unsnapped the top of her coverall and ran her bloodied hand across her breast, her scatting melting into honey humming.

Daniel stopped at a red light, put the car into parking gear, leaned over, and seized the open edges of her coverall. He shook her, once, then tossed her back against the car seat. "What did you just do?" he shouted.

The CD skipped from the force of his voice.

Sybil winced but kept smiling. "Thanks for the hearing loss, OK?"

"Sybil, if I have to shake you again, you won't survive."

"Look, OK, I didn't mean for *that* to happen necessarily," she said, her voice so dry he didn't need to see into her mind to know she was lying. "I didn't think it would do that. It was just a smoke bomb. I was gonna add to the party atmosphere. That couldn't have been me; musta been a gas leak or somethin' . . ." She shrugged. "Too bad. The station was gonna get demolished anyway; no big loss. Better me than the city, though, huh? You should go." In agreement from behind them came a few sharp cries from a car horn.

Daniel didn't move. "You killed forty people with one stupid prank."

"The light's green, man."

"They're all dead," he said thickly. "Some of those people were *your* friends. Didn't you read the signs? Didn't you?" The car horns behind them rose to a thunderous, multitoned scream.

"Go!" she screamed, her hands over her ears.

He shifted from *P* to *D,* and they crawled forward into a mass of nearly immobile traffic.

"I don't *have* any fucking friends. Remember?" She stretched her spine against the seat. "How does it feel to be crushed to death?" she asked, her hand moving back to her breast. "In the bombed buildings? Oh, God, does it hurt? Is it over quickly or is it . . . Do you know? You *must* know."

"Alexandra." Daniel tasted blood in his mouth and realized that he was biting the inside of his lower lip. "Joachim."

Sybil shook her head. "Alexandra wasn't even there. And Joachim got out. I told you; he took off. He sketched when he saw me and I watched him leave."

He wanted to believe that; it was easier just to believe it, it just made sense, really. "Where did you get the bomb?"

"I made it. My dad taught me how to make smoke bombs. It's really easy."

"And how did the car get all fucked up?"

"I ran into a newsstand," she said with an impatient sigh, "near Central Park. Do you care? It's just a car."

"And why did you run into a newsstand?"

"I'll tell you when we get home," she mumbled. "Which will be forever tomorrow. Will you give me a bath?"

"Yes," he said. "It'll be a while before the water's hot."

"I'll wait."

It was nearly 4 A.M. when they arrived, the last ninety minutes spent without words. In the dark warehouse, she sat on the concrete floor with her arms around her knees, her face empty and expressionless. Daniel tried not to look at her as he fired up the propane-fuelled water heater. Days before, she had hauled four giant clear blue plastic bottles of drinking water in the deformed shopping cart into the warehouse; slicing into them with a six-inch serrated knife, Daniel added their contents to the melted snow water already in the heater.

Four-thirty, and dawn still hours away. Sybil lit a candle, pale, long, and thick as her forearm, on the construction table. The tin bath now rocked unsteadily on a wheeled pallet; Daniel filled it ten inches deep with the steaming water, adding a box of baking soda to defeat the dirt in the melted snow. Sybil pulled off her clothes and boots and shivered into the tub, her teeth chattering. Tears had streaked white lines through the layer of grime on her face. Daniel poured a plastic bowl of water over the top of her head. "You're so muddy," he said mildly, lathering his hands with runny liquid soap. "What were you doing to get so filthy, Sybil the Slovenly?"

"I was hunting," she said. A smile slowly returned to her face. "I was bringing the second coming to people who forgot that it was supposed to happen tonight."

"Yeah?" said Daniel noncommittally; he rubbed the lather into her hair.

"Yeah," she agreed. Her voice was low and husky, like she'd been screaming all night. "I killed every homeless person I could find."

"How did you know they were homeless?"

"I could tell," she said. "You can . . . see it in their eyes. You can smell it on them. The despair."

"Is that where the shit came from?" Daniel grasped the back of her head with one hand, tipping it back, and with the other hand poured more water over her head to rinse out the soap. Her neck was covered with fine bruises.

"This one guy—totally past it. He's the one that got me by the neck. We had a good fight and the motherfucker almost had me down. He was too far gone to even consider running. He'd probably been running all his life and he figured that this was it—maybe he knew that his life was on the line. . . ." The bruises bobbed and pulsated as she swallowed. "I flipped him and shoved his head into the ground and he shit his pants and there was a hole in his pants and it got me. He got me in the end, the crazy bastard. Reminded me so much of my dad . . ." Her laugh was a bubble breaking. "He gave me a brown souvenir. Awesome. He was awesome.

"Oh! And there was this old lady . . . she was fuckin' tough! She just would not cooperate! She did *not* want to have her neck broken! And she was making so much noise that I panicked when I saw the cops, and that's when I ran into the newsstand. I should have just bricked her ass. I mean, I got her, but . . ."

He lathered his hands again and passed them around her shoulders, arms, and breasts. "Burn your coverall," he said. "I can't stand the smell of it. And you'll have to lose the parka, too, probably."

"You do it," said Sybil. "Set the fire. Light some more candles. Light some incense. Light me a joint. Burn it all down . . ."

Daniel left her soapy, kicked the clothes into the burn pile, then lit a thick twist of newspaper and settled it on top. Her clothes were fairly flammable, for being damp and muddy; all of them had been liberally splashed with butane. "Very dangerous and very stupid. I wish you had told me." He sighed. "I wish you had . . . been with me."

"I was there. I saw the whole party. I could tell you weren't having a particularly good time. Don't you know it? You're with me all the time," she said, and then again, insistently, "you're *with* me—all the time."

Daniel watched the fire, struggling with the leather; he tossed more newspaper at it and chewed a new wound in his mouth. "So you decided to waste an entire party just because I was there."

"No," she said. "Not because you were there. I *was* going to . . . but I just . . ."

"You should have."

"But I decided when I saw you that I didn't want to." Her teeth were chattering again. "I'm clean. I'm going to bed. Come with me."

Daniel felt the Saturday-ness as soon as he woke up; he stretched against sheets delightfully cool against his hot skin, swung his legs down, and stretched out his shoulders, a warm hungry glory of being awake and alive.

Down on the next level he caught sight of the girl, wearing his pants and nothing else, adding newspapers to the arrangements of the rich woman's Christmas and the parking garage woman's clumps of hair, now glued in an even layer on one of the fang canvases, and it all came back to him like a sudden vicious hangover: *Oh God Oh God what did I DO, what in the world was I involved in last night?*

Sybil looked up at him and began in midstream, "I mean, can you fucking believe it? I mean, I can believe it, but I think—I guess I was hoping for something—aw, fuck, you know?"

"What?" Daniel sighed.

"Look at this." She ran upstairs with the paper and handed it to him. At the bottom of the front page ran a piece about the collapse of the long-abandoned Worth Street Station. How dozens of bodies lay trapped under several layers of concrete and pipe, but that no identifications had yet been made. How an investigation was beginning, how terrorism had not yet been ruled out. Daniel folded the paper and handed it back to her. "If Joachim's dead—" he began.

"C'mon," she said wearily. "You were gonna kill him anyway."

Daniel blinked at her. "What makes you think that?

She smiled. "You think I don't know you?"

She trailed her fingers against his lips.

"They're going to find out." He sighed.

"Like they're going to find out that you drink people's blood?" She was sober, as far as he could tell, her eyes clear, her body smelling of cheap laundromat soap.

"I can't hypnotize an entire city's worth of forensics . . . people," Daniel blustered.

"What's it matter?" Sybil said. "There's no mention whatsoever of the other people who died last night. All those people without credit cards or color TV or cabfare." Tears wet her cheeks suddenly. "Is anybody ever gonna know?"

"Besides me, you mean?" Daniel put in, his voice quiet. "Is that what you were creating?"

"If a person falls in the park and there's nobody around to hear, does it make a sound?" She abruptly laughed at herself and rushed back to her arranging work downstairs. She had his shoulder bag with her, and she took her wire sculptures out and set them on the ground, next to his spent glow stick and a party hat, neither the one that he'd chosen, or her propeller beanie. "By the way," she called up, "these"—tapping one of the sculptures—"are mine. They are not yours to give. Don't try to give away my things without asking me first."

"I could say, 'Don't murder scores of my friends without asking me first,' " Daniel muttered to himself, reaching for clothes.

"You could say that," Sybil agreed, in tones almost as quiet. "OK. These are yours. But please leave them right here; this is an installation and it's not fair to disturb it while it's in progress." She set down the last newspaper. "Now, the question is, do you want to go play outside, or do you want to stay and play inside?"

Daniel thought of the snow, and he thought of the hangover traffic, and he thought about forensics people, and put the clothes back down.

Scene Twenty-four: Survivors

"The Supreme Gina has been trying for ages to get hold of your ass."

Sybil had told him not to answer it and now she glared at him, hands on her hips. Daniel motioned with his fingers for her to keep walking. "I've been busy, darling," Daniel explained to the uncooperative phone, squinting at the shadowy forms and pinpricks of light swimming across Bowery Street.

"Your home phone [static] doesn't work any [static], for some reason."

"I don't live there anymore," said Daniel, frantically angling his head and body this way and that, seeking reception. "Look, could I call you back? My phone really isn't cooperating right now."

Sybil stomped into the intersection and pretended to direct traffic. Somehow, the herd of taxis and trucks swerved to avoid her. Tucked capelike into her collar, a long trail of silvery-white glitter tulle, a recent Dumpster find, whipped the air behind her.

The Supreme Gina didn't seem to have heard his last few words, barreling on, her voice chopped into odd, loud, bitchy chunks. "Still, [static] not considerate. The

Supreme Gina would [static] that, since you were unable to [static] with her before the first of the year, Frau Herr will no longer [static] performer at Gemini."

A massive yellow delivery truck snagged the glitter cape and ripped it from Sybil's shoulders, the wake tossing her sprawling onto the icy-wet street.

"Fine," Daniel bit out, threw the cell phone to the ground, and darted into the intersection. A Subaru wagon driver rubbed her eyes; did she really see a man jump off the sidewalk, skip across the hood of her moving car, and then disappear into traffic? A few hops and a grab, and Daniel set Sybil down onto her feet on the sidewalk.

Sybil, nonplussed, wiped dirt and blood off her hands onto the thighs of her olive-drab pants. "I'm fine, asshole," she snapped at him. "You didn't need to act like a fucking superhero."

"Who's the superhero? What is it with you and traffic?"

"It's my planet; I ought to be able to walk wherever I want to. And like it wouldn't be so fucking nice and convenient for you to have me killed. Isn't that what you really want? Since you can't kill me yourself?" She had spent the afternoon in a frenzy of broken-glass and paper assemblage, interspersed with rails of cocaine; as night deepened and the clouds broke open to reveal a terribly black and starless sky, she all but ran across the bridge into Manhattan, with Daniel following close behind her.

"How do you know what I want?"

She spat a copious, frothy wad onto shards of opaque ice in the gutter. "I know better than you do, O, utter insane love of my life."

"You need to come down. Right now." He grabbed the shoulder of her coat and hustled her down the sidewalk. "If I have to poison you with alcohol, you're coming down."

Thank God for dark-wood-paneled bars and tired bartenders; Daniel procured a bottle of Wild Turkey and two glasses and gently suggested to the people sitting in the farthest-back booth that they should move. Their toddy-addled brains barely acknowledged the presence of the anguished-looking Daniel and the tweak-goggled Sybil.

Sybil chugged the first four fingers of whiskey, pausing between gulps to pull air through her nose. "I don't think I ever want to do coke again," she mumbled.

"I don't know why you can't just do a little at a time," Daniel said, pouring her another. "I don't know that there's any left."

"I wanted to get rid of it," she explained, taking a mouthful and grimacing painfully. "It's Sonic Ruth's drug. She's in me right now. Running out my nose." Sybil took a much smaller sip. "Did I ever tell you about the time we almost killed a cop?"

Daniel mutely shook his head.

"It's like this. Sonic Ruth traded her ass for free coke. She got all her blow from this one guy, James, this ex-lawyer who got busted and did some time but managed to white-collar his way out. He controlled most of the coke that came into or went out of Colorado Springs. And that's like, a shitload of coke. Kilos and kilos of the shit. Coloradans love cocaine—those rich, conservative Yuppies who live there have to have some way of cutting loose, y'know? Not to mention the fraternity jocks. That's the weekend: Coors, tits, and coke. I mean, there's no way I'll ever know just how much James dealt, but plenty of times I saw guys come and go with duffel bags so heavy they walked lopsided. And I don't know if it was coke or cash money in there, but it was—Anyway. Sonic Ruth hooked up with James through her parents; her folks were so dumb they didn't know where all his money came from, they didn't know *why* he had this humongous house with two swimming pools and a lawn that looked like a fucking golf course. And six cars. Ruth's dad's a doctor, and he knew James through another doctor friend, this plastic surgeon who I guess was into something legally shady. Golf buddies. Anyway, James started giving Ruth coke when she was like, I don't know, eleven or twelve, and by the time she was thirteen or so, he started fucking her, and giving her tissues for presents afterwards. This is about the time when I met her; it was the summer between middle school and high school and we were the two freaky chicks who hung around record stores, and one day she invited me over to listen to music and . . ." Sybil groaned faintly. "She didn't start bragging to me about the fact that she fucked for blow until she was about fourteen; she thought it was really cool, this status symbol, to be fucking this guy who's like forty and drives a silver Lexus, gave her free drugs."

Sybil erupted into inappropriately loud, metallic laughter. Daniel forced the other bar patrons' attention away from them, and stared hard into Sybil's eyes, daring her to be so loud again. She smirked at him and went on. "And so she brought me with her over to his house one day, since she'd told him all about me and he wanted to meet me. I mean, this is the sleaziest character, still looked like a lawyer, you know, the light-colored suits, the loafers, the hair; and he just fucking *loved* me. The way that guy looked at me made me want to have a sex change. I escaped and went out and sat by the pool and wondered how the hell I was going to get home. When I got sick of waiting I went back inside. Sonic Ruth's sucking James's dick in the middle of the living room while a bunch of other assholes stood around and made commentary."

She paused to toss down more Wild Turkey. "That isn't even the point of this story, but it happened on the same day, so I had to mention it. So Sonic Ruth gets her coke, and I'm all like, 'Let's go, now, please,' and so we get in Ruth's car and start driving. Of course the bitch has had like forty lines of coke, and she decides it'd be a really freaky glam punk rock Courtney Love thing to do to smoke some weed. So she's fumbling around in her purse and steering with her knees and not watching the road, and there's this big dip leading down into the outskirts of town, and at the bottom of the dip is this cop writing out a ticket. So I grab the wheel and try to swerve out of the way, but we're going way too fast; we clip the edge of the cop's back bumper and knock down the cop. And by this time Sonic Ruth has a clue, and she brakes her car and it stops about five hundred yards away from the cop. I look back and the cop is getting up—he's all right, it looks like—and Ruth's like 'Shit! Shit! Shit!' and I have this amazing flash of instinct and I grab her bag that's got all the drugs in it, open the door, and run for the hills; there's trees by the side of the road, and I go get lost. The cop never saw me. I walk back home and it takes me about two and a half hours, but I make it all right with no hassles. Sonic Ruth got arrested, but since she didn't do anything worse than reckless driving and going like eight miles per hour above the speed limit, and she wasn't drunk and managed to hold it together enough that they didn't test for anything else she was on . . . it was, like, two weeks before we left—"

"Ssh!" Daniel held up his hand to silence her, and she actually obliged, halting her increasingly slurry mumble. "Do you hear it?" he asked.

"Hear what?"

Daniel stood up, looking over the tops of the booths toward the door. He saw only large haunted dark eyes and the glint from the zipper of a familiar coat, but it was all he needed; Daniel bolted out of the booth, headed after.

"Joachim!" he gasped, tumbling outside. The night wind smacked him, slamming the door shut. "Joachim!"

Joachim turned to face Daniel, his eyes as starless as the black night sky, and said, "I'm leaving."

Daniel grasped the fleece-jacketed arms, palpating them, assuring himself that the flesh was real and solid, touching Joachim's face with his hands. "I thought I heard you! You're alive—you're all right! Oh, thank God!"

"You're alive, too, huh," said Joachim flatly.

Daniel blinked and reeled back. "I never thought I'd see you again—"

"If you cared so much, why didn't you call? It's been five days. It's been five days of *me* being questioned by cops and *me* trying to identify bodies from chunks and pieces!" Joachim's voice dropped to a furious hiss.

Daniel shook his head and found that he couldn't stop doing it. Five days of lying with Sybil, only getting up to fetch her food, only alone while she emptied her chamber bucket outside. Reading to each other. Fucking. Crying. "I couldn't . . . It's too new, too recent . . . I didn't want to be reminded . . . Did you tell them about me?"

"I told them that you were there. That you didn't leave either with or before me. They've been trying to get in touch with you ever since, but you're not at your apartment, you're not answering your phone . . . So now you're missing, presumed dead." The fathomless eyes flicked back at the bar. Sybil peeked over the top of the booth. "I didn't mention her."

"We were last out," Daniel said soothingly. "Do you know who else made it out?"

Joachim slowly shook his head. "I don't know. If people left, I didn't notice. I was rolling balls," he confessed ruefully. "I was so high I wouldn't have noticed anything all night if I hadn't smelled shit all of a sudden."

"Please come in. Sit down. There's a bottle of whiskey. Please."

A galvanic response jerked Joachim's relaxing posture rigidly upright. "I will not sit down and drink and pretend to be nice to *that—person!* Not even for you!"

Daniel glanced back toward the bar; under the gas-flame hair, Sybil's face wore an innocent, discreet smile. He turned back to Joachim with a sigh. "Yes, yes, of course. I forget that I sometimes can only see the best things in someone and forget all their problems."

"You could say that."

"Please. Please. If not tonight, can I still get in touch through your old number? I'd really like to see you. I'd really like to keep in touch." Daniel stared deeply into Joachim's dark irises, angling his head until his reflection was visible. *Please.*

Joachim, nodding, extended one gloved hand; Daniel gently pulled the glove away and pressed his hand against Joachim's. Daniel put his arm round Joachim, bringing their foreheads together. "It'll be all right," Daniel whispered. "It'll all be all right in the end."

Don't tell them anything more about me. Don't tell them anything about Sybil. You've done your bit and I'll take care of everything else, my dear puppy. Smile to let me know you understand.

Joachim looked up and allowed a smile to play at the corner of his lips. "I gotta go," he said.

"I'll call you tomorrow," said Daniel.

He kissed Joachim on both cheeks and hugged him as tightly as he dared, tucking his nose into the delicious space behind Joachim's ear where the richest scents collected, reminiscent of fresh olives, good paper, Hindi incense. In the end, he let Joachim walk away, hail a taxicab, slip inside, disappear.

With a heavy step, Daniel returned to the booth where Sybil sat. She had finished her second glass of whiskey and was now playing with the water droplets on the table, slid over diagonally with her head resting against the wall. "I drove him away," she sang.

"Oh, so now you feel better about yourself." There was no sting in it.

"No, you do." She traced an anarchy symbol in spilled whiskey. "You came in here because he was here. You didn't even know it. You love him so much it's embarrassing to watch."

"Only because you don't know what love is," Daniel retorted.

"Is that supposed to hurt?" She grinned and showed her palms, bright pink and scraped and swollen, thin red scabs dotting the mounts. "No, see, *this* hurts. I don't think there's anything you could say to me that would hurt more than skinning my hands." She put her palm down on the anarchy symbol and her eyes rolled to the ceiling, the only outward show of pain. "So who was on the phone earlier?"

"Oh, Gina. I mean, The Supreme Gina." Daniel quirked his fingers in the air. "I've been kicked off the drag revue. Watch the tears roll down my cheeks."

"Shed the nonessential." She licked her palm, then held it out to him; the taste of the thin blood, adrenaline and cocaine and a sort of numb wordless rage, diluted in alcohol, sliced through him, snaking like metal filaments through his blood vessels. Sybil smiled at him. "Jonesing now, huh?"

Daniel found himself unable to speak, instead staring at her, dissecting her face into damp pink skin, wet flesh of lips, glistening jelly eyes, soft fragile entrances into her nose; all of it so delicate, so tearable, with so much blood inside, underneath. He closed his eyes, struggling to maintain control.

"Let's go," she said.

On the street, Sybil looked at her hand with incomprehension. "Wow, it's all better," she slurred, feet stepping sideways.

Daniel caught her and took her other hand and ran over it with his tongue; this one was no longer bleeding, and he tasted only the dry smooth aftereffect on the sealed skin. "Now that one'll be better, too," he said.

He sighed and took both her hands in his, massaging the backs of them, the smooth moist skin with soft flexible sinews and knuckle bones succulent enough to chew. "I need to be away from you," he confessed, squeezing his eyes closed. "I'm afraid I'm going to hurt you if I'm around you for a moment longer. I need to be angry with you for a while and I haven't had the chance, and I don't trust my anger right now. I'll hurt you, I know it. I'll kill you if I touch you anymore. And"—he chuckled faintly—"I want you alive."

Sybil kissed Daniel's chin, lips, neck. "Go on," she told him softly. "Leave me alone. I'll be all right. We've done nothing but fuck and cry for five days. Go away. Sanity's sake."

"I love you," he said.

"Please don't," she responded, pressed her raw, healing palm against his cheek, and turned away, her head bent low. Daniel watched her for the entire block, clenching his fists until his claws punched into the skin, willing himself not to follow her so thoroughly that he forgot to breathe.

The days that followed had a surreal cast; the sky was as clear as plastic wrap, painfully bright during the day and as black as the void at night, and no Sybil. Daniel avoided the warehouse. He took a room at a cheap hotel in Noho, wore the same clothes over and over.

When he woke up after the first day's sleep, he called Joachim, and Joachim's roommate informed Daniel that Joachim had not been home all day.

"Please let him know that Daniel called," Daniel said.

Even over the phone, he could feel the mood change. "Oh . . . *Daniel.* OK. Yeah. OK. I'll let him know." As in, *I've already forgotten this.*

"Don't fuck around, pal. This is important."

"Oh, yeah, yeah, I know, I wasn't fucking around."

"Is he there?"

"No, man, I told you, he was gone when I woke up and I've been here all day, and he hasn't shown up. When he shows up, I'll tell him you called, so why'n't you chill, yo?"

Daniel hung up. He hated being called "yo." He went downstairs to get some Hunan Chinese from the café on the ground floor, then returned to his room, arrayed the boxes on the bedside table, and picked up the phone again, this time calling his accountant.

"Is this Daniel?" Gestwirt answered Daniel's greeting.

"Yes, it is," Daniel said in German, as they always spoke together.

"Marvelous! How were your holidays?"

"Exciting," said Daniel.

"So were mine, although not in the way that I might have chosen for myself."

"I know what you mean. At any rate, I must discuss business with you. Are you free this evening?"

"Please come! I should probably be asleep, but I haven't been doing much of that lately. There's too much to do!"

Daniel poked at his food with a pair of chopsticks. "I'll be a little while, I just got dinner," Daniel said. "An hour? Do you think you can stay awake that long?"

"For you, certainly."

Daniel sampled each of his boxes, then closed them up again and set out. On his way to Gestwirt's, he cut through a gay dance club, danced, and had his fill of blood, culled from seven different men. All seven survived, though one ended up in the emergency room after he'd fallen unconscious in the lavatory and cracked his skull on the linoleum floor.

This evening, Gestwirt wore pewter-colored satin pajamas, sheepskin-lined slippers, and a kind of weird turban made from a reversible terry-cloth towel fastened with a gaudy paste-ruby brooch, askew on his forehead. He welcomed Daniel at the side door of his condo and led him up the tall, narrow flight of stairs. The old man crept forward one careful step at a time, and Daniel respectfully followed behind, noting that the rich scent of Gestwirt's cologne did not entirely mask an undertone of antiseptic and, even fainter, urine. Daniel had just begun to jauntily comment, "Are we very stiff today, friend?" when Gestwirt stopped and struggled for breath. The comment came out instead, "Are we very—are you all right, Heinz?"

Gestwirt gestured emptily for a moment before he could speak. "I'll be all right," he panted. "For the first time in my life, I wish I lived on the ground floor."

As painful as it was to watch, Daniel didn't offend the man by offering to help; he only crept along behind, wishing there was something else to be done. Gestwirt was old; he wasn't a child. He was still a man. Younger than Daniel, but still, a man.

In the soft yellow- and green-tinted light of the office, Daniel saw that in the weeks since he'd last visited the accountant, something inside Gestwirt had gone wrong. Gestwirt tugged off the turban and dropped it distastefully onto the desk. The lines in his face seemed deeper, wider, full of shadows that shouldn't be there; the sparse white hair had gotten sparser, patches missing awkwardly at the sides of his head. "My God, what happened?" Daniel breathed, stifling the urge to reach out and touch the grotesquely exposed pink-gray scalp.

Gestwirt smiled ruefully, settled on the low couch beside his desk, and lifted a glass of water to his lips. "I spent *my* holidays in the hospital," he admitted, a touch cockily. "Hooked up to tubes, full of sedatives. . . . It wouldn't have been so bad without the catheter. I think that's what I could stand the least."

Daniel, immobilized, stood in the center of the room.

"My granddaughter Cecily was the only one on my side," Gestwirt continued, slipping on a pair of impossibly thick trifocal glasses and shuffling through the sheaf of paper in Daniel's file. "Everyone else wanted me to stay there with a tube in my penis and a mask on my face, watching television with a head full of dope—have you watched Sally Jessy Raphael? The things people consider to be acceptable! Once upon a time people actually got dressed up to be on television. It was a special, once-in-a-lifetime experience. They were on their best behavior. Now . . . horrible teenagers, hideous fat women like the ones in a circus. Screaming and tearing at each other like wild animals." Gestwirt toyed with his turban. "Cecily made this for me. I'm supposed to wear something on my head all the time to avoid chill, but it's so ugly . . ."

Daniel tried to laugh but it dried in his throat before he could voice it. "So what is it?" He did finally sit down on the guest's couch, a softer, wider affair in a dark maroon velvet. Antique, Victorian; older than them both.

"Let's see. A mild stroke, which isn't really a problem, but in the hospital I got chilled and my lungs began to fill with fluid. Apparently, I have less than half my lungs working at the moment; maybe it's worse now, I don't know. They are simply too damaged to keep working much longer." He threw up his hands philosophically. "Oh, and cancer, to be certain; that's been around for years and years, but it's never given me much trouble until now. It must have been the strain of Thanksgiving dinner. I ate so much turkey I could hardly move! Eh . . . I have nothing to complain about. I brought it upon myself, trading blow jobs for cigarettes."

That wretched word—*Krebsgeschwür*—resonated throughout Daniel's mind, blotted out everything else he'd said. Cancer, eating his friend. He flinched and shook his head, unable to be titillated. "Oh, God, Heinz, this is terrible."

Gestwirt frowned, his face a Braque configuration of huge, faceted eyes and gnarled skin. "I'm here, aren't I? I'm breathing; I can think; I can work. So. Shall we get to business? And not discuss this morbid nonsense any further?"

"You should be in a hospital."

"And you should be at home making love. I think your concern is very charming, but you're repeating the things said by my family that I hate most. I ignored them. I'm ignoring you. Business?"

"Heinz . . . it's just that . . . I don't want to lose you. I don't want to imagine the world without you in it."

Gestwirt relaxed and smiled, and in profile, his face was almost the same one that Daniel had come to love, worn and grooved from concern and laughing. "Yes, Daniel. But this has to happen. Everything that lives must die. And we're human beings. We do everything on a grand scale, don't we? We take decades to die, and it costs a great deal of money. I would prefer to continue with the work that I enjoy, seeing the clients who have come to depend on me, instead of taking up bed space that would be better used for people who are so weak that they cannot live on their own, or who *want* to die that way. That has never been the case for me—I have always preferred excitement to relaxation. I think you are the same, which is why we like each other so much. I wish to die on my feet, and I think you do as well, don't you? Neither of us wants to die, but if it must happen, it should be on our terms."

Daniel nodded slowly, looking at the toes of his shoes.

Gestwirt waved his hand. "Anyway, you won't have to worry about that for a good long time yet. You're thirty; the best years of your life are still ahead of you. You don't even have children yet." Gestwirt sighed. "I sacrificed the pleasures of my youth for children," he murmured. "I swore that if I made it out of Poland alive, I would have as many children as I could to make up for the ones that I saw die. I gave up . . . boys. I found Sarah, God rest her. We had an understanding. We created children."

Daniel allowed himself a soft laugh. "I could never give up boys," he said. "I've never even tried."

"Oh, but it's easier now, isn't it? Everything's changed. The world . . . Ah. Well. Business."

"Business. I need to sell my flat."

"Do you? Have you found another place?"

"I'm staying in a hotel for the time being. And then I think I'm going to travel, stay with friends. Be a vagabond for a while."

"Adventure. Marvelous. Do it while you can. Well, the place should sell as soon as I list it; I shall do it first thing tomorrow morning."

"Furnished."

"All right . . . perhaps you can provide me with a rough list of the furnishings."

Business passed between them, gleefully on Gestwirt's part, painfully on Daniel's. He listed all the furniture he'd selected with the help of his assistants, and the things he'd found on his own in his first few months of living in Manhattan, all the objects running through his mind with their tags of memory—the individuals who leafed through catalogues with him in bed, skipped around trendy furniture stores, or weren't there, and the color reminded him of her eyes. Just things. Only when Daniel had finished did he feel the tickle of salt-wetness on his face drying.

Gestwirt had only made quick and quiet sounds of acknowledgment as he wrote the descriptions in shorthand on a yellow legal pad, but now he set down his pen, took off his glasses, and sighed heavily. "I'm afraid that I've broken your heart without meaning to," he said.

"You could hardly help it," Daniel said, scrubbing his cheeks with his knuckles. "I did ask."

"I remember getting that flat for you. You were staying at that dreadful hotel, and every day it was 'I was out shopping—did you find me a place?' "

Daniel chuckled. "I needed everything," he said. "I came to New York with nothing. Nothing except account numbers."

"And isn't that all you need?" Gestwirt laughed, but

Daniel looked so stricken that he stopped, holding out his quivering, leathery hands. "I'm so sorry! Please, put it out of your mind. And don't insult me by crying! I'm still alive right now."

"You're my oldest friend in this city," Daniel murmured, wiping his cheeks again. "When I came, I had nothing. You've given me so much."

"I helped you to embellish and control what you already had, that's all."

"No," Daniel said, rising and taking Gestwirt's hands in his own, "that is *not* all. You helped me to remember the good things about Germany. You showed me that there is something good and hopeful in the world that survives. You were a friend to me when I didn't have a single one in the world. You aren't just someone I hired."

Gestwirt sighed. "You and I both know that, in the end, that is all that I am, and that's all the emotion you should have concerning me. And you saw a Germany far better than the one that I ever lived in. I haven't been back there and I don't think I'm going to go. Everything that I loved there is gone now."

"You're right," said Daniel heavily. "I can see there's going to be no comfort in sentiment with you tonight. I'll go. Please, get some rest and take care of yourself. My old phone number doesn't work anymore, but let me give you a more current one. I might not answer it immediately, but I want you to let me know right away when you've found a buyer for the apartment."

Daniel felt a panicked desire to tell Gestwirt to forget it, that he wanted to keep the flat after all, that he could just move back in, forget Sybil, and if she dared show her face at his door, run her through with the fireplace poker. Instead, he scribbled down the hotel room's phone's number on the same yellow legal pad as his list of furnishings, picked up Gestwirt's left hand, the one with the yellow-gold wedding band slipping easily up and down an emaciated finger, and brought it to his lips. He focused all his love for Heinz Gestwirt, all five years of conversations, arguments, giggly sherry-fueled late nights, into the kiss. When he looked up at the old man, Gestwirt's eyes glazed with a helpless, stricken desire.

"I'm not what you think I am," Daniel whispered with a flickering, hesitant smile. "Not at all. And I could keep you from dying. I could save you, just as you are, to last forever."

Gestwirt arched an eyebrow, his expression free of alarm, fear, or surprise. "Even if you were telling the truth, I wouldn't want it. Why would I want to be like this forever? An old man with a sore back? Now, if you could make me young again, maybe I'd be interested." The desiccated hand stroked Daniel's hair. "If I'd met you when I was your age, I might not have gotten married."

"Bullshit," Daniel said, standing up, letting go. "Then you wouldn't have had the grandchildren, and everyone knows that they're the best part of being alive. You made your choice."

Gestwirt, as ever, immune to sarcasm, wagged his finger and grinned. "When I was young, I would have gotten into trouble to see someone like you. I was hardly more than a child, but I knew what I wanted."

Daniel left, substituting a smile for the good-bye that he was afraid to speak aloud.

When Daniel rose the next evening, the message light on the hotel phone was blinking. He put the receiver against his cheekbone without rising from where he lay, face-down, his pillow in shreds underneath him. There were two messages—one from Gestwirt, reporting that the apartment had sold at its listed price within four hours of its posting. "Three point one five million, furnished; not so bad," Gestwirt half-laughed, half-coughed into the phone. Gestwirt always took his ten percent before he told Daniel anything about the sale. "I took the liberty to shelter the money in Portugal again, which makes five million you have there. And I think that's all I have to say today. We should talk again before too long, however, so, please"—and here he paused to cough—"call me and schedule an appointment. We should get loose ends tied up. Good night."

The other message was from Joachim.

It was very brief and halting; hello, what's up, you called. "I'm gonna be out of town starting in February," Joachim added abruptly, as if cutting himself off. "It'd be kinda cool if we got together before then. Call me tonight on my cell and we can set something up."

Daniel recalled to Joachim, over coffee, the waking up alone on a nest of chopped polyfill. Joachim laughed, poking the bottom of his cup with a spoon. "So why isn't Sybil with you?" he asked at the end of the laugh.

"Because I wanted to get the *fuck* away from her," Daniel said forcefully; they both laughed. "I mean, I know I'm going to go back eventually. But I really, really have to get away from her sometimes. She's just so . . . overwhelming."

Joachim shook his head. "I just don't like the fact that she showed up at the party, and then the place . . ."

"She had nothing to do with that, Joachim. It's just a . . . bad coincidence." Daniel's coffee had gone cold and sour. He put it on the counter and pushed it away with his fingernails.

"Daniel, it's *too* bad."

"Yes, it's too bad, but nonetheless, it's a coincidence." Daniel swiveled a little on his tall, round stool, changing postures as he changed subjects. "So where are you going next month?"

Joachim also shifted on his stool. He had never taken off his coat; that, and the decision to meet with him at this incredibly busy, yuppie coffee bar, combined to tell Daniel that Joachim feared being alone with him. "I'm going to Sydney," Joachim said.

"Australia?"

"I got a job."

"In Australia? With who? Doing what?"

He blushed, flattered by Daniel's consternation. "I'm going to be doing set design for the Radley Theatre Company. I might get to do set design for things inside the Sydney Opera House—that's gonna be a hell of task. Still, it's pretty cool. It should be really fun."

"So you'll be gone for a while, huh?" said Daniel.

Joachim smiled a little. "A good while," he said. "As long as I can."

"Darn it . . . I was gonna leave the country. We can't *both* leave the country." Daniel shifted on his stool again, facing more toward Joachim.

"Sure we can," said Joachim. "Go ahead. You don't have to stay anywhere. You're an international citizen. I mean . . . you have dual citizenship, don't you?"

Daniel chuckled away that awkward question, and Joachim shook his head, rubbed his temples, and forgot about it. "I think it's good to get out of New York once in a while," Joachim went on. "If nothing else, it helps you appreciate what you actually like about it. And it's good to just . . . you know, get a fresh start." He stood up and pumped his coffee cup full again. "I mean, that's what you're doing, isn't it? I've never seen you change as much as you have recently. Selling your place and busting up the studio."

"I always stay the same for years and years," Daniel said, "and then something happens and everything changes. It's always really sudden. Like earthquakes."

"Or bombs," said Joachim.

Daniel swiveled on his bar stool, now mostly away from Joachim. He toyed with a napkin dispenser for a minute, trying to remain calm and focused. "So what's the deal?"

"Oh. My friend Igor is going to spin a set for me at Almighty on February 12. You can come over to my place for dinner first if you want to, I'm having some other folks over, or you can meet us at the club. Igor says the earliest he'd start would be ten, but it'll probably be closer to midnight."

More large social settings. "Don't I get to see you without having to arm-wrestle for your attention with your super cute young friends?"

It was Joachim's turn to laugh away the awkward answer. "I'm just really busy, Daniel."

"No, I understand. Kidding. I'd be delighted to. Thanks for inviting me."

"We are still friends, right?" Joachim raised his coffee

cup; Daniel lifted his and obligingly clinked the rims together.

Daniel awoke in the dark again, facedown on an intact pillow, glanced at the clock radio on the bedside table, and found it to be 6:30. Mostly for purposes of illumination, he switched on the television as he got dressed. He kept his back turned to the commercials but favored the blaring fanfare of orchestral brass of the evening news theme song. "Tuesday, January 18, 2000," spoke a disembodied voice.

Last night had been January 13.

Daniel rang the front desk in terror.

"What day is it?" he demanded.

"It's January 18," replied the desk clerk, used to such things.

"This is room 1403. I'm checking out."

"Very good, sir."

Daniel turned on all the lights in the room and stared at himself in the mirror. He looked essentially the same as he had the morning he'd gone to sleep, if a little paler and more jagged around the edges; no beard growth had happened, his eyebrows were still separate and distinct. He hadn't gotten old. It was still the same year. He wondered how long it would be possible to remain in state on that unforgiving mattress with the DO NOT MAKE UP THIS ROOM sign facing out on the doorknob. Perhaps they would have let him sleep for weeks.

The boxes of Chinese food were moldy. No phone messages. He had been forgotten.

He returned to the warehouse in a taxi, curled up in his seat with his arms around his knees. The driver said nothing to him, only scowling when Daniel didn't tip. Daniel knocked carefully on the door; when no response came, he tried the knob and found it turned and admitted him.

Sybil stretched out on one table, supine, arms hanging slack over the sides, near-naked, covered with fine cuts and small round cigarette burns. Her eyes were open, but she didn't move except for infrequent shallow breaths, unresponsive to the sound of his footsteps or his voice saying her name. On the end of the table, a few inches from her head, a dead brown rat lay on its side in a glass aquarium topped with a stretched, unmarked canvas and a haphazardly arranged stack of bricks. The floor around the table held a devastation of torn magazines, empty plastic sandwich bags, unconscious butts of cigarettes, broken crayons, broken brushes, broken glass.

Daniel carried Sybil's limp, heavy body upstairs and settled her gently on the bed. He licked her tiny wounds and wrapped her in the blankets, rubbing and breathing on her palms to warm them. She shivered minutely, the delicate hairs covering her body standing up in response to the change in temperature. Her dilated eyes focused on him briefly, then closed, and she frowned and grumbled.

"What happened?" Daniel whispered.

Her slack fingers attempted to draw the blankets closer around her but couldn't. Daniel did it for her. "Mmmm . . . desperate measures," she replied, her voice like smudged text on crumpled newsprint. "I was trying to force a vision through blood, burning, delusion . . . I caught the rat, offered his freedom for a sacrifice. Ate a shitload of mescaline. And then there she was. Sitting right next to me. Wanted to know where the money went. She touched me. Have you ever felt that? I didn't mean to have a vision of *her,* I didn't mean to evoke *her.* I wanted her gone . . . I wanted you here. But you were gone. I couldn't . . . I couldn't hear you."

"I was asleep," he said.

"Please don't leave me again," she mumbled, slipping back into unconsciousness. "Even if you have to kill me, please don't leave me again . . ."

But he had to leave her, sleeping and safe in bed, to feed his blood-starved body. He compromised by staying in the neighborhood; he found an elderly couple huddled in sleeping bags in the warmth spreading from the back of a bakery. After draining both of their sleeping bodies, he wrapped their limp arms around each other and covered them up again.

Scene Twenty-five: The Center of Silence

The dreams that occur just as the brain begins to return to consciousness are the most vivid and strange, as they are not properly dreams but the jagged twitches of the conscious mind struggling to be reborn, and are closer cousins to the opium phantasies of Coleridge than the opaque self-conversations of deep sleep. Daniel's waking mind conjured a vision of the subway tunnels, filthy light fixtures and an ichorous drip from a broken sewer; he pressed against the walls, glancing nervously down the tracks for approaching trains. At his feet he found a thick tail of indigo silk so infinite and dense that it drenched his fingers. He wrapped the length around himself as he went so that it wouldn't dirty. It terminated in a loose toga around the body of a dark-haired woman, a beautiful movie star; Lucia Bose, Italian temptress of the sixties. She took the tail end of the silk from Daniel's shoulder slowly, smiling seductively, reeling him in. Instant tangle of soft lip and tongue flesh and the texture of her nipples, so maddeningly detailed he could feel every cell. She reeled him tighter against her, throwing back her head, offering her sleek porcelain neck.

So he bit down.

Then he was awake; by Jove, was he ever awake, a painful ringing in his ears from a blow to his head. He sprawled on the floor, on his ass on a pile of bedding. Sybil stood against the wall, one hand cupped over her throat and the other still clenched into a fist. "What?" he demanded, his voice harshened by disuse. He blinked and continued, in a more normal voice, "Happened."

"You bit me, asshole," she hissed.

He shook his head, licking his teeth. He didn't taste anything. "I was dreaming," he wondered. "I wasn't biting you, I was biting Lucia Bose."

"Sure felt like you were biting me. Shit. I was trying to kiss you because I could see that you were starting to wake up." She looked at the hand cupping her neck.

"*Not* smart, actually, Sybil." Daniel grasped the edge of the bed and straightened up, shaking his head.

"Duh, I know that now." She looked at her hand again, relaxing against the concrete at her back. "You just barely broke the skin. Ow. You're too dangerous. You want me to start bringing you people to bite when you wake up?"

"Yeah," Daniel said jokingly, "or dogs." He glanced up at her expression. "Just kidding. No dogs."

"I'll remember that." She meandered back over to the bed. "Who's Lucia Bose?"

"An Italian actress. One of the most beautiful women who ever lived. I first saw her in an Antonioni movie in the fifties and I thought my heart stopped. She's also in the movie *Satyricon*. You know, Fellini."

"Never saw it." She rubbed the poke marks in her neck with her fingertips. "Show it to me sometime."

"Are you better today?" He felt it now, not so much her thoughts or what her body felt as the combination of all of those things that made up Her. He felt elation that her self, the self that she was willing to let Daniel experience, was not as opaque, as guarded, as it had been before. She was refreshed, in a joyful mood, wearing clean, attractive, and comfortable clothes. The horror and pain of the night before seemed to have evaporated, leaving only the cuts and burns and a vicious headache as evidence. Sybil stretched out her hand and touched his fingers with hers, and the corners of her mouth kept hinting at a smile.

"I'm mostly better. Freeze-dried."

"I'm really sorry I bit you," he said softly.

"I know," she replied. "It's all right."

"I want to go out, though. I'm a couple of days behind and my body's letting me know about it." He didn't tell her that he'd gone out the night before as she slept.

"That's just what I was going to suggest. I have some ideas, actually."

"Oh, do you?" He laughed and allowed himself to be hauled out of bed, have clothes handed to him, have his bed-tangled hair brushed and dressed with styling wax. She'd picked out an immaculate, simple dark twill suit, a white Brooks Brothers shirt, a charcoal vest. "Ah! Something nice, I'm guessing. And what are you wearing? *New* clothes? My goodness, how you've changed."

"Like I said," she murmured, holding up one tie against his lapel, then another, "I have some things in mind. Hmmm . . . What shoes are you going to be wearing?"

"Sybil, I can pick my own tie. I do know a thing or two about fashion. I bet you still can't tell a Galliano just by looking at it."

A delicious smirk battle ensued. "Gaultier's better," she said, dropping the ties on the floor and walking away. She padded downstairs in stocking feet.

"My God, I've created a monster." He chuckled and picked up the ties. The black tie with the gold sunburst would be an excellent choice. Sybil returned from the lower floor. "Were you attempting to 'force a vision' of style?"

"This is one of my ideas," she said, thrusting a massively thick fashion magazine under his nose. "I ran across this yesterday while tripping, and I thought . . . 'Wow, cool.' " Her smudged fingers gripped it open to a particular page, a strange neosurrealist photo, showing a whippetlike model, mostly consumed by an enormous pink satin dress, digitized into a landscape of blue sand dunes and orange sky.

"It's a . . . decent photo," said Daniel.

"No, goober, the dress."

Daniel took a closer look. "Oh. *That.* I think it's really dreadful." The dress seemed to be eating the model. "Who would wear that?"

"Uh, *me?* No, it's awesome. I mean, it's perfect. Yeah, it looks dumb right there, but I think I could improve it."

"You can't *make* that, can you?"

"No, but we can buy it."

"Sybil, there's no guarantee . . ."

She took the magazine and read from the index pages in the back. "Page two-twenty-three. Rosepetal organza dress, six grand, Dallas Koyatsuzama, New York." She shrugged. "Just think, he could be in Tokyo. But no, you can buy it, off the rack, here in town."

"Six grand." Daniel grimaced. Then he remembered the sale of his flat, the money in Portugal. "I mean, what's it for? Just to wear around the house?"

"I'm thinking of a very specific purpose," she said, sitting beside him and pulling on knee-high galoshes. "When was the last time you had an art show?"

"I'm having one right now," said Daniel, "in Portland."

"No, I mean, in person. Not just an opening—I guess what I mean is a *performance.*"

Daniel went to the mirror, closely examining his face for stubble.

"Seriously," insisted Sybil.

"Seriously?" Daniel shrugged. "Seven weeks ago. You were there. At Gemini."

"That? Oh. I mean . . ." She grunted softly with frustration. "I'm talking about immersive theater. Like my approach, no script or anything, just impact . . . but in an enclosed setting, kind of."

"Oh—theater."

"Could be, could be, yes. But the most important thing would be to completely transform the environment. Sets and props and costumes. This is what I want to do."

Daniel smiled indulgently. "And who will build these sets? Who will make these props?"

"We will. We already have most of them. Even though you've never done a show here—"

"Not theater. I've shown here." Sold two of the fifty treated photographs.

Sybil rolled her eyes. "Even though you've never done *theater* here, you've still got some kind of name recognition to get people to come. And you have the money to make sure it happens. I'll take care of most of the rest. But I really want to wear that dress for it. I want to do . . . something really fleshy. A real concentration on *flesh.*"

"Yeah. Meat . . . skin," Daniel guessed.

Sybil nodded, her hand spinning out further elaboration. "Bruises. Organs. Cannibalism. Uh . . . carnivorous sex. You get where I'm coming from?"

He laughed and nodded. "Yeah, yeah, I think I do. I almost could have anticipated it."

"Oh, you're just saying that because it's a good idea and it didn't occur to you. But yeah, you understand what I'm talking about now." She picked up the magazine and consulted the index. "Hopefully they're still open—it's kinda late, but if traffic is good, we should be able to get there before they close. I wish you'd wake up earlier."

"Are you ready to go yet? I'll call a car to meet us at the créperie."

The boutique where Dallas Koyatsuzama's designs were sold closed at seven o'clock; Daniel's watch read 6:04 when they left the warehouse.

At 6:05 Daniel said, "Sybil, you know you can't keep this up much longer."

She replied, her voice squeezed tight to be pleasant, "I know."

At 6:07 Daniel went into the créperie, followed a young male patron into one of the two single-toilet rest rooms, and smiled at the man in the mirror. "I'm sorry," he said. "I'll just leave you alone now." He didn't.

At 6:09, Daniel let himself out, pocketing the rest room

key. He joined Sybil on the sidewalk and together they flowed into the back of the service car.

"We also need to go to the store where you bought the camera," Sybil said. "I have a plan."

Daniel laughed and clutched his temples. "Good Lord. Well, I thought you wanted a show, but instead you pretty much want to get arrested."

"I don't want to get arrested," she said, not entirely convincingly. "I just want to bomb. I'm tired of hiding. I mean, it's been good, it's been nice having time to think. To figure out if I'm in trouble or not."

"I don't think you're in trouble," said Daniel. "Everyone who could connect you with Worth Street Station's . . . dead." He glanced over to answer her unspoken question. "Except Joachim. But he's not saying anything. I made sure of that."

Sybil stared at the floor. "You can get out any time you want."

He sighed. "But I haven't."

Traffic was not good. Daniel and Sybil leapt out of the car in front of the boutique to find the neon sign asleep, the store deserted. "Those jerks," Sybil bitched, stamping her foot. She splayed herself against the front window, peering in. "I don't see it. Oh, well, too bad. I'll come back." She dropped her arms and turned her back on the store, slowly beginning to walk away. Daniel fell into step with and slightly behind her. "The first thing we need to do about this show is decide *when* it should happen," she said. "The date should not be chosen lightly. It should be a date of tremendous importance."

"March fourth," he said immediately.

She seemed surprised at his sudden, definite decision. "OK," she said. "Why?"

"It's the day Artaud died," Daniel said. "I have the feeling that we'll symbolically be killing him again."

"If you don't die, you can't be reborn. And a violent death is the best way to guarantee that. Ghosts, the spirits of those who die violently?" She turned around to face him, her eyes wild. "Flesh *and* ghosts . . . !"

"Naturally."

Although the electronics store lay a good twenty-five blocks away, they walked rather than searching for a taxi in the soup-thick gridlock on Eighth Avenue. The clouds had returned, bringing tiny, infrequent, discreet afterthoughts of snow. "We should leave this city as soon as possible after the show," Daniel said, squinting a snowflake from his eyelashes. "I'd prefer sooner, but it'll wait until then."

"We? And where?"

"Well, you certainly shouldn't stay here. Since you don't want to get arrested." She lazily rolled her eyes again. "As for where, I haven't decided. I've been thinking someplace like . . . Mexico. Or Brazil, maybe."

"Brazil? No."

"Mexico?" he attempted.

"Oh, I dunno."

"We could go to Africa," said Daniel. "I've never been there before. Nobody knows me there. It'd be easy to disappear."

"It'd be easy to get your ass shot off. Unless you want to declare yourself the dictator of a small country, become a voodoo god. Now that'd be really funny to watch." She laughed and poked his ticklish spot. "We can worry about that later. Right now . . . we have fun to do."

The electronics store was famous for being open until eleven o'clock; teenagers and young families crowded the aisles of beige and silver plastic-encased merchandise. "Go distract that guy," Sybil murmured, slipping her hand inside her coat. "And be ready to disappear."

Daniel approached the video section manager, a fresh-faced young man in a starched blue shirt and name tag. "Excuse me, do you work here?" Daniel asked.

"Yes, can I help you with something?"

"Um, yes. Brian. Thanks. Could you please show me how to use this . . . this . . ." Daniel gestured at a table in the computer section. "This thingy here." He pointed with a gloved finger at a laptop, at the tiny protuberance at the base of the keyboard, like a dark-gray pencil eraser.

"Well, that's not really my section—let me get Kim to come and help you—"

Daniel touched the laptop screen with the bare skin on his wrist, watching the display of words and rectangles slowly warp out of shape. "Why's it doing that?" Daniel demanded.

The laptop screen abruptly blanked, its humming silenced.

"That's weird. . . . Let me get Kim to help you; she's our computer expert. Hey, Kim!"

"No, please, I would like for *you* to help me," said Daniel, smiling at Brian.

Brian's lips opened and closed a few times, silently, before he said, "Sure, sure, let me see what I can do." He slid the laptop toward him and poked a few buttons authoritatively. Nothing happened. "Wow, it's really dead. I wonder what happened."

"Hmm," said Daniel innocently, moving to the next computer. The touch of his skin destroyed the image on the screen, flipping lights and darks into reverse and laying a strip of violent orange across the center. "What's wrong with *this* one?"

"I really don't know . . ."

A thickset woman with eyeglasses approached them; her name tag read KIM LANG. "What's the deal, Brian?" she queried.

Daniel smiled at her before she had a chance to say anything else. "I can't seem to get my computer at home to work," he said. "I can't figure out this weird little wiggly thing." He manipulated it with his fingertip, trapped inside the thin suede gloves. With his other fingers, he stroked the unresponsive keyboard. "I keep on rubbing it and moving it around and around . . . but I can't seem to make it work. Do you know what I'm talking about?"

Kim wet her suddenly dry lips. "Um . . . yeah, I think I do."

A sudden violent burst of laughing from the television section superseded Daniel's next innuendo. The population of the store looked up simultaneously, flowers turning toward the sun; on the rack of wide-aspect televisions, six-by-six-by-forty-two-inches wide, Sybil spread her legs wider for the girl in the wig, thrusting herself against the muscle, pushing up the hem of Sybil's short skirt. These were moments Daniel hadn't witnessed; the camera's tiny light neatly illuminated Sybil's spread vulva. "Mmm, sexy bunny," the girl moaned. "You are *so hot*."

Brian, and most of the other young males in the area, watched fascinated, didn't seem to mind at all. Kim, however, had gone white and wild-eyed, still frozen where she stood. Her panicked eyes darted to Daniel.

Daniel smiled at her. "Isn't *that* something," he said.

"Gross!" commented a young boy, being herded away by his anxiously hissing mother. Hungry female moaning blasted from the television speakers.

Store security scrambled. Sybil came walking up to Daniel with a fast, deliberate stride, her expression one of barely suppressed elation. "I'm ready, darling," she said.

Brian stared at her, then back at the screens, then back at her. She smiled at him, "Hi," then seized Daniel's arm and herded him through, down the stairs, out onto the street.

"You're leaving your tape there?" he asked her, walking quickly beside her running.

"I made a couple of copies," she panted.

East Village, a safe distance away, Sybil gnawed on strings of cheese pizza, angling the slice away from the photographs spread on the table. "So these are the ones I took of you," she said, muffled with crust. Daniel pulled them across the varnished tabletop toward him. The pictures were too candid to be particularly flattering, but his wiry, chalky body looked all right, and his facial expressions, in the photos where his face was present, ranged from unbearably pompous to tenderly vulnerable. He held up his favorite. Sybil nodded. "I like that one best, too," she said. "Do you have prints of the pictures you took of me?"

"No, just negatives."

"If you give them to me, I'll have some prints made. I

have ideas for promotional materials. Like a poster, and some postcards. Imagine what kind of response we could have gotten if we'd had postcards tonight and started handing them out—wouldn't that have been rad? So . . . if you give me the seven hundred you're supposed to be giving me every week, I'll go get those made."

"Ah," said Daniel. "Remind me again. I'll go to a cash machine."

"Don't worry about it right now. We should talk about the next couple of happenings."

"Oh, let me guess. You have some ideas."

Sybil wiped a dab of tomato sauce from the corner of her lips. "I'm gonna go grab another slice," she said.

Daniel looked over the photos again in her absence. He would have liked to take some of them to add to his nostalgia album. These would be photographs of a man he used to be. It seemed so long ago that he had sat in that chair and palmed his balls for a strange girl, offering her anything, everything. Outwardly he supposed that he looked the same, but he remembered her calling him "an empty suit of clothes," and it seemed more true now than it ever seemed possible before.

Sybil came snaking back, sporting a mouth that butter wouldn't dare to melt in, arm in arm with a young, savagely dressed Latino male with a forty-ounce bottle of beer in one of the pockets of his pants. "Hey, yo, Daniel," he called out. "Remember me? It's been a long time. I haven't seen you since you kicked me an' my peeps out of the studio in November."

"Ennio," Daniel replied with a slow smile. "How could I ever forget Bastard Son? The money man. You're my pride and joy."

"Yeah, I know," said Ennio nonchalantly. "So you know, since then, I'm running this theater space just a coupla blocks from here. Teatro Resurreccíon. We ain't producing nothing right now because half my folks are out of town. Your girlie's telling me about something y'all might wanna do there."

Daniel's glance left Ennio and went to Sybil, making no attempts to conceal her glee. "You don't know how lucky you are that you ran into us tonight," he said. "Need any money?"

You are a citizen of New York City. You live and work there. You know where things are—the grocery, the deli with the superb rice pudding, the bank. Bus stops and public sculpture do not move around, do not disappear, do not suddenly cease to make everyday sense.

You walk down Broadway quickly, eyes at shoulder level, careful to avoid excessive eye contact. The slightest thing will set people off these days. The world in 2000 is collectively insane. You, like many weekday deskbound others, have been gossiping at the watercoolers about the lesbian videotape that shows up again and again in Manhattan department stores and street-level television vendors. You've seen the two-inch square, bit-choppy replay on your computer screen at least four times this week; you've sent it as an e-mail attachment to your buddies in middle America to display the outrageousness of New York.

The cleaning up of the city under a strict, hypocritical mayor hasn't stopped the culture of showing off, something that can never be fully bred out of the residents of New York City. On a well-deserved fine day in January, Broadway hops with agitated shoppers, each of them desperately swerving to avoid a mime, in black-and-white striped top, black leotard, and beret, miming in front of the Space store. You have to go to the Space to buy clothes; there's no way to avoid walking past the mime. You hate mimes with a vicious passion, although you have no idea why—everybody hates mimes, don't they?—and the whole process never made any sense to you, the silence, the beret, the whiteface and smudgy eyes. This is the mime-est mime you've ever seen, except for the bright red lipstick. The mime is trapped in an invisible box, his hands bumping against nothing, millimeters away from the Space's window display. You hesitate with your hand on the door, wondering if the mime will actually touch the glass. Impatient bodies press you forward.

You buy good, plain, well-made clothes at the Space. They are the clothes that everyone wears. No one leaves the Space unhappy or disappointed. They knew what they wanted when they came to the Space, they knew it was located at the Space, and indeed it was there for purchase. Even the bags are good, plain and well-made. But now you are hungry.

Not much to do except walk past the mime again.

Now this is a problem. Walking past the mime once, vaguely interested in what the mime was doing, was one thing, but doing it a second time—you will have to run past the mime and hope to God the mime doesn't follow you. Before you can do this, you stand and wait a minute, looking back at the racks of clothes and shoes, wondering if there is anything else you need, perhaps something that would require a changing room, buying you time. Why doesn't the mime leave?

Other people loiter just inside, hesitating before going past the mime again. You read the distaste in their faces as they watch him, staring at his own reflection now, cocking his head in tiny mechanical birdlike ticks. From where you stand, the mime is looking at you through the glass, his empty eyes locked on yours, around the edge of the window display full of Space-clad metal suggestions of human figures, headless, angular. A forgotten childhood memory teases loose; a raven with a worm wriggling in its beak, staring at you. Gave you nightmares for weeks.

A tall young woman in new black denim Space jeans and a white down jacket, carrying a Space bag, breaks free from the hypnotizing effects of the mime's robot-bird impersonation. "To hell with this," she declares with a grin, marching to the door. The standing group seems to shake itself awake, laughing a little, following her. Relief. Joan of Arc. Salvation.

The young woman bursts out the front door, the dawdlers following her, approaches the mime from behind, and taps him on the shoulder. The mime reacts like a normal person, startling slightly; maybe he had been looking at the people inside, the bastard, just pretending to study his reflection. You hope desperately for her to give the mime a piece of her mind, and a piece of yours by proxy. It's partially your battle, too.

She shows the mime her hand, turning it over once or twice with fingers outstretched—see this, it's my hand, see—then slowly forms a fist, one finger at a time. With the fist, she punches the mime in the gut. The mime crumples forward onto the fist, which draws back for another one, his face a pantomime of shock so exaggerated, red mouth and eyes open in huge *O*s, that you can't help laughing. Somebody watching goes, "Yeaaah," and applauds. You feel relief and exhilaration, combined, dashing aggressively through your veins. What a good show. You decide to keep watching; everyone else is.

After the third punch leaves his torso, the mime's striped shirt soaks through red. After five, blood gushes from his midsection; underneath his white clown makeup his skin has turned a ghastly white. He vomits gobs of brilliant crimson blood. You have forgotten all about eating anything.

The tall woman steps back, a gore-stained blade between the fingers of her fist, and the mime falls onto his face on the pavement.

"Pretend you're dead," she screams.

And you think you've seen her before. Mmmm sexy bunny.

Nobody is shouting to call the cops. Nobody is helping. A localized silence, then a generalized din; chaos. You are shoved backward into the anonymous crowd, some of whom shove back. You quickly lose sight of the girl and the mime. You fumble for your cell phone; it falls out of your hand and disappears. You lose your balance, slip on the slick sidewalk, go sprawling under legs and coats. Above you, the signs are sideways, upside down, buildings sliding and warping into malevolent faces.

You lose your bag of clothes from Space.

Daniel released Sybil from his exhausted clinch and stepped back, breath fogging in the semidarkness of the maintenance tunnel. With her stocking cap, Sybil wiped the smudges of lipstick and ejaculate from the insides of her thighs, then put the hat back on her head and pulled up her pants from around one ankle. She reached over and caressed the unmarked, rosy skin of his belly.

"Success," she said.

Daniel wiped lipstick off the corners of his mouth, his cheeks. "Just barely. That blade you're using is rusty. Still, I wish we'd had the camera," he said, hoisting his own trousers.

"No." She shook her head. "There's no point in recording it; those people are going to have the image in their heads until they die, or get lobotomies. That's better than any videotape." She regarded the slumped dead body, his back to the concrete wall and chin drooped limply to his chest. "Just think—we were the last thing on his mind."

An hour before they had been performing a little street theater at the store on Forty-second Street; now they were uptown, in different clothes, with a dead innocent bystander Daniel snatched from the confused and half-stampeding crowd. "It'd be cool if we did that at every single Space store in town," she mused, gently removing the man's wallet from his pocket. She handed Daniel the credit cards, clucked over the absence of cash. "They could use it as part of their advertising campaign. Wouldn't that be hip?"

"I wish I knew why people hate mimes so much," said Daniel.

Sybil shrugged. "A mystery man was not meant to understand," she declared with a wide dramatic gesture of her hand, bending down and shouldering the backpack that contained her change of clothes. "Good thing you woke up before dark. I know that hurt, but it was worth it, huh? The adrenaline? I'm gonna go get the postcards figured out with Bastard Son. See you tomorrow." She grabbed the pipe ladder leading up to street level and hauled herself up. At the street she moved aside the metal grill and flung herself onto the sidewalk, dropped the grill back into place.

Daniel looked at the body, at Tom, remembering the taste of his thoughts frozen in a solid block of panic. Sybil's brick had left a fat dent in his skull, too blunt even to bleed.

The last face Tom saw, looking at Sybil, was not hers.

Daniel bent down to Tom and stared into his eyes, one of them a dull-glossy billiard ball red, but saw nothing there but pinprick pupils and congealing retina. All that he had to go on was the fading impression from his mind. Long, tangled, artificially golden hair, wide watery blue eyes, snub nose. Talking. A disembodied face in stark focus against a coursing backdrop of running human forms and quivering neon.

He put on his cowboy hat and followed the service walkway through the darkness for another block before hauling himself up onto the street, dampening perception so thoroughly that a teenager on a bike ran into a fire hydrant and went sprawling. Daniel hurried along the street, not listening to the boy's barrage of swearing, anxious to be back inside. Even through the thick layer of white zinc oxide he'd worn on his face, sunburn slapped his skin.

He was in his old neighborhood, near enough to walk to the building where his art collection slept in carefully climate-controlled storage. A security guard greeted Daniel warmly as he let himself in with a key card, his right to be there encoded in a mysterious silver stripe. "Hey, nice burn," said the security guard. "You ski? Vermont's supposed to be excellent right now, what with all the snow."

"Yeah," said Daniel edgily, "Vermont."

"Have a good one."

Daniel thought, *I've already got a bunch of good ones.*

In the long, well-lit, sterile hallway, each storage room number was marked out in embossed graphite on a black background. Daniel found his room by memory, how many steps from the elevator, the specific quality of the light angling from a few rooms over. He punched in a combination of numbers to get in the door. It shut behind him with an air-tightened shush of rubber and steel.

His own works rested calmly in racks, suspended individually from the ceiling, swaying slightly with the sudden air current caused by his entrance. He shook his head at how many there were, sitting here in obscurity, some of his best paintings and collage, works that he himself adored—the ones that perfectly captured a memory or evoked an emotion—but no one wanted to buy. He singled out an engraving, a portrait of Gilda leaning backward over the arm of a chair, that still quickened his heart with the vibrant immediacy of the lines, the quiet calm of her expression; he had made it in 1959, shown it eight times, and it had never sold.

Farther back, behind his things, hung Daniel's Kurt Schwitters collection, what he'd really come to see. Each page, each scrap of notebook paper, hung pressed between sheets of glass, just like his own; but these quick notes and scribbles were wildly valuable, highly desirable, too much so for him to ever touch them again. But they belonged to him. Envelopes addressed to Daniel Blum, Karlsbadstrasse, Berlin, postmarked 1932. To Daniel Blum, Berlin, 1939. A fast drawing of a chair with a man's head from an advertisement hovering above the seat, and a brief note: *What are you still doing there? You shouldn't cling to Germany.* He hadn't thrown any of it away, not even the most insignificant scraps. Schwitters was the only one who wrote him back. Daniel had compulsively written letters to all of his heroes—Tzara, Arp, Ball, Grosz, even the sublime and untouchable Marcel Duchamp—but no one replied except Schwitters. *Your work shows great promise,* on the back of a dairy receipt, from Norway. *You're better with a pencil than with words.*

Eighteen pieces in all. Ten pieces, all of them drawings, had already been sold, one at a time, to the Schwitters collection in Hanover. Now all that was left was the writing, the personal notes, the proof that Schwitters knew him, cared enough to put pencil and postage to paper. Daniel checked his watch—it would be eight hours before he could get in touch with anyone in Hanover by telephone. But it would be done.

Shed the nonessential, said Sybil.

He lay on the floor in the space that divided the desired works from his own, watching their minute swaying slow to imperceptibility, willing his own breathing to stop, seeking stillness. It didn't work, of course. He had a body full of living blood that craved oxygen, and in the climate-controlled environment, oxygen was at a premium. He found himself on his feet and his hand on the door, leaving behind the gym bag full of mime clothes and pre-moistened towlettes, before the vertigo from standing up had a chance to catch up with him.

An enjoyable sensation, not being in mental control of what his body did, being an immaculately honed machine that operated without ever having to consciously want to do anything. His legs walked, his spine held his body straight, his throat said good-bye to the security guard and his lips shaped it. His arm gestured, beckoning a taxi. He gave the address of Heinz Gestwirt's home.

When he arrived, he wasn't sure what to do. He had never visited Gestwirt without an appointment before. Sunday evening, supper time, the lights upstairs spilled a warm, human glow. Just a visit couldn't hurt. Stop in and say hello.

A slim, well-dressed, attractive brunette in her thirties answered the front door when Daniel buzzed. Her eyes flitted over him from head to toe and back, expertly collecting details. "Can I help you?" she asked, her voice pleasant and reasonable but tightly controlled. She made eye contact and was lost.

"I'm Daniel Blumenthal," said Daniel. "I'm a friend of Heinz. Is he in?"

She averted her eyes and wet her lips. "Yes . . . he's just . . . finishing a meal." She stood aside to let him in, following him up the stairs. "Have you known him long? I don't know that he's ever mentioned you."

Daniel said, "I don't know that he would . . . I'm a client of his. He manages my finances. And we have a lot in common."

Gestwirt, in his makeshift turban, half-sat, half-lay on a sofa in the sitting room off the kitchen, eyes closed, mouth open. Daniel tiptoed for a moment, wondering if he was asleep, but Gestwirt stirred, dragging himself upright. "Hello?" he said, patting his robe for his glasses;

with them on, he broke into a bright smile and stood up. "Daniel! What a pleasant surprise! I'm afraid you're too late for dinner."

"No, I was in the neighborhood, and I thought I'd stop by to see how you're doing." Daniel found Gestwirt's hand moist and chilly and laced with an alarming number of brittle sinews.

"In the neighborhood," Gestwirt echoed, winking. "Visiting the Supernova? Looking for love?"

"What?" startled Daniel. Gestwirt giggled. "Oh, God, no. That place? You'd have to put money into *my* underwear for me to go there again."

"Daniel, this is Cecily, my granddaughter." Gestwirt hustled Daniel back to where the brunette stood, wiping her hands with a dishcloth, forcing them to shake hands. Cecily blinked at Daniel's fingernails. "The very dearest of my dear family."

Daniel looked her up and down, not as subtly as she had done to him in the doorway. "Nice to meet you," Daniel said. "Any great-grandchildren to make Heinz's life even more joyous?"

"I'm a lesbian," said Cecily flatly.

"So?" Daniel smirked. "That didn't stop your granddad."

Gestwirt interrupted by laughing. "I knew you two would *love* each other," he said. "Cecily, why don't you run along home now? I think I'll be fine tonight on my own."

"Altpapa . . ." Cecily protested. "What if you need me in the middle of the night? What if there's an emergency?"

Gestwirt rolled his eyes. "What if, what if? If I need you, my precious, I'll call you. I have the phone with me all the time—see?" He brandished a wireless telephone handset, then replaced it in a pocket of his robe. "Don't worry. Mr. Blumenthal's a good friend and he's no fool. Go home. Thank you for supper. It was delicious. And very healthy." He kissed her on both cheeks and then on the lips.

The woman grimaced and recoiled like a reluctant toddler. "Make sure he's got something on his head to keep away the chill," she muttered to Daniel. "And don't let him into the liquor cabinet."

"I'll do my best," said Daniel humbly.

Cecily gathered up her coat, gloves, and hat, glancing nervously behind her at the two men. "Please call if you need me," she said again from the foyer.

"Get lost, Florence Nightingale. I can empty my own bedpan." Gestwirt settled on the sofa again, pulling off the towel/turban and dropping it beside him with a heavy sigh.

"She's out of her mind with worry," Daniel said, sitting on the other side.

"Cecily? No, Cecily's never out of her mind with anything. She is a person very in control of herself, and the things around her. Especially me. I'm surprised that she let you in, actually."

"I can charm my way into anything," said Daniel.

Gestwirt's smile grew. "Yes, you can, can't you? With that face, that smile? You've come quite far, haven't you—farther than you yourself thought you could go."

Daniel reached over Gestwirt and picked up the turban, toying with the brooch holding it together. "I'm going to sell the rest of my Schwitters to the collection in Hanover." The pin unfastened, the turban unraveled, revealing the faded, threadbare reverse side of the towel.

"What? Really? Why?"

Daniel shrugged minutely. "What's the point of keeping them?"

"Because, Daniel, they're valuable now, which means that in ten years they will be even more valuable. Those notebook pages are more precious than gold. You give those up in your will. Or is it that there's something more promising that you're interested in?" Gestwirt cupped his hand over his mouth to catch a cough. He opened his hand to check the result, grimaced, and reached for a box of tissues.

"Look at us," said Daniel. "We're not touching. We sit here, right next to each other, not touching."

"You wouldn't want to touch me right now," Gestwirt

said, wadding the dirty tissue and tossing it into a paper bag on the floor, already half-full.

"I do, before it's too late," said Daniel.

Gestwirt said nothing. Daniel, restless again, stood up and stretched his legs. Gestwirt slowly eased himself off the sofa and went to another room, closing the door behind him, as if giving Daniel permission to snoop. Daniel accepted the invitation, stalking around Gestwirt's sitting room, glancing at the restored sepia photographs of Gestwirt, a year before he was sent to Birkenau. He had been a slender sly rake of a boy, only seventeen, with wide pale eyes, dimple, a hint of blond mustache. The mature man emerged from the toilet to the soundtrack of a flush, wrapping his quilted robe around the alarmingly thin body underneath, and nodded at Daniel. "That picture again," Gestwirt said, smiling. "Whenever I have you over, if I disappear from the room, I find you in front of it."

"You had a very interesting face," Daniel explained. "Have."

"No, no. I once had a pretty face. It remains interesting."

"Do you mind if we . . . I mean, I hate to make you work right now. I know you're tired and you just ate."

"No, no, ate? That wasn't eating. I might as well have been taking vitamin pellets. Green vegetables with no butter or salt on top of sticky rice? That's not dinner. I want a corned beef sandwich and a bottle of Belgian *doppelbock*. Perhaps even two bottles. And I would love to look at figures for a while. All this relaxing depresses me." Gestwirt led Daniel down the hall that ran the length of his apartment to the door of his office. Daniel glanced into the other rooms. The doors had always been closed when he had been here before, but now he could see into them, dark and neatly arranged with antiques, and each room had its own individual scent. Daniel felt a terrible pang of longing for his flat across the street from the Met, the soft blue study full of fascinating books, the infinite bathroom. He missed the cleanliness, the luxury of comfortable new furniture, oceans of running water.

Once inside the office, Gestwirt thrust a sheet of paper at Daniel. "Your account numbers," he proclaimed.

"Oh! How did you know?"

Gestwirt sighed. "I know," he said. "Tying up loose ends, like I said."

Daniel scanned the page. He didn't recognize half of them, having been opened by Gestwirt on his behalf. "I don't suppose there's time to consolidate these."

"I have all the time God gave me to consolidate them, but do you? It will require a lot of research, as some of these are more stable than others, and some have nastier tax penalties than you're probably comfortable with."

"No, no, never mind. I'll deal with them later. Money. Sometimes I wish I didn't have any. Life would be so free."

"Unfortunately, food and rent most certainly are not." Gestwirt sank down onto the visitor's couch, sighing heavily. Daniel followed, sitting on the floor beside Gestwirt. Gestwirt stroked Daniel's hair. "I don't suppose you will indulge me by going to the deli to get me a corned beef sandwich?" Gestwirt asked.

Daniel chuckled. "No, I won't. I'd hate to think that I was responsible for killing an old man with a corned beef sandwich. How about, though, you trade me a blow job for a cigarette?"

Gestwirt laughed, a full belly laugh that he should not have been physically capable of. "You're joking," he gasped.

"Yes," said Daniel. "I'm joking. I don't have any cigarettes."

The old man lay and watched raptly as Daniel stood up and slowly undressed, the yellow-green light casting peculiar shadows over his angular body. He remained silent when Daniel lay on the couch beside him, untied the robe, and slid his arms inside it. Daniel ran his fingers through Gestwirt's hair, shaking off the strands that came loose. "Is your head warm?" Daniel whispered.

"Quite warm, yes, thank you." Gestwirt's voice was reasonable, pleasant, ordinary; but after he spoke, Daniel felt him holding his breath.

"Please remember to keep breathing. Cecily would be very upset if I forgot to remind you to breathe."

"Yes, thank you."

Daniel angled himself up on one elbow, gently pulled Gestwirt's trifocals from his face, and set them on the floor. He stroked both sides of Gestwirt's face, pulling back the wrinkles, examining him. "I still see a pretty face in here," Daniel told him. "With long, pretty eyelashes."

"Cecily would be very upset if she saw what you're doing right now," Gestwirt said.

Daniel pursed his lips, unbuttoning the shirt of Gestwirt's silk pajamas. "Somehow I think she'd understand," Daniel said. He passed one hand over Gestwirt's sunken chest, stroking erect nipples with his fingertips. "I think I saw you," he continued, listening to the soft hiss of Gestwirt's breath through his teeth. "I think it was you. You went to Haus Vaterland at least once, didn't you? You would have been about ten—"

"Twelve," Gestwirt said. "With my uncle Karl."

Daniel pulled down the elastic waist of the pajama bottoms and pressed himself against Gestwirt's hot, sweat-moist body. Gestwirt breathed, but with difficulty, in abrupt fits and starts. "It was the week after Christmas. You were dining in the Grinzing—"

"Because—Karl and I both loved trains . . . but that was before—"

"Before Poland, yes. But forget about Poland. Forget about it." He pressed his hands against Gestwirt, one against his heart and the other his groin, and concentrated as hard as he could on crumbling the mental architecture, on forgetting. He tore down the buildings, the faces, cleared away the broken glass, replacing it with the sensation of warm hands, a comfortable couch, the caress of silk. Gestwirt relaxed all at once with a huge sigh. "In the Grinzing. Having a divine meal and laughing. Watching the model trains going round and round the restaurant. And you were laughing at a man who had just spilled a tower of dishes that came crashing all around him. Do you remember that?"

"Oh," sighed Gestwirt with a smile, "I do remember that. The whole restaurant was laughing."

"Do you remember the man? Do you remember what he looked like?"

Gestwirt's foggy eyes traced Daniel's features. "He looked just like . . . like you." One of his wrinkled hands reached over and tucked Daniel's hair behind his ear. "I thought he was very strange to look at, because his hair was so long. . . . Uncle Karl and I joked after the mess was cleared away that we couldn't tell if he was a man or a woman."

"But you could tell, couldn't you?" said Daniel. "You could tell I was a man."

"You moved like a man . . . cursed like a man," Gestwirt said lightly, then his face fell and his eyes closed. "I must be imagining things. It couldn't have been you. I'm old enough to be your grandfather. You're just a child. Cecily's older than you are."

"How old was I when I first came to you here?" Daniel pressed himself harder against Gestwirt. Both of them were erect now, cocks trapped against thighs.

"Th-thirty. Oh, Daniel, you don't know what you're doing."

"And how old am I now?"

Gestwirt frowned.

"I'm thirty, aren't I? Isn't it strange how every year I seem to stay the same age? Do you even remember setting my date of birth back a year every year? It's because I told you to. And I told you not to remember. To be quite honest, I'm actually twenty-seven, or so it seems." He rested his head against Gestwirt's shoulder, listening to his fast, erratic heartbeat, and a faint gurgling that must have been his lungs trying to pump air through the fluid collecting in them. Gestwirt's breath emerged with a high, falling note, was brought back in with a rattling wheeze. "I was born October 27, 1902 at four o'clock in the morning, in my parents' kitchen, in Berlin. And twenty-two years later, I was the worst busboy Haus Vaterland ever had."

He showed his teeth.

Gestwirt gasped, then gasped again; his hand flew to his chest and patted against it, trying to clear a path for air to his lungs. This did not work. His streaming eyes begged Daniel, and Daniel obligingly helped him sit up a little, allowing his chest more room to move. Gestwirt's face went through several changes of color before settling on a shade close to his normal flesh tone. "You . . . impossible," he whispered. "Immortal."

"No," said Daniel. "But close. I won't preserve you forever like this. I'm cruel, but I'm not that cruel. I'm too fond of you to be that cruel." Gestwirt's trembling hand sought the pocket of his robe where the phone was, but Daniel caught the hand and held it down on his own belly. "Now, now. Why call Cecily? What could she do? Back to the hospital? Another catheter for this tender flesh?" Daniel grasped Gestwirt's prick, still erect and hard as a pistol. "I think not. I think that if you go back to the hospital tonight, you won't ever come out again. If I were a doctor, I would never let you go."

Gestwirt lifted his other hand, held it up to Daniel's smiling face, and touched the sharp point of one of Daniel's fangs with his fingertip. The tooth smoothly slid into the skin. Gestwirt looked at the heavy bead of blood balancing on his finger, then wiped it onto Daniel's outstretched tongue. "You don't . . . want to drink *my* blood," Gestwirt said. "It's old and . . . sick."

"Your blood will always be precious to me." He pressed his lips against Gestwirt's neck, speaking against his larynx, his voice echoing around Gestwirt's throat. "You won't survive this. You won't make it through the night, no matter what I do. But I can take the pain away. You have nothing to worry about. And neither do I."

The old blood was thin and slow but high in adrenaline and a huge variety of fascinating chemicals, some of which Daniel had never tasted before. And so much lust. He shifted himself to get a better position to hold his own neck, and found their joined loins slippery with semen and urine. "Heinz?" Daniel asked softly, licking his lips, and, enchanted with their flavor, licked them again.

Gestwirt still sat up, but his chest lay still. His half-lidded eyes dilated to the point of blackness. Daniel reluctantly let go and stood up. He had left two big holes in Gestwirt's neck; he bent down and whisked his tongue around them. Gestwirt's thready heartbeat continued, although Daniel had sucked away his consciousness, and his body had begun the downward spiral. He kissed Gestwirt's lips, whispered, "*Gute nacht,* Heinz," and gathered his clothes from the floor and his file from Gestwirt's desk. Now there was only one thing left to do.

He took a long, hot bath.

Scene Twenty-six: The Prince of Bones

The rat and the aquarium were gone, and in its place sat a note in green crayon on lined notebook paper. *Join Me & Bastard Son at Teatro.* When Daniel arrived, he understood that the green crayon had not been an accident—Ennio cracked the door of the tiny theater and an opaque fog of cannabis smoke roiled out. "Get in here, man, hurry up," Ennio muttered in a strangled high voice; he turned his head and exhaled a lungful back inside.

Daniel slid into the dark room, closing the self-locking door behind him. Slow-tempo beats played faintly over the P.A. "Me and Sybil's upstairs," Ennio said, elaborately clasping and releasing Daniel's hand. "You wanna smoke weed?"

"Yes," said Daniel, taking Ennio's shoulders, jaunting through the open doors of Ennio's mind, and bending his head to Ennio's neck. He drew two good mouthfuls from just below the skin, licked the wound, then pushed Ennio a safe distance away. No pretend kisses with Ennio, whose very first words to Daniel had been "I'm straight, man. I know you ain't, that's cool, but . . . nah-ah." Daniel let the hypnotism fade, leaving only a gentle cannabis befuddlement behind. "So how's it going?"

Ennio shook his head and blinked. " 'S good, man, good. We been get'n some work done up on the computer. But still, we kinda need you to get finished. I woulda called, actually, but I don't know the number. Damn, I got a headache."

"Never mind that," Daniel said. He started upstairs, sparing a look behind him at the interior of the theater space. It wasn't large, only the size of his living room back at the old flat, entirely painted black from the ceiling and over the built-in speaker cabinets to the floor; the only light for the entire room came from a single "black light" bulb hanging from a cord in the back of the room. When Daniel and Sybil had come after meeting Ennio at the pizza joint, the theater had been essentially empty but for some overhead light racks that had not yet been installed; now, the lights hung up above in the gloom, and large bolts of patterned cloth and plain muslin, a couple of tall, spindly homemade four-legged stools, and several TV sets in various stages of age and repair had been stacked against the walls. "Spending the money?" Daniel asked pleasantly.

"Aw, yeah, man. I got some supplies 'n' shit . . . bought some props . . . I need to get started on this mural, y'know, but I want to finish up the computer stuff first."

Upstairs, Sybil lounged in thrift-store underwear on a pile of handmade velvet pillows, weakly clasping the stem of a huge Moroccan hookah, surrounded by humming, blinking computer drives. The very tips of her blue hair had been dyed orange and styled into a soft peak at the top of her head; she looked like a melting, lit vanilla candle. "Oh, good, you got my note," she said, scrambling to an upright position atop the pillows. "Hey, you want to see something amazing?" She stood, balancing herself on the table that held four large computer monitors, and pointed at another table to Daniel's left. A familiar aquarium, lit from without by a low-wattage, white incandescent bulb, contained a familiar rat devouring a pile of seeded whole-grain bread. "See? His name's Victim. Ennio named him. We got some plans for him."

"I thought it was dead," remarked Daniel, leaning in closer to examine the aquarium, now topped with a heavy wire rack and eight concrete cinder blocks. The rat's eyes followed him, but it didn't stop eating. One crumpled, swollen foreleg curled up against its compost-colored body.

"No, he's never been dead. He was in a coma. Oh, and in case you're wondering, I didn't do that to his arm. I wouldn't have been able to catch him if his arm wasn't all fucked up." Sybil leaned against Daniel and blew smoke into his ear. "I saw what you did down there. You think you're slick," she murmured in his ear. "Did you have a good night out on your own?"

He kissed her, touching just the tip of his tongue to the roof of her mouth. "I tied up some loose ends with my accountant," he said.

She gave an insinuating hum. "Did you miss me?"

"Aren't you with me all the time?"

Ennio shouldered past them and slung himself into an ergonomic chair before the computers. With a swipe of his hand across the table, the monitors snapped from coruscating fractal designs into windows, two full of pink text on a black background, one with the photo of a nude, inquisitive Daniel, and the other, the negative of Sybil, arched defiantly in the same chair. "Do you think we should do a front and back?" Ennio asked. "I dunno. I can't figure it out."

"What do you mean, you can't figure it out? You're Bastard Son," said Daniel. "You've got more visual talent in your big toe than I've got in my whole body."

"I don't got your talent for exaggeration," Ennio said. "Man, you don't *make* art. You *be* art. Just standin' there." He swiveled in his chair and stared at Daniel and Sybil. "Look at the two of you. It's fuckin' eerie, man." He turned back to his computer screens. "Notice your girlie's bigger than you are?"

Daniel scoffed. "Not possible."

"Tell 'm," said Ennio.

Sybil scoffed back. "Five eleven."

"Six feet."

"One eighty."

Daniel gaped. "You do *not* weigh a hundred and eighty pounds."

"She does, man," said Ennio. "I saw that scale, man. That's a big girl. And what do you weigh?"

Daniel hesitated for a moment, then confessed, "All right, so I'm skinny."

Sybil wrapped one arm around Daniel's head and wrestled him down to the pillows. "I win!" she crowed, sitting on top of him.

"I let you," said Daniel, enjoying the pressure. "Don't tickle me or else."

"Oh," Sybil replied, slipping her hand into his shirt, "I know better. You should bite other people, not me. I'm good for other things." She spread her legs until she was straddling his right thigh. "Remember this pose?" She spoke to Ennio. "Where have you seen this before?" she asked, grinding her pubic bone into Daniel's muscle and rubbing her palms against her crotch. "Mmmm, sexy bunny," she groaned, impersonating the girl in the wig. "God, she was stupid."

Ennio laughed, reaching over next to them to pick up the mouthpiece of the hookah, on the end of a long, flexible thread-wrapped tube. He took a deep gulp of smoke, swallowed it, and exhaled through his nose at Daniel and Sybil. "If you two feel like bonin', go for it. Just know I'll be watchin'. Not to mention the camera."

"Camera? Where?" Daniel asked. Sybil pointed at her videocamera, resting on the tabletop but not pointed at them; instead, it focused on a large jar, buzzing with fruit flies. "Science project?" He bounced under Sybil.

"Reproduction, man," said Ennio.

The flies buzzed over a gobbet of raw meat.

"Flesh and ghosts," whispered Sybil.

Daniel slipped his hand into the gap in her underpants. Ennio watched this violation for a moment, then rummaged in a pile of hardware until he found a flat, blank plastic tablet. He plugged it into the back of one of the computer drives and hit a button on the front of the drive. As Sybil slid the camisole over her head, he began to stab and sweep the surface of the tablet with a translucent plastic stylus. "Keep going," he said. "This your thing. You gotta inspire me to create."

"You mean, you didn't fuck her, just to see what it was like?" Daniel asked. Sybil unzipped his pants—two side zippers—and peeled them down, scraping her fingertips against the delicate trail of hair leading from his navel.

"I 'int say that," said Ennio.

"Don't be nosy, Daniel," Sybil said, kissing his bare belly. "*You* fucked someone else last night."

"I didn't fuck him. I don't think he could have handled it."

"Quit talkin'," Ennio commanded. He took another hit from the hookah. "You distractin' me."

Daniel hated to think that they were showing off for Ennio, but there was no denying that he and Sybil did things that they had never done before, and in more outlandish ways. Daniel bent Sybil's knees up over her shoulders. She duplicated the position from their first time, then, without breaking contact, turned around until she was facing him. He aimed his ejaculate at her breasts. Ennio provided occasional commentary and direction. His stylus trembled and wavered over the tablet; on one of the computer screens, a complete portrait of their coupling emerged, bit by bit, not seeking to portray any particular moment in time but instead incorporating all of it.

He sought specific points on the scanned photographs, then merged the two images together. "Looka this shit. Looks like Francis Bacon or some shit."

Sybil grasped the edge of the table with sweat-slickened fingers. "Oh, hey, Dan . . ." She grunted softly; he was still inside her and had continued the thrusting in her distraction. "Check it out. He's right."

Daniel mumbled, "I want you to come, Sybil."

"Again?" Sybil whined.

Ennio glanced over at them, eyebrow arched. Daniel smiled to himself. So even the famous Bastard Son, god of graffiti, prince of bones and light, couldn't get her off. "Yes, again," he insisted. "I never want you to stop."

"Quit fucking me, then," she said, her voice a carbon copy of Ennio's, "and go *down* on me, bitch."

Ennio chuckled and turned away again, concentrating on the computer images and the hookah. Daniel, lulled by the cannabinols swirling in his blood, complied with Sybil's demands, sinking in, meditating on her vagina (the *flesh,* the delicious smoked reek of her, still smelling very faintly of latex and spermicide from the day before) until she yanked his hair and sobbed for him to stop.

"Busy, busy, busy," murmured Ennio.

Exhausted, Daniel and Sybil curled together on the pillows, now scattered and in disarray and several of them ruined, catching breath and cooling down, and watching Ennio's postcard design come to life. He superimposed translucent layers of image over text, and vice versa, added the mutated image of Daniel/Sybil to the front of the card and the digital sketch to the back side. In the aquarium, the rat had eaten all the bread and struggled against the wire mesh at the top of his cage. "You know, rats can chew through wire," Daniel murmured.

"That's OK," Sybil said. "We've got lots of mesh, and besides, he won't be around long enough for it to be an issue. Besides, watch him."

The rat grasped the wires above it and hung from the one good forepaw, then dropped back to all fours and began sniffing and kicking around the thin layer of newspaper at the bottom. The twitching, whiskered muzzle held still for several seconds, then twitched a few more times. The lids of glass-bead eyes drooped, and it spilled the water in its dish when it tried to drink. It burrowed into a dry section of newsprint and stopped moving. "Drugged bread," Sybil declared with satisfaction. "We sprayed it with ketamine in a water suspension and then toasted it. He should be out until tomorrow, at least. And then he'll get some more."

Ennio swayed back and forth in his chair, in time with the music, fondling the dry top skull of a small dog, a cocker spaniel perhaps. He owned a huge collection of skulls, bones, shrunken heads, taxidermied birds, small mammals and fish. His tags and murals were all over town, on buildings and subways; in addition to his gorgeous, ornate signatures and texts, he was most famous for being able to photo-realistically depict skulls in spray paint. His transition to "legitimate" art, through hiphop CD sleeve design and thence to the galleries, had been seamless, but although he now had a six-figure income, he still bombed the streets with his spray cans on a regular basis.

He added a thumbnail-sized image of one of his human skulls to the bottom left corners of the postcard, front and back. "I think this is done," he said.

"It's beautiful," Daniel replied. He felt genuine excitement for the performance for the first time. "It's fantastic. I can't wait for people to see this." He cuddled Sybil and kissed the soft protuberances of her shoulder blades.

"Oh, yeah," said Sybil, sliding away from him and standing up, "I got something to show you. I got it today. I'll be right back."

She ran down the stairs, naked.

"Damn," whispered Ennio ruefully. "Man, she digs you."

"I think she digs you, too," said Daniel.

Ennio shook his head, continuing to speak under his breath. "Nah, man, not like that. She got down with me, but that don't have nothin' to do with what you an' her gots goin'. Man, she's a monster. She had me up all night."

"She's just new to sex," Daniel said. "She'll grow out of it."

"What's she, like eighteen? I'm glad you can put it to her, 'cos I can't keep up. Man, can you picture her in her sexual prime? When she's, like, thirty-five an' shit? I'm scared of that."

"Yeah, you should be," said Daniel.

"She's fuckin' intense," Ennio murmured. "Did you see where she was puttin' out cigarettes on her tits an' shit? Fastin', eatin' paint, and disappearin' down her own hole. She showed me that warehouse where you been livin'.

You better keep an eye on her or she's gonna kill herself, take you with her. Think she'd go alone? Hell, no. She'd take the most precious things with her. Like a Egyptian queen."

"Are you ready?" Sybil yelled from the staircase.

"Please hurry," Daniel responded. "The anticipation is killing me."

"Be careful," Ennio said. "She got a ulterior motive."

She'd bought the Koyatsuzama dress. With it on, she could barely fit through the narrow walkspace at the top of the stairs; Daniel could see from where he sprawled on the pillows that the body of the dress was made of a framework of plastic coils, each one larger, until the bottom coil was easily five feet wide. Hundreds of coils or tubes of pink silk organza hung slackly down like tentacles, rolls of fat.

And she'd "improved" it; the dress had been liberally smudged with yellow paint, charcoal, and used motor oil, so that the rolls of fat seemed to be bruised or rotting. It was the most hideous thing Daniel had ever seen, and the stench was terrific. "Jesus God!" he said.

"Fuckin' *nasty,*" Ennio added, awe in his voice.

"It's repulsive, isn't it?" Sybil swayed over.

"You look like a birthday cupcake made out of freshly ground pork," said Daniel.

"Not really *freshly,*" she said. "Or if it is, a couple of rats got into the grinder." She burst out laughing at the image.

Daniel grimaced. "People are going to vomit when they see you."

"Good," said Sybil. "That's the plan. I'm thinking of having like, a trough, just in case people need to hurl."

"My God . . ." Daniel stood up and circled her, so that he could see it from all angles. None of them was even slightly flattering. "What the hell am I gonna wear?"

"Whatever you like."

"Get that piece of shit out of my lab," Ennio said. "I can't deal with that smell. Put it back in the closet." He turned back to Daniel. "I'll take this to the printer in the morning and we should get back cards by day after tomorrow."

"Get six thousand," Sybil called from downstairs. Ennio glanced at Daniel for confirmation, and Daniel nodded once. "I hope you got plans for 'em all," Ennio said. "That's a lotta postcards."

"I'm sure Sybil has ideas. And I want to keep some of them, of course."

"Yeah." Ennio stood up and stretched his body, bending backward until his hands touched the floor, kicking his legs over his head into a handstand. Daniel sat still, fighting the urge to imitate him. "So what up now? We got some shit to build. You guys wanna help me paint?"

"I wanna make a bomb," Sybil said, returning upstairs, now more warmly dressed in a thermal shirt and cargo pants. "I've got all this plastique—"

"Where did you get plastique?" Daniel demanded.

She pursed her lips and rolled her eyes. "I made it," she said. "I made it a long time ago. The old apartment. When I was blocked and couldn't concentrate on painting, I would make plastique. I told you, my dad taught me. That was our family bonding—knife-fighting techniques and making explosives." Ennio glanced at Daniel and arched his eyebrows, angling his head in her direction. She put her hands on her hips. "*What?* My dad made explosives for his army division. That's all he's any good at. But he taught me everything he knew . . . how to make nitro, how to build a timer . . ." When Daniel and Ennio remained silent, she threw up her hands. "OK, fine, we'll paint. I won't make incendiaries here, I'll do it at the warehouse. Don't worry, you can keep your bitch ass theater safe."

"Thank you," said Ennio, unfazed. "Check it out, Sybil, if you want to do a show, you have to make it happen. You can't keep gettin' distracted. You'll fuck it up if you don't buckle down and get the shit done. Now, c'mon. You a artist or a terrorist?"

"What's the difference?" she muttered.

Scene Twenty-seven: Angels Are Dreaming of You

John F. Kennedy has bowels of chrome struts, glass, and nubbled gray plastic.

The bowels are crawling, infected with rushing, anxious people, clutching tickets, dragging black nylon bags on tiny wheels, cursing the twists and turns of the gate areas, ignoring the vast sweeping vistas of air soaring forty feet over their heads.

He is not ignoring the architecture; he has the luxury of time, a three-hour layover, not enough time to justify leaving the miniature metropolis, spending an hour each way to travel into the city. He has a certain appreciation for the place, the sterile ultramodern chill of it, like electrically treated water gulped at two degrees centigrade. He wanders. He has already spent an hour in the airport chapel, the only worshipper, gazing at the stained glass and feeling nothing in particular, no more religiosity than he would have felt in a grocery store. Mass happens on other days. A Protestant chapel, no matter how lovely its artworks and the sincerity of its chaplain, lacks the grandeur and majesty of Real Church. With his remaining two hours, he seeks secular amusements.

He lingers for a long time at a "newsstand," standing and fondling the slick paper of fashion magazines, lost in the subtle texture of offset ink on paper. The butch, defiant female model on the front of the Italian magazine looks so much like him that he holds up the magazine next to his face and gazes into the mirror.

Androgyne. Heavy velvet eyelids. Short hair in wispy spikes, a sharp nose turned up toward the ether, and ears jutting out. Inside the magazine is a short biography and a collection of photographs of the model in various bizarre, revealing clothing. She is the daughter of film star Lucia Bose; Italian, too, like him.

He lowers the magazine and rubs his heart. He feels an almost, but not completely, painful tugging there. Apprehension. He does not enjoy airline travel. Outside the JFK cocoon, the afternoon sun has emerged from the clouds briefly, and he won't be allowed to sleep again for a while. This, for him, is a red-eye flight. He hopes that he can make it all the way to Rome—how terrible it would be to sleep and shrivel in the cabin, how much panic it would cause.

He selects the Italian magazine, and several more of the thickest, glossiest volumes he can find—more fashion, lifestyle, art magazines, from Britain and France and America. He pays with cash. "Do you have anything smaller?" asks the shopgirl, the words drying in her throat even as she speaks them. Later today the cash-drawer count will be over by sixty-one dollars, and this is not a problem.

"Not a problem," he replies crisply, and walks away.

He returns to his own departure terminal, skipping neatly and invisibly from the path of a disheveled woman and two blond students running flat out to catch a plane, and slips into the bar and grill four gates away from his focus. Part of the bar has large windows, drawing in watery sunlight, but to his relief, most of it lies in deep shadow lit only by tiny electric bulbs and the blue-pink-gold flicker of televisions showing basketball and hockey highlights. He settles at a dark table by himself, relaxes, isolates. He is ignored.

He chooses the American art magazine first, as a form of good-bye, good riddance. He is looking forward to living in a land where tackle football is not a given graphic influence in every tavern and pub, where the buildings are older than he is. Going home, returning, to see if any of it remains. As he picks up the magazine by its spine, postcards slip out of it and onto the tabletop. Two of them are subscription reply cards on dull ecru paper with red text. One of them is glossy and larger.

That tug in his abdomen abruptly transforms into a stabbing, and he jerks his head left, west, summoned, *Over here.* Holding it with one hand while the other rubs his chest where the pulling originates, he handles the postcard by its edges, examining it more closely. An action/Cubist sketch, red and white, of multiple bodies coupling—no, only two, but in a dozen different ways, pale-blue text on the sides violating the picture, dates and an address and a beautifully rendered, tiny human skull.

admission $10. leave inhibitions at the door. emotion potluck. bring enough to share.

On the other side of the postcard, two overlaid photographs merge, translucent, so that the center of the nude bodies renders as solid high-pale fleshtone. Male and female. The female, eyes averted, is a stranger to him. The male, his child, not of flesh but of blood. Daniel Blum, gazing heavenward, fingers on his belly pointing downward to the dark tangle of intermingled male and female genitals.

No names, but fat, disease-pink graffiti-style lettering, designed to be challenging to read, shadowed in blood red. *FLESH. From the sublime to the absurd. If there's a soul, we will see it escape.* Disguised, veiled, but visible underneath the bodies floating in darkness anchored only by an antique chair, more words in the same typeface as was used on the back of the card—*Carne. Prepucio. Membrana. Fantasma.*

He looks to the west again, slipping the postcard into

the inner pocket of his coat, next to his boarding pass for the flight to Rome.

He's here. Here, in this city.

He stands up and, leaving the magazines on the table, walks with grim purpose to the Alitalia ticketing counter, thousands of yards away, one straight unbroken line, forcing the running people to go around him. At the counter, the olive-skinned man in uniform, harried and unpleasant from dealing all day with harried and unpleasant customers, glances at him with distaste. "Your final destination?"

"Rome."

"May I see your ticket, please?"

"I need to change my flight," he says, withdrawing the ticket and the postcard at once. He hides the postcard in the ticket envelope. "I will reschedule my flight for a later date. I am willing to pay whatever it costs."

"Very good, Mr. Ricari. Let me see what I can do."

Daniel awoke, panicked, on his feet, in the warehouse, the same place as he'd fallen asleep to the sound of Sybil's snoring beside him. The bedding space was empty, indeed the entire upper floor was empty, and he spoke into the air, assuming himself alone, "Please, God, tell me that was just a dream."

"It's not just a dream."

Sybil's disembodied voice rose just below him, from the area where stolen bottled water was stored. She said, "Do you hear it?"

"I don't—" Daniel cut himself off and fell silent, holding his breath, until he heard the disturbing roar of machinery, screams of tearing concrete and breaking glass. The dream evaporated. "What is it?"

"They're demolishing the next block."

Daniel hurried to dress himself and swung himself downstairs. Sybil sat curled up next to the stash of blue plastic bottles, smoking a cigarette. "It's coming," she muttered. Her voice was corrosively bitter. "Our block is next. I know it."

"Don't let it happen," Daniel said.

"I'm not. I'm taking a break. I'm working over on the table. Go check it out. But don't touch anything."

Cautiously he approached the two parallel long tables, former home to boxes of crayon-pastels, brushes, canvas, and now almost completely cleared except for piles of tiny industrial fuses, scraps of machinery and wiring, a glass dish half-full of thick, colorless putty. A portable compact disc player, a personal data assistant palm-sized computer, and an opaque glass perfume bottle lined up on the opposite table, chillingly innocuous. Daniel kept his distance.

"The workmen might leave the machinery there at the end of the day," she said, "since it's too much of a pain in the ass to drive it all the way back to the yard. But no matter what I do, it won't buy us much time. I told you, you should have bought the place—this wouldn't be happening now."

"But Sybil—"

She ignored his protest. "I suggest you get out of here, just in case I'm caught and they trace me back here. Maybe you should take your books, too. I know how much they mean to you."

"All right," said Daniel quietly. "But . . . sabotage is . . . always better when you have backup, don't you think? Safer, anyway?"

"I *don't* want to leave here," she said tightly, crushing out her cigarette in a hubcap already spiky with butts. "Not yet. And I don't want you getting caught. You're too rare. I *need* you."

"Really?" said Daniel. "You love me *and* you need me. How wonderful the world is."

She spit into the hubcap and wiped her mouth with her sleeve. "You know what I'm talking about. Take your books, take a taxi, take 'em someplace safe. Like where you keep your art or whatever. I would say the Teatro, but people come and go out of there all the time, and I can just see one of Bastard Son's crackhead buddies thugging your precious shit and selling it."

Daniel thought of the Schwitters collection, already packed and shipped and gone to Hanover, where the curators undoubtedly cartwheeled with joy at coming that much closer to having everything, everything the artist had ever done, every note and every sketch that he'd sent away, and he felt cold, sick regret. Not for having sold the Schwitters, but for keeping them so long, for having them in the first place, for having ever tried. "I had a very alarming dream," he said. "But I don't remember what it was about. Something about JFK."

"The president?"

"The airport."

Sybil stood up and dusted ash from the thighs of her cargo pants. "You're thinking about escape," she said. "You're feeling anxiety about the show. It's normal. Last night I dreamed that I was crucified upside down, nailed to these planks with giant knitting needles. So I was falling and drowning at the same time, trapped by tools of creation. And then I wake up to these fucks destroying the most beautiful place on earth."

Daniel returned to the upper floor, hoisted the boxes that contained his first editions, bringing them down to the door two at a time. Six in all. He piled them into the sagging, twisted shopping cart. "What's today?" he asked.

"Saturday." She settled herself gently into a chair across from the unfinished bomb. She pulled on pale-gold translucent latex gloves.

"The twelfth?"

She nodded, already absorbed in the minutiae of her dainty, fragile porcelain tools, poking through the innards of the disemboweled technology. "You have something to do today, don't you? Go do it."

"I'll see you later," said Daniel.

He stood outside with the shopping cart in the dusk, watching the massive, rumbling, mud-stained, violating trucks, and bent-necked industrial cranes, and workmen in stained yellow jumpsuits and hard hats crawling on the surface, rushing in and out like ants. They were not so much demolishing the warehouse on the next block as gutting it, tearing out chunks of bricks and drywall and pulling off the broken windows. The piles of debris being pushed from inside contained empty plastic soda bottles and a crumpled poster of Snoop Doggy Dog. So there had been squatters living there, too. He glanced up at Sybil's warehouse, and it wore a large yellow paper notice from an architecture firm, marking it for "RENOVATION." "RETAIL OR RESIDENTIAL." They didn't even yet know what they wanted to do with the building. Daniel tore down the sign, wadded it as tightly as he could, and tossed it into the Dumpster.

He brought his books to the storage space, eliciting the help of a different security guard, this time a tall, massive Asian woman, Hawaiian or Polynesian, as stoic as he'd ever seen. She easily wrestled the heavy boxes onto and off the elevator without a comment. Daniel enjoyed her simple, healthy brute strength, her defiant quiff of lustrous black hair. The sight of the smooth golden flesh of her neck above the dark-blue uniform blouse made his mouth water, but he was too preoccupied to act on it.

He did have something to do today.

He didn't particularly want to go dancing, or have dinner, just to see Joachim and bask in his utter sanity, probably for the last time. Australia. Daniel had never even had curiosity about the country—it seemed so absurd, an entirely different hemisphere, with sunshine, surfing, and barbecues at Christmas, savage wild animals, and vast expanses of arid nothing, with the humanity desperately clustered to the temperate perimeters. The idea that there was opera in Australia simply didn't make sense to him. But it was good enough, cultured and beautiful enough, that he was losing Joachim to it.

He stood at the door to Joachim's apartment building, chipping gummy silver polish from his fingernails, shuffling his feet, reading the lists of names underneath the row of chewed-looking black plastic buttons. Daniel lightly tapped the appropriate button and waited for the answering buzz that would open the door. Joachim was just a boy, just a human being, not the love of Daniel's life, not even the most brilliant artist he knew. Daniel didn't know why he felt this tearing emptiness inside him. But not emptiness, as such; just a very strong sense that something was wrong, the atmosphere had changed, variables had shifted. His mind flashed again to JFK, to the newsstand, the face reflected in the mirror next to the Italian model's.

Joachim himself came to the door, wiping his hands on a half-apron tied around his waist. His eyes grew so wide, they threatened to leap out of their sockets. "Daniel!" he gasped. "Hi! You're . . . early." He stood frozen in the doorway. "Nobody's here yet—I'm still making dinner." He made no move to stand aside, remained staring with his hands flat against the green-stained apron. The scent of garlic and rosemary hung around him in a cloud.

"Is it all right if I come in?" Daniel asked politely, one hand on the doorjamb and directed thought, and stronger yet, directed desire, already flooding down barriers in Joachim's mind.

Joachim's eyelids fluttered and spasmed, and he squeezed his eyes shut, shaking his head. "Oh . . . yeah, yeah, c'mon in."

Daniel rarely visited; he didn't like Joachim's apartment, a third-floor walkup, a tangle of cramped angles and switchbacks, as if dividing one apartment wasn't good enough, but each room in it had to be chopped into uneven thirds. He liked the decorations, a combination of exquisite photographs (some of them Daniel's landscapes of an alienated, emulsion-scraped Manhattan skyline), large unframed paintings with plush toys stapled to their surfaces, and battered vintage posters of 1970s pop idols. But the tiny front room was cluttered with objects, leaving only a narrow strip to walk through. "I haven't had time to clean up yet," Joachim explained, returning to the kitchen. "Busy cooking. Before that, of course, I was packing."

"I could straighten up for you," Daniel offered.

Joachim smiled through a sheet of steam rising from the stove. "There's no place to put anything," Joachim said. "There will be on Tuesday, when I'm out of here. Poor Billy—he's gonna have the place all to himself. He's gonna just *hate* it." Joachim reserved sarcasm for special occasions of frustration.

"Is he here?" Daniel glanced around him, hoping to find the roommate, so that he could take more direct revenge for being so rude to him on the phone.

"No," said Joachim. "He's in Queens with his girlfriend. He's gonna meet us down at the club tonight. Actually, he's probably going to have her move in here, so he can eliminate that amount of transit time in his life. Jesus. I'm going to be so glad to get away from him in some ways. I mean, Billy's a cool guy and all that, and he's liberal with his recreational substances, but . . . he can be such a thoughtless little swine. Like, he could have straightened up before he left this morning, but . . . noooooo."

Daniel followed Joachim as far into the kitchen as room would allow. "So what are you making?"

"Quiche."

"Oh, really? So does that make you a real man or not?"

Joachim arched his eyebrow. "Daniel, that is so fifteen years ago."

Daniel stood still, and silent, until Joachim had filled his pastry crusts with layers of beaten eggs, bacon, and spinach, and packed them into the oven, shoulder to shoulder. "So you're leaving on Tuesday?" he asked.

Joachim glanced over his shoulder at Daniel, sliding the cooking pans into the sink and washing his hands. "Yeah."

"What airport?"

"Um . . . Kennedy; why?"

"I just had a bad dream about that airport last night. I've got a really bad feeling about it. God, I wish you weren't going."

"Well . . ." Joachim shrugged. "Too late now, isn't it? I mean, the plane ticket's're bought, the apartment's rented, and I start work next Monday. I got my visa and my booster shots. Whatever happens, happens. It's fairly set in stone at this point."

"No," Daniel said. "Nothing's ever set in stone. And, even if it is, stone can be destroyed, can't it? I don't know what I'm gonna do when you're gone. Joachim, my life is insane. My life has always been insane, but . . . right now . . . I'm afraid."

Joachim untied his apron. "Daniel. You're going to have to just deal. For God's sake, you're a man, you're a grown-up, you control your own destiny. If things are too weird, just get out, go somewhere else, start over again."

"It's not like that," Daniel insisted. "I can't. I can't get out now. I'm in it too deep."

"You yourself just said that nothing's set in stone. If you're mixed up in some bad shit, I'd say go to the cops, come clean, and just get *out*, you know?"

"I can't go to the cops," Daniel said. "A lot of other people who haven't got anything to do with this would get hurt. The drugs alone—Jesus, you know how many drugs are involved in our lives. And right now, in this country, drugs are worse than murder." Daniel paused to catch his breath and lower his voice. "I can't get out of this now. My life isn't like that. I'm doing this performance with Sybil and Bastard Son, and I can't just run out on her like that."

"Right. You're doing this for Sybil. It's all about what Sybil wants. It's all about what Sybil needs. Listen to yourself. You're scared shitless. I've never seen you afraid of anything in the world, ever. I've seen you face down cops and leave them shitting their pants. I mean, what the fuck is this? A psychotic teenage girl? A psychotic teenage girl who doesn't even *love* you? She's probably fucking Bastard Son, too, just as an *experiment* to see if all Latin guys have dicks or something." Daniel burst into a rueful laugh before he could stop himself, and Joachim hurled the rolled-up apron across the room, knocking over a vintage egg-shaped lamp. "Look, man, do what you want. But I'm going to do what I want. You can't stop me, for God's sake."

"I *can* stop you," Daniel murmured, "and you know it."

Joachim stood his ground, waving his hand in front of his face like he was shooing away a mosquito. "Stop messing with my head, Daniel. You give me headaches. You gave me a headache as soon as you walked in here. You manipulate people. I've seen you do it! I've seen you lie to people. And then I see them believe you, and so you just get whatever you want. Well, guess what—you can't have me. You *can't* stop me from going to Sydney and getting out of this diseased shithole. You're a big part of it, you know? You thrive on the disease, the whole atmosphere of using people. So, all right, I'm never going to make it in the New York art world because I don't take any pleasure in hamstringing other people. I don't like to fuck other people over, Daniel. You obviously do. You admire that ability in other people. I think it's ugly. I won't let it happen to me."

"You've let it happen to you for years," Daniel said heavily. "You bought into it. You accepted it. You were complacent. You got ahead by closing your eyes and your ears and coasting along on the wave. Don't get on a moral high horse, like you've never benefited from the exploitation of other people."

"I never said that," Joachim retorted, but he was visibly flustered. "I never said that I was totally innocent. That's the problem. I've recognized it. But unlike you, I'm putting a stop to it. I'm getting out."

"Into the beautiful golden sunlight of Australia, where nobody ever uses anybody. My God, Joachim, you know that human ugliness is everywhere that human beings are. If you think that Australia is going to be any better—"

"Australia will be better," Joachim said, "because you won't be there. Because where you are, Sybil is. And I won't put up with her anymore."

"This town's not big enough for the two of you," Daniel mused, picking up the fallen lamp and settling it back onto the overcrowded table with the magazines and the pipes and the empty beer bottles. "And this is the biggest town there is."

"Not really," Joachim replied, his voice quieter now. "There's a link. There's you. *You* always find me."

"You don't ever have to see her again," said Daniel. He reached into the inside pocket of his coat and withdrew the Future Sound of London CD that Sybil had taken. "Here. I stole it back for you."

Joachim came closer, accepted the disc, smiled and shook his head as he turned it over and over in his hands. "Wow. I never thought I'd see this again. She's gonna beat your ass."

"It wouldn't be the first time," Daniel confessed.

"You didn't have to do that."

"I wanted to see you smile at me one last time."

Joachim's smile slowly dissolved. "Nice try. But I think you should leave. It was a mistake to invite you."

A violent surge of desire rose in Daniel's chest, and he tried to clench his fists to fight it off, but instead he gripped Joachim's wrists. Joachim opened his mouth, but no sounds came out; his mind screamed *No, please, let go. I'm not the one you want.* Daniel relaxed his grip but didn't release him, and whispered, "You *are* the one that I want."

Joachim slackly shook his head, eyes glassy. "Please don't do this," he croaked.

"Don't do what? What am I doing?" Daniel asked softly, caressing the bones under the fragile tissue skin, rubbing away the red marks left by his hands, soothing Joachim, transmitting waves of calm, pleasure, well-being, staying, *please stay.*

Joachim spasmed with the force of his resistance.

The walls of Joachim's mind crumbling, doors shaking loose from their hinges.

Daniel felt a quick snap of static electricity between their skins as he let go.

Joachim struggled away, staggered, and slumped against the kitchen counter. He slid down onto the floor. His eyes were open, but the inner image of Joachim's mind was a featureless white void, reflecting infinitely back onto itself.

"I didn't *do* it," Daniel whispered. "Oh, Christ. I did do it. Oh, Christ, Joachim, I'm so sorry. I didn't *know* I could do it."

That tugging inside him, reminding him that he was not alone.

Joachim's guests would be arriving soon. Daniel scanned the room quickly for evidence, picked up the CD where it had fallen, and put it back into his coat. Billy's bedroom had a window that led out onto the fire escape. Careful not to disrupt the bed, the television set, the video game console and teetering stack of game cartridges, Daniel hiked up the long tail of his coat and opened the window, struggling to push past the swollen wood. He slipped out sideways, pulling it shut behind him. He had disturbed the layer of dust and pigeon droppings on the sill, but it was too late to do anything about that. The alley below stood deserted but for sullen rows of dull, dusty black garbage bags and flattened cardboard boxes.

Silent as a hawk, he dropped to the pavement, landing on his toes, the impact pounding the cartilage in his knees until he wanted to scream. He stood for a moment and wiped the dirt and guano from the surface of his coat as best he could, then walked out of the alley, head held high, disseminating a cloud of incognito.

He hailed a taxi a few blocks away and told the driver, "Kennedy Airport, please."

He wasn't sure what he was looking for there, what he would find. Mostly it bought him time to think. A pang of full-body distress reminded him that he needed blood. He hadn't even taken any of Joachim's blood. At the airport, perhaps . . . He met the glance of the taxi driver, and then his own reflection; he looked inhuman. He kept his mouth closed and his hands in his pockets.

In one of the airport parking garages, Daniel found that he had no time or strength for subtlety; he took a chance on a middle-aged man walking by himself toward his car, a gray sedan parked between a massive truck and an even larger sports utility vehicle. As he bent to put his keys into the door, Daniel swept up behind him and thrust his claws into the back of his head, partially severing the brainstem, caught the man's collapsing body, and rolled with him underneath the sedan.

No time for subtlety. He tore open the man's shirt and sliced through the skin and fat at the juncture of arm and torso, a hole just big enough for his mouth, and fitted himself to it like a lamprey. As long as he didn't make a mess, he could have it all . . . No name, no life, no family, all of it trapped in the disconnected brain, just the meat and the fluids and the knife taste of drugs from an asthma inhaler, food salt, blood salt, blood sugar, and sweetly dissolved oxygen. When the body refused to yield any more blood, Daniel pushed himself from underneath the car, stood up, and brushed down the legs of his pants, checking his face in a rearview side mirror.

Daniel performed the same maneuver again twice more, two men on their own, cars parked between other cars, then staggered toward the elevator that would take him into the airport. He leaned against the walls of the elevator car, quivering and gulping deep breaths, lost in vibration from the flickering light from above.

Inside the airport, in a violent flash, he found himself at the Alitalia ticket counter, without remembering the steps that had taken him there. The ticket agent, olive-skinned and impeccably groomed, asked him, "Flight information?"

"Oh, I'm sorry," Daniel stammered, walking stiffly away.

He wondered if he should cancel Joachim's plane ticket but realized that he didn't have the information anyway. He kept meandering through the airport. He wanted to throw himself on the X-ray machine at the metal-detection checkpoint to see what the guards would find, if they would let him stand up before they shot him or just let his riddled and soaked body ride the conveyor belt to the end.

He went to a newsstand. Bastard Son had been here the day before, slipping the postcards advertising the show into all the issues of art magazines. He had chosen the airports, while Sybil patrolled bookstores and newsstands in town. Daniel left stacks of cards in the foyers of clothing boutiques and cafés. Even after all that, they were left with five thousand postcards. Daniel opened a magazine to the center and found his image there, hand on his groin, between Sybil's scarred legs. Four nipples blurred together across a wide pallid chest.

His hands shook and he dropped the magazine. Without picking it up, he fled the newsstand, rushing back through the airport in quick eye-baffling bursts. He threw himself against the side of another taxi, thrust his hand through the rolled-down window of the driver's side, and touched his hand to the driver's temple. He took a deep breath and held it.

Not like lightning, not like a bulldozer controlled. A soft, silk-wrapped bullet.

Take me home.

"Front and Pearl, Brooklyn," the driver said. "I'll get you there in half an hour."

Out in front of the next warehouse, the unmanned machinery appeared intact. The sign on his own had not yet been replaced.

He found Sybil inside reclining on the Craftmatic, feet up, writing in her block capitals in a cheap school notebook. She glanced over, smiling.

"You didn't blow up the trucks?" he muttered.

"I put sugar in the gas tanks. They'll figure it out in the morning. So . . . tell me . . . was I right?" she asked.

Daniel stood with his back to the wall. "Right about what?"

"You did it, didn't you?"

"I didn't kill him," he said softly.

She raised her eyebrows. "You didn't? You did something worse, didn't you?" She shook her head, closing her eyes.

"I . . . *love* . . . him," Daniel struggled.

"Loved," Sybil corrected. "There's nothing left to love, is there? No more Joachim? Well, there's this body, baptized with the name Joachim Trueba, who once upon a time made a bunch of cool paintings with teddy bears nailed to them. But he got mixed up with the wrong crowd, and now he's a frickin' vegetable." She swung her legs over the sides of the bed. "You should have killed him. What's the point of leaving him alive? He's just gonna be a burden to the system. A bed jockey. You left a shell. What the fuck were you thinking? Were you thinking?"

"Leave me alone," Daniel said, going upstairs and lying on the bed.

Sybil followed him up and sat next to him. He turned on his side, back to her, away. "Look, I'm sorry, but it's true," she said softly. "He's living dead now. I mean, is he ever going to recover?"

"I have no idea," said Daniel. "I never stuck around to find out. I've never done it before. I've never been *able* to do it before. It was an accident. I just wanted . . . If only he hadn't resisted . . ."

She lay down alongside him without touching him.

"You'll never leave me, will you," he said dully.

He felt her shake her head, and her fingers crept over his chest until she touched his exposed neck, stroked the stubble growing over his throat.

"Joachim wasn't what you're looking for," Sybil whispered. "What did you find at the airport?"

"Blood," said Daniel. "And the postcards in the magazines—Ennio did a good job. How did you know I went to the airport?"

She sighed heavily and pressed her fingers to her forehead. "I'm *with* you, Daniel."

"Then what am I looking for?" he asked. "Don't you know? Why don't you help me?"

"I can't help you," she said. "I don't know. I know it's a *who* and not a *what.* Unless you think of a connection as a *what.* Definitely a connection. But I don't understand what that is. Because you don't understand. I feel you, but I can't know more than you know."

He rolled toward her and held her chin in his hand. She was sober, more or less, her eyes clouded only by fatigue. "How did you get this way?" he whispered. "Have you always been this way?"

"No," she said. "Only with you. I can only see . . . I don't know how to describe it. I can only see through you." She kissed his palm.

"And I can't 'see through' you," he sighed, letting go and rolling back. "Sybil, please tell me the truth. Do you love me?"

She sighed and shook her head. "No matter what I said, I wouldn't be telling the truth," Sybil said.

Scene Twenty-eight: Sybil Spank

Now, many places in New York forbade themselves to Daniel.

Forty-second Street, near Broadway and the Space, was off limits; his old neighborhood was a bad idea; East Midtown, between skyscrapers and the Park, where Heinz Gestwirt had shared a neighborhood with the Supernova Gentleman's Club, could never be truly safe again, no matter how tall the buildings or dense the humanity. And anywhere that artists were likely to be about made him nervous; his face and his naked body, as mutated as it was, was everywhere in Manhattan, from the infernal postcards that were now stacked everywhere, to the posters that Ennio had pasted up layers thick around the theater. He had to admit that he liked the design of the poster blitz; extremely localized—twenty-one posters all on the same wall, arranged in a frame around a spray-painted silver-white shark with jagged jaws agape. But he wavered back and forth between a defiant, delicious egotism and shriveling anxiety.

Nonetheless, there was much shopping to be done.

No set needed to be built, only objects to be arranged; there would be no division between the audience and the performance, nothing to sit upon, nowhere to hide except to leave. Some props had already been constructed, like a crown of thorns twisted out of eighteen wire hangers, a four-foot papier-mâché pork chop with a Nazi swastika clearly visible in the spray-painted "grill marks" on one side, and the familiar circled K of kosher food on the other. There would be propane barbecue grills, a split steer with the skin still on it (specially ordered from an upstate farm), baskets of doll parts and bowls of dry pasta in the shapes of penises and breasts. No script, only some vague directions that Sybil had written in her notebook: *sexual magic tricks. impersonations. blood-drinking from a silver cup. salome's first dance in hell for beelzebub, lord of the flies.*

Sunday afternoon, in rapidly fading light, Daniel and Sybil bought Christmas lights at a 75 percent discount, candles and frankincense, the naughty pasta, and a white Tyvek cold-weather-survival jumpsuit, white Tyvek stovepipe hat, and white plastic platform clogs for Daniel. When he had tried on the entire ensemble, he and Sybil began to laugh hysterically and couldn't stop until he'd taken it all off and bought it and left the store. "I never really pictured myself as the chef of the apocalypse," he admitted.

"Yeah, but somebody's gotta do the cooking, don't they?"

He leaned forward and kissed her forehead. "Hungry?"

"Yeah."

"Feel like Northern Euro?"

"You thinking about that place we went to that one time?"

"Where you totally blew me off, yes. That's the one. Nobody dangerous will be there."

On Sundays, the grill was even more deserted than usual, and in that dead space between lunch and dinner, Daniel and Sybil found that they had the place to themselves. They chose the largest booth, space for eight, piled their coats and shopping bags on one side and shared the other.

The single waiter emerged from behind the long driftwood bar, pulled up a chair, and sat in it backward at their table. "How's it going today?" he asked. He was young and cute, and behind his stylish narrow glasses, the whites of his eyes bore a faint telltale redness.

Sybil leaned in close to him, examining him with similar eyes. "Are you stoned on weed?" she whispered to him.

The waiter sniffed dismissively. "Does it matter?" he asked.

"No," Sybil said, shrugging. "Just curious. I'd offer to smoke a bowl with you, but you're the only one working, so I guess that's kinda out of the question."

Daniel smiled and patted Sybil's hand. "Isn't she nice?" he said. "Well, some menus, if there's anybody cooking back there."

The waiter glanced back through the restaurant toward the kitchen. "Mark and Heidi are back there doing prep for dinner," he said. "They should be able to whip something up for you, but it might be a little while, depending on what you ask for."

"That's fine," said Daniel, "I like it here. Um, anyway. Menus."

"Menus. And could I start you out with something to drink?"

"I'd like a pint-sized White Russian," said Sybil. "Him, too."

The waiter saluted and went back to the bar.

"Uh-oh, Daniel, I see the long face coming out," Sybil chided. "What have I told you about the long face?"

"I'm sorry, Sybil. I can't help it. My friend is . . . my friends are . . ."

"Dead," she finished for him, in a voice more compassionate than he thought she was capable of. She twisted a strand of her blue-and-orange hair into a spike. "You kill people all the time. So what if you happened to get to know and like them beforehand? It's the same in the end. You do what you have to do. You do what you want to do."

When the brimming cocktails arrived, they ordered a large, simple meal, which the waiter/bartender quickly shuffled to the kitchen before resuming his seat, and his book, behind the bar. A distant church bell chimed six times. Sybil promptly created a liqueur-milk mustache. "I think we should go out clubbing tonight," she said, licking the mustache off. "We can hand out more postcards."

"We'll never get rid of them all." Daniel sighed.

"Oh, I think we can. We just have to be more ambitious. Maybe we should go clubbing in Jersey—we need New Jersey people to come to this. Or Long Island."

"Are there clubs on Long Island?"

"There must be. Oh, hey! We should invite our helpful waitron. And the kitchen staff. Have you got your stash?"

"It's in my bag."

The door of the restaurant opened while Sybil rooted around in the shopping bags, and a group of seven people entered, all of them in sober expensive suits. The grill's regular clientele, European business travelers, it seemed; but one of the women caught Daniel's glance and held it. "Daniel?" she inquired.

"Miranda?"

Madame Miranda Martin, wearing a quiet navy suit with a long skirt, the only hint of her nighttime existence in the form of four-and-a-half-inch stiletto-heeled boots, murmured to the rest of her party, separated from them, and approached Daniel's table. "Daniel," she said again with a dry wisp of humor in her voice, "you're at *our* table."

"Well, since I've been here for twenty minutes, technically it's my table now." He stood up, took her hand, and bowed over it to kiss the horse-pill–sized emerald on her middle finger. "I'm terribly sorry, my dear. We haven't gotten our dinner yet; it would be simple to move."

"Thank you," said Miranda.

Sybil emerged from the bags with a handful of

postcards, almost colliding with Miranda as she straightened up. "Oh, shit!" she gasped. "I didn't even notice you were there."

Miranda Martin drew herself to her full height, which, even with the boots, wasn't quite comparable to Sybil in pillow-thick platform shoes. In Miranda's world, not being noticed was inconceivable. "Good evening," Miranda said lightly. "Daniel said you were just moving to another table."

Sybil looked askance at Daniel, who shrugged, picking up his cocktail and moving it to the next booth, a more modest affair for four. "You remember Sybil, don't you?" he asked.

"Yes," said Miranda.

Sybil handed her a postcard. "Daniel and I are giving a groundbreaking performance on March fourth," she said. "You should come."

Miranda examined the card. "I'll check my calendar. I might well have previous plans."

Daniel moved the shopping bags and his and Sybil's coats to the next booth. "Out and about this evening, Miranda?" he asked breezily.

"Just gathering some sustenance before the evening's fun." Miranda's face broke into a smile. "I plan to entertain my visiting guests at Daddy Spank this evening—will you be joining us?"

Daniel glanced at Sybil, whose chin jerked up and down so fast that he thought she might sprain something. "Oh, yes, absolutely," he said. "We'd be delighted." Miranda went slightly pale; Daniel insisted, "The *two* of us. Same place, same time?"

"Er . . . yes," Miranda stammered. Her face went from pallid to pink. "I trust that you'll be on your very best behavior."

"Oh, don't worry about us," Daniel said, sitting and putting his feet up onto the seat across the booth from him. He took a huge gulp of his White Russian. "I'll even bring gifts for you and your guests."

Sybil bent slightly at the knees and clasped her hands

together. "I'll be good, Mommy," she wheedled in a child's voice, "promise."

Miranda glanced at her guests, who stood watching and amused, and the pink of her face flamed alarm red. "Yes, well," she said, "excuse me." She arranged her guests and herself in the midst of them, unable to ignore the fact that Daniel and Sybil were at the next table.

At length, the waiter/bartender brought out their food. Sybil handed the waiter a postcard, and he glanced over it, blushing slightly and grinning. "Oh . . . hey . . . is your name Daniel?" he asked suddenly.

Daniel nodded, cutting into his fish with a fork.

"There was a guy in here yesterday asking for you," he said. "It was really weird. He was like, fairly short, wearing a Prada suit—I'm a fashion student, so I naturally remember the suit. He was really intense. Had kind of an accent, I'm not sure what kind."

"Did he leave his name?" Daniel murmured, eyes focused on the nut-brown surface of the seared meat and potatoes on his plate. All appetite, all desire to put the cooked food into his mouth and chew and swallow and process it, drained out of him into the center of the earth.

"No . . . well, he might have, but I don't remember. Sorry. I just thought it was odd. I told him you hadn't been here for a while, but that you used to be fairly regular, and that you were a nice guy, we all like you." The waiter slipped the postcard into the pocket of his black apron. "Anyway, if he comes in again, I'll let you know. And I'll see if I can come to this—it sounds pretty interesting."

Daniel lifted a flake of fish to his mouth and promptly bit the inside of his lip. He dropped his fork and pressed a napkin to his mouth, spitting the fish into it.

"Definitely try to make it," Sybil said. "It'll be a total atmosphere. Hey, Dan, aren't you hungry?"

After Sybil had eaten both plates and Daniel paid for the meal, they gathered up their things without speaking again to Miranda or the waiter and bolted for Teatro Resurrección. "Oh holy shit," Sybil kept repeating in the taxi. "Oh holy shit. This is so perfect. Daniel, just think of what we could do. Oh holy shit."

"You are forbidden to kill anyone tonight," Daniel said sternly.

"Oh, man, Daniel, c'mon, please?" She shook her head and laughed. "Yeah, OK, I can see your point. Kind of. But oh man, this is gonna kick ass. I wonder if I can score some coke beforehand?"

Ennio was working on the mural when they arrived. "El Bastardo!" Sybil cried. "Body paint and an airbrush, and hurry!"

"Hurry? Shit," Ennio drawled. "What for?"

"It's a happening!" She had already unbuttoned and slid down her pants.

"I'm going to go to the warehouse and change," Daniel said.

"Could you bring me—fuck, I'll just write you a list. Meet me back here." She hobbled to the stairs with her pants around her ankles. "We are gonna *kick ass!*"

When Daniel returned to the theater with one of the large paper shopping bags full of the things Sybil had requested, he found Ennio patiently airbrushing green tendrils around Sybil's thighs while she stood naked and spread-eagled with her hands balanced on the bathroom sink. "I'm going costumed as the Androgyne Deity of Weeds," she explained to Daniel. "How does it look?"

"Astounding. Gosh, Ennio, you should hire yourself out for parties." Daniel set down the bag.

"I do it at Burning Man every year, man," Ennio replied in a quiet mutter, concentrating on the tight, tiny vine swirls snaking around the hollow of her buttock muscle.

Daniel settled himself in the microscopic dressing room, more of a large closet, took off his clothes and eased himself into seamed-back black stockings, a black vinyl miniskirt, and a corset. Pushing the hair back from his temples with an elastic band and covering his chest with the shirt he'd worn earlier in the day, he plucked his errant eyebrow hairs, smoothed a double handful of Sybil's white shimmering powder over his face, added liquid eyeliner, curled his eyelashes and applied mascara. He got so lost in the glorious minutiae of creating an idealized face that he didn't notice Ennio and Sybil standing in the doorway and watching him. Daniel did a double take at their grinning faces and frowned. "Stop spying on me."

"You are *such* a girl," said Sybil.

"My God, *what* are you wearing?"

She glanced down at herself. "You've never seen this before, have you?" She proudly smoothed out the wrinkles in the hot-pink, fine plastic mesh bodysuit that covered her from neck to ankles. "I used to wear this to dance in at the first place I worked. I had it specially made—this is the stuff that they bag vegetables in."

"I ain't sayin' *nothin',*" Ennio said, waving his hands.

"We're going to a really boring fetish night," Daniel explained. "And as this is probably the last time I'm going to go there, I figured we might as well make it special."

"Fetish?" Ennio scoffed. "What, are you gonna eat dooky or something?"

Sybil laughed so hard she couldn't speak, and Daniel just shook his head. "No, no, Daddy Spank has a strict no defecation rule."

"So if you gotta take a shit, you have to leave," Sybil gasped out.

"Damn," remarked Ennio, and that started her off again.

Daniel stood up and held up his arms. "Would someone please lace me?"

Cinched in the sweet prison of a twenty-six-inch vinyl waist, balancing steady on the five-inch platform pins of agony pumps, Daniel wet and parted and combed his hair while Sybil and Ennio slammed tequila shots with salt and shared a blunt made from a hollowed Cuban cigar. "Oh, to be young and drunk off your ass," he sang. Hair completed, he touched up his nail polish. "I *am* such a girl," he remarked to himself.

"Can I wear your new shoes?" Sybil asked Daniel.

"Time," Daniel called out.

It was eleven o'clock. Ennio had gotten back to work

on the mural, singing softly to himself in Spanish. Sybil helped Daniel on with his Soviet military-issue wool coat. "Hey, you're taller than me," she said. She kissed his neck under the stiffly gelled swoosh of hair, the natural curl at the bottom of his hair calcified there. "You look really pretty."

"Pretty as a girl?" he murmured.

She grinned at him. Her eyebrows were colored the same orange as the tips of her hair with melted orange crayon wax, and her lips were a full, luscious deep green. "I would kiss you, but red and green don't mix," she said.

She wore Daniel's usual long black leather trenchcoat, cutting an absurd figure in which none of the stylistic elements fit together, but somehow, through sheer force of will or bloody-mindedness, it worked. The way she looked made matching utterly passé. Daniel kissed the tip of his finger and held it to her lips. "I wouldn't ruin you for the world."

In the Daddy Spank service car, Daniel leaned forward to the driver's seat. "We have to make a quick stop on the way," he said. He gave the address of his art storage space, and the driver nodded and gunned his engine into traffic.

Sybil squinted at Daniel. "Where are we going?" she asked.

"Remember the presents I was referring to?"

"Oh, I thought that meant you were going to do something really outrageous."

"Oh, I am," said Daniel. "But this is in addition. And I'm going to need your help, so if your mesh thingy is delicate, you'll want to keep buttoned up."

In fact, Daniel enlisted all the help he could—Sybil, the driver, and both the security guards on duty at the time; without questioning him, they took the paintings down from where they hung suspended, opened the glass cases, and took out the paintings and collages and photographs and lithos and monoprints. There were too many of them to fit into the trunk of the service car, so Daniel chose the ten he loved the most. "We're bringing them with us?" Sybil asked, watching him carefully stack them, collages on top, since, even with their multiple layers of yellow-brown varnish, the pasted elements might still flake off or shift.

"And leaving them there," said Daniel, slamming the trunk and shaking hands with the security guards. "We'll see if anyone wants them if they don't cost anything."

Back in the car, headed south on Park Avenue, Sybil nuzzled the top of her head against Daniel's shoulder. "I never sold anything either," she said.

"Except the sight of your lovely body, of course." Daniel riffled through the inch-thick stack of postcards in his beaded handbag.

"Aw, hell. That was like making money by pissing into a cup. I actually really miss dancing."

"You still dance."

"Yes, but there was something really . . . I don't know . . . I mean, yes, it was icky, the men were icky and the other women were just kind of desperate and repulsive . . . but I have to admit, I enjoyed the power. Really explicit power. How I could change an entire room just by shaking my shoulders a little bit so that my tits would wiggle." She relaxed and laughed. "That just goes to show you—you get away from anything long enough and you start feeling nostalgic for it."

He kissed her forehead. "I think you're just baked."

Even on a Sunday night in Manhattan, 11:30 P.M. is still early. The penthouse of the midtown high-rise, decorated tonight in a Fellini-style Roman decadence complete with plaster Ionic columns, massive clusters of grapes, and a perfumed fountain, had everything necessary for a grand fête except for a crowd of guests. Perhaps ten people, standing around talking and eating grapes, had arrived before Daniel and Sybil. Sybil set down the stack of paintings she had brought up with her and huffed impatiently. "What the hell?" she complained. "This place is the size of a fucking football stadium and there's nobody here!"

Daniel gave the driver, who had also helped to bring the art upstairs in the elevator, a twenty-dollar tip and sent him away. "Oh, get over it," Daniel said. "They'll come. It's really early. Anyway, let's go disseminate this stuff."

Miranda, in queen bitch mode, stalked over to greet them. "Thank you for joining us," she said. "What are those?"

"These, my pet, are party favors, from me to you. And your guests." He propped a collage against the nearest plaster column. "Take 'em or leave 'em. Or throw 'em away. Or call them yours and sell them. They're out of my hands now."

Madame Martin looked Sybil up and down, her steely facade fragmenting slightly at the edges as her eyes traced the spiraling vines and lovingly depicted seven-lobed cannabis leaves decorating Sybil's body under the nearly invisible pink mesh. It was the closest Daniel had ever seen Miranda Martin to actually laughing. "That's a very interesting costume," she said, modulating her words carefully.

Sybil stuck out her tongue and grinned. "I'm the Mistress of Weeds," she said. "I'm stronger than anything man-made. You can call me Kudzu. Honey, I don't know about you, but I'm here to have fun tonight, and right now, this is grim."

He and Sybil set the pieces around the room, checked their coats, and began to dance. Encouraged by the better-than-usual tracks played by the unobtrusive DJ in black hooded sweatshirt and sunglasses, Daniel danced alongside Sybil (it was not really possible to dance *with* her) for so long that it came as a shock to bump into another person, and see that the room had filled up. Almost no one was dancing besides them, instead engaged in their pretend agonies and cruelties and admiring each other's new outfits. Daniel stopped in his tracks and Sybil careened into him, nearly knocking him over. "Oops!" she said. Her painted torso gleamed with sweat, but it had only smudged the designs circling her breasts and tracing delicately up her spine. She clung to him, catching her breath, and the two of them looked around the room, noting the positions of the artworks. Two of them were already missing, and the crowds slowed and murmured as they passed the others. "I think it worked," Daniel said.

"That was very brave of you. And smart. The worst thing you can do is sit there looking at stuff you did years ago wondering why nobody wants it—you should get rid of it as quickly as possible. I mean, who cares? It won't be worth anything until after you're dead anyway. Now, shall we put on a show?" she murmured in his ear. "Now that I'm warmed up and you're no longer artistically constipated?"

He held out his arms to her. "Enslave me, smoky Goddess of Weed," he intoned.

She took him on a tour of the dramas happening in the room: spanking with paddle, spanking with bare hand, electrical shock, candlewax, the riding crop across his exposed nipples, alternating feather and pinprick on the skin. Sybil was all charm tonight, and most of the patrons who had seen her before didn't recognize her, naked and painted and meshed and with different hair. Daniel, in a ticklish sensory haze, wondered if the eyebrows made all the difference. At the end of each visit, Sybil smiled daintily and offered a postcard from Daniel's handbag. "We're having a show," she said. "You'll dig it."

She found an empty velvet couch with a T-shaped bar on one end fitted with stout steel loops, and Daniel gratefully collapsed on it, facedown. Sybil sat on the arm of the couch, lovingly tracing the crook of his elbow with a grape leaf she'd torn loose from the now decimated tower of fruit. "I never got a chance to punish you myself tonight," she murmured.

He opened one eye. "I should think it's your turn for it," he replied. "You punish me all the time. Or is it that you always have to be in control of every situation?"

"I think that's the case," Sybil said.

"Then you should give it a break. At least for a little while." He glanced around. "Shame we don't have any toys. But I think I can solve that problem. . . . Stay here."

He got up again, stalked toward a couple of men engaged in a very deep kiss, and ran his hands along their bare backs. As one, they parted from each other, each kissed him, and the taller of the two unlocked the slightly outsized handcuffs from his belt and handed them to Daniel. "I'll bring them back, I promise," Daniel whispered.

He returned to Sybil, a shimmering hot-pink odalisque on the couch. He swung the cuffs lightly on his fingertip. "Just a little surrender?" he suggested. She shook her head slowly. He edged onto the couch next to her and kissed the cuffs, then kissed her neck. "You've done it before. You think I'd let you come to harm? I'll rip the guts out of anyone who tries to bother you. Remember that trust. Remember when I first fucked you. You trusted me enough then. Not now?"

She didn't speak, but she relaxed, and she didn't resist when he fastened one loop of the cuffs onto her wrist. They were big enough that they didn't cut into her flesh. "Have you ever been arrested?" he whispered to her.

Sybil nodded a little, swallowing. She was nervous. He kissed the lump in her throat. "Just a little trust, just for a little while," he murmured. "Remember safe words?" She grinned and nodded more. "Do you want to use one?"

"You'll know when you should stop," she said.

Daniel shrugged. If she wanted to be that way, he would extend a little trust her way. He looped the cuffs' linking chain around the T-bar and snapped the other ring onto her other wrist. Abruptly the expression in her eyes transformed into something so complex that he knew he could never get to the bottom of it—fear, anticipation so intense that it made her body vibrate, a blasting tumble of memories. He could smell her adrenaline and it made his mouth water so violently that he had to suck the moisture back through his teeth before it ran out the corner of his lips. He wanted to look behind him at the people who had already come to stand around and watch them, but he didn't dare break the connection between his eyes and Sybil's. She needed him to focus or the evening was over.

The couch's back stood flush against the wall, so instead of doing what he wanted and straddling her, he sat next to her and extended one leg along her body so that his ankle rested on her shoulder, the vicious tip of his stiletto heel next to her ear. She began to breathe through her hastily licked lips. "Quite different to be on the other side of this, isn't it?" he murmured.

"I *did* get arrested," she said, the words tumbling out in a rush. Daniel began to massage her upthrust arms with his hands, finding her muscles as tense-hard as bamboo. She took a deep breath and her eyelids lowered. "I've been arrested three times. One time for breaking curfew and resisting arrest. I got off easy on that one."

Daniel ran one hand over her breasts, then, hooking his claws into the fine mesh, he sliced through it, just enough to expose the whole breast. Underneath him, Sybil gasped and shifted her body, but she couldn't go far, between the cuffs and Daniel's leg.

"One time for shoplifting at the mall," Sybil continued, her breath coming in jagged pants. "I was stealing underwear for my mom."

Daniel sliced the mesh again and lifted out the other breast. He was delighted at the sensual wrongness of the sight, green-smudged perfect grapefruit tits on a bed of shimmering pink. He bent his head and sucked the airbrushing off the surface of her nipple skin. His prick pushed its way up and out from under the vinyl miniskirt. A single droplet of translucent fluid ran down from the head and landed on Sybil's enmeshed belly. He reached across her for the beaded handbag.

"And one time," Sybil said, "for beating the shit out of the captain of the football team in a parking lot."

Daniel withdrew a long, hollow-tipped 12-gauge needle from the handbag. Sybil did not see it; she had her eyes closed and her lips moved sluggishly, as if she was talking in her sleep. "I broke his cheekbone," she said. "I broke his collarbone. I dislocated his shoulder. It felt . . . so . . . good."

Daniel gripped her right nipple in his fingernails, gently, just to hold it still.

"Sonic Ruth made me do it," Sybil hissed. "She sucked

him off and wouldn't swallow and he smacked her for it. And so she said, 'Go kick Glenn Lovell's ass.' Have you ever dislocated a shoulder? Have you ever heard that pop?"

Daniel set his teeth, tongue safely back and out of the way, and punched the needle through the soft pink meat of her nipple.

She bucked underneath him, right leg thrashing and kicking the white shoe off her foot and across the room, screamed at the top of her lungs, but there was far more than simple pain in her voice. Her head arced back and the skin of her face and chest blossomed bright red, blood rushing to the surface of her winter-white skin. Daniel stared greedily at the twin beads of blood running from the emergent sides of the needle, but all the people behind him gasped at once and he looked up out of reflex.

The blond teenage girl in pink, the one he'd seen in Worth Street Station, stood right next to him, the pompoms in her hair delicately fluttering in a breeze that wasn't there. Her bulbous blue eyes were not looking at him, but instead down at the howling Sybil, and her lips were moving, throat bobbing, but in silence. She pitched forward violently and blurred into nonexistence.

Daniel sat frozen with his fingers on the needle, staring at the space where, a minute ago, there had been a little girl with a big head, in a dress too short, electric-blue fishnet tights, brand-new sneakers, talking, talking, talking. He glanced at the little audience, who were also still and silent, all of them with their mouths open.

Finally one of them broke the silence. "Did you just see that?"

"What the hell?"

"Cool," said one.

Daniel slid the needle out of the now limp and sweat-soaked Sybil and bent his head forward to sip the blood that welled out of the two new wounds. She made no more move to stop him than to weakly shift her body underneath his. "Daniel," came her voice in a husky croak. "Now, please."

He grimaced on the tiny tongueful of her blood in his mouth. Too much to take in. Intense vertigo from the sick sea of endorphins and adrenaline and breaking-down inside her. He fumbled with the handcuff keys and dropped them, and someone else had to unlock the cuffs and set Sybil free. As soon as her wrists—cut, chafed, bloody—had been released, she sat up, threw her arms around Daniel, and burst into tears. "Please take me h-h-home," she begged with her lips against his ear.

The spectators seemed very pleased that they had witnessed a breakthrough.

Scene Twenty-nine: The Truthful Precipitates of Dreams

"I'm sorry I pierced your nipple."

"Well . . . you could have at least put a ring in it or something. But no, don't apologize. You were only copying me. You forced a vision."

"We all saw it, Sybil."

"I'm not crazy."

"You should know that label is meaningless to me."

"But now you know I'm not making it up. When I tell you I see her, I really *see* her. And she won't go away; I was hoping that you being there would make her go away, but she likes you, I think . . ."

"I've never seen anything like that before. She was so . . . vivid . . . I could see her breathing . . ."

Shuddering. "She's not there. She's dead. I saw her die. I made sure. What's gonna happen to me, Daniel? I'm not sorry. I'm not fucking sorry. If she's waiting for an apology, she's gonna keep waiting. I mean, what, do I see a priest? Get an exorcism? Am I possessed? Is it real?"

"Ssh. Ssh. You're not possessed. You're not possessed any more than I'm possessed." He paused for a second before continuing with the litany of comfort. "Don't be afraid. I won't leave you. I won't leave you."

"You can't, anyway," she said.

Under cover of darkness, in a truck requisitioned from a man who now, neck badly askew, rested facedown in the East River silt, Daniel and Sybil moved out of the beautiful warehouse. All of Sybil's art projects had long since been moved to the Teatro Resurreccíon, and Daniel's books rested in their airless room on East Seventy-fifth Street, which left only clothes and bedding. Daniel abandoned his heavily damaged car on the brick promenade under the Manhattan Bridge and kissed Sybil in the driver's seat of the truck. "Go to the Sally Bond Hotel," Daniel said, handing her a matchbook with the address printed on it, palmed from the nights that he stayed there without her. "It's just off Broadway. Just double-park and wait for me. I won't be long."

She was too tired to ask him why he wasn't coming with her. "I'll go get something to eat on the way," she said. "I don't want to be stuck there waiting for you."

He watched her drive away, looking back at long, wet Front Street, the infinite darkness, shadows reflecting on shadows. The sun had come out that day, warming the earth and melting the snow, now freezing against the pavement in a crackling cellophane layer. A remarkable stillness reigned here, a starless half-past midnight and not a soul on the icy streets, with only the soft roar of cars on the bridges bracketing him, the dark pressing down on him until it became difficult to walk or breathe.

Faint laughter from Jay Street, but when he turned the corner and walked up that way, no lights were on in any of the buildings, and the corner convenience store sat silent and imprisoned behind layers of steel grating. He stood at the base of the crumbling building, listening for the laughter to come again (and it did, faintly, from the back of somewhere) and wondered when it would be their turn to be demolished, have the laughter gutted and the bones carted away in a mud-spattered yellow dump truck.

The neighborhood felt like a desecrated grave, like the old Jewish cemetery where he walked alone, in obfuscation, combing the ground over and over again for anything more precious than cracked stones and violently churned earth. Most of the valuables had already been plundered, but one evening Daniel found gold teeth, still embedded in the jawbone, and scattered, scratched pearls. He wished his mother and father were there in the cemetery, at peace, together, underground. He did not know where either of them were; unlikely they were still together, unlikely they were alive. During the thickest part of the war, years after Ricari had left him, Daniel had wandered back to his childhood home and found a different family living there, fair-haired Christians from Bonn, with frozen, terrified smiles. They didn't know anything. They hadn't wanted to leave their home and move into a house where Jews had lived; they had abandoned their beloved pet dog while they were being transported, unsure of being able to feed it, but brought their children, a little girl and boy too traumatized to speak. Daniel left none of them alive. The next week, all the buildings on that block were bombed and he hid in the ruins of a general-goods store, under the counter, laughing, ticking off the seconds between explosions. He passed the time wondering if the British would level the city and put up a new one in its place, or just salt the earth and wash their hands of Germany altogether.

Daniel began the run across the Brooklyn Bridge, first turning back toward Brooklyn and then mounting the swell onto the bridge itself. He had been having the nightmares again, but now they happened every time he closed his eyes. They weren't really nightmares; in fact, they were generally pleasant journeys through all the parts of Manhattan to which he no longer allowed himself to go, touching things and experiencing their textures as if for the first time. But they weren't his hands with which he caressed fabrics and thumbed through old books, and it wasn't his face he saw reflected in store windows as he went past. That was the nature of the nightmare.

He hated waking up from these reveries to find that he was still tethered to the body of Daniel Blum, the same body he'd had for decades. His body never changed much, except to grow hair, shed flakes of dead skin. Even his toenail had finally grown back. His body always went back to the same state. He wondered what the limits of it were. What, for example, would happen if his heart was torn out and could no longer propel the blood through his body? What if he lost his spine or his brain?

He saw a flash out the corner of his eye and paused in the center of the bridge walkway, the wind tearing the breath from his sinuses. The yard where the construction and demolition vehicles were parked seemed to be on fire in two, no, three places. It was almost too far away for him to be able to see the green truck peeling out of there and gunning for the Brooklyn Queens Expressway.

He made it across the bridge in ten minutes, including a minute admiring the leaping orange flames and the delayed booming of the explosions. He carefully avoided the neighborhood of the former Worth Street Station, which forced him slightly out of his way and through Chinatown. He thought about hailing a taxi, but a cursory examination of his wallet stopped him cold. He had only a hundred and eleven dollars, the remnants of his most accessible account. To get more cash, he would have to physically enter a bank and demand it, and banks were full of cameras that couldn't be charmed. "All my money is in Portugal," Daniel said out loud, laughing as he passed rows of restaurants and outlets for cheap shoes, all closed. "Fuck you, Heinz . . ."

He had a good credit card under the name Daniel Blumenthal, with which he could access money held in Switzerland, and he used that when he arrived at the Sally Bond Hotel. He rented the largest room they had available, which was a two-room suite with a double bed; the Sally Bond didn't place much stock on luxury, being primarily residential and renting rooms to those who lived hand-to-mouth, for whom coming up with $150 a day was par for the course. Daniel went up to the room and turned on the lights, tested the water taps, then, satisfied, went back down to the lobby to wait for Sybil.

He waited there on the green-and-gold, faded-to-beige lobby couch, tapping his nails on an issue of *Reader's Digest* for an hour before he deigned to pick it up and begin reading it. He had gotten to the vocabulary-building section toward the back of the magazine before Sybil actually trudged in with the bedding bundle over her shoulder. She thrust it at him. "Let's get your shit," she said.

The truck stood double-parked on the street. Together they piled the boxes and cases in the lobby. The desk clerk raised an eyebrow but said nothing and made no move to assist. Sybil sat down heavily on the couch and blew out her breath in a stream. "Holy fuckin' moley," she muttered.

"Did you get food?" Daniel couldn't help asking.

She stared at him blankly for a moment. "Oh, shit, I forgot."

"You . . . forgot?"

"I'll be right back," she said, heading for the door again.

"You'll be right—? Wait!" He handed her one of the set of room keys. "Sixth floor," he said imperiously. "I'm gonna take a bath."

"You'll need it," she grunted.

Daniel settled himself in the too-short tub, slid head and torso under the water, and blew bubbles up to further distort the acoustic-tile ceiling. He wasn't thrilled about the expression on Sybil's face, or her tone of voice; it sounded like the weary hindsight of a big-game hunter who called it quits after the Big One took off his leg at the knee. And yet, she'd been intact, unbloodied, unbruised even. He surfaced and let his head cast off steam, reaching for the paper-wrapped, heavily scented little soap on the bathroom sink.

He heard the outer door open and smelled mustard, beef, and onions. Sybil slouched into the bathroom and ripped open a paper bag, spreading it across her lap. She began to stuff French fries into her mouth, three or four at a time, no more, no less.

"Whatcha got there?" asked Daniel, wadding lather between his palms.

"Dogth," she said with her mouth full. She swallowed and licked her lips and smiled. "Kosher dogs. Kinda a tribute to you."

Daniel threw the soap at her, and it hit her chest and disappeared into the collar of her sweatshirt. She chuckled and took a bite of one of her franks. "Sorry," she murmured, wiggling the soap through her clothes. "Bad joke." She finished one of the dogs and all of her fries, and waited until Daniel had washed himself head to toe before she spoke again.

"So I ran into your friend," she said.

"Which friend?"

She hummed faintly to herself, picking one of the grilled onions from the second dog. "Your dad," she said.

Daniel blinked at her for a moment, then rubbed more soap-milky water over his face. He edged the water-outlet switch with his toe. "You don't say," he replied airily. "Did he scare you?" The escaping water made a slurping, sucking sound, and Daniel felt a part of his cockiness go with it.

"Yeah, he fuckin' scared me," Sybil said, and took a huge bite. She swallowed, grabbed the soap from where it had settled in her lap, on the edge of the brown, grease-dotted paper, and tossed it into the sink. She wiped her hand on her pants. "He scared me so much I forgot I was hungry. And I haven't eaten all day."

"Did he try to hurt you? Where is he?"

Daniel stood up, gasping in the sudden cold air, and Sybil tossed him two towels. She shook her head and chewed some more. "He didn't try to hurt me. He was just . . . there all of a sudden. I had, like, gotten out of the car in front of Joseph's, you know, I was gonna go in and get a pizza for us, just in case you were hungry, too. And he just walked up and stood in front of me."

"Did he speak to you?"

"Yeah, he said hello." Sybil shrugged. She finished her meal and tossed the garbage into the plastic trash can next to the sink. "It's like that's all he needed to say. 'Hello, Sybil.' That's the part that freaked me out, the fact that he knows my name. How does he know my name?"

"If he spoke to you, he knows everything about you," Daniel muttered.

He went into the other room, wrapped himself in the now stained down quilt, and flung himself out on the bed. Sybil calmly unlaced her boots and began shedding layers of clothes. "He wants to see you," she said.

"He told you this?"

"No . . . well, I mean . . ." She stared into the distance. "He didn't say it. But . . . I mean, I tried to slow him down, like I did you. But . . . fuck. He's the fastest thing I've ever seen."

"He's very old." Daniel sighed to the pillow. "He was older than I am now when we met."

"He's *fine,* though," Sybil said wistfully.

"So he wants to see me," Daniel repeated. "Where? When?"

"Tomorrow?" Sybil replied, as if she were guessing, but Daniel knew that she wasn't, although it felt that way to her. "I dunno, seven, seven-ish, Russian Tea Room, third floor?"

"Jesus Christ. He would." He laughed softly to himself. "He would, wouldn't he? I hate that place."

Sybil, undressed, pulled the quilt away from Daniel's body and inserted herself into the space. "Daniel," she murmured, "today I lost my home, I performed probably a million dollars in property damage, I helped throw a body into the river, and I just got mentally raped by a little weird pixie dude. Who used me as fuckin' voice mail." She gave a single-breath laugh. "And I'm going to get up tomorrow and make a giant, headless naked woman out of papier-mâché. This is Sybil the Soon-To-Be-Sleeping."

He sighed and nodded and kissed her head, and she curled against him, inundating his soap-smelling body with the odor of her sweat and the homeliness of grilled onions. She warmed him.

After she had fallen asleep, he moved as gently as he could to switch off the lamps and turn on the television with a remote. On the screen, news helicopter cameras circled and focused on the devastation at the truck yard. "Police officials have given no official cause of the fires," said the voiceover with firm, concerned resolve. "They have not yet ruled out terrorism, although why this would be chosen as a target is unknown at this time."

The Russian Tea Room was, naturally, packed to the gills with tourists and regulars, their gentle conversational chatter multiplied to a dull roar. Daniel had been a few times before, years ago, out of curiosity and on an occasional luncheon date with art patrons who appreciated the history and spectacle of the place. He thought the whole thing was too busy, and it reminded him awkwardly of Haus Vaterland, with its multiple floors and restaurant areas and the slightly hysterical atmosphere. He stepped lightly through the place, careful of the waiters carrying food, sending out a headache-inducing barrage of *Hi, I'm your buddy, don't mind me.*

Last night, with Sybil snoring faintly in his arms and infomercials on the television, he felt his comfortable cowl of denial melting away. So, the dreams. It was new to him. It was different with everyone. He could still push Ricari out of his mind, if he spent all his energy and concentration on the task, but . . . Ricari had found Sybil.

And the third floor . . . the room with all the bears and bunnies! Good Lord! A madman had designed this kaleidoscope of gold and tapestries and mirrors, going on and on backward into a brain-twisting infinity. Daniel, between the illusion-generating and the visual onslaught, almost lost his balance and had to grab the edge of a table to steady himself.

"Please," spoke a voice from the table, thumping Daniel like a hundred pounds of velvet. "Sit down. Don't worry, we won't be here long."

Orfeo Ricari looked much the same as the last time

Daniel saw him, shorter hair, but that was about all; he still looked like an angelic altar boy with the mouth of a harlot, almost completely immobile, like a most detailed mannequin. His gray eyes were so light and calm that they reflected like mirrors, and any expression could be read in them without conclusion. With a delicately mechanical gesture, he lifted his hand and indicated the empty seat across the table from him. "Sit, Daniel," he said again. "Or you'll just stand there and be fascinated for hours. Don't embarrass yourself."

Daniel sank down into the chair. He wanted more than anything to lay his head in Ricari's lap, have his head petted, find comfort in the simplest and most fundamental human contact. But Ricari was stronger than Daniel was, or Ariane was, and he remained a safe distance away, across the table, too far away to reach, and the wide oval tabletop with its neatly arranged condiment tray a vast gulf of space.

"We have to *talk?*" Daniel croaked. "Out loud?"

Ricari blinked slowly. "I don't trust myself to touch you. I would tear you to pieces."

"Angry at me as usual." He didn't mention the lust, the terrible sexual craving, which Ricari felt as surely as Daniel did.

"You never improve."

Daniel sighed and squeezed his eyes closed. "I've never cared what you think. What I want to know really is what you're doing here. Did you fly out all this way from wherever you were just to lecture me some more?"

"Not exactly," said Ricari. He reached into his jacket and withdrew a familiar postcard, which he held between his fingertips, then dropped on the table. "What is this, pray tell?"

"Where'd you find that?"

"You know where."

Daniel stared at Ricari. "What do you mean, what is it?" he retorted huffily. "Isn't it obvious? Or can't you read? I'm giving a performance. With my lover, Sybil."

Ricari shook his head. "I'm not here to lecture you," he said. "I'm here to . . . oh, Daniel. This is when your existence becomes torture. Everything you know and love is gone, and so you search about, trying to find something that matters. What you must understand is that none of it matters. There is nothing you can do to make your existence any easier. And I am sorry. For the first time, I am sorry that I did this to you. And not in a way that I regret having done this because it inconveniences me, but because . . . if I could ease your suffering, I would. If there was anything I could do, I would do it."

"You could tear me to pieces," Daniel muttered, his throat suddenly thick. He felt two tears run hot into the hollows under his eyes and wiped them impatiently away.

"I won't kill you," Ricari said simply. "I refuse."

"Then I'll-I'll-throw myself in front of a train. I know that'll kill me."

"It won't work," said Ricari. "I tried that. Remember? I was knocked out of the way and it broke every bone in my body. But . . . it didn't work. You nursed me back to health." He closed his eyes. "With strong young German soldiers." He opened his eyes again and set his head to one side. "You don't remember, do you? What's the matter with your memory, Daniel? I never forget anything. Do you only remember the things you want to remember? Or are even those gone?"

"I don't want to remember." Daniel wiped his face again.

A waiter approached their table, then suddenly stopped in his tracks and went back the way he had come. Ricari allowed himself a smirk. "He didn't drop even one plate," he said.

Daniel held his head between hands slippery with tears. "Orfeo . . . please . . . what do I do?"

"Die. Go to the grave. Let them bury you." Ricari's expression did not change. It was frozen there; he was so barely alive, weeks from blood, his skin like waxed silk. "Go on and die as many times as you like," he said. "It doesn't matter. You'll just come back. Eventually you will meet a natural end. But it won't come soon enough to save your soul from damnation."

"Fuck my soul!" Daniel bit out. "I want out!"

"The classic cry of the suicide," Ricari said, and with a minute twitching and softening, his face registered the subtlest amusement. "No, my dear, we are a special case in the eyes of God. His punishment for us is extraordinary in its brutality, as it is fitting for our sins."

"You and your fucking Inquisition," Daniel muttered. "If you'd been born four hundred years earlier, what kinds of tortures would you devise for your sinners? I can read you like a book. You're an evil son of a bitch, and if you can't find someone else to torture, you torture yourself—but you need that sadism, don't you? You'd stab yourself just to stab somebody."

"And the only thing that matters to you is to make sure someone's looking."

Daniel shuttled past the steel sphincter corridors of Ricari's irises and into the black depths at the centers of the eyes, searching for light at the end. The only light was that which reflected from their smooth glassy-wet surfaces. "You know, we had this same conversation exactly before," Daniel said.

"Yes," Ricari said, "I know. In 1931. I suppose that means that what we say is true. You and I are archetypes."

"No, we're just boring, and we never change." Daniel pressed his temples again.

"She's using you, you know," said Ricari.

". . . What?"

"The girl. Sybil. She has you by the throat and you can't even tell."

"Nonsense," Daniel replied with a brittle laugh. "She's mine."

"No, you're hers. She controls you. She could control me, too, if I wasn't smarter. Stronger than you. She's not like the others."

"I know," Daniel admitted. "She can see through me."

Ricari leaned forward across the table. "She *controls* you. Think about it. Why are you still here? Why have you done anything for the last few months? Why do you make decisions, and then suddenly do the opposite?"

Daniel glanced nervously over the tablecloth.

"You must enjoy this. You enjoy not having to be responsible for the things that you do. Oh, Daniel. I had some hopes that, as you got older, you would stop being so selfish. But the only way you've been able to do this is to . . . hand the reins to someone worse than yourself." Ricari sat back and blinked a few times. "Oh. Now I understand. Now I understand completely. It might just work for you."

"It might just," Daniel said. "You've seen inside her mind. You know what's she's made of. I know what I'm doing."

Ricari shrugged. "Yes, I believe that you do," he admitted. He folded his hands. "Forgive me. I made an incorrect assumption. I should never have come. I should take myself back to Napoli as I had originally planned. It's been a pleasant side journey." He gazed around the room. "I've always wanted to visit this place. And now I have."

"This place is awful. I feel like I'm gagging on gold. You wanted to see me again; admit it." Daniel smirked. "To see if I still look the same. And to show yourself off."

Ricari's faint smile evaporated. "As if I could be proud of being the way I am," he hissed quietly. "As if I could take pleasure in seeing you the way you are." He stood up, and Daniel rose with him. "This is good-bye," he said, drawing himself to his full height, just under Daniel's chin. "I wish you luck in finding the peace that you seek. And may God have mercy on your soul."

"You, too, eh," said Daniel.

He extended his hand, and to his surprise, Ricari extended his hand as well. The spark struck between them crackled audibly; they never touched.

Ricari's thought was *I trust you to do the right thing.*

Daniel's thought was *I forgive you.*

Daniel allowed Ricari to leave first, standing next to the untouched table and losing his mind in the detail of the sixteen-pointed sunburst on the ceiling.

He went directly from the Tea Room to the Teatro Resurreccíon, craving the dark, the grime, the incessant bump of Ennio's music. He expected to find Ennio and Sybil smoking pot and up to their elbows in paper and glue, but only Sybil was there, meditating in silence, wearing her meat dress and holding a fourteen-inch straight machete. She stood on a newly built wooden platform in the back of the room, the raw unpainted wood glowing in the semidarkness like bleached bone.

"Good, you're here," she said. "We should rehearse."

Scene Thirty: Renewed Exorcisms

On the fifty-second anniversary of the death of Antonin Artaud, some freaks are putting on a performance at the Teatro Resurreccíon in Noho. There have been some interesting shows put on there in the past, usually sound and video installations created by the ultra-hip artist Bastard Son, and occasionally improv theater sketched out in the round to an audience seated on metal folding chairs. Advertisements for the Flesh and Ghosts happening have been all over New York for the last month, and the naked female pictured on the postcard is recognizable as the girl from the sexy bunny video clip. Bastard Son's signature skull rides shotgun on the postcard, and therefore it seems like a worthwhile event to visit as a precursor to a night of serious clubbing. Doors at ten, performance at 11:59, according to the card, ten dollars admission, not too bad. Stop in and have a look around.

At eleven o'clock the street outside the Resurreccíon is thick and impenetrable with people, going in, trying to go in, staggering out, standing on the sidewalk talking and smoking cigarettes and being Society. Celebrities galore—artists, patrons, journalists, club kids, socialites, pop stars—you even see Kim and Thurston from Sonic Youth, emerging from the door with baffled expressions on their faces. You want to stop them and ask what could possibly be inside, but they are already gone down the street at a pace more run than walk. You look at your companions and shrug.

A sullen Latina in a nude-colored nylon bodysuit and heart-shaped pink sunglasses guards the door, accepting money and stamping wrists. She looks enough like Bastard Son to be his sister. "No reentry," she litanizes. "If you leave, you can't come back in. No reentry." You ask her if it's all right if you smoke inside, and she smirks and gives a single quick nod of her head.

You lose the urge to light a cigarette as soon as you're inside the door; the room hangs opaquely fogged with frankincense and the smoke from meat sizzling on a grill in the center of the room. Mostly the low light is red, though shot through with yellow flames from the grill. On your way toward the grill, you hit your head on a giant pork chop hanging from the ceiling. Your girlfriend laughs at you. "This is just gross," she says. "I thought this might be more gothic, but this is just . . . there's too much smoke in here. It's making me sick."

The door opens again, shunting more people in, and in the momentary clearing of the air the artwork in the room swims into view. Besides the spinning pork chop, there's a very realistic side of beef, mannequin legs strung from the ceiling like a chain of pale misshapen sausages, a fifteen-foot mural of a man having the skin on his face blasted off from the left side, the right side with enough flesh left to display panic. It's definitely the work of Bastard Son, but also shows another artist's hand, as if Bastard Son detailed the newly flayed skull and someone else painted the intact side of the face. On the wall opposite this mural is a ten-foot white screen made of a gently waving curtain of plain muslin, and, projected onto it, a massively magnified image of hundreds of sibilant flies clustered on a cow's eye. The sound of the buzzing of the flies has also been magnified, and the sound substitutes for music. Rising up from time to time is a low harsh roar that you recognize as the sound of a passing subway.

You take a better look and realize, as you're standing right next to it, that the side of beef is a real one, that you can smell it beginning to warm and soften in the stifling room, that underneath it is a metal washtub collecting the blood that runs out of the cleft organs and down the dangling hoof.

You recognize the male from the postcard, in person, his skin a few shades warmer than the paper fabric of his clothing. He walks up to you and smiles. "Gobble the flesh and spit out the soul," he says to your girlfriend, his black lips grinning, a mouth full of pointed teeth. He bends down to the washtub, dips a glass mug into the blood, and raises it to his lips.

Your girlfriend claps her hand to her mouth and blunders toward the exit; you wish you could do the same, but you're frozen there, watching the vampire drink the thin mixture of blood and melted ice from the surface of the steer. He makes a face. "I gotta admit, this is really nasty," he tells you conspiratorially. "But, then again, you eat beef every day, don't you?"

He takes a bite of the glass mug and crunches it like ice, gore dripping from his lips.

The frankincense is too much. You turn your back on the vampire, walking stiff-leggedly toward the exit, but you can't see it through the crush of people gaping at the videoscreen flies stabbing the cow's eye with their proboscises, wings glinting and iridescent. Now, visible at the bottom of the screen, you see the words, painted on the muslin in drippy block capitals, I CAN SEE THROUGH YOU.

You begin to push people with your hands to get them out of the way. Someone pushes back, cursing you, and you bump your thigh against a glass aquarium, topped with Christmas lights, and inside the aquarium is an obese sewer rat, spread-eagled on its back on a doll-furniture antique sofa covered with red velveteen. The rat's four paws have been affixed to the doll sofa with heavy brass screws. You really, really hope that the rat is dead, but the rat breathes feebly, its muzzle twitching as it dreams. Anesthetized. At least that.

You reach the door at last. Bastard Sister repeats again and again, "No reentry. If you leave you can't come back in. No reentry," shuffling piles of money into a black steel box. You stand there agape as the curious hustle past you into the freak show, and she turns toward you, her eyes suddenly enormous, slicing curses into you.

"No *resurreccíon!*" she shouts in your face. "You leave this world, you can't come back in!"

You feel a light hand on your arm and turn to face the vampire again. There is no trace of blood on his face or on his suit, and his eyes seem so gentle, so reasonable. "Please stay," says the vampire. "We begin the show in twenty minutes. Please stay." You can't help but return his smile, and you follow his gaze back into the room and see the girl from the video, wearing a most improbable dress and a white chef's hat, standing by the grill, brushing what looks like barbecue sauce onto what looks like burgers. It's not so bad after all—you've seen Damien Hirst's sectioned cows and sheep floating in formaldehyde. This is definitely do-able. This is the art of the extreme. You will never accomplish anything without facing down fear and disgust. The man you thought was a vampire (c'mon, really, fake fangs are twenty dollars at the mall) smiles at you and squeezes your arm. You've made him happy. You pays the money, you takes the ride.

At 11:50, the front door is closed, and no further people are admitted or released.

Daniel and Sybil stood together, hands clasped in front of them, on the platform, now covered with a black plastic tarp. A packed house, overpacked in fact, standing and crouching room only, with only a slight berth given to the growling grill and the slowly swaying raw beef. Only the strongest and most perverse had remained, rewarded by the frankincense running out and a return to breathable atmosphere. Ennio and his sister had gone, taking the money with them; the video loop of the flies and the audio loop of the subway continued unmanned.

Sybil raised her head and stared out over the heads of the audience. Her voice forced itself out of her belly and into the smoke. "Flesh," she said, barely audible, "your body, my body, just an aggregate of proteins. Barely held together. Decaying. We make more flesh out of lust and coat the world."

Daniel spoke in an ordinary voice, but with such projection that he could hear the words echo from the far wall, and he watched the audience flinch at the sound. "The soul is electricity," he said. "Ghosts populate the earth, wearing suits of meat. To believe that your consciousness is worth more than an animal's is idiotic and untrue. Every living creature produces a charge."

"But to call any of it sacred is a joke," Sybil replied more loudly, turning her head toward Daniel.

"The riddle of existence is a joke," said Daniel. "And you never get to hear the punch line."

Sybil met Daniel's eyes. "Ever?" she asked plaintively.

He let go of her hand and ran his finger along her forehead. "Well, I don't know," he said honestly.

"Yeah, you do," Sybil said. "How many deaths have you witnessed? How many deaths have you caused?"

The audience sat rapt and unmoving.

"How many have you?" he countered.

Sybil broke away from him, winding with difficulty through the crowd in her wide dress, the organza already ripped, the plastic reinforcements underneath bending and snapping. She went over to the aquarium where the rat lay insensate on its couch. She picked up the whole doll sofa and brought it through the crowd, urging the audience to look closely. The majority of them couldn't do it, but a few bold souls actually touched the fuzzy brown body with fingertips. "He's still alive," Sybil murmured to them. "Do you think I should kill him? He won't be able to survive with his paws injured like that. He's been pumped full of drugs for a month. Should I put him down in the street and let a car run over him, let the other rats rip him apart? Or should I take care of him now?" Sybil slowly made her way back to the platform, where Daniel crouched with his arms around his knees. "What do you think, Daniel? Angel of Mercy?"

"Define mercy," he said, standing up with a smirk. "You saved his life just so you could use him as a torture object. Look at him. You named him Victim. You crucified him. Are you going to inject him with morphine? Take him off life support?"

Sybil stared at Daniel, chin wobbling with suppressed tears, turned away from him, and set the sofa down on the platform. "He won't live much longer anyway," she said.

"Give him to me," shouted a woman from the audience, sparking guilty laughter from the others. Sybil obediently walked back down among them and handed the woman, a willowy girl with long purple yarn braids, the rat on the sofa. The woman looked down at the rat with a compassionate eye. "Oh, he's dead," she complained, evoking more laughter.

"He's still useful," Sybil pointed out. "If you boil him down to the bones, you can sell the skeleton to Bastard Son." More laughter.

While Sybil bantered with the audience, Daniel calmly picked up the glass mug he had bitten into earlier and crushed it between his hands. "Ouch," he murmured pleasantly. He had cut into the big veins on the mounts of his thumbs. Dark blood ran thickly over his wrists. Amid sounds of astonishment, he wiped his hands on his Tyvek suit, marking thick smudges that looked black in the red light.

Sybil stomped back onstage. "Dammit, Daniel, why do you have to be such a showoff?"

Daniel pulled a fragment of glass from his hand and tossed it into the crowd. "Let's not get off track, shall we?" he said. "What were you saying about a punch line?"

Sybil stared at him for a long time. "Are you sure?" she murmured. The subway soundtrack swelled, receded, and was gone.

"God, yes. God, yes, I'm sure." He threw back his head and laughed. "Why else am I here? Why else . . . have I been here? I want to see if it's different. I want to see if I've got a punch line. I want to see if I have an answer. And I want to see if it'll work." He took her into his arms and touched his forehead to hers. "You know I'm sure."

"OK, then," she said. "Put on a show. I'll be right back."

Sybil fell onto her belly, the dress ballooning up over her legs, and crawled away, disappearing into the back room. Daniel performed a semi-striptease, slicing his way out of the surprisingly tough Tyvek; his healing hands were painfully stiff. At last he freed himself of the paper suit and stood before the crowd in a sequined silver maillot, cut high on the hips and plunging in the front almost down to his navel. He loved the piece—completely useless as swimwear, impossibly tacky, unflattering to any figure except one where the hips were smaller than the chest, or, in other words, a man. The audience, a little baffled by Sybil's absence, gave him a round of thunderous applause and whistling as he stood with his fists on his hips, doing a few high kicks and shimmies for the sheer pleasure of their response.

"Hands up, who likes pork!" he shouted. More laughter and applause. "Hands up, who likes sodomy! Hands up, who likes Queens! Hands up, who likes war! Hands up, who likes . . . looking at the back of your own brain, standing on the edge of the void, feeling the pathway of your spine . . ." Daniel ran his hands along the sequined path of his torso, wrapping his arms around himself, sliding his hands along his arms until the hands were joined in points and then joined and flying away, like swallows. He let his hands drop to his sides and stalked back and forth along the platform, meeting gazes and burning them until they fell. "How many of you here tonight are virgins?" he hissed. "Oh, there are many types of virginity. There is the virginity of sexual thought. The virginity of masturbation. The virginity of orgasm. The virginity of sexual touch with another. The virginity of penetration. The virginity of sodomy. The virginity of death." He paused in the center of the stage, glanced around at a roomful of averted eyes. "Oh, there are even several varieties of that. Not just your experience of your own death, but that of others. How many of you have seen an animal die? All of you here did. You saw Victim when he was alive, and then suddenly he wasn't. And how many of you have ever seen a man die? Did you see his soul escape? No, I guarantee you did not. This is not to say that there is no soul to escape, only that your pathetic eyes aren't good enough to see it. Do you see the electrons stop when you throw a light switch? You only see that the light is no longer there. Precisely the same. However, tonight, you will all lose your virginity, in ways that you could not possibly previously imagine."

He fell silent, smiling grimly, and read the audience. They were reverent but juicy; they wanted to see what would happen next. They came expecting theater, thus theater was what they saw. Daniel gave a little sigh and a shrug. "Or perhaps I'll just sodomize a volunteer."

"How are you gonna do it through that suit?" piped up a young man in the front, releasing a new stream of laughter, heartier even than before, releasing tension.

"Why don't you come up here and find out?" Daniel responded, giving the crowd the banter that they craved, though he shot daggers from his eyes at the little upstart. The boy laughed again, and Daniel felt himself relax, his bruised dignity soothed by humor. "I don't think it'll be *too* hard to find my way in," he added. "From here, all I can see is asshole."

A sudden pattering on the platform caught Daniel's attention, and he turned to see Sybil running back up onstage, completely naked except for a coating of iridescent glitter. "Sit," she bellowed at Daniel, pushing him off his feet and into a nearby reclining chair on the stage. Straddling his legs, she snapped his wrists into restraints, made from intricately twisted heavy-gauge wire, on the armrests. She bent over, displaying her genitals, to clamp Daniel's ankles to the chair. Daniel glanced over her shimmering back at the audience, who were torn between amazement and titillation. "I made this chair," Sybil announced to them, straightening up and turning her back to Daniel. "Well, I *stole* this chair, but I modified it, made it special. Especially for my purposes here tonight."

She bent and slid a portable CD player, connected to a guitar-effects pedal by a slim wire, underneath the chair. He stared up at her, a chill sweat of apprehension tickling under his arms and across his breastbone. She had not mentioned anything under the chair before. He glanced down at the wire restraints; twisted and knotted in layers, he might be able to break free from them, if he was willing to sacrifice his hands.

She smiled charmingly and settled the wire-hanger crown on his head. It snagged his hair a little, and she took the time to adjust it so that it rested just above the temples. He caught his reflection in her eyes and found it extremely charming.

You're a gorgeous bitch, he thought.

Sybil bent down again, next to the chair, and with a thrilling *shing!* pulled loose the machete from its scabbard, mounted on the side of the chair. She had had the knife sharpened earlier that day, the cutting edge a little smaller than it had been before, but so keen that Daniel could smell the freshly exposed metal. Sybil turned the machete back and forth before her eyes. "Isn't this beautiful?" she boasted to a room silent but for the humming soundtrack of the flies. "This was my fifteenth birthday present from my father. He liked to give me knives for presents. This was the last gift he gave me before he made the mistake of using a gun. See, with a gun you don't think; you're hot; you shoot, bam, guy falls down dead with holes in his face. With a knife, you have to stop and think. You have to plan. Calculate. Know how to use it." She walked around the back of the chair, swinging the machete lightly in her hand. "My father loved me in the only way that he knew how—by making me enjoy acts of violence. Did your father teach you anything, Daniel?"

Daniel glanced at her, but he wasn't looking at anything in particular. "He taught me that . . . it doesn't matter if you think you're a Jew or not. If someone else thinks you are. And they're willing to kill you for it."

Sybil kept her eyes on the frozen audience. "I think that's a pretty valuable lesson," she said. She turned to face him, ran her hand gently over his bare, moist chest. "Daniel, how many Jews have you killed?"

"Hundreds."

"And how many gentiles?"

"Hundreds. Thousands. Tens of thousands."

She kissed the corner of his mouth. "And did you ever see a soul escape?"

Daniel closed his eyes. "No."

She turned again to the audience. "Ladies and gentlemen, I give you . . .

"The soul of Daniel Blum."

He watched the shining arc of the machete coming down with an idle interest, and then felt a thickness in his throat, like the first stages of crying. She had to scream as she wielded the blade to give herself enough power to pass through completely with one chop; he knew she wouldn't be able to bear having to do it again. And he loved the sound of that shriek—her own variety of compassion.

Daniel was pleasantly surprised at how little pain there was, that the worst part was a terrible urge to swallow and being unable. His view of the red lights in the ceiling diffused, slowly and delicately like the petals of a flower spreading. And music; he supposed that, technically, it was screaming, commotion, anarchy, but with an underlying order and rhythm to it all. He moved his hands and his arms and his legs—he was standing up, walking, he was free and dizzy, just awakening to a cold evening full of the smell of burning leaves. And a lover's hand on his face, lips on his (he felt that very distinctly, he knew that was real, and that his sensation of walking and standing was illusion), Sybil's raspy voice calling out, "Taste the blood! Transform yourselves! Remake the world in your own image!" In harmony with further whistling from the throat of the machete.

Their fingers felt like feathers on his chin.

The dark petals by far outnumbered the red petals; the

poppies had gone to seed, begun to sink under a shimmering surface of oil. . . . Daniel wished that he could see. He wished he knew what they were doing to his body. He began to feel bored and edgy, and the pain rose up, clawing as if the wire crown encased his entire head and neck, down to the edge, below his pharynx, he could feel the line now, exposed to the air and trying desperately to heal itself while the blood that would help him accomplish this still poured unabated from his head. He forced his lips to move, and a macabre whisper forced breath through his severed throat—

"Sybil, I'm sick of this."

Against his ear, the velvet of her lips as painful as shreds of asbestos. "Yeah," she whispered to him, "me, too."

He could still see light, bursting faintly in a corona on the edges of his mind. He could still smell the distinct chemical scent of fuming nitric acid and sawdust. He could still feel his eardrums implode from the impact.

To be spared the screaming, he was grateful.

VOICE OF THE BLOOD

JEMIAH JEFFERSON

Ariane is desperate for some change, some excitement to shake things up. She has no idea she is only one step away from a whole new world–a world of darkness and decay, of eternal life and eternal death. But once she falls prey to Ricari she will learn more about this world than she ever dreamt possible. More than anyone should dare to know . . . if they value their soul. For Ricari's is the world of the undead, the vampire, a world far beyond the myths and legends that the living think they know. From the clubs of San Francisco to a deserted Hollywood hotel known as Rotting Hxall, the denizens of this land of darkness hold sway over the night. Bur a seductive and erotic as these predators may be, Ariane will soon discover that a little knowledge can be a very dangerous thing indeed.

___4830-2 $5.99 US/$6.99 CAN

Dorchester Publishing Co., Inc.
P.O. Box 6640
Wayne, PA 19087-8640

Please add $2.50 for shipping and handling for the first book and $.75 for each book thereafter. NY, NYC, and PA residents, please add appropriate sales tax. No cash, stamps, or C.O.D.s. All orders shipped within 6 weeks via postal service book rate.
Canadian orders require $2.50 extra postage and must be paid in U.S. dollars through a U.S. banking facility.

Name____
Address______________________________________
City____________________State______Zip__________
I have enclosed $__________ in payment for the checked book(s).
Payment must accompany all orders. ❑ Please send a free catalog.
CHECK OUT OUR WEBSITE! www.dorchesterpub.com

IN THE DARK

RICHARD LAYMON

Nothing much happens to Jane Kerry, a young librarian. Then one day Jane finds an envelope containing a fifty-dollar bill and a note instructing her to "Look homeward, angel." Jane pulls a copy of the Thomas Wolfe novel of that title off the shelf and finds a second envelope. This one contains a hundred-dollar bill and another clue. Both are signed, "MOG (Master of Games)." But this is no ordinary game. As it goes on, it requires more and more of Jane's ingenuity, and pushes her into actions that she knows are crazy, immoral or criminal–and it becomes continually more dangerous. More than once, Jane must fight for her life, and she soon learns that MOG won't let her quit this game. She'll have to play to the bitter end.

___4916-3 $5.99 US/$6.99 CAN

Dorchester Publishing Co., Inc.
P.O. Box 6640
Wayne, PA 19087-8640

Please add $2.50 for shipping and handling for the first book and $.75 for each book thereafter. NY, NYC, and PA residents, please add appropriate sales tax. No cash, stamps, or C.O.D.s. All orders shipped within 6 weeks via postal service book rate. Canadian orders require $2.00 extra postage and must be paid in U.S. dollars through a U.S. banking facility.

Name____________________

Address____________________

City____________ State______ Zip______

I have enclosed $________ in payment for the checked book(s).

Payment must accompany all orders. ☐ Please send a free catalog.

CHECK OUT OUR WEBSITE! www.dorchesterpub.com